*To my grandmothers, Marguerite (Bobbi) Hensley
and Gloria Belle Plentl. For always loving me
and encouraging me, even when I was sassy.*

Delicious Double-Cross

"There are things you do not understand."

"No." The brother stepped forward, looking as though he might like to take Thomas by the throat. "I am afraid it is *you* who does not understand."

Only, it wasn't a man's voice delivering the words.

It was a woman's.

And that was when Thomas took a closer look.

Two blue eyes glowered at him, nowhere close to a cry. Her blond hair was a short, unschooled tangle about her ears. She radiated an energy that made him take an involuntary step backward.

"Miss . . . ah . . . *Lucy* Westmore, I presume?" he asked weakly.

"Yes." She stalked toward him, her fists clenched.

He took a deep breath, trying to sort out how to defuse the situation.

But it turned out that breathing deeply around Miss Westmore was a mistake, because she smelled of the outdoors and fresh laundry, not at all the way a proper young lady was supposed to smell.

Now *he* was the one feeling off-balance. And it wasn't only because she'd taken the upper hand in this meeting. This young woman stirred something long dormant beneath his skin. He'd thought he'd grown out of such adolescent urges. That he could look at a woman and not wonder what was under her skirts.

What was beneath those trousers, however, was a different story entirely.

By Jennifer McQuiston

JENNIFER McQUISTON

The Spinster's Guide to Scandalous Behavior

THE SEDUCTION DIARIES

AVONBOOKS

An Imprint of HarperCollinsPublishers

This is a work of fiction. Names, characters, places, and incidents are products of the author's imagination or are used fictitiously and are not to be construed as real. Any resemblance to actual events, locales, organizations, or persons, living or dead, is entirely coincidental.

AVON BOOKS
An Imprint of HarperCollins*Publishers*
195 Broadway
New York, New York 10007

Copyright © 2015 by Jennifer McQuiston
Excerpt from *Diary of an Accidental Wallflower* copyright © 2015 by Jennifer McQuiston
ISBN 978-0-06-233512-8
www.avonromance.com

First Avon Books mass market printing: December 2015

Avon Trademark Reg. U.S. Pat. Off. and in Other Countries, Marca Registrada, Hecho en U.S.A.
HarperCollins® is a registered trademark of HarperCollins Publishers.

Printed in the U.S.A.

10 9 8 7 6 5 4 3 2 1

Acknowledgments

As always, I want to thank the usual suspects: my agent, Kevan Lyon; my wonderful editor, Tessa Woodward, and the fabulous Gabrielle Keck; the publicity team at Avon, especially Caroline Perny; the Avon art department, especially Tom Egner, who has a knack for creating the perfect covers for my books; my friends and critique partners, who know who they are; my amazing readers, for cheering me on and anxiously awaiting the next book; and of course, my patient and enthusiastic family.

This time, however, I want to extend my thanks further.

In particular, I feel compelled to thank everyone who followed me on my journey as I travelled to Sierra Leone in October 2014 to fight the Ebola epidemic, as part of my day-job with the CDC. I was incredibly touched by the outpouring of support, the thousands of new Facebook followers, the people who told me my posts helped educate them and relieved their fear. That was a long, hard, unforgettable deployment. I didn't get any writing done: it is hard to conjure drama on the page when you are working twenty hours a day on something as dreadful as Ebola. But I did feel closer to the romance community than I ever had before, thanks to so many new friends. Thank you for your prayers, your support, and your kind words. They meant the world to me.

Prologue

London, 1850

It was a closed casket by necessity, not protocol.

But that didn't keep people from coming.

They milled about the drawing room, somber clothing and whispered voices coalescing into a dark smear of sight and sound. Some had come to grieve, others to gawk. He was far too drunk to remember their names but not yet drunk enough to drown them all out, so he took another surreptitious swig of whisky from his flask and tried not to scowl.

Through the din of the room's murmured speculations, his mind added its own rehearsed explanations for his sister's closed casket.

She suffered terribly, in the end.

She'd not want to be remembered that way.

Ensuring, unfortunately, that Josephine would be remembered the other way.

Young. Pregnant. *Unmarried.*

Damn it all, but what was he supposed to say to these

people? That Josephine had *wanted* to die? That perhaps now, at least, she could find the sort of peace and respect she had been denied in life? The guests might be here in his home offering their condolences, but there was an edge of macabre fascination to their voices. They'd never have forgotten the scandal as long as she had lived among them. Well, Josephine had solved that problem, hadn't she? The entire room believed she had died in childbirth, the babe along with her.

The truth, however, was somewhat more damning.

"I must speak with you, Lord Branston."

Thomas was startled enough to momentarily forget the siren's call of the whisky. Here, at least, was a name he could remember, even dead drunk. *Miss Gabrielle Highton.* He turned his head until his bleary gaze focused on the face of the woman he still hoped to marry, despite all that had transpired. "Gabrielle?" he croaked.

"Yes." She wrinkled her pretty nose. "Are you . . . unwell?"

Unwell. That was one way to put it. He breathed in, wishing the room wasn't swaying. "I . . . I am glad you came." He hadn't been sure she would.

She stepped closer, until he could smell her perfume, a floral scent that reminded him now, too much, of the flowers draped across his sister's casket. *Lilium candium,* his brain helpfully supplied. It was telling, perhaps, that he could remember the flower's name in his drunken state, but not the names of half the people in the room.

How long had it been since he'd studied botany at university?

A far less important question than how many minutes he ought to wait before taking another swig of whisky.

His fingers tightened against the flask as Gabrielle's gaze hovered to the left and right, but wouldn't quite meet his. "I came because I needed to tell you." She drew a deep breath, making dread shift in his stomach, pooling alongside the whisky. "And because I knew you would be here." Her eyes finally met his and held. "You've not been at home the other times I tried, you see," she accused.

Thomas gritted his teeth. No, he'd not been at home. There were arrangements to make. Funerals to organize.

Bottles to drink.

And tell him what, precisely? He could understand if Gabrielle had a desire to speak with him, considering the depth of his sister's scandal. But whatever his betrothed had to say was a conversation best had in private, not at the foot of a casket. He deserved a chance to explain.

Beg, if necessary.

"I will call on you tomorrow," he said, his voice hoarse, his hand outstretched. "We might speak then."

But she was already twisting the betrothal ring from her finger. He felt the cold press of it against his open palm. "I am sorry, my lord. But I think it is best if I do not see you again."

His fingers curled over the ring. *Bloody hell.* Would she no longer even call him Thomas? He'd kissed this woman, for Christ's sake. Offered her his hand and title in marriage. But apparently his intended considered the title of marchioness a poor payment for enduring the taint left by his sister's ruin, because she was already turning for the door.

Gabrielle's departure had not gone unnoticed, either. Around him the crowd was stirring, the whispers shifting. It was one thing to be left at the altar, but this was a different notion entirely. As the vultures circled closer and the woman who had once been his future slipped out of the drawing room door, he took another generous sip of whisky, not even bothering to try to hide the flask this time. Let them gawk. Let them *talk*. It no longer mattered.

Perhaps his sister had found the right solution after all.

And perhaps it was time for him to disappear as well.

Chapter 1

London, April 1853

ilson, the aging butler who ruled Cardwell House with a glove-covered fist, sometimes acted as though there was a metal prod shoved up his bum. Not that good posture wasn't an essential element of the position, and by all accounts Wilson was excellent at his job.

But today that prod looked to have been heated in a fire prior to insertion.

And that meant someone—most likely her—was about to catch a scolding.

Lucy Westmore sighed into the silence of the greenhouse, resenting this small intrusion more than she should. Wilson didn't say a word as he pulled to a halt in front of her, carrying his omnipresent silver tray. Not that he had to. His scowl was loud enough. But years of dealing with the old butler's frowns had taught her the best recourse was to head off his lecture with a well-placed apology. So she brushed the dirt from her hands, peered up from where she was kneeling, and tried to fit a repentant smile to her face.

"I know I missed calling hours again, Wilson. And I am sorry, truly I am. I just need a few more minutes." She shoved a fistful of blond hair out of her eyes while she waited for his response. Damn, but it was hot in the greenhouse today, the air thick and musty and oppressive. Perhaps she *had* spent one too many hours here, sweltering over the sweet pea seedlings she was preparing for the St. James Orphanage community garden.

A drop of sweat slid down her nose, and Lucy's gaze settled on the butler's balding pate. It would be heavenly to do something similar with her own unruly hair. She was tempted to giggle as she imagined what his scowl might look like then, but giggling never helped her cause where Wilson was concerned.

He'd been butler to her father for seventeen years, and to the previous Lord Cardwell for twenty-odd years before that. As such, he commanded a familiarity none of the other servants dared. She might be twenty-one years old and of an age to mind her own affairs, but he never failed to scold her, should the circumstances call for it.

Which, admittedly, they usually did.

But couldn't he see this was important?

Growing impatient now, Lucy rocked back on her heels and gestured to her dirt-stained trousers. "Surely you wouldn't have wanted me to receive callers dressed like this? It would have been ever so much worse." When his scowl deepened, she switched tactics. "Would it help if I promised to apologize to Mother and Lydia later?" Although, she was quite sure Lydia wouldn't mind. As far as sisters went, she was the lovely, forgiving sort.

Mother, on the other hand . . .

The thought of her mother's reaction to her tardiness—and her trousers—was enough to make Lucy wince. She should have quit the greenhouse hours ago, but she'd simply lost track of time. Yes, that was what she would say.

Hopefully, it sounded like a more reasonable excuse than the truth, which was that she'd rather extract Wilson's metal prod from his bum and shove it in her eye than suffer through another round of prescribed calling hours with Mother. For Lucy, they were an excruciating reminder of just how awfully her life was about to change. She might have agreed to go through with it but she'd be damned if she delivered herself trussed and bound for the upcoming Season one second earlier than necessary.

"I will change before dinner," she added. "And I promise I will try to remember calling hours next week. But these seedlings are wilting and I must—"

"Miss Lucy," Wilson interrupted, which would have seemed a terribly rude thing for a butler to do if she hadn't been so relieved he was finally speaking to her. "Save your explanations for your mother. I suspect you will need them this time."

She bit her lip. "She is very angry?"

Two bushy brows lifted high, like gray mustaches above his eyes. "Lady Cardwell spent half the afternoon making excuses for your absence, and the other half bemoaning your future. I even saw her look out the front window, no doubt to see if you were swinging from a tree."

Lucy flushed. "I haven't done that since I was a child."

Wilson cocked his head, his silence deafening.

"Fine. Since I was seventeen." She sighed, realizing how awful that sounded. What self-respecting seventeen-year-old still climbed trees? But she'd never been like other girls. And despite her best intentions, despite constantly stifling her natural impulses and trying to behave the way a proper lady would, she was beginning to reach the conclusion she probably never would. "Honestly, I am not trying to upset her, Wilson. I just have different interests."

He shook his head, as though she were a hopeless case. "Well, I have not come because of your mother, or even be-

cause of the calling hours you have so predictably missed."
He leaned forward, slowly extending the tray he carried.
"You've a package. It came in today's post."

Lucy was startled enough to fall silent. Not quite the vehemence of his usual objections to her penchant for wallowing in dirt and trouble, but then, Wilson was as slippery as an eel. No doubt he was biding his time, waiting for her guard to drop.

She climbed to her feet and eyed the proffered tray. At first glance the package seemed rather innocuous. About ten inches square and wrapped in brown paper, it sat on the butler's silver salver like a large, plain cousin to the dainty white letters that surrounded it. Its appearance sparked some mild curiosity, but then again, most correspondence did.

She regularly received letters from her brother, Geoffrey, who was partway through his first year at university. She also maintained a vigorous communication with several philanthropic organizations, and a felon or two besides, if one considered her campaign to improve the conditions for prisoners in Newgate.

But as her eyes settled over the handwriting on the outside of the package, she felt a sudden quiver in her stomach. Because the parcel was addressed in the same distinctive scrawl that adorned the Christmas cards Aunt E sent every year from Cornwall.

And a package from Aunt E engendered more than mild curiosity when you considered the woman had died two weeks ago.

Her fingers reached out and Wilson jerked back the tray. "Oh, no, Miss Lucy. Not until you wash your hands."

She glared down at her fingers. *Bugger it all.* They were only a little dirty. Not to mention the fact she was a goddamned grown woman of twenty-one years.

"You are a cruel beast of a man, Wilson."

A smile finally claimed his broad, wrinkled face. "I am

at least a *clean,* cruel beast of a man." He pointed a gloved finger toward the washstand that waited at the greenhouse entrance. "And I'll not have you sullying my tray. We've just polished the silver."

Lucy stalked toward the washstand, grumbling out loud—mainly because she knew Wilson expected her to. As she scrubbed her hands, she pondered what the arrival of such a parcel could mean. For years, her aunt's only correspondence with the family had been a single annual Christmas card, signed with an impersonal "E." It was unconventional at best, coldhearted at worst, an annual reminder the woman cared so little for her family she couldn't be bothered to think of them more than once a year.

She didn't even wait for the butler's footsteps to fade before tearing open the brown paper wrapping. Several items fell to the greenhouse floor, tinkling on the Egyptian tile, but she was too intrigued by the series of leather-bound books emerging in her hands to pay them much mind. Why had Aunt E sent her books? And more to the point, *how* had she done it, given that the package clearly must have been posted after her death?

Lucy opened the cover of the top book and read the inscription on the first page.

The Diary of Edith Lucille Westmore
January 1, 1813

Though the air in the greenhouse was warm and heavy, a chill rippled down her spine. Apparently, her mysterious Aunt E had a name. A *real* name, not just a single, detached letter.

Part of it, at least, was Lucy's own name.

Why had no one ever told her?

She closed the cover, suddenly feeling nervous. There appeared to be four volumes, and in her hands they felt terribly old, with small cracks in the leather and gaps in the stitching. But the physical history of the diaries paled in comparison to the history of the woman they represented. Lucy was holding a more intimate knowledge of her aunt than she had ever been permitted to know in real life, and she didn't know whether to lock the books away unread or fall upon them voraciously and read them from cover to cracked cover.

She glanced down at the drooping seedlings, suddenly feeling far less enthusiastic about the orphanage's garden. Her gaze shifted to several other items, scattered about her feet and glinting amidst the spilled dirt. There was a folded letter of some sort, as well as a key and a piece of jewelry. She bent down and reached out her hand, gathering them up.

The necklace intrigued her, a pendant strung on a black velvet ribbon. Lucy ran a finger over the shifting colors in the stone—green, gold, and brown. She'd never seen anything like it on the necks of women in London.

Then again, she'd never seen her aunt on the streets of London either.

Unfolding the letter, she held her breath.

Dear Lucille,

Her fingers tightened against the paper. Anyone who knew her understood she preferred to be called Lucy. But her aunt was a complete enigma to her.

It served that the reverse might be true as well.

I know you must be surprised to receive this package, given that by now I am quite dead. But I suspect someone—probably a man—will try to thwart my wishes, and so I have taken this step to ensure my intentions are honored.

The life of a peer's daughter is difficult. Believe me, I understand, more than you know. But to be the eccentric daughter of a peer is harder still, and even as a six-year-old child it was clear you marched to your own tune. My hope is that in reading my diary, you will understand the choices I have made. It is up to you to sort out whether your own independence is worth the price I paid for mine. Probably someone will try to convince you I was mad—or worse, that you are yourself. But I lived my life the way I wanted, and vow I shall greet death in a similar fashion.

My only hope is that you find the courage to as well.

I am leaving you more than my journal, Lucille. I am also leaving you Heathmore Cottage. It isn't much, I know, but perchance it might offer you the freedom to choose your own future. Guard its secrets well, Lucille.

And remember me fondly, as I have always remembered you.

—E

The air pushed from Lucy's lungs in a confused rush.

Aunt E had left her Heathmore? And what was this nonsense about secrets and fond memories? It was all so odd. She barely knew her aunt, certainly not well enough to have shed more than the perfunctory tear when news of her death had reached London. The family had not even traveled to

Cornwall for the funeral, save for Father, who was more or less morally obligated to see his older sister buried.

Confused, Lucy lifted the key to a skein of sunlight streaming through the greenhouse roof, studying its ridges and angles. She possessed only the dimmest memory of Heathmore Cottage, from a summer visit when she had been about six years old. She could recall a whitewashed home overlooking choppy green waters, and the steady beat of wind in her face. Though she could no longer remember the curve of her aunt's cheek, she retained a clear memory of a set of glass figurines, lifted down from a mantel and placed in her chubby hands.

Unsettled by the sudden rush of memories, Lucy shoved the key and the necklace into her trouser pocket, then folded the letter and stowed it between the pages of the top journal. She'd been a fanciful child, and those memories of Heathmore were murky at best.

She remembered far better the things that happened *after* that summer.

Soon thereafter, Grandfather had died and her father assumed the title. Governesses and curmudgeonly butlers had been introduced into her life. And all contact with her aunt had contracted to that single, lonely card at Christmas.

More's the pity.

From what little she could remember, it had been a fun visit.

Then again, Wilson hadn't been part of her life yet to spoil her fun.

As FAR AS handshakes went, it was a fine, firm one.

But firm or not, Thomas's mind was not entirely eased. According to his understanding of Miss E's last will and testament, which had been read just this morning by the solicitor up from St. Ives, he was not shaking hands with the correct person.

"You are *sure* your daughter will approve the sale, Lord Cardwell?" Thomas glanced uneasily at the two-story crofter's cottage which was now—for better or worse—his responsibility. Built on the most exposed part of the cliff, Heathmore Cottage braced itself against the wind like a stooped old soul, leaning ever so slightly off center. The front door lay open, its broken latch dangling. They'd had some difficulty gaining entrance without a key, a fact remedied by Thomas's forceful shoulder applied against the salt-weathered wood.

That had sparked his first twinge of guilt, as if he was somehow trespassing to conduct a buyer's inspection without a proper key. The second twinge of guilt had come over the price. There had been little by way of actual negotiation. He simply named a figure—four hundred pounds, to include both the cottage and the surrounding property—and Lord Cardwell immediately accepted.

Not that the dwelling he'd just purchased inspired much by way of confidence. He might have even paid too much. The stone walls of the old farmhouse had once been plastered white but now appeared a sickly gray, and in some places the plaster had fallen completely away to show the darker stone beneath. The roof's thatching was infested with mold and vermin and would need to be completely replaced, preferably with something a bit more modern. And thanks to the leaking roof, the floorboards in the bedrooms abovestairs were rotting. Miss E hadn't even lived here in several years, preferring instead to take cleaner and drier rooms in town.

Of course, he wasn't interested in the condition of the dwelling. His real interest lay in the property itself, and the hundred or so acres surrounding the cottage.

Thanks to his time at university, Thomas was the only formally educated soul in Lizard Bay, save the vicar. The townspeople seemed largely oblivious to the potential in the coastal soil, but he knew the true value of the property, thanks to his scientific curiosity and the long hours he'd spent prowling the surrounding fields and cliff tops.

But admitting he coveted Heathmore for reasons beyond making his home here wouldn't help his cause, and so he kept those thoughts to himself.

Lord Cardwell waved a hand toward the ramshackle cottage. "Oh, I can assure you, Lord Branston, my daughter has no need for a falling-down house. She has her first Season nearly upon her, and a husband to find. Until then she has her charities to keep her busy."

Thomas felt a slight easing of his conscience. If, as her guardian, Lord Cardwell found it prudent to handle his young daughter's more distracting affairs, who was he to gainsay the decision? Miss Westmore sounded very young and naive, likely just eighteen if her first Season was looming large. Probably one of those flighty London beauties who lived and breathed for her debut. He'd known a girl like her, once upon a time.

Thought, even, to marry her.

It had been three years since his sister's funeral. Three years since he'd left the cruel gossip and the whispers of those who would judge her. Josephine had been all the family he'd had in the world, and he failed her, utterly. The disquieting reminders of London and the ghosts that lingered there were good enough reason to seal this deal in the most expedient way possible. Lord Cardwell was leaving tomorrow, and Thomas didn't want the negotiations to stretch back to the city if he could help it. He'd been able to forget, in a fashion, secreted away here in Cornwall. Or if not forget, at least *accept* the painful path his sister had chosen. But he suspected he would remember all too well should he be forced to return to London.

Or worse, someone *else* would remember, put together the

pieces, destroy what little solace he had been able to cobble together.

"Besides," Cardwell went on, "I suspect my daughter will appreciate the money. She's always sending various charities her pin money."

Thomas didn't have to force the smile that rose to his lips. At least he could identify with *that* sentiment. A certain spinster he had known also enjoyed such things, once upon a time.

"As I am sure you know, your sister was also a staunch supporter of worthy causes," he said. In fact, Thomas himself had once *been* one of Miss E's worthy causes. She'd been the first to welcome him when he arrived at this barren outpost three years ago. Others in town had initially viewed him with suspicion. Not that he blamed them. He had been silent and sullen, the stink of London and whisky clinging to him like a miasma.

But Miss E had befriended him, and there was no denying the townspeople respected *her*. Her reputation in town had been a strange, perplexing phenomenon, one Thomas was never able to properly sort out. She was clearly an outsider, eccentric and outspoken, regularly interrupting the vicar's Sunday service with her own contrary thoughts on the sermon.

Cantankerous was the word that came to mind.

But once Thomas had been taken under her prickly wing, there was no longer any question of his acceptance in Lizard Bay. Miss E had forced him to look beyond his drunken solace to the world beyond. He missed her a good deal.

If only her brother did as well.

"Sounds like my sister," Cardwell agreed, showing few signs of mourning beyond a ring of dark circles below his eyes. "She was forever trying to right the wrongs of the world. But I still can't imagine what possessed Edith to think this an appropriate bequest for my daughter." His voice trailed off, doubtful. "It's falling to pieces."

"Perhaps Miss E thought your daughter had fond memories of the place," Thomas offered, though he'd not seen Lord Cardwell—nor the man's daughter—once in the three years he lived here. How many memories could the chit have?

Cardwell shook his head. "My daughter was quite young the last time we visited. I doubt she even remembers the journey. More likely Edith has some plot afoot, God rest her soul. She always did."

"A plot?" Thomas raised a brow, his mouth twisting with surprise. "Surely it's just her way of showing a kindness."

"Perhaps." Cardwell sounded tired. "But with no money to cover the repairs, this seems more of a burden for my daughter than a boon. I can't help but wonder what my sister was thinking." He looked back at the house, frowning. "I hadn't realized Edith had permitted the house to fall into such disrepair. Why didn't she *tell* me she was in need of financial assistance? I sent her twenty pounds a quarter, but I would have gladly sent her more money if she'd asked."

Thomas bit back a retort. Twenty pounds a quarter might have been enough for a frugal spinster to live on, but it couldn't cover the upkeep of an aging cottage. And if he knew Miss E, she would have felt guilty for accepting her brother's charity and been far too proud to ask for more. The fact that Cardwell called his sister Edith was proof enough the man scarcely knew her. Everyone in the little town of Lizard Bay—from the grocer to the vicar—had called her Miss E. If Lord Cardwell had bestirred himself to come down from London to visit his sister once in a while, he might have seen Heathmore's decline with his own eyes and intervened before it reached this sorry state. But given the fact that the home's dilapidated condition was the cause of this quick sale, Thomas held his tongue.

"I feel a bit guilty," Lord Cardwell went on. "I should probably pay *you* to take Heathmore Cottage off my daughter's hands. It's out in the middle of nowhere, with not even a proper road to get here. You'll need the devil's luck to turn it into something usable."

"No need to worry." Thomas forced a smile to his lips. "I like the solitude the property offers. With a little work and polish, I think it will shape up as a nice escape from . . . er . . . town."

Not that Lizard Bay was much of a town. And one scarcely needed to plan an escape from the few hundred souls who made their home there. But he vowed he would try to make Heathmore Cottage livable again, if only to breathe truth into the deception he felt so uncomfortable about fostering. "I admired your sister, Lord Cardwell," he added, hoping to ease the man's conscience. "Miss E was always kind to me. I am happy to help her family by removing this burden from your hands."

And if Heathmore's hidden treasures had been left in the hands of a flighty young thing from London, a fine, firm handshake with the girl's father was surely a reasonable means to an end.

From the Diary of Edith Lucille Westmore
January 1, 1813

Dear Diary,

I had always planned to start the New Year by keeping a journal. I simply hadn't counted on having to start a new life as well. But I cannot see a different way forward. No matter Father's vile threats, I refuse to marry a gout-ridden peer who is twice my age.

In truth, I think I would be deranged to carry it through.

A wife belongs to her husband. By law, by nature's edict.

But a woman alone belongs to herself.

I want Father's approval, truly I do. It feels as though I have spent half my life trying in vain to please him, and the other half utterly failing. But if he thinks to control me with threats of an asylum, he doesn't know me at all. I will make my own choice in this.

I must, if I am to remain sane.

Chapter 2

*L*ucy pushed her food around her plate and stole a sideways glance down the dining room table. Father had returned home today, looking worn-out and weary from his travels, as though he'd gone nearly to hell and back.

Well, not *hell*, precisely. Hell was at least a few degrees farther south.

On every map she'd ever seen, Cornwall stretched away to the west, all the way to the ocean. But knowing where Heathmore Cottage lay on a map wasn't the same as seeing it with her own eyes. She was bursting with questions over the inheritance Father still hadn't mentioned, though they were now well into the fourth course of dinner.

What little she had read from the first of Aunt E's diaries had left her with more questions than answers. Was her aunt truly mad? Her diary entries hinted she'd possessed a passionate, determined nature. Lucy couldn't imagine being committed to an asylum simply for refusing to marry. But sane or not, the person Aunt E had been was coming alive through the scribbled pages of her journals. Why did no one speak of her death?

Why did no one speak of her *life*?

As her mother discussed plans to visit the modiste for yet another mind-numbing fitting before the start of the Season, Lucy slid a hand into the pocket of her skirts, running a finger over the slim iron key she had taken to carrying about like a talisman. If she didn't soon take matters into her own hands, she was either going to be forced to strangle the modiste or her mother.

Neither murder would get her any closer to Cornwall.

So she put down her fork and cleared her throat. Her mother's head swiveled in her direction, her brow pinched in annoyance. "Lucy," she admonished. "How many times must I tell you? A lady does not clear her throat. It sounds very common."

"But I have something I wish to say."

"Well, a lady should never say too much, particularly during dinner. It would never do to interrupt the conversation of the gentleman seated next to you."

Lucy stifled a groan, recognizing the familiar pattern of this conversation—namely, how disastrous the upcoming Season was bound to be, given the sorry state of her manners. "But there isn't a gentleman seated next to me." She lifted a hand in her sister's direction. "There is only Lydia. And no one would ever mistake *her* for a man."

"Probably because she doesn't wear trousers." Her mother's eyes narrowed. "Pity we can't say the same about you."

Lucy bit her lip to keep from saying something she would regret.

Damn Wilson and his interfering gossip.

Her mother sighed and placed her fork down next to her plate. "Can't you see how important this is, dear? For heaven's sake, the Season is only two weeks away, and you should be seizing every opportunity to practice, not prowling about the greenhouse in trousers. Do you *want* to be a disaster?"

"I am sorry," Lucy mumbled automatically. "I will try harder."

"Well, you must start tonight. If you wish to engage in conversation with a gentleman, you must first listen." Her mother tilted her head, demonstrating. "Wait for a break in the conversation and then catch your partner's eye." She fluttered her eyelashes—a nonsensical bit of artifice for any able-bodied female but particularly outrageous when wielded by a forty-odd-year-old viscountess who lectured her daughters like a Roman general. "When they acknowledge you, speak quietly and demurely."

Lucy rolled her eyes. The gentleman she must meet during the coming Season sounded very dull indeed. "Then how will anyone hear me?"

"We hear Lydia when she speaks," her mother pointed out. "You might take a page from her book. Listen more. Practice a little self-restraint." She paused, her gaze scattering across Lucy's hair. "Let your maid curl your hair, for a change."

Beside her, Lucy could feel Lydia stiffen. Most young women would preen under such praise, but Lydia's obvious discomfort was just another reason why Lucy loved her half sister to distraction. The illegitimate daughter of Father's former mistress, Lydia had been brought to Cardwell House after her mother died. She and Lucy had grown very close in the four years since Lucy's older sister, Clare, had married a prominent London doctor and moved into her own home. Lydia deserved a Season of her own, and there was no denying she possessed a sweet, gentle temperament far better suited for the role of hopeful debutante.

But circumstances being what they were, she was to be relegated to the shadows this Season, so as to not steal the spotlight away from Lucy's sure-to-be-disastrous come-out.

Though she didn't envy Lydia her former life, Lucy did

sometimes envy her current position. Illegitimate daughters didn't need to have Seasons if they didn't want to.

And no one cared whether or not they curled their hair.

Father cleared his throat, which was apparently a fine sound for a *man* to make. "Well, Lucy. You've got the entire table's attention now. What did you wish to tell us?"

"It is just . . . I am glad you are back," she said, apparently too loudly, given the way her mother glared down the table. She drew a deep breath, striving for quiet and demure. "Do tell us, Father," she said, feeling as false as her voice. "How did the trip to Cornwall go?"

He grimaced. "It was not particularly pleasant. I am glad it is done, at any rate." His attention drifted back to his plate.

Lucy squirmed in her seat, though she knew it would probably earn her an admonishment from her mother to sit like a lady. *Surely* there was more to the trip than that. "Oh, to hell with it," she muttered under her breath, causing Lydia to cower. She leaned forward and braced her hands on either side of her plate. "Is Heathmore Cottage the same as I remember?" she blurted out.

Father looked up. "Heathmore?"

"Yes." Lucy nodded. "Aunt E's house."

He blinked at her from behind his spectacles. "I don't even see how you remember it. You can't have seen it since you were, what, four years old?"

"I was six," she told him, not liking the downward slope to her father's brow. "It's a white stone cottage, perched on a cliff."

My white stone cottage, her mind insisted on adding. *My cliff.*

"Er . . . yes." He rubbed the back of his neck. "I mean, no. Heathmore is not at all the same. You wouldn't recognize it, I fear. Fortunately, I left things there well settled."

Lucy stared at her father with a growing sense of unease. *Settled?*

Things were anything but settled.

In fact, she was feeling decidedly unsettled. Behind her father's spectacles, his eyes weren't meeting hers. A wisp of unease uncurled in her stomach.

"I ask because I received a package from Aunt E this week," she told him.

"A package?" Surprise sharpened Mother's voice. "How is that even possible? The woman died two weeks ago."

"She must have had someone mail it in the event of her death," Lucy reasoned. She slid a hand into her pocket, her fingers dancing over the key. How much to reveal? The journals seemed a terribly private gift to mention. If Aunt E had wanted others to see them, she wouldn't have taken such pains to see the pages delivered in so surreptitious a manner. The necklace, too, was something she didn't want to share. God knew it wasn't the sort of jewelry one wore to church. Heathmore Cottage, on the other hand, was a gift that could not be hidden.

She pulled out the key and held it up. "Apparently, she's left me her house."

There was a moment of shocked silence, where Lucy was quite sure she could hear the air settle in her lungs. But then her mother made a strangled sound that was anything but demure. "Oh, for heaven's sake! The woman was mad."

Lydia clapped her hands together. "Oh, Lucy, your own house!" she exclaimed, not a trace of envy in her blue eyes. "What a generous bequest."

"It isn't generous, it's ludicrous," Mother snapped. "I declare, that woman was always tottering on the edge of insanity. For her to reach out now, when it might sully Lucy's reputation just as her first Season is about to start . . ." Her voice hitched. "It's . . . it's *unconscionable*."

Father offered a weary sigh. "So *that's* what happened to the key to Heathmore Cottage," he murmured. "I had wondered what my sister was up to." He held out a palm, beckoning for Lucy to pass the key forward up the table. "I'll just send the key on to Lord Branston. I'd hate for him to have to buy a new lock when we've a perfectly good key in hand."

Lucy closed her fingers over the key. "Who is Lord Branston?"

And more to the point, why did he have need of her key?

Her father frowned. "Now Lucy, be reasonable. Branston's offer to buy the place is a bit of a relief. The house is falling down. And it is miles from the nearest town, without even a proper road to speak of. I can't understand why he wants to buy it, but he says he likes the solitude."

Lucy's face grew warm. Oh, *bugger it all*, Aunt E had been right. Someone was trying to thwart her wishes. And bless her aunt's no-longer-beating heart, it *was* a man.

Two men, in fact.

"You've sold my property?" she demanded. "To a *hermit*?"

"Not a hermit." Her father's frown deepened. "A marquess. I admit, it was a bit of a surprise to find someone so cultured in a town like Lizard Bay."

Lucy swallowed the growl that wanted to escape her throat. "Cultured or no, how can he buy Heathmore when I've never even spoken to the bloody man? Aunt E left the property to *me*." She shoved the key back in her pocket. "I am of age, and I am in possession of the key. It should be *my* decision whether or not to sell it."

Beside her, Lydia made a small squeak of protest.

Lucy ignored her. She didn't want to upset her sister, who always grew pale and nervous during domestic squabbles, as if the family she'd been fortunate enough to find was in danger of disintegrating before her eyes. But this wasn't a battle she could back down from.

Not if she wished to claim her inheritance.

Father stared at her as though she had grown two heads. "Frankly, I am surprised to hear of your interest in the place.

I've never seen you show the slightest interest in anything beyond your petty distractions in London."

Lucy felt a familiar spark of anger to hear her work so described, as though her philanthropic pursuits were some form of childish amusement. She wanted nothing more than her father's approval, lived and breathed for the occasional word of praise. Why couldn't he for once acknowledge her accomplishments? Had he any notion of how hard she worked? How many sleepless nights she'd spent, penning letter after letter, hoping to change the course of the world? "They are not petty," she retorted. "And one has nothing to do with the other."

"Lucy," he said, chidingly now, "truly, I have done you a favor to dispose of Heathmore Cottage so expeditiously." He reached into his jacket pocket and drew out a bank note, waving it as though it was a flag of truce. "And you've four hundred pounds for your trouble." He handed it to a footman, who brought it down to Lucy. "Perhaps you might like to send it on to one of your nice charities, hmm?"

Lucy glared down at the bank note. Nice charities? Oh, for heaven's sake.

Didn't he understand she corresponded with *felons*?

"How could it only be four hundred pounds?" she demanded. She might not remember much about Heathmore, but she did recall how the fields above her aunt's house had seemed to stretch to the moon. She glared at her father. "Why, there must be dozens of acres."

"Around a hundred, I think. But it isn't arable land. A more useless bit of heath and bog I've never seen. Trust me, I've done you a favor."

Lucy's nails dug deep into the skin of her palms. "Whether or not I sell it—and who I sell it to—is a decision I will make for myself." She lifted her chin. "I insist on inspecting the property myself. We can leave tomorrow."

Her mother's hand flew to her throat, fluttering in agitation. "Lucy, you *can't* be serious. Your father just returned from that godforsaken place, and your Season is about to start!" Her voice rose a hysterical notch. "We've waited for this year for too long already. Any longer and you'll be too far on the shelf to have any chance of a good match!"

"And what a pity *that* would be," Lucy grumbled mutinously.

Her father leaned back in his chair. "Don't be obstinate about this, Lucy. It's an impossible idea. The cottage is falling down. And it is infested with rats and vermin. Quite uninhabitable."

Lucy glared at him. Had her parents any notion that, to her, the thought of the coming Season—an archaic process that more or less sold young women of good breeding to the highest bidder—was enough to give the idea of living in a rat-infested cottage a good deal of appeal?

"If it is so terrible," she pointed out, "then why does Lord Branston want it?" She crossed her arms over her chest. "I would like to see Heathmore for myself. Only then will I know whether selling the property is the right choice. And I must remind you, I am twenty-one years old. I am of an age to make my own choices on this matter."

At that, her father's face turned an unfortunate shade of red. "And how do you think you will you get there?" he asked, his voice a tangle of irritation. "You'd need train fare to Salisbury. An overnight stay at the inn, and then a coach to take you on from there. All of that costs money, and that is the *one* thing my sister didn't leave you."

"I will use my pin money," she declared hotly.

"If you have any saved, I suppose you are welcome to try." At Mother's squeak of protest, her father raised his hand, as though asking for a moment to explain. "But I refuse to give you a penny more."

Lucy gaped at him. "You would take away my pin money?"

"As you have so enthusiastically pointed out, you are of age." He raised a brow in challenge. "But I know you, Lucy. You haven't any money saved. Perhaps, if you put it away like Lydia does, instead of sending it to every lost cause in London, you might have a nice sum to set by, but you've never been able to hold onto a farthing."

This time Lucy was too angry—and too hurt—to ignore the slight.

"Lost causes?" she choked out, wishing that for once Father could be supportive of her interests, rather than merely tolerant. "And here I thought they were merely 'petty distractions.'"

He frowned, but that didn't mean she had won the point.

Because . . . he was right.

She *didn't* have the money to fund a trip to Cornwall. She ought to, given that she received three pounds a month in spending money and had no interest whatsoever in ribbons and clocked stockings and the like. But as he had pointed out, her pin money had a habit of falling through her fingers, straight into the coffers of her charities.

She had always thought she was saving the outside world with her generosity.

But now she wondered if she might not have been ruining her own future instead.

Her father tapped a firm finger against the table. "Lucy, you can't afford this house. You haven't the money to travel, much less the funds to make it livable." He picked up his fork, the redness in his face easing now. "These sorts of antics were tolerable when you were seventeen, but you are a grown woman now, with responsibilities to your position. You've the coming Season and your entire life ahead of you. Your mother has gone to great expense to prepare you for your come-out, and you might be a bit more grateful for the opportunity. Heathmore is sold, and you'll just have to accept it, hmm?"

The usual sounds of dinner slowly resumed. Forks against china, the low hum of conversation. No doubt it was a relief to the rest of them to have the matter so handily dismissed.

But Lucy felt as though the walls of the dining room were closing in on her.

Smothering her.

She knew she was being impulsive—indeed, she'd been accused of such proclivities her entire life. And she wasn't entirely foolish. She knew that in her present financial state, she very likely *couldn't* afford the property. But that didn't mean she didn't want to try.

Something about this fight stirred a recklessness in her that felt far more real than the looming Season. The fate of Heathmore Cottage—indeed, the fate of her own future—was hanging in the balance. No other cause had ever felt quite so necessary to her very survival.

She pushed away her plate. "May I please be excused?" she asked.

Quietly and demurely.

Just the way she had been ordered.

When her mother nodded, Lucy waited for a footman to hold her chair, then stood up, smoothing a hand down the front of her silk skirts. It was wasteful, she knew, leaving her plate half full on the table. Many in London lacked food tonight, much less gilt-edged china to eat it from. She ought to know, given that feeding the unfortunate poor in East London was another one of her "petty distractions." But tonight the thought of staying at the table one second longer than necessary made her stomach churn in anger, not hunger.

She made her way meekly out of the dining room, head down and hands clasped in front of her. But despite the outward façade, her inner thoughts tumbled about, gaining speed and shape. No, she didn't have money of her own.

But livable or no, Heathmore Cottage was *hers*. A gift from Aunt E, to restore or sell as she saw fit. This Lord Branston fellow needed to prepare himself for disappointment.

Because by Father's own damning words, lost causes were her specialty.

Chapter 3

Lord Branston
c/o Postmaster, Lizard Bay, Cornwall
April 12, 1853

Dear Lord Branston,

Despite whatever agreement you believe you have reached with my father, he lacks the legal authority to act on my behalf. I am of an age to make my own decisions, and if I decide to sell Heathmore Cottage, you can be sure it will not be for so paltry a price. I am returning your bank note, with my regrets. Please return the home and the property to the condition in which my aunt left them. Any further association with the property will be considered trespass.

I will not hesitate to involve the authorities if necessary.

Yours Sincerely,
Miss Lucy Westmore

Thomas stared down at the letter, the bank note crumpling in his hand.

Well, this was . . . unfortunate.

Scarcely twenty feet away, the cottage's newly replastered walls gleamed white in the sunlight. The dusty parlor furniture had been pulled out and scrubbed down. Mrs. Wilkins, the proprietress of the boardinghouse down in Lizard Bay, had spent yesterday morning washing the cottage's dusty windows with vinegar-soaked rags. And above his head the new roof was slowly taking shape, though he'd only been able to find one roofer willing to take the job, and the slate had to be carried up the narrow, twisting path on the back of an obstinate donkey. But now the letter from Miss Westmore threatened to undo it all.

Return the home and property to the condition in which my aunt left them.

How was he supposed to do that? Rip off the new slate roof?

Through his irritation, a reluctant bit of respect tried to intrude. Whoever else she was, Miss E's niece was not quite the frippery-minded miss he'd imagined. The girl must have a core of steel to cross her father in this way. In fact, there were elements to her letter that reminded him suspiciously—painfully—of a certain deceased spinster. Miss Westmore sounded like a very determined young woman, and if she was anything like her aunt, he'd made a misstep in negotiating with her father instead of her.

As he shoved the letter and bank note into his coat pocket,

Thomas eyed the boy who'd brought the letter up from town. The lad was the smallest of the Tanner orphans, with a shock of red hair and a face full of freckles. It was good to see he was wearing shoes today. In January, Thomas had seen Danny tripping about town with naught but socks on his feet—and not because he'd lacked the shoes, either, because Thomas had personally seen the entire lot of Tanners shod around Christmas time. It seemed, upon further interrogation, the boy had thought shoes were too fine a luxury to wear to anything but church. But today, shoes were clearly not the worst of the boy's problems. The lad's left eye was red and swelling.

"Have you been beaten then, Danny?" Thomas could scarcely imagine the postmaster lifting a hand to the lad, or old Jamieson, the town grocer who sometimes had odd jobs for the Tanner boys. "You can tell me if someone's been hurting you."

The boy shook his head, his eyes focused somewhere in the vicinity of his scuffed shoes. "Just some roughing around from one of my brothers."

"Would you care to tell me which one?" Thomas waited for a further explanation. Seemed like more than the usual sort of fisticuffs, but it had been a while since he was a boy of that age. Twenty-odd years, in fact. And even then he had been nothing like Danny.

Oh, there were enough similarities to give him pause. He, too, had been an orphan, but instead of three feisty brothers, he'd had a sister. And instead of growing up surrounded by townspeople who knew and loved him, he and Josephine had been granted only a cold, uncaring guardian, followed by a relentless string of boarding schools.

When Danny remained mutinously silent, Thomas sighed. He could respect wanting to protect one's siblings, if nothing else. "Well, if you're determined to protect your brothers, I suppose I can respect that. But try to be more careful." He dug a coin from his pocket and tossed it to the boy. "And give the postmaster my thanks for having you bring the letter on so quickly."

Danny caught the coin in the air. "It weren't *so* quick," he admitted, looking down at the ground. "None of us wanted to come and deliver it, and we got into a bit of a row about it." He touched a finger to his swollen eye. "I'm the smallest, you see, so I lost."

"You fought to see who *wouldn't* have to bring the letter?" Thomas asked, perplexed. That hardly made sense. He always tipped them well. "Why?"

"Well . . . that is, you see . . ." Danny glanced nervously toward the cottage. "It's the haints."

"You think Heathmore is haunted?"

Danny took a step toward the rocky path that meandered the two miles or so back to Lizard Bay. "I heard Mrs. Wilkins tell Mr. Jamieson she could hear Miss E moaning up here, pining for her lost love."

Thomas had to work to control the bark of laughter that wanted to work its way out of his throat. *Miss E, pining for a man.* It was about the most ridiculous thing he had ever heard. Why, Miss E had eaten men for breakfast. She'd had Mr. Jamieson, the local grocer, cowering at her feet in fear of messing up her monthly order of snuff, and her long-running feud with the town vicar had been the stuff of legends.

"You don't need to worry." Thomas smiled. He supposed he'd had his own fears at Danny's age, when ghosts had seemed a far more terrifying prospect than the threat of inner demons. He'd only been eleven when his parents died in a carriage accident, and he'd imagined them as ghosts more than once. "Miss E is in heaven now, not a ghost come back to haunt you." The devil seized him then. "If anything, I think she'd come back to haunt Reverend Wellsbury, don't you?"

Danny's eyes flew wide, and Thomas mentally kicked

himself. Clearly, one didn't joke around about ghosts with eight-year-olds.

"But Mrs. Wilkins said—"

"Mrs. Wilkins likes a bit of gossip, hmmm?" Thomas interrupted. In fact, most of the townspeople who lived in Lizard Bay did. "You shouldn't pay her any mind."

The wind chose that moment to rear up, an eerie, howling sound that whistled through the nearby rocks. The boy jumped like something flushed from the heather. "C-Can I go now?" Danny stammered. "This place gives me the woolies."

Thomas cocked an ear toward the edge of the cliff. Woolies was a rather unscientific term, but he supposed he could understand the sentiment, given that the hairs on his own neck had pricked to attention. With Miss E's permission, he'd spent many an hour here, hiking the moors above the cottage, exploring the cliff walls, noting the area's unusual geography and studying the plant life. In all those hours of introspective study, he'd never before paid the sound of the wind much mind. But then, he didn't believe in ghosts.

Not unless they were of the living variety.

"It's just a natural scientific phenomenon," he explained to the boy. "I suspect the sound is produced by the shape of the cliff face and the updraft from the ocean."

Danny gaped at him, his mouth wide enough to catch flies. "Phenom-what?"

"The wind." Thomas pulled a hand through his hair. How did one explain such things to an uneducated eight-year-old? "It's just the sound of the wind."

"Gor. You know a lot of big words, Lord Branston."

"So would you if you would apply yourself more diligently to your studies."

"Dili-gent?" the boy mouthed uncertainly.

"It means to work hard."

Danny's lower lip protruded in a definite pout. "I don't need to study hard. Who needs books and numbers, anyway? I'm going to be a fisherman, like my da was."

Thomas shook his head, feeling bad for the boy. It had been less than a year since Danny's father died at sea, and he supposed that wound was still raw. But if the boy thought he had a fisherman's future in Lizard Bay, he was sorely mistaken. "Danny, we've been through this. I am willing to pay for you and your brothers to go to university when you are older, but you must study hard now in order to qualify. I would encourage you to think beyond fishing. What if you had a chance to become a barrister? Or a doctor?"

"Barri-what?" came the boy's mumbled response.

Thomas hesitated, knowing his words probably sounded hollow, given that he himself provided no useful contribution to the world at large. Who was he to give such advice to a boy of eight? He had gone to university because he'd *wanted* to, not because he had to. After all, he'd become a marquess at the age of eleven, and acquiring a higher education wasn't a prerequisite for the job. Moreover, looking back, it had been a supremely selfish decision. He'd left his sister behind, alone and unprotected.

And when he finally came of age, it turned out that a knowledge of botany and geology had not in any way prepared him for the dissolute life of a peer. He'd have done better studying probabilities at the hazard table, or fermentation and distillation techniques.

Danny took a decided step toward the path that would carry him back down to town. "Well, I still say I want to be a fisherman." He jumped as the eerie sound echoed again up from the cliff face. The boy's face turned white. "It's her gh-ghost," he stammered, "not the wind!" And with that, he turned and sprinted back toward the safety of town.

Thomas watched the back of the boy's head disappear

through the break in the rocks. Part of him wanted to follow. Leave the cottage to the feisty Miss Westmore and be done with it. That would certainly be the easiest path, and Lord knew he'd already dealt with enough family drama in his lifetime.

But he'd already run away from too many difficult decisions in his life, and he supposed he owed it to Miss E's memory to safeguard the land she had loved.

As he turned back and looked out over the moors stretching up above the cottage, he thought of all that the property held, and all that might be lost if he let it go. The repairs to the structure aside, the real value of the property lay beneath its soil, not within its walls. He couldn't believe Miss E had meant to endanger it by leaving it to neglectful relatives, but then, she'd grown a bit senile in her later years. He'd thrown himself into procuring it for honorable reasons, and he was loath to let it go so easily, now that the seeds to save it had been planted. Worse, the most damning line from Miss Westmore's tersely worded letter kept swimming through his head.

If I decide to sell it, you can be sure it will not be for so paltry a price.

She had all but threatened to sell the property to the highest bidder. That meant if he wanted to save Heathmore from those who would exploit it, he was going to need to take the negotiations to London. And so Thomas trudged back to the cottage to call off the roofers, already mentally calculating his route to London, dreading every agonizing mile.

God, he hated London. Was there a hope in hell he could manage this trip without falling apart? Thanks, in part, to Miss E's insistence on temperance, he felt more in control of his life now. More capable of resisting the bottle, at any rate. But he knew he was untested in his current state. There was little enough by way of temptation here in Cornwall.

London, however, was a different beast entirely.

Perhaps he'd spent too long avoiding this decision, too long trying to convince himself of all the reasons why he shouldn't set foot in the city. It had been three years, after all. Three years since he'd fled his sister's funeral and his fiancée's betrayal, heartsick and confused and more than a little inebriated. He knew *he* had changed, largely for the better.

But had London changed?

Had *she*?

Heaven help them all, he was about to find out.

Today, Father called in our family doctor. After questioning me at length and completing a cursory examination, Dr. Bashings withdrew from the room to confer with my father for a good half hour, their voices hushed and urgent. When I pressed my ear to the door, I caught only one word, but it was more than enough.

Bedlam.

That most terrifying of threats, the asylum where the ton disposes of their unwanted women. But would Father really do it? I know I am too outspoken for my own good. According to my father, it is one of my most significant flaws. In retrospect, I probably shouldn't have rapped Dr. Bashings on the head and told him to mind his own bellows when he asked about my menstrual cycle, but honestly, I can't see what one has to do with the other. For now I'm to be given a prescription, some vile-tasting powder that is to be mixed with my milk at night.

Apparently my humors run too hot for Dr. Bashing's comfort.

Well, they are certainly running hot now.

I may not be a pliable sort of young miss, but I refuse to be a drugged one.

Chapter 4

"The post has arrived, Miss Lucy."

Lucy looked up, immediately on guard. Ever since penning her letter to Lord Branston, she'd felt on edge whenever Wilson brought the post. Something told her the man who wanted Heathmore Cottage would not be so easily put off.

But why was Wilson smiling?

"Am I to presume a letter has come from Geoffrey, then?" she asked warily, closing her aunt's diary and tucking it into the pocket of her day dress.

"Yes, your brother is proving remarkably dedicated to his correspondence these past few months." His bushy brows rose in amusement. "Shall I fetch your gloves?"

Lucy picked up Geoffrey's latest letter by one corner, sniffing it suspiciously. "No, I am sure that won't be necessary. He never pulls the same prank twice." Although repeating the mischief when someone didn't expect it would be a prank in and of itself, wouldn't it?

Geoffrey was famous for such things.

Or rather, he was *infamous*.

Last month, he'd sent her a letter whose pages had been soaked in the juice of hot peppers. After she accidentally touched her face, her eyes had watered for hours. Last week he'd sent a letter containing a sachet of ink cleverly hidden behind the wax seal. When she opened it, the ink had gotten all over her hands and ruined one of her favorite dresses.

Who knew what horrors this one contained?

"I'll just let you open this one." Lydia giggled from the sofa where she was bent over her embroidery. "Read it out loud, if you would."

"Coward," Lucy laughed, though she could understand the need for caution. She carefully slid a fingernail beneath the wax seal, half expecting the thing to burst into flames. She'd never admit it out loud, but it felt good to have Geoffrey prank them by letter. He'd escaped to university this past autumn—ostensibly to further his education, though she suspected he did so primarily to extend his career as a professional trickster.

She missed him more than she'd thought she would.

She looked up from her careful task to find Wilson peering down. She smiled, knowing the servant missed Geoffrey every bit as much as she did. "Don't you have something to polish?" she asked, though her words held no heat. She *did* so enjoy catching Wilson engaging in poor manners, given that the reverse was so frequently true.

"Only you, Miss Lucy." He gave her a freshly forged frown. "Only you."

As he puttered away to wherever Wilson went when he wasn't harassing her, Lucy leaned back into the chair to read the letter in peace. Geoffrey's handwriting was a tight, familiar scrawl, but the paper itself looked as though it had been written out of doors, with noticeable grass stains along the edges. Probably on the cricket field, if she knew her brother.

She felt a frisson of irritation to see the evidence of his

carefree leisure, given that she was being cloistered indoors due to her mother's fears that the spring sunshine would ruin her complexion ahead of next week's come-out. God, she'd give anything to climb a tree the way she used to. She'd even do it quietly and demurely if she had to.

But that would no doubt ruin her carefully buffed fingernails, bugger it all.

Dear Lucy,

Father wrote to me to say Aunt E has left you a rat-infested house in Cornwall. What jolly good luck! I always thought she was a bit mad, but this surely confirms it. Father asked me what I think about your insistence on keeping it, and I had to laugh. Perhaps it might help those poor marriage-minded fools take notice of you this year.

You could be known as the Rat Lady from Lizard Bay. Why, they'll be lining up for a chance with an heiress like that!

In all seriousness, I wish you good luck in the coming Season.

You are definitely going to need it.

Yrs with affection,
Geoffrey

"What has he done this time?" Lydia asked, her head still bent over her embroidery. "You've gone very quiet."

Lucy folded the letter, suddenly less enthusiastic about reading it out loud. There was no obvious prank to impart—it seemed an ordinary enough letter. She couldn't fault him for ribbing her about the coming Season, given that such teasing was part of his dubious charm.

Geoffrey knew she was dreading the coming drama, with its scratchy ball gowns and interminable waltzes. Knew she hated the idea of the fumbling, eager gentlemen—men so desperate to have her dowry they were even willing to pay court to the awkward, mannish, *plain* Westmore daughter. He must know, too, that she didn't want to marry. She had been outspoken enough on her views of marriage and such through the years.

But the mention of Heathmore Cottage—and the fact her father had asked Geoffrey for his opinion on the matter— stung.

"It's just Geoffrey." Lucy shoved a wayward strand of hair out of her eyes, tucking it behind one ear. "Up to his usual antics."

"More hot peppers?"

"No." She rubbed her forefinger against her thumb, as if testing for heat, relieved to find none. Still . . . perhaps she should wash her hands. Just in case. "He's teasing me about Heathmore Cottage. But if *he'd* been the one who was given the property and then had it sold without his permission," she muttered darkly, "you can bet he'd not be so glib."

"Probably because he would be tripping over his feet to sell it as quickly as possible." Lydia looked up from her embroidery hoop. "Remember, he's been terrified of rats, ever since that prank at Harrow went wrong. And why are we still talking about this? I thought the matter had been resolved at dinner last week."

"Just because I stopped speaking of it doesn't mean it's resolved. And Geoffrey's an idiot." Lucy scowled at her sister. "*I'm* not afraid of a few bloody rats."

Lydia arched a fair brow. "Is such language really necessary? You are supposed to be trying harder to sound like a lady."

"For heaven's sake, sometimes you sound just like Mother." Lucy stood up and began to pace the length of the drawing room. It wasn't as though she didn't *try* to look and sound like a lady. She and Lydia were less than a year apart in age, and shared a remarkably similar appearance—the same wispy blond hair, the same unobjectionable blue eyes. People were forever mixing them up at church and the like. But physical similarities aside, no one who *knew* them would ever mistake them. Their mouths might be similarly shaped, but Lucy's was usually running amok, while Lydia's seemed to know just what to say.

Or rather, what *not* to say.

Lucy reached the fireplace, then turned back, her skirts twitching angrily about her ankles. "The point is, it would be Geoffrey's choice whether or not to sell Heathmore. He's not even reached his majority yet, and Father already treats him as though he is capable of making his own decisions. I cannot believe Father wrote to him to ask his opinion." She threw up her hands. "It isn't fair. It's *my* property. And I am twenty-one years of age."

"To be perfectly honest, I doubt Father would encourage Geoffrey to keep a rat-infested cottage either," Lydia pointed out. "Have you considered that perhaps the house is really as terrible as he says? That you are fortunate to have sold it at all?"

"Well, I *can't* know that, can I?" Lucy halted in front of the window and stared out onto the Grosvenor Square streetscape. The newly budding trees stood like sentinels, their skeleton branches hopeful against the blue April sky. But she herself felt no such patience. Come next week, the trees might be in bloom, but *she'd* be launched into the Season that was barreling down on her like a runaway horse.

Nausea swirled in her stomach at the thought. She wasn't even sure which bothered her more: the thought that she was to be denied her inheritance, or the forward march of her imminent, unwanted Season. Her debut was something her mother had planned for several years, waiting for the perfect time, long past the usual age young women were presented. It had been necessary, everyone said, to let the gossip around Lucy's older sister's "disastrous" marriage to a mere doctor die down first, to give the crowd time to find other diversions and rumors to occupy their tongues. But Lucy hadn't minded. In fact, she had savored that blissful, four year reprieve. A Season had never been something she wanted, though she'd grudgingly come to accept its inevitability over the years.

But now, thanks to Aunt E's diaries and the key to Heathmore, she'd been given an alternative view of her future, a bit of independence dangled before her eyes like the rarest of jewels. And she wanted it with a desperation she couldn't quite explain.

She rubbed her neck, her fingers stiff with anger. "I'm expected to blindly trust everyone else's judgment in this without being credited with enough sense to make the decision on my own. But something doesn't feel right. This Lord Branston fellow seems far too keen on acquiring the property, especially if it is in such terrible shape as Father says. Aunt E trusted me with the property when she didn't trust anyone else."

And had claimed there were secrets to guard as well.

She turned away from the window and met Lydia's eyes. "That is why I need to get there. To see Heathmore myself, and understand the man's interest in it."

Lydia's forehead creased with worry. "Father forbade it."

Lucy shook her head. Her memory of last week's dreadful dinner conversation was still fresh in her mind, probably because she'd rehashed it no less than a dozen times, examining it from every possible angle. "He didn't *forbid* it so much as imply I couldn't afford it."

And she couldn't. She had scraped and scrimped and tallied every penny she owned, most of which had been rolling about forgotten in the bottom of her desk drawer. Father was right: she could count less than a pound to her name. Worse, he had proven true to his word and refused to give her any pin money this week.

No doubt he thought she'd hie herself straight off to Cornwall.

No doubt he was right.

She considered whether she ought to just ask her older sister, Clare, to loan her the money. Clare, happily married now, was expecting a second child in August. While her sister and brother-in-law lived sensibly, they had enough money to spare.

But aside from Mother, Clare had been one of the family's most vocal champions of Lucy's coming Season. She had accompanied them to every dress fitting, supplying her bountiful fashion advice on the merits of each gown Lucy had been forced to choose. She'd encouraged her to steer clear of the sort of friends who put others down, explained how to repair a torn hem and go on dancing into the night. Clare seemed determined to make her a smashing success—no doubt on account of her guilt over the delayed Season.

No, she couldn't ask Clare for help. The risk that her older sister might tell Father—or worse, Mother—was too great.

Lydia, on the other hand . . . now there was a sister she could always depend on.

Lucy fixed her with a hopeful stare. Lydia hardly *ever* spent her pin money. And that meant she probably had over one hundred pounds squirreled away, just waiting for someone to need it. Lucy took a step in her sister's direction. "Couldn't you just loan me a few pounds? I don't have need of much, just enough to get me to Cornwall and back. Father would never even need to know where I found it."

"I can't." As soft and fragile as Lydia looked, her voice was stern. "I will not lie about this. I owe this family far too much."

"I would give *you* the money if you needed it," Lucy pointed out, stung by her sister's quick refusal. And she would, too, if only she had money to give. She was nothing if not charitable, apparently to the point of idiocy.

"You have less at stake than I do," Lydia said quietly.

On that point, Lucy found she had no argument. Father had been unfailingly generous to Lydia, going so far as to publicly acknowledge her as his daughter. Lydia might not have a grand Season in her immediate future, but she'd been given a respectable dowry that might eventually tempt a third son or prosperous tradesman to overlook the circumstances of her birth. If she'd been in Lydia's shoes, with the same domestic-minded hopes and dreams, she supposed her loyalties would be very similarly aligned.

But Lucy's dreams weren't of the domestic-mind variety. At least, she couldn't imagine having such dreams while shackled to a man who only wanted her dowry. No, she dreamed of adventures, not titled husbands. She wanted a life full of grand causes and charities that needed her, not a husband who had need only of her money.

And the thought of abandoning *her* hopes and dreams just because she was female made her want to smash something.

"I suppose I can understand your loyalty to Father," Lucy muttered. "And I should not have asked you. It was not fair of me."

"It isn't only about Father," Lydia sighed, picking up her embroidery again. "If you do this now, with the Season nearly upon you, it will break your mother's heart." She lowered her head. "I cannot be a party to that."

"Surely you don't owe my mother such loyalty," Lucy protested.

"Don't I?" Lydia looked up, her expression sad but firm.

"She welcomed me into this house four years ago, when she had little reason to. When my very existence posed a threat to her own children's reputations. She may not be my true mother, but in a way, I owe her more than any of you." She shook her head again. "So, no. As much as I love you—as much as I usually admire your fierce sense of independence—I won't betray their trust. If you are determined to go to Cornwall, you must find a way to do it on your own."

"And how am I supposed to do that?" Lucy replied bitterly. "Father has refused to give me any pin money this week."

Lydia lowered her embroidery again. "Honestly, Lucy, for all your grand causes, have you ever stopped to think how the world outside your door really lives? Are you really this naive? Do it the same way the world outside Mayfair does, every single day. Earn it, the way my mother and I did. We took in mending each week."

"But . . . you know I can't sew worth a shite," Lucy countered weakly, imagining how many stitches she'd need to manage to even afford train fare. Why . . . it must be *thousands*.

Her fingers twitched, making their objections known.

"Well then." Lydia's smile turned grim. "I suggest you find something to sell."

A woman in search of freedom is a woman in need of funds.

It hurt to sell my jewelry, especially the pearls that had belonged to my grandmother, but once I had the money in hand there was no turning back. I went as far as I could. The northern coast of Cornwall, to be exact. The townsfolk of this small coastal village looked at me queerly when I arrived. No doubt they are unused to fashionably dressed young ladies arriving in Lizard Bay and purchasing vacant properties without a husband or parent in tow.

But if I am going to be a spinster, I vow I shall be a spectacular one.

A lady doesn't require pearls for that.

Chapter 5

*L*ucy walked home, head down, hurrying the length of Oxford Street.

It wasn't exactly a fine day for a walk. The overhead clouds were threatening rain and the temperature seemed closer to early March than half-past April. A wind from the west buffeted her trouser-clad legs and found the gaps between the seams of her borrowed felt jacket. She might have liked to hail a cab or wait at the corner for the Bow and Stratford omnibus.

But for the first time in her pampered life, every penny counted.

And today a public conveyance was an extravagance she could no longer afford.

Seeking solace from the cold wind, she shoved her hands in her pockets, jingling the few coins that waited there. Despite the weather, and despite the fact that her pockets were far lighter than she needed, it still felt strangely good to be walking about the streets of London with only her own thoughts for company. She couldn't remember the last time she'd felt such freedom. People might stop and stare in horror at a young women traipsing these streets unchaperoned, but no one gave a young "man" a second glance.

But despite the pleasure to be found in such subterfuge, she still felt a faint queasiness echoing through her belly. Probably on account of what she had done, rather than what she wore, but it was far too late to second-guess her decision now.

She was determined to reach Cornwall and inspect the property her aunt had left her. She knew it was disobedient and possible even reckless, but she felt—she *knew*—that if she didn't at least see the cottage her father was insisting be sold, she would regret it for the rest of her life. But to reach Cornwall she needed money, and there were only so many ways a young woman could do that—and still hold her head up—in London.

In the end, it had been Aunt E's diary and Lydia's sage advice that had given Lucy the vital clues as to how to go on. She didn't have any jewelry to speak of, an unintended consequence, she supposed, of being the sort of girl who had never wanted or appreciated such things. But she didn't need enough money to *buy* Heathmore, simply to travel to see it.

And she'd had at least one thing of value to sell.

As she rounded the last corner toward home, she lifted a hand to try to tuck her chin-length hair back beneath the slouched felt cap. She sighed as the strands refused to stay put, recognizing the telltale signs of what she knew was her deepest flaw: the propensity to charge headfirst into an idea without first thinking it through.

Take those seedlings for the St. James Orphanage, for example. She'd gotten the bright idea to start the project after seeing bowls of pea soup sitting on the long communal table where the children took their meals. Only later, after she'd started the project, did she realize the poor orphans were served pea soup nearly every day . . . and, as a result, dearly *hated* peas. Now she'd gone and sold her hair to the wig makers, only to end up with hair too short to pull back and pockets still not full enough to carry her to Cornwall.

Stupid, stupid.

As the long shadow of Cardwell House reached toward her, Lucy realized with a start of dismay that hiding the evidence of her new short hair was no longer her greatest worry. She was returning to Grosvenor Square later than she'd intended, thanks to the long, punishing walk. An unfamiliar coach waited outside, and a finely dressed matron was being helped into it by a young man. *Bugger it all.* She'd missed calling hours.

Again.

Head down, she slipped past the coach, trying not to attract undue notice as she aimed for the servant's entrance. All she needed was to be recognized by one of her mother's so-called friends. But she stopped dead in her tracks as she heard the light patter of laughter coming from inside the coach. "Didn't I tell you she'd be nice, dear?" she heard the woman say over the creak of springs in the seat. "And she's old enough to probably be desperate."

"Nice and wealthy." The young man chuckled, making Lucy's cheeks heat in indignation. "And really, that's all that matters, isn't it?"

"She's pretty enough," came the woman's voice again.

"I suppose." The young man laughed again. "Of course, it won't matter. I don't intend to spend any more time with her than necessary to get an heir."

Lucy's hands tightened to fists. Who on earth were they talking about? If they were talking about Lydia—dear, sweet, *deserving* Lydia, who dreamed of a husband and children and happiness—she was going to need to warn her sister against this bloody fop and his mother. But the pieces didn't fit. Lydia wasn't usually invited to calling hours, on account of her illegitimacy.

But Lucy couldn't take the time needed to puzzle it

through. If today's visitors were leaving, that meant her mother was inside, spitting mad.

And that meant she needed to get inside and change as soon as possible.

Lucy dashed away from the coach and slipped inside through the scullery entrance, dodging the curious stares of the kitchen staff, who were already busy preparing for the evening meal. She lifted a finger to her lips, begging their silence. Then she plowed down the first floor hallway, hoping to make it upstairs and change before Wilson or her mother were any the wiser. Just when she thought she might actually succeed, a hand snaked out of the drawing room doorway and closed tight about her wrist.

"Lucy Westmore!" Lydia hissed, dragging her inside. "Where have you been all afternoon?"

"*Shhhh.*" Lucy twisted away from her sister's grip. After a furtive look down either side of the hallway to make sure she hadn't been seen, she shut the door firmly.

Lydia put her hands on her hips. "You missed calling hours again."

"A fact I cannot bring myself to regret." Lucy grinned as she unbuttoned her jacket. "I saw our visitors as I was coming in. They seemed awful. And why are you so upset? It isn't as though this is the first time I've missed them."

Lydia's face flushed red. "No, but it is the first time your mother has made me pretend to *be* you during calling hours!"

Lucy's fingers stilled over the buttons. "You pretended to be me? On *purpose*?"

"I didn't have a choice, thanks to you." Lydia's eyes flashed a warning. "The Baroness Whittle stopped by today, and even though the Season hasn't started yet, she brought her odious son with her. He specifically asked to meet you."

Lucy frowned, thinking back to the coach she had just seen, and all she had heard there. *Oh God.* She didn't need to warn Lydia to be careful.

She needed to warn herself.

Not that much warning was needed. She'd always suspected her Season would go a particular way, that gentlemen would only be interested in her money, rather than her thoughts. How could they be interested in anything else, as disastrous as she was with a hairbrush? But to have this uncensored confirmation of it made her stomach pitch in distress.

"But . . . *why?*" she asked. "Why pretend to be me? Why not just meet him yourself?"

"He doesn't want an illegitimate daughter for his wife, you ninny. He's going to be a *baron*. Your mother was nearly desperate to make a good impression, and when she couldn't find you, I suppose she felt I was better than nothing. We look enough alike that they never guessed."

Lucy swallowed. She wasn't even out yet, and already the thought of meeting a gentleman like that across the battle lines of a drawing room made her skin crawl. Was this how it was going to be? She was about to be presented as publicly available and looking to make a match, thank you very much. And to the eyes of countless greedy gentlemen, she was a walking, talking ten thousand pound dowry.

No wonder the baroness had brought her idiot son.

He probably wanted an early peek at the circus.

"Are you listening to me?" Lydia demanded. "Your Season is scarcely a week away, and you don't seem to care at all. And don't tell me you've been in the greenhouse, because Wilson already checked there." Her gaze scooted lower, and that was when her eyes finally widened. "Why are you wearing Geoffrey's old hat and jacket?" Her voice inched louder. "What on *earth* is going on?"

Lucy shrugged out of the borrowed garment, wishing she could shrug off her simmering anger as easily. The damned fop had actually admitted he was only interested in her money. She couldn't imagine a life shackled to someone so shallow. "I went . . . out."

Lydia gaped at her. "Do you mean you went *outside*? Dressed like *that*?"

"You've seen me in trousers before."

"Yes. Trousers to work in the greenhouse, which is scandalous enough," Lydia choked out. "But to go out, where someone could see you . . . You look like a—"

"Boy?" Lucy finished. She removed the hat, and several pieces of her newly cut hair swung forward to just barely graze her chin. "'Tis rather the point. Better to be thought a boy, I think, when one traipses unchaperoned through the streets of London." She smiled cheekily. "I need to guard my reputation, you know."

Lydia turned pale as new milk. She reached out a trembling finger to touch Lucy's hair. "Oh, Lucy . . . what terrible, awful thing have you done now?"

Lucy shook her head, testing the feel of it against her neck. Her hair didn't *feel* terrible. Neither did it feel awful. "I've sold it." She blew several insistent wisps of hair from her eyes, wondering how to contain them. Now that she'd removed her cap, the shortened strands seemed a bit . . . *excited* by their newfound freedom. "In fact, it was your idea."

"How, exactly, was this *my* idea?" Lydia sounded close to hysterical.

"You encouraged me to find a way to earn the money to reach Cornwall on my own. You told me to find something to sell, so I visited the wig makers. Did you know they pay more for blond hair?"

Though . . . not *much* more. She had a total of fifteen shillings in her pocket. By her calculations, if the sum was added to the loose change from her desk drawer, she had enough to get her to Cornwall. Now she just needed to find enough to either keep her there or get her back.

"I didn't mean you should sell your hair," Lydia cried. "I *meant* you should sell the silver buttons off your old cloak. Or perhaps your pen and ink set."

"Don't be silly. I *need* my pen set."

"You need your hair, too!" Lydia retorted, her voice incredulous. "What about your Season? Your mother will be devastated. What were you *thinking*?"

Lucy's lungs tightened, as though someone had yanked a rope tight about her chest. For heaven's sake, this wasn't about Mother, or the Season, or Lydia either.

It was her choice. Her life. *Her bloody hair.*

"No one will notice when it's pinned up," she protested, though a niggling doubt argued the counterpoint. She'd known from the moment the wig maker had made his first snip with the shears that hiding this was going to be a potential problem, but by then it was too late to change her mind. She'd hoped that with a few hairpins no one would notice. But judging by the way the ends refused to stay in even a simple queue at the back of her neck, the wig maker must have cut it even shorter than she'd thought.

Lydia sank down onto the sofa. "You are ruined," she whispered. "If you go out in public now, you'll never recover."

"Oh, for heaven's sake." Lucy rolled her eyes. "I'm not ruined." Surely being ruined would involve more than a trip to the wig makers.

And be a bit more fun in the making.

Take Aunt E, for example. According to the first volume of her aunt's diary, she'd taken herself to Cornwall without her parents' permission and lived for more than four decades as a scandalous spinster. To Lucy, that sounded like the *right* kind of ruin, one that was earned outright, rather than merely presumed. But judging by the tears welling in Lydia's eyes, her sister's definition of ruin was rather different.

"You mustn't tell anyone," Lucy warned, suddenly realizing that between her hair and Lydia's knowledge of her plans, a good deal of havoc could be wrought. "I still need to find a bit more money if I am to do this properly, and that means I need to hide this from Mother, at least for the near future." She looked pleadingly at her sister. "Do you promise not to say anything?"

"You are really going to Cornwall, then?" Lydia choked out.

"Not yet. Soon, though. When I can earn a bit more money. And I won't be gone forever." Lucy sat down beside her sister and placed a hand over hers. "I only want to have a look at my property, to make the decision for myself. In fact, I predict I will be back before the Season has even properly started."

But Lydia pulled her hand away. "And what good would coming back do, with your hair shorn and your reputation in tatters?" she asked bitterly. "Did you even think this through before you charged into it?"

Lucy bit her lip, the question hitting a little too close for comfort. No, she hadn't thought it through. She'd simply read Aunt E's diary entry last night, and woken up this morning determined to find something to sell. As per usual, she'd set her sights on a grand goal and ignored the smaller difficulties, such as how to explain—or hide—the evidence of what she had done. She might be impulsive, but she at least had enough self-awareness to look back now and recognize her usual pattern of impetuousness.

"I probably should have done a bit of research into how much I might earn first," she admitted. "And I should have waited to visit the wig makers until I had enough money to leave immediately after I had done it."

Lydia's face turned red. "*That* is what you see as the lesson learned here? For heaven's sake, Lucy, how can you be so . . . so . . . *blind*? I would give anything to be in your position, you know. To have a chance to find a proper husband, and to find real happiness." A tear rolled down her cheek. "And yet you are throwing it all away for a rat-infested cottage?"

Lucy felt a spark of irritation. Why couldn't Lydia see her side of it? For as long as she could remember, this threatened Season had hovered above her head like a guillotine. And now, with the encounter with the visiting coach, it was clear her fears were well-founded. She had only ever consented to suffer through the drama of this Season to silence her parents' expectations. It wasn't as though she had any intention of procuring a husband anyway—especially not one who only wanted to give her a ring in exchange for ten thousand pounds. She might be a female, but she wasn't an idiot, and she knew an unfair bargain when she saw one.

"This isn't about a cottage, Lydia. It's about my future, and what I want from it." She hesitated, thinking with a small cramp of regret of how long her mother had been planning this Season, and how hurt she would be if she did something to ruin it. "I know this is hard for you to understand, but I can't imagine myself happy with a husband." *Particularly not a greedy arse with a sour-faced baroness for a mother.* "And what is the point of a Season, if not to find a proper match?"

"But what is the point of a future without someone to share it with?" Lydia countered through her tears.

"Why would I want to share my future with someone who will make me miserable?" Lucy protested, shuddering at the thought. "Why must I marry at all?"

"Not all marriages are miserable. Your parents seem to muddle along, even though they have their differences." Lydia's cheeks flushed, no doubt on account of the fact she was living, breathing proof of some of those differences. "And Clare seems wildly happy in her marriage to Dr. Merial," she pointed out. "You could hope for a love match."

"Could I?" Lucy glanced toward the window, unable to imagine it. She shook her head slowly. "I am not like Clare." Her older sister was poised and beautiful and brave. She had chosen a man she loved, but Lucy couldn't think of a single other marriage based on such an anomaly. With her too-tall figure and mannish ways, she couldn't imagine ever being gifted with such a choice herself. Which meant she was facing precisely two possible paths for her future: marry a penniless fop like the one from the coach.

Or don't marry at all.

Outside, night was starting to fall, and through the window she could see the glow of the gaslights on Grosvenor Square. A servant would be coming in soon to pull the drapes, which meant she needed to scurry up to her room and figure out what to do with her hair before dinner. But she hesitated, wanting to make Lydia understand.

"Can't you see?" Her gaze swung back to meet her sister's tear-filled eyes. "I don't have the same dreams as you and Clare, Lydia." In fact, she couldn't imagine a more miserable existence than being shackled to a man she didn't know, forced to conform to a stranger's expectations of what a suitable wife did and said. She thought about her now-confirmed fears for the Season, the certainty of an unhappy marriage if she accepted her fate.

And then she thought of her aunt's diaries, full of passion and adventure.

Resolved, she shook her head. "Haven't you ever wanted something so much it hurt? Something that was refused you, even though you knew it ought to be your birthright?"

"How can you ask me that?" Lydia answered, swiping at her face. "*I* won't have a grand Season, you know. And I'm at least *half* a Cardwell."

Lucy sat silent. It was true. Thanks to the vagaries of her birth, Lydia's hopes for a future and a husband were of the ordinary variety, lacking the glittering ballrooms and pinched slippers and polished peers in her own future nightmare. There would be no grand Season for Lydia, no presentation at court.

But Lucy had never wanted this Season. It was her mother's dream, not hers.

God, they were a hopeless pair, each wanting what the other had.

A knock came at the door, making them both jump.

"Miss Lucy?" came Wilson's booming voice from the hallway.

Oh, bugger it all.

Lucy brought her finger to her lips, begging her sister's silence.

"I know you are here," Wilson warned from outside the door. "The kitchen staff told me they saw you come in."

Lucy groaned. Could no one be trusted to keep a secret around here? Slowly, she stood up. Slowly, slowly, she opened the door to face Wilson's predictable scowl. But as the butler's frown dissolved into a look of abject horror, her lips flirted with a smile.

She *did* enjoy vexing the man.

"Do you like it?" she asked, touching the new rough edges of her hair. "I think it complements my trousers."

Wilson made a wheezing sound deep in his chest. Lucy stepped forward and clapped him on the back, suddenly worried. She wanted to annoy the man, not kill him.

"You've a caller, Miss Lucy," he rasped, punctuated by a series of halting, gasping coughs. He straightened, regaining a bit of his usual starch. "A *gentleman* caller."

Lucy's skin began to itch along the collar of her borrowed shirt. "I . . . I do?"

"The gentleman specifically asked me not to involve Lord Cardwell." He handed her a card with a disapproving frown. "I don't mind saying I am uncomfortable with the request."

Lucy looked down at the card.

The Marquess of Branston.

"Oh, my God," she whispered. Her knees buckled and she had to lean against the door frame for support. *Oh, bloody, bloody hell.*

"A visit such as this requires a proper chaperone. Shall I

inform Lord Cardwell?" Wilson frowned. "Or perhaps you would prefer Lady Cardwell provide attendance? Calling hours have ended, but perhaps an exception could be made."

"No!" Lucy cried, beginning to panic now. If her parents found out about the letter she had sent, she'd have far more to worry about than a lecture on missing calling hours. When Wilson's frown lengthened, she tried to temper her voice. "The gentleman is here about something to do with one of the charities I work with." The lie tasted sour on her lips, but she plowed ahead. "I shall be fine with Lydia as chaperone. You may show him in now."

Wilson looked down at her trousers.

"He is no one of consequence," Lucy insisted, squirming now. And she didn't dare leave Lord Branston alone in the drawing room for the half hour or so it would take to dress and curl her hair. It was better to see him quickly and be done with the matter, before her father caught wind of his visit. "Please show him in," she insisted.

With one last frown, Wilson did as she asked, saving her from a spate of further lies.

Because Lord Branston *was* someone of consequence. And while she'd felt empowered dashing off a scathing letter, she felt ill-prepared for a face-to-face meeting.

"Lord Branston," Lydia mused from the sofa. Her tears were gone, though her eyes still bore traces of redness. "Isn't that—"

"Yes." Lucy knocked her head once, twice, against the door frame, but the violence did little to clear her thoughts. If anything, it muddled them further. She dug at the unholy itch that had sprung up beneath the collar of her shirt, almost as though her skin were telling her to run far and fast. She turned around to face her sister. "It's the man who tried to buy Heathmore."

Lydia's forehead wrinkled. "Lucy, what else have you done besides cut your hair?"

"I *may* have sent him a letter demanding he vacate the premises," Lucy admitted. She blew wisps of hair out of her eyes. "And accused him of trespass."

And threatened to summon the authorities.

What was the bounder doing here? Why would he have come all the way from Cornwall, especially given the tone of her letter?

Not to thank her for her good manners, or to compliment her on her penmanship.

Oh, God, she needed a solid plan. And apparently an entire army of hairpins.

Unfortunately, neither were in ready reach.

"Are you really going to meet Lord Branston dressed like *that*?" Lydia asked, sounding horrified by the notion.

Lucy looked down at her clothing, relics left by Geoffrey when he escaped to university. Though she wore trousers when digging in the dirt, it had been years since she'd truly dressed as a boy, and then she most often pretended to be a groom to climb trees in Hyde Park. The subterfuge no longer came easily. She would have preferred to be dressed in her own clothes for this meeting, especially given how Geoffrey's waistcoat bunched in the wrong places and strained in others. And good *God*, how this shirt made her itch.

But as awkward as she felt, she refused to give Lord Branston the pleasure of dressing properly for his company. The man was trying to force her hand in a direction she refused to go, and she would see this to an end, once and for all.

Hopefully, before her father found out.

From the Diary of Edith Lucille Westmore
January 31, 1813

One only gets a single chance to make a first impression, and I fear I have made mine all too well. I attended church down in town today, intending to meet my new neighbors. When Reverend Wellsbury offered to walk me home after the service, I foolishly accepted.

Looking back now, I can't imagine what I was thinking. I even let him steal a kiss. I might choose to be a spinster, but that doesn't mean I can't kiss a handsome man every now and again. But now I suspect the vicar kissed me only to illustrate the potential moral perils of the life I have chosen. When I explained I had no intention of ever marrying, he said it was unnatural for a woman to choose to be alone, and that the town was worried about me, living alone on the edge of a cliff.

Worried more about me, or my influence on their daughters, I wonder?

Still, he is much respected here in town. If everyone in Lizard Bay subscribes to the handsome young vicar's views, my reputation here will be as doomed as it was in London. Well, I shall endeavor to be myself, no matter the cost to my reputation.

Indeed, I can scarcely wait for church next Sunday.

Chapter 6

A stiff-shouldered butler led Thomas into a drawing room, the walls papered in intricate blue flowers. After his three year sojourn in Cornwall, where his feet spent more time out of doors than inside, the carpet felt obscenely thick beneath his polished shoes. His eye fell upon a crystal decanter of brandy, mocking him from a sideboard.

Damn, but he could use a drink right now.

He hadn't had a drink in three years, not since Miss E collected his drunken secrets and threatened him with a bit of well-meant blackmail if he didn't dry out his sorry hide. He'd done it, too. There was too much at stake to not obey. But it was telling that in the two hours since he'd stepped off the train at Waterloo Bridge Station, he considered stopping for a drink no less than a dozen times. He was beginning to wonder if the easy sobriety he enjoyed in Lizard Bay was more a lack of temptation, rather than any strength of character on his part.

He'd only been in London a few hours, but already he felt adrift, as though returning to sea after a long absence to find he no longer knew how to swim.

He forced his gaze to the center of the room. Brandy might ease the tightness in his spine, but it would not further his cause. This wasn't a casual business meeting between peers, handled over drinks at a gentleman's club. He was here to meet—and negotiate—with Lord Cardwell's flighty young daughter. He suspected he'd do better to pour himself a cup of tea.

He scanned the room's occupants, sorting out the battle lines. A girl was seated on the sofa, staring at him with wide blue eyes. A sour-faced brother played chaperone to one side, digging at his collar and looking none too happy to see him. Thomas ignored the lad and concentrated on the primary business that had dragged him here from Cornwall.

His gaze settled more firmly on the girl. She was pretty enough, he supposed, in a bland, British sort of way. Blond curls were piled on top of her head and she was wearing a demure pink gown that would no doubt find a welcome in any fine drawing room in London. The pallor of her skin told him he'd found his quarry and managed to surprise her.

Good. Always better to start these things with the other party off-balance.

"Miss Westmore," he said, bowing from the waist. "Thank you for seeing me. I imagine my appearance comes as a bit of a surprise."

Her eyes widened even more. "I . . . That is . . . I am certainly surprised. By your . . . ah . . . appearance . . ." Her voice trailed off, trembling at the edges.

Odd, that. She sounded unsure of herself. She'd seemed more confident in her letters.

More of a bollocks-bruiser, actually.

Thomas studied her profile as she darted a nervous glance toward her brother. She looked as though she'd suffered a recent cry, judging by the redness of her eyes. He'd prepared himself for a feisty exchange, given the tenor of her written correspondence. But he hadn't prepared himself for tears and stammers and silence.

"I am sure you can imagine why I am here," he said, wondering why she wouldn't meet his eyes. "Your letter suggested you might consider a different offer, and so I have come to negotiate. I would offer you five hundred pounds for Heathmore Cottage."

She sat frozen like a leaf in ice, even though she'd practically dared him to come to London with a better offer. And why did she keep looking away? He was negotiating with *her* now, not her father, and certainly not her brother. Wasn't this what she had wanted?

Or was this silence part of her act to extort more money?

He was tempted to tell her about Heathmore's nearly barren soil. About the second floor of the cottage, rotting and treacherous because he'd not been able to find carpenters brave enough to come in to do the work. About the eerie whistle of the wind and the townspeople's whispered speculations of a haunting. But the speech he'd planned felt forced, the words a pale shade of the truth. Because there were good things about Heathmore, too. Sweeping ocean vistas, and acres of hidden beauty, a rare explosion of color come summer, fragile flowers somehow finding a toehold in the reluctant soil.

But *she* wouldn't know any of that.

"I understand Heathmore Cottage might hold great sentimental value for you," he began again, more softly now, "given how much it meant to your aunt. But there are things you do not understand."

"No." The brother chose that moment to insert himself into the conversation. The lad stepped forward, looking as though he might like to take Thomas by the throat. "I am afraid it is *you* who does not understand."

Only, it wasn't a man's voice delivering the words.

It was a woman's.

And that was when Thomas took a closer look.

Bloody hell, it wasn't a brother playing chaperone at all. It was a young woman who, if you took the time to look beyond the poorly chopped hair and the ill-fitting waist-coat, looked very much like the demurely stylish young lady seated on the sofa.

Only, there was nothing demure or stylish about *her*.

Two blue eyes glowered at him, nowhere close to a cry. Her mouth was a wide slash of disapproval beneath a rounded snub nose, and her blond hair was a short, unschooled tangle about her ears. She was nearly as tall as he was, and appeared to harbor some sort of twitch, scratching at her neck. But despite these things—which might have made another woman appear unbalanced—she radiated an energy that made him take an involuntary step backward.

"Miss . . . ah . . . *Lucy* Westmore, I presume?" he asked weakly.

"Yes." She stalked toward him, her fists clenched. He wondered if perhaps she meant to strike him. She was certainly *dressed* for a brawl. The first time he met Miss E, she'd done that very thing, pulled back her gnarled spinster's fist and popped him in the left eye, for no greater a transgression than accidentally trespassing on her property.

He took a deep breath, trying to sort out how to defuse the situation. But it turned out that breathing deeply around Miss Westmore was a mistake, because she smelled of the outdoors and fresh laundry, not at all the way a proper young lady was supposed to smell. He wasn't so rusty he'd forgotten *that*, how Gabrielle, his former fiancée, had drenched herself in eau de cologne and expensive perfumes. Now *he* was the one feeling off-balance.

And it wasn't only because Miss Westmore had taken the upper hand in this meeting, surprising him with her trousers and unlikely scents. Unlike his bland reaction to the pale, nervous young woman on the sofa, *this* one stirred something long dormant beneath his skin. He'd thought he'd grown out of such adolescent urges. After the heartbreak of a failed betrothal and three lonely years in Cornwall, he'd become accustomed to his celibacy. He could look at a woman and not wonder what was under her skirts.

What was beneath those trousers, however, was a different story entirely.

He gave himself a mental shake. This train of thought was unproductive at best, dangerous at worst. The future of Heathmore depended on these negotiations, and he needed to get his head in the game. So he smiled at the strange, glowering girl, trying to recall the charm he had once wielded like a potent weapon, even though that life had long since dissolved into nothingness.

"I will offer you five hundred and *fifty* pounds," he said, trying to be generous.

Her mouth turned down in a frown. "I am afraid Heathmore isn't for sale, Lord Branston," she told him, her voice dripping with disdain. "At least, it isn't for sale *yet*."

LUCY GLARED AT this gentleman who was not at all a gentleman.

A true gentleman would not have come without due notice. A true gentleman would not be trying to steal her inheritance for a pittance. And a *true* gentleman would not be standing in front of her, thick curls rakishly disheveled, skin tanned where his neck met his collar.

He was not what she had expected. From the sofa, Lydia seemed to hold a similar opinion, because she kept sneaking round-eyed glances toward the man.

Cultured, her father had called Lord Branston that night over the dinner table.

He prefers his solitude.

Well, her father had forgotten to mention young and handsome.

Lucy had somehow conjured an image of a stooped, gray-haired hermit with false teeth. But Lord Branston's mouth, she couldn't help but notice, had its full complement of teeth, because he was flashing them at her in a lopsided smile that made her knees tremble in an alarming—and unacceptable—fashion. His hair was auburn, not gray. And not a single shade, either, but a kaleidoscope of color, as though nature couldn't quite decide whether he was dark-haired or ginger or something more complicated.

She realized with a start she was staring. In fact, she realized with a curl of dismay she could quite happily stare at this man all day.

Well, he might be handsome and young, but he was also a man. Aunt E had already proven herself correct on many things, and the pages of her diary were filled with good advice. The *least* she herself could do was trust her aunt's judgment on the matter of men.

"I only agreed to see you today to set the matter straight," she informed him, drawing herself up to her full unfortunate height. She dug at her collar again. "I have no intention of selling Heathmore until I visit the property and assess its worth myself."

He crossed his arms, making the seams of his frockcoat strain about his shoulders. "I have already invested a good deal of money in the property. That money would need to be returned to me if we cannot arrive at a satisfactory outcome." His smile stretched higher. "But I am nothing if not willing to negotiate. Would you consider five hundred and seventy-five pounds for the property?"

Lucy glared at him. The *nerve* of the man! Just who did he think he was, trying to buy her acquiescence with a higher offer?

And telling her she owed *him* money?

Oh, but this was war. The man had no idea who he was dealing with.

"If you have invested money in property you do not own, the folly can be laid at no feet beyond your own," she snapped. "I believe I have already made myself clear, Lord Branston—"

"Six hundred." He uncrossed his arms. "Or if not that, name your price."

Damn it all, but he was tenacious. And apparently wealthy enough to toss money around as though it were a pittance. Either that or he knew something about the property's value she didn't. In her letter, Aunt E hinted that Heathmore had secrets.

What did Lord Branston know about the property that she did not?

"Why aren't you offering this to my father?" she asked, trying to temper the bitterness that wanted to creep into her voice. "He was eager enough to accept your initial offer of four hundred pounds. Presumably for six hundred pounds he would deliver me and my dowry along with the property, tied up neatly in a bow."

Lord Branston raised his brows, two auburn slashes of surprise. Hazel eyes slid down the length of her body, making her momentarily forget about the discomfort of her borrowed clothing. Her breath caught in her throat as his gaze slowly climbed back to her face again. "Are you offering yourself as part of the trade, then?"

Lucy's mouth fell open. Was he *flirting* with her? She had little enough experience in the process to know whether or not this exchange qualified as a flirtation.

He was a scoundrel. A thief.

And still her heart leaped treacherously.

"No!" she somehow managed to choke out. "I refuse to barter myself for any man. I want my freedom. My independence. Heathmore, perchance, offers me that."

His gaze sharpened to something beyond wolfish appreciation. In fact, his eyes seemed to pry beneath her skin.

"You are refusing my offer," he asked, "because you want to live there yourself?" He sounded surprised.

Presumably he knew about the rats, then.

"I do not yet know if I want to live there." She lifted her chin. "But if not, I would sell the property for a price that would at least permit me to pursue other choices in life."

"So it *is* about the money then." He sounded almost disappointed. "Six hundred and fifty pounds."

Lucy bit her lip. He'd gone beyond what she imagined the property was worth now. And why, oh why, had she told Lord Branston those things? Her freedom and her independence made no difference to him—indeed, they were pieces of her hopes and dreams that even her own parents refused to consider. He didn't need to know a thing about her, beyond the fact she was refusing his offer.

She scowled, resenting his easy wealth, given that she had just sold her hair for fifteen desperate shillings. "I won't consider any offers until I have a chance to inspect my property, Lord Branston." And her suspicion that he knew something she didn't was now quite thoroughly roused. What about the property had him so fixated he had come all the way to London to continue these useless negotiations?

Something smelled like a . . . well, like a *rat*.

And not one of the ones she ostensibly owned.

"I am afraid you have wasted your time in coming to London," she said, summoning her best glare. "So you may as well return to Cornwall. Wilson will show you out now."

Except . . . Wilson was nowhere to be seen.

Lucy glanced toward the open drawing room door, searching for Wilson's familiar balding pate. What good was a butler if he wasn't there when you needed someone tossed out? The servant usually hovered over her like a persistent gnat, but he'd left her alone with only Lydia to guard her reputation? Judging by the way her sister was still gaping moon-eyed at their handsome guest, there would be no help from *that* quarter.

She caught the familiar sound of Wilson's shoes then, clicking on the hallway tiles. Relief poured over her. There he was. Just in time.

But as Wilson came through the door, Lucy realized he hadn't come alone. Behind him came her father, his face dark as thunder.

Oh, damn Wilson and his meddling.

It had been this way since she was a child. She'd do something—sneak a pie from the kitchen, let loose a pair of frogs down the first floor hallway—and Wilson would somehow, some way, inform her father. He might be a treasured part of the family, but he was also a bloody spy, and it seemed as though he was always on whichever side was not her own.

And while *she* might be through negotiating with Lord Branston and wish him gone, judging by the look on her father's face, things were just heating up.

"WHAT IN THE blazes is going on here?" Lord Cardwell stalked into the drawing room.

Thomas found himself without a ready answer.

Not that he needed one, given that the question was not intended for him.

Which was six shades of wrong. *He* was the one who rightly deserved Lord Cardwell's condemnation. After all, he had come here unannounced. Procured an audience with Cardwell's young, unmarried daughter without the man's knowledge or permission. But Cardwell's blustering anger wasn't being directed toward him.

It was being aimed at his trousers-wearing daughter.

"Father, I can explain—" she began.

"I am not interested in your explanations, Lucy."

"But I only wrote to him because—"

"Be *quiet*." Cardwell's voice boomed through the drawing room, making the fine curiosities on the mantel rattle. "You should be ashamed of yourself, greeting Lord Branston looking like this."

Her shoulders slumped. In spite of himself, Thomas cringed for the girl.

Lord Cardwell turned to Thomas, shaking his head. "I must offer my most sincere apologies, Lord Branston. If I might beg your discretion over whatever she has said or done, and most particularly, for what she is wearing, my family would be grateful. Her Season has nearly begun, and we'd like to avoid any unfortunate rumors, given the delicacy of her position. Lucy is . . ." His voice trailed off, as though he himself was at a loss to describe his hoyden of a daughter.

Quite unexpectedly, Thomas's mind readily supplied a string of missing adjectives.

Stubborn. Surprising. Brilliant.

He'd come prepared to dislike her. To trick her into selling Heathmore, if necessary. He'd presumed she would be like his former fiancée.

Spoiled. Self-centered. *Beautiful.*

Instead, she had turned his preconceived notions of what a viscount's daughter should do and say and turned them on their side.

"Perhaps you should be apologizing to your daughter, instead of me," he told the man.

Cardwell's head jerked backward. "I beg your pardon?"

"Your daughter. After, all, she's the wronged party here. I believe apologies are customary in those situations."

"The wronged party?" Cardwell echoed, blinking in confusion. "She's greeted you wearing trousers!"

"Her manner of dress is irrelevant to the discussion at

hand," Thomas growled. "You attempted to sell me a piece of property that belonged to your daughter, without her authority. And yet, she is of age, is she not?"

"Yes, but—"

"I presume she is considered sane and is therefore capable of making her own decisions?"

"Er . . . I suppose." Cardwell's face reddened, and his gaze slid to his daughter. "Although one has to question her decisions of late."

Thomas bristled at the edge of doubt in her father's voice. Three years ago, when his sister turned up on his London doorstep—unmarried and pregnant—there had been some in London who encouraged him to have her committed to an asylum. After all, he was her guardian, even if he'd proven a poor one, and no sane woman would fall prey to such folly, particularly not the sister of a marquess. It would have been the most expedient solution to the scandal she presented, and was a decision that *might* have even convinced his fiancée to stay.

But he'd refused to listen to them then, and he refused to tolerate Cardwell's uncertainty now, no matter that it was the fashionable way to deal with headstrong females.

"You owe your daughter an apology, Lord Cardwell." He crossed his arms, waiting.

"Just who do you think you are, coming into my house and telling me how to behave toward my daughter?" Cardwell blustered.

Miss Westmore stepped forward, her face pale. "I assure you, there is no need for an apology, Father," she said hoarsely. She cut Thomas a terse glance, though her gaze felt different now than it had during the heat of their earlier argument. More speculative, somehow. Either that or now she thought *him* deranged. "I think it best if you go now, Lord Branston."

He hesitated. His heart told him their business was not through. But if she abdicated the apology he'd just fought for on her behalf, he could allow that was her decision.

And quite honestly, so was the decision regarding the disposition of her property.

"Miss Westmore," he told her. "I understand your desire to make sure you know the value of the property before you make any decisions about its sale. I only ask that, when you eventually reach a conclusion on the matter, you give me first right of refusal."

Her eyes flashed. "I would not depend on it, my lord."

Thomas gritted his teeth. He'd thought, perhaps, that she'd been wavering. There had been a moment before her father stormed onto the scene when he thought things might be leaning toward a different solution. If she lived at Heathmore herself, rather than selling it to the highest bidder, the property would be safe.

But damn it all, there was no mistaking the stubborn glint in her eye.

He'd seen it more than once, when someone had tried to cross her aunt.

Not wanting to inflame the situation further, he nodded in Cardwell's direction, who at least was glaring in *his* direction now, instead of his daughter's. Then, knowing he had angered them both, he turned on his heel and left.

That drink was waiting.

And he still had thirteen bloody hours left in London.

Though it is tempting to lay my troubles at the feet of my father, I didn't escape London simply to thwart his wishes, or merely to avoid an unwelcome marriage. Neither did I leave only because I was afraid of Bedlam, and the horrors that might await me there.

I left for a more important reason than that.

I came to find myself.

Already, I have a fair idea of who I am not. I am not someone who can change myself at the bequest of some man—be he a father or a vicar. I cannot pretend to be something or someone I am not. I may be a spinster by choice, but I will not be an unhappy one. There is plenty to keep me occupied in Lizard Bay beyond the distraction of vexing Reverend Wellsbury, and I am determined to immerse myself in the possibilities.

If I can improve someone else's life, perhaps I can improve my own.

Above all, I shall make my own happiness, even if it makes others cringe.

Chapter 7

Locked in her room—presumably for safekeeping—Lucy did not waste time licking her wounds. No, she put her anger and isolation to a better use. She packed her bag.

Her parents' voices had shaken the house into the wee hours of the morning, tossing about words like "troubled" and "willful" and "unstable." Mother had even proposed calling in old Dr. Bashings for an evaluation, a suggestion that sent Lucy's thoughts spinning in a pattern that might well be argued as mad. The prophetic words from Aunt E's diary swam drunkenly through her head. *Would* Father have her committed for refusing to obey him?

And writing to Lord Branston?

And cutting her hair?

She didn't know.

But she wasn't going to stay locked in her room and wait for the axe to fall.

Her parents' worried tones had settled sometime after midnight, but the resulting silence hadn't eased Lucy's mind. Outside her bedroom door she could hear the clock in the hallway strike the four o'clock hour. As the last chime trailed off, she mulled over her choices—scant though they were. She could forget about Heathmore, suffer her Season, and accept the repercussions of her willfulness . . .

Or, she could seize the opportunity that now presented itself.

She wasn't entirely naive. She hadn't nearly enough money. It wasn't going to be easy. It might even be dangerous.

But it wasn't *impossible*.

She had enough money—if she was frugal—to get herself to Lizard Bay. Once she was there, she felt sure the rest would sort itself out. She could take a position in town to cover her living expenses. Possibly even sell Heathmore if it proved the uninhabitable disappointment her father had described. But at least the decision would be her own to make.

And at least then she would have no regrets.

A sensible girl would wait for the first streaks of dawn to make her dash for freedom.

Well, she *wasn't* a sensible girl. Or at least, isn't that what her parents believed?

Her decision made, Lucy dressed hurriedly in one of her new walking gowns, fashioned by London's most exclusive modiste for a Season she had never wanted. Feeling daring, she fastened the green stone necklace Aunt E had sent her about her throat, then slipped Heathmore's key in a pocket, her fingers curling around the promise of it. Over the past two weeks the key had become something more than just a key to her. Somehow, by carrying it around in her pocket, it had become a symbol of hope. For her future, for her happiness. But to procure that future, she needed to do more than carry it about in her pocket.

She needed to slide it in the damn lock and open the door to her house.

Nearly ready now, she placed her aunt's diaries on top of the single change of clothes in her valise. She'd only made it through the first volume so far but had already read enough to know she was more like her aunt than she'd ever imagined. These yellowed pages were proof enough of her path.

Aunt E had done it, once upon a time. Packed her bags and left in the night, not telling anyone where she was going. Aunt E had made her choice and never looked back. She could do this. She *would* do this. Even Lord Branston had acknowledged her right to make this decision without interference.

That had surprised her almost as much as her father's more damning words.

But not even Lord Branston's unexpected show of support could ease her troubled mind. Make no mistake—she was quite sure she hated him. But her curiosity was roused as well. Why did he want Heathmore Cottage so badly he would come all the way to London to extend the negotiations? What secrets did Heathmore hold? Nothing about her inheritance made sense, and she was through trying to sort it out from London.

But first she had to escape her room.

Lucy pressed an ear to her door, listening to the sounds of the house at sleep. She felt quite sure she could pick the lock. She had plenty of practice being locked in her room as punishment for her varied transgressions through the years. Hairpins were good for at least *something*, though their value in containing her short hair was now thoroughly moot.

But picking the lock carried an element of danger. Had Father put a guard outside her door? If he had, she presumed it would be Wilson, and that meant she couldn't risk it.

So she threw up the sash on her window and leaned out, scanning the shadowed street below. Not a soul was out yet, though the milk sellers and carters sometimes used this route early in the morning, on their way to the market. That was why she needed to leave now, before there were witnesses about. She eyed the oak tree outside her window, the bark rough with promise. The leaves were not yet out, which meant it was hard to tell which branches were healthy and which were not. She'd have to trust fate, she guessed.

Just yesterday, hadn't she wished for a chance to climb a tree again?

Well, *wish granted.*

She tossed out her bag, wincing as it crashed off the limbs. Then, with a muttered oath instead of a prayer, she swung a leg over the sill, yanking at the heavy skirts of her walking gown as they tangled about her feet. This was not going to be as easy as the last time she had done it. Then again, that had been more than four years ago.

And she had been wearing trousers at the time.

Somehow, she launched herself into the branches of the tree. And somehow, though she sacrificed some skin on her palm and a patch of lace on her sleeve to the effort, she managed to lower herself to the ground. As her boots touched down, the breath left her lungs in a slide of relief. Giddiness washed over her.

She had done it.

Now all she needed to do was walk the dangerous, dark streets of London and reach the train station without being gutted by a brigand.

She picked up her bag and turned around, only to run smack into a silent wall of servant.

"Going somewhere, Miss Lucy?" Wilson's big voice cut through the quiet of the street.

Lucy scrambled backward, her heart thudding against her ribs. *Damn Wilson to hell and back.* She should have known he'd guess her plans—he had an uncanny way of knowing exactly what was running through her mind. Well, she had clearly miscalculated this time.

It would have been better to pick the lock.

Could she outrun him? Wilson was old, but he wasn't wearing skirts and carrying a bag. She didn't like her odds.

"And where might you be going this fine, early morning?" he asked, as though their meeting was a casual one.

Lucy took another frantic step backward, until the bark of the tree dug against her back. He was part of the family, but he was also a servant. He couldn't stop her, not really.

He could only tell her father.

But that would mean disaster, given that the train didn't depart the station until eight o'clock. She expected her father to eventually come after her, of course. But she hoped to have at least a day's head start. "I'd rather not say," she told him tersely.

"I see. Do you mean to tell me you've found enough money for the journey?" Wilson inclined his head, his broad face awash in doubt "I was led to believe you lacked the funds to reach Cornwall."

Lucy bit her lip. She should have known Wilson would be aware of all of this. The man knew *everything* that went on at Cardwell House. "I've enough to get there," she told him defiantly. "That's all that matters."

"I see." He crossed his arms. "And how will you eat once you are there?"

"Well, there are rats, aren't there?" As his bushy brows rose, she sighed. "Honestly, I will sort it out when I get there. You can't stop me, Wilson. So you may as well bid me good-bye."

His familiar frown made her chest squeeze tight, reminding her that in spite of their long history, she was going to miss the man. He inclined his head. "I haven't come to stop you."

She blinked. "You . . . you haven't?"

"No." He stepped forward, and she tensed. But instead of grabbing her arm, as she had feared, he picked up her hand and pressed something cold and metal into her palm. "Safe journeys, Miss Lucy."

She looked down. In the dim gaslight, she caught the glint of two gold sovereigns.

"But . . . you . . ." she stammered through a sudden wash of tears. "You can't mean to do this. You could lose your position," she protested.

"I wiped your father's nose when he was a lad," he scoffed. "I wiped his sister Edith's nose as well, God rest her soul. He's not going to sack me." He gave her a rare ghost of a smile. "And I'm not trying to help you *reach* Cornwall, Miss Lucy. I don't imagine I could stop you with a pistol and a length of rope." His big voice shook with emotion, and if she wasn't mistaken there was a sheen of tears in his eyes as well. "No, I'm trying to help you get back safely, you see."

Lucy's fingers closed over the precious coins. "Thank you," she whispered, swallowing the lump in her throat.

Wilson regained a bit of his usual frown. "And I insist you take a cab to the station. 'Tis too dangerous to walk this time of morning. All sorts of suspicious sorts lurking about."

"But . . . I need every penny," she confessed.

"There's a hackney waiting on the corner of Oxford Street. I've just come from paying the driver."

Lucy gaped at him. "How did you know—"

He smiled again. "Your next steps are never that hard to guess. I just imagine the most impulsive path possible, and there you are, tripping along it, brave as anything." His smile fell away, leaving him suddenly looking more like the old Wilson she knew. "If you like, I will tell your father you are skulking about in your room and don't wish to see anyone. That should buy you a day or two's head start at least."

Lucy stared at him, speechless. Not even Lydia had been willing to do this for her.

And Lydia was *family*.

He jerked his head toward Oxford Street. "Go on, then. Quickly, before I change my mind."

Lucy took several steps toward freedom, hugging her bag to her chest. At the corner, she could make out the shadowy shape of the cab and horse that would carry her to the train station. She turned around to look at the servant she'd known nearly all her life one last time. "Wilson?"

He stood like a dark rock in the street. "Yes?"

With a soft cry, she launched herself into his arms. She hugged him fiercely, as though this good-bye could stretch to the rest of her family. Somehow, in this moment, knowing she had Wilson's approval was enough.

"Thank you," she whispered.

"Just promise me you'll try to stay out of trouble," he said gruffly over the top of her head, patting her back.

"I'll *try* to," she promised, pulling back with a smile. "But we both know my efforts don't always end well on that front."

And then, with her bag in one hand, she ran like the dickens for Oxford Street.

STREAKS OF DAWN were just appearing on the horizon as Thomas made his way out of the hotel. Or at least they *should* have been appearing.

If he had been back home in Lizard Bay instead of London, he was quite sure he could have seen it. Instead, soot-streaked buildings obscured his view. When he breathed in, the morning breeze smelled of coal fires instead of salt air and sea grass. And the muddled pounding of his head told him that even had the sky been more promising, he was still too knackered from last night's dive into the bottle to properly appreciate it.

Wincing from the effort of breathing, he lifted a hand to hail one of the cabs sitting in a line. A voice pushed from behind his shoulder. "Branston?"

He stiffened but didn't turn around.

The voice came again. "Excuse me, but are you perchance Lord Branston?"

Thomas gritted his teeth and forced his feet to turn. A

well-dressed gentleman grinned up at him, umbrella in hand, hat perched quite properly on top of his head. The man was close to his own age and looked vaguely familiar, but then, all of London did.

He'd once imagined himself friends with half the ton. It had taken his sister's scandal to realize that friendship was a term best used loosely in London. The discovery of the true friendships he'd formed in Cornwall had shown him that such memories of his friends in London were based on little more than smoke and mirrors.

Thomas tried to school the surly expression that wanted to settle on his face. "Are we acquainted, sir?"

"Wellingsford. Edward Wellingsford. Come now, don't say you don't recall?"

Thomas shook his head.

"We went to university together?"

"Did we?" Thomas responded bleakly. He still didn't remember. And while he didn't remember many details of what came after graduation, given his rapid descent into dissolution once he'd entered London's social scene as a marquess who'd reached his majority, he remembered very well his years of study during university.

He'd bet his right hand he had never seen this man in a single, solitary class.

"Well, I was there the first year. I was thrown out for doing poorly." The man shuffled his feet. "But we both belong to the same club. And I came to your sister's funeral."

Thomas forced himself to give a curt nod. He still didn't remember, but perhaps pretending to might send the man scurrying off.

"How long has it been?" the man mused. "Two years?"

"Three," Thomas murmured, turning back to the street and raising his hand again. Damn it, but why was the hackney taking so long?

"I was sorry to hear about your sister," Wellingsford said next, glib as punch. "Though, from the gossip I heard, I have to say it was probably for the best."

A red haze of anger descended over Thomas's line of sight, and he had to force himself to stare straight ahead, to not react. For Christ's sake, it had been three bloody years. Were the gossips still talking about Josephine as though she were a parlor joke? A cautionary tale, meant to scare young women into prudish compliance?

It happened to the sister of a marquess, it could happen to you, too.

Christ, but this visit had devolved into everything he'd feared encountering in London. The incessant gossip. The false smiles.

The now-empty brandy bottle, rolling about the floor of his hotel room.

He'd promised himself he wouldn't fall into old habits. That he was better than that, different inside. But his hard-fought sobriety in Cornwall had apparently made him forget this piece of his former life. From the moment he stepped off the train yesterday, the sounds and scents of the city had crept beneath his skin and stirred unwelcome memories. The disastrous meeting with Miss Westmore hadn't helped.

Here he was, not even twenty-four hours in London, facing the mean-spirited censure of former friends and clawing his way out of a bottle.

A better man would swear never again. A lesser man would seek out a dose of laudanum to shave the edges from last night's mistake.

He counted himself somewhere in between, and so he did neither.

"Have you seen Miss Highton yet?" Wellingsford pattered on, pulling Thomas's thoughts reluctantly toward his former fiancée. "I hear she's doing all right for herself, though she's facing her fourth Season now. Angling for a duke, to hear the tales." The bastard actually laughed. "Must have been a blow for you to lose a woman that beautiful. I know *I* wouldn't kick her out of my bed on a Monday."

Thomas turned slowly, his hands clenching. "I don't care to hear such things said about my former fiancée, thank you very much." He glared down at Wellingsford. Gabrielle's callousness might have once left him reeling, but she didn't deserve such slander.

Something in Thomas's expression caused Wellingsford's eyes to widen, and he took a quick step back, his hands held up in defense. "No need to get testy. I didn't mean any harm to the girl. I'm just making polite conversation." He pushed a nervous laugh from his lips. "She wouldn't have me anyway, old chap. I'm only a second son. Too lowborn for the likes of Miss Highton." He glanced toward the cab, which was finally rolling to a stop at the curb. "Say," he said, brightening "can we share a cab?"

"No." Thomas clambered up into the hackney, feeling strangled by his high collar and necktie. Feeling, too, disgusted with the Wellingsfords of the world.

"Come on, then," the man whined, placing a hand on the cab's runner. "Just a quick hop across town. We could catch up. Lots to talk about. It's been three years, after all."

Thomas leaned down, beckoning the man closer. Wellingsford stupidly tipped an ear toward him. Though it was probably a terrible idea, given how quickly rumors flew through London, Thomas grabbed the man's coat lapel and hoisted him closer. "If I let you up in this cab," he growled, "and have to listen to one more disgusting word out of your mouth, I can promise you your face will be rearranged before we even reach your destination." He released his hold on the man's coat and patted the man's hat for good measure.

Wellingsford stepped back, his face a ghastly white. "Er . . . n-never mind," he stammered. "I think I see another cab."

As the bastard hurried away, Thomas settled back in the

seat, a grin settling on his face for the first time all morning. He knew he had likely just started a new train of gossip that would soon be spread through every club in London.

Mad Marquess Threatens Idiot.

Well, that was a change of headline he could live with, at least.

"Where to, governor?" the driver asked, far too cheerfully for seven o'clock in the morning.

Though Thomas had intended to go straight to the train station, for some reason—no doubt on account of his encounter with Edward Wellingsford—his tongue now took an unexpected detour. One he had promised himself he wouldn't take.

Then again, his judgment had never been trustworthy when rendered down the barrel of a bottle. "Golden Square, if you please."

As the driver chirruped to the horse, Thomas slouched down into his seat and lifted a hand to his temple, pressing gingerly. What had made him say that? There was no doubt the unwelcome encounter with Wellingsford had stirred his emotions, but was this a good idea? He'd left three years ago as much to protect *her* as to protect himself, and distance was an essential element to that unspoken agreement. He didn't know what he might be capable of if he saw her again. Perhaps he was still drunk.

Although . . . he was quite sure his head would probably feel better if he was.

Too soon, they were at Golden Square. The driver tied off the reins, but Thomas didn't get down. Instead, he leaned back against the cracked leather seat and stared up at the red brick town house he had last seen three years ago.

It seemed different, somehow.

Whatever else he'd expected of the address, it wasn't this starched, residential street lined with its spindle-limbed trees, the branches patiently waiting for the warmth of late spring. Then again, those days around his sister's funeral and Gabrielle's scathing betrayal had been almost insensible. He recalled coming here, of course, to meet with her.

To beg her to change her mind.

To come with him to Cornwall, if necessary.

But one by one she had rebuked his suggestions, standing firm, preferring to choose her own path. It was odd how he could remember how she had looked, the tears swimming in her eyes, but couldn't recall the look of the town house.

But was it any wonder? It had all been conducted in a drunken haze.

No doubt *that* was why the actual look of the place took him by surprise this morning.

As the morning began to lighten around him, the house slowly came to life. A light flared in the downstairs window, a servant stirring about. Then a light appeared abovestairs, in what he presumed was her bedroom.

"Shall I go and knock for you, gov'nor?" The cabbie sounded confused.

"No." Thomas shook his head, but stilled as the curtains on the second floor moved. He heard the sounds of the sash coming up, and his eyes stayed sewn to the spot. He'd not seen her since the day after the funeral, when he came by one last time, determined to make her see reason. But as the muslin stirred and the sound of light laughter reached him through the window, he caught a glimpse of a profile he'd once known as well as his own, and his breath caught in his throat.

She'd changed. Grown less slender.

But there was no doubt it was her.

The sound of her morning laughter through the open sash plucked a nerve inside him. He felt tautly strung, ready to burst. Once upon a time, he'd have done anything to pull laughter from those lips. He'd make up limericks. Tell terrible jokes. Tickle her arm, if the teasing didn't work. How long had it been since he'd made someone laugh?

God, did he even possess the skills anymore?

"Gov'nor?" the driver asked again

Thomas shook himself from his stupor. It hadn't been a good idea to come. Christ, but would he ever be able to move on from this? It was clear she'd carved a new life for herself, one that didn't involve him. He had no business intruding when she'd made her wishes quite clear.

"My business here is done," he answered briskly. "To Waterloo Bridge Station, if you please. Quick as you can, I need to make the eight o'clock train."

With a sour glance—no doubt on account of the stupidity of such a detour when time was marching by—the cabbie set off. Thomas leaned back in his seat, closing his eyes.

She'd looked . . . well. Happy, even.

That was something at least. It was a relief to know she had a normal life, and lived in a normal house. He wondered if she was as happy as she sounded, if she might eventually find someone she could love. He hoped so.

No matter the nature of their parting, no matter even Wellingsford's vile words, he'd never wished anything less for her. It was the closest glimpse he'd had of her in three years, and already he couldn't help but wonder how long it would be before he had another.

Bloody hell, he could use another drink.

Second impressions give one a better understanding of a person than first impressions, I think. A peek behind the curtain, so to speak.

Well, Reverend Wellsbury has been given a peek he won't soon forget.

After the audacity of his kiss—followed by his unwelcome lecture on propriety—I made sure to sit in the front pew of church this week. I also sewed a bright red ribbon along the edge of my crinoline, and shortened the hem of my skirts. Sure enough, the pompous windbag stumbled over his sermon every time I flashed my ankle.

Proving, of course, that men are imminently untrustworthy.

They all say they want a pure, obedient wife, but then lose their heads over a bit of red ribbon. I wonder if the good vicar realizes the potential moral peril in staring at a woman's unutterables? He should be pleased that he now has something more significant to worry about than me living alone on the edge of a cliff.

Now he has to worry about me coming to church.

Chapter 8

*T*homas trudged his way down the boarding platform. The entire trip was a failure. He'd failed to convince Miss Westmore to sell Heathmore Cottage, with all its hidden secrets. He'd broken down and visited the one address he had sworn to avoid. And the reek of brandy on his breath and his pounding head were reminders enough he'd failed in that respect, too.

Just three more reasons to hate London.

Damn, but it was crowded at the station this morning. A schoolboy in plaid wool tossed a ball from one hand to the other, and as he passed, Thomas was reminded enough of Danny to glance down to make sure the boy was wearing shoes. At the edge of the platform a young man in a checked apron tried in vain to sweep up the castoffs of humanity, pushing paper wrappers and discarded flyers on the edge of his broom. But much like the people themselves, the detritus just circled back around to fill in the empty space.

Thomas had never liked crowds, preferring instead to lurk amongst libraries and gardens. But when his time at university had ended, he'd felt adrift, unsure of what to do with himself. He'd been almost pushed toward the teeming streets of London, his preferences be damned. He was a marquess, after all, and there were certain . . . *expectations* . . . to the position.

And instead of peaceful gardens and greenhouses, clubs and racetracks had become his proving grounds. And instead of books on botany and geology, bottle after bloody bottle had filled his life. He couldn't even point to when it had become a problem. He only knew it had.

He preferred the solitude of Cornwall now. *Needed* it.

Too many people made him twitch.

All too soon these worn-out souls would be packed elbow-to-chest in third class seating, sweating and miserable. Thank God he had a first class ticket and would soon be sleeping on his own upholstered seat to the rhythm of the rails.

A bell rang out, fair notice the train was boarding. With it, the crowd began to push and hum. Through the frantic swirl of people, a woman caught his eye. Perhaps it was her height, standing several inches above the other women on the platform. Or perhaps it was because he could just see an inch or so of blond hair peeking out from the bottom edge of her bonnet. Whatever the reason, it was enough to make Thomas turn and stare as she hurried toward a third class car. It *couldn't* be her. She was a viscount's daughter.

She wouldn't be riding in third class.

But as her face turned to greet the ticket taker, he caught a glimpse of that wide mouth that had argued with him so vigorously yesterday but then failed to stand up to her father. *Bloody hell.* It *was* her.

Miss Westmore was boarding the train to Salisbury. *Alone.*

Perhaps he shouldn't count his failures just yet.

At least she was wearing a proper dress this time—and a very fashionable one, too, though his skills in that arena were rusty with disuse. It was a bright canary gold, clearly meant to draw attention to the wearer, and was nipped and tucked in places that highlighted her generous curves. Definitely not the sort of gown—or the sort of woman—one usually saw in a third class car. About her neck, he spied a distinctive serpentine stone, a defiant symbol of Lizard Bay and the unusual geology of the coast.

Its appearance gave him pause. It told him her destination better than any map.

Holy hell. Did she really mean to go to Cornwall without suitable accompaniment? He could see no servant trailing her. No glowering father at her heels. No stacks of trunks and hatboxes towering in wait of loading. He couldn't figure her out. The girl was trouble incarnate. He ought to bundle her back to Lord Cardwell's house, the consequences of facing her father be damned. Or better still, he ought to leave well enough alone.

But as she disappeared into the depths of the third class carriage, he found himself drifting toward the point where he had last seen her. What was she doing?

Damn it, what was *he* doing?

She'd made her position clear yesterday. She had no interest in dealing with him. But something about this girl piqued his interest. She seemed . . . *alive.*

Not much else in his life did.

Thomas made to follow her into the carriage but found his way blocked by the ticket taker.

"Tickets, please!" the man barked, holding out his hand.

Thomas shook his head, which had the misfortune of making it pound more fiercely. "I just want to speak with a woman who's just gone into the car. I'll only be a moment."

"You must have a ticket to board," the man said sternly.

"I only want a word—"

"And I only want your ticket."

With a snarl, Thomas pulled his ticket from his jacket and handed it to the man. "Now may I pass?"

The station worker began to sputter. "But . . . this is a first class ticket, sir." He pointed toward the other carriage, just ahead. "Your car is there. This is the *third* class car."

"Oh, for heaven's sake," Thomas growled. "I presume a first class ticket holder can sit anywhere they please?"

"There are only a limited number of seats—"

"Then give someone else my seat in the first class car." Thomas pushed past him. "I choose to sit here."

WITH AUNT E's second diary volume clutched in her hand, Lucy found an empty seat and settled into it with a small sigh of relief. Wilson, bless his big heart, must have kept his word, because no one had shown up to intercept her at the station. The wooden seat felt hard as a slab of granite beneath her bum, but it couldn't dim her enthusiasm.

She was finally on her way to Cornwall.

She took off her bonnet and leaned her head back against the wooden bench, briefly closing her eyes. She was too excited to sleep, but suspected she was also too tired to read. Through the seat back, she could feel the steady vibration of the engine and the jostling of fellow passengers as they shifted about on the bench, each seeking to find a comfortable position to carry them through the portending nine hour ride.

Perhaps, once the train started moving, she might have a hope for a nap.

"Does your father know you are on this train, Miss Westmore?"

Lucy's eyes flew open and her fingers tightened over the journal as she saw who had uttered such a damning phrase.

Oh, bugger it all. She bit her lip to keep from saying it out loud.

Could she really have such poor luck?

Lord Branston towered over her, his auburn hair back-lit by the morning sun streaming through the train's grit-covered window. If this was a dream, she hoped it ended in something more interesting than another tiresome offer for Heathmore Cottage.

But given the man's persistence, she suspected he was all too real.

"As we established yesterday, I am of age," she replied crisply, sitting up straighter and shoving her aunt's diary in her valise. "My father cannot dictate my actions."

"Ah." He sounded unconvinced. "So having reached your majority, you simply bade him good-bye and walked out the front door?"

"Not that it is any of your business, but I climbed out a window. You'll find I am persistent enough to do nearly anything once I've set my mind to something. I've set my mind to see my property and understand what has you sniffing after it." She glared up at him. "And given that you are a marquess who tosses about offers of hundreds of pounds as though they mean nothing, shouldn't you be seated in the first class car? Or perchance own your own train?"

"No trains." He stepped forward, out of the sun, and his features shifted into sharper focus. She could see, then, the light brown of his eyes, golden flecks swirled with green, and the light stubble across his cheeks, suggesting he'd not shaved this morning. He chuckled softly. "I prefer to spend my money on falling-down cottages, you see."

Lucy swallowed at the sound of his light laughter. "Not *my* cottage."

Unperturbed, he lowered himself onto the bench beside her and stretched out his legs.

As though he meant to *stay.*

As he filled the space beside her, she caught the faint scent of brandy. Perhaps his valet had splashed some on his skin after shaving? Although . . . he didn't appear to have used the services of a valet this morning. Though his clothing was quite respectable—the sort of frock coat and trousers you might find on any well-bred London gentleman—the points of his collar were drooping, and his necktie was slightly off-center.

Not that those small signs of dishevelment detracted from his appeal in any way.

Already, he was making her heart thrum faster and the skin itch beneath her collar.

He sidled closer to her as he made space for a last, straggling traveler, a woman with a fussing baby in her arms. He even took the woman's bag and stowed it for her under the seat. The gesture, while kind, caused his thigh to brush up against hers and sent her stomach jumping like a nervous kitten.

"Surely there are other places you might sit," she said in exasperation.

A crooked smile appeared as he settled back against his seat. "I don't see any other seats, Miss Westmore."

"I would imagine there is more room in the first class car."

"Yes, but the company there is so much less enjoyable." Warm hazel eyes met hers and lingered. "The view, as well."

Lucy slouched down against the hard bench. He wasn't doing anything untoward, exactly. And he'd extended a kindly hand to the woman with the baby. But that was evidence he was mannered, not nice. She didn't trust him any further than she could throw him.

And then it was too late to fix.

With a mighty groan, the train began to pull out of the station.

Bugger it all. Now she was stuck with the man for the length of the journey.

She inched away from him, though that brought her flush against a portly man to her right who reeked of pipe tobacco. She cleared her throat purposefully, given that she had no intention of making a good impression. "Speaking of views, I remember the view of the ocean from the front door of Heathmore Cottage," she said, determined to both regain the upper hand and circle the conversation back around to the point.

Which was that she was *not* going to sell him the property, so he might as well toddle on to a different seat in the car and leave her in peace.

Lord Branston shrugged, seemingly unperturbed by her rabid throat-clearing. Or was he hard of hearing? But no . . . he was smiling. "The view is about the only thing to recommend it, at present. I assure you, my offer of six hundred and fifty pounds is more than fair."

"It is worth more than that to me."

"I can see you appear to harbor a sentimental attachment. Your aunt was similarly fond of the place." He hesitated and leaned closer. "Would you consider six hundred and seventy-five pounds?"

Lucy drew in a sharp breath. *Bloody hell.* He'd only sat down next to her to continue the negotiations. "If Heathmore is in such terrible condition, why are you so interested in it?" she asked. "I suspect you could buy any home in England. Why is *my* house the one you want?"

Though the train car rocked and swayed as it gained speed, his eyes didn't waver as they met hers. "Why is anything the one we want?" he said softly, and the varied interpretations of his words kindled a warmth in her stomach.

"That is hardly an answer," she protested.

"Very well, then. There is something about it that appeals to me, something others don't see when they look at it." He inclined his head. "It has . . . hidden depths. If I thought you meant to live there and see to its upkeep, I would leave it be,

I assure you. But as long as there is a chance you might sell it, and as long as there is a chance someone else might buy it, I am afraid I must continue to offer."

Somehow, she found the presence of mind to shake her head. "And I am afraid I must continue to decline, Lord Branston." In fact, in this moment, on this train, she wouldn't imagine selling it, no matter how high the man's offers escalated. Though she'd claimed to Lydia that she wanted to inspect the property to have a better sense of its worth, now that she was finally on her way, freedom tingling beneath her skin, the thought of selling it felt six shades of wrong.

His low-throated chuckle slid over her like a warm bath. "We'll see, Miss Westmore. We'll see."

Reverend Wellsbury seems up to his usual tricks again.

Today's sermon was on loving your neighbor, and he met my eye more than once from the pulpit. When I winked at him, the man turned as red as the devil himself. I have to admit, he's a handsome thing—it's no hardship to go to church, even if my mind's not always on God.

But I can't help but wonder . . . just who does he intend the advice for?

It is no secret around town that I've received three separate proposals of marriage from Mr. Jamieson, the town grocer, and more mooning glances from Mr. Bentley, the postmaster, than I can count. They are both kind—if a bit too persistent—but I cannot bring myself to imagine anything beyond an innocent flirtation with either of them.

Now Reverend Wellsbury . . . there's a man with whom I can imagine a not-so-innocent flirtation. But despite his appeal, I cannot quite bring myself to trust his intentions. He seems determined to save my soul from spinsterhood.

But unfortunately, he seems unwilling to martyr himself for the cause.

Chapter 9

To keep his mind off the fact he was still half drunk and hurtling through space in an iron box with no hope of stepping outside for air, Thomas kept his attention focused squarely on Miss Westmore's face.

Not that it was a hardship to do so.

In staring at her as much as he liked, he discovered something peculiar about her. Well, *more* peculiar. She filled out a pair of trousers nicely, after all, and had hair of a length that would inspire envy in a monk. Nothing normal about *that*.

But he couldn't help but notice she chewed on her lower lip when she was thinking, and he found himself wanting to see it again. But that wasn't going to happen if she kept those rather lovely lips pressed together, tight as a slipknot.

A porter came down the aisle, carrying a basket of items for purchase. Thomas lifted a finger, summoning the man, and then dug in his pocket for a coin to purchase two apples. *"Malus domestica,"* he said, presenting one to Miss Westmore with a grand flourish.

Her eyes narrowed on the proffered fruit, but she shook

her head. A beat passed, and then those lips miraculously opened. "Why did you call it that? It looks like a plain old apple."

He turned it into his palm, the yellow-red skin slightly mottled. He could tell by its color that it was a Ribston Pippin variety of apple. He could tell her its entire history, including its original cultivation from an orchard in Yorkshire. But given the disdain in her voice, he decided to keep that information to himself. She seemed none too impressed by his knowledge anyway.

He stared down at the apple in his palm, wishing she would just take it. She looked hungry, despite her refusal. Or was she turning up her nose at the apple itself? It looked different than the apples he'd been served on the way to London. He supposed they must serve only polished apples in the first class cabin, the ones with no evidence of interest from insects and the like. But he liked the look of this one, as though it was somehow more real than the carefully chosen, polished variety. Much like Miss Westmore herself.

He frowned, suddenly realizing she was still waiting for his answer. "*Malus domestica* is the scientific name for apple," he explained. "I enjoy . . . odd facts." At her resulting scowl, he added, "I studied botany at university, once upon a time."

She rolled her eyes. "If you are trying to impress me, Lord Branston, you should just leave off. Botany is hardly a subject of note. Now, philosophy, religion, law . . . *those* are subjects a marquess might use to advantage. At least, the *useful* variety of marquess." By her tone, it was clear that she roundly considered him one of the nonuseful varieties.

Not that he disagreed.

She wiggled down into her seat and stared straight ahead again, though her lips muttered a last, final thought. "And the fact that you know the scientific name for a bloody apple won't change my mind about Heathmore."

Thomas sighed at the dismissal. He bit into his apple and pocketed the one he'd intended for her. This was a bit like trying to squeeze blood from a stone. He thought of his discarded first class seat, with its lovely cushioned bench and its copious space. And then he thought of how close Miss Westmore was sitting to him, and how the scent of her reminded him a bit of this apple: fresh, tart, and entirely unexpected in the car of a filthy third class carriage.

As far as trades went, he suspected it was worth it.

"Do you know much about your destination, Lizard Bay?" he asked next, thinking, perhaps, she simply needed an avenue to less confrontational conversation.

She ignored him.

"It is a small town," he went on. "And I've never seen a lizard there, myself. I suspect the town's name derives from some older, Cornish word. Or perhaps it was named after the lizardite rocks that litter the coast." She kept her eyes focused straight ahead, as though the elderly couple sitting on the opposite bench was the most fascinating thing she had ever seen.

But . . . there it was.

Her mouth shifted. The line became softer and her lower lip slipped between her teeth.

She was *definitely* more aware of him than she was letting on.

"Do you always bite your bottom lip when you are thinking?" he teased.

She made a grand show then of *not* biting her lip and inched her tall frame a little farther to her right. Thomas stifled a laugh. If she continued in that direction, she would be sitting on the lap of the gentleman beside her all too soon. Not that the man looked as though he would mind. It had not escaped Thomas's notice that she'd captured interested glances from most of the men in the car. She seemed oblivious to the attention.

That told him she was rather naive about the intentions of men.

And that made Thomas want to stick tight as a burr to her side.

"No witty retort?" he asked mildly.

"You should not be staring at my lips," she muttered.

Now *that* was about as ludicrous as the idea he might willingly abandon his hopes to acquire Heathmore. She might not be the most striking woman in a train car, but there was something about her that drew the eye. It was true that her mouth turned down, all too frequently, but that made him want to force a smile.

Thomas shrugged, hardly knowing which devil had seized him, but all too willing to give himself over to it. How long had it been since he'd tried so hard to make a woman laugh? He'd once been considered rather funny, in the days before he descended into that dark, London drunkenness, but he scarcely recognized the skill that was emerging in slow, rusty turns.

"I am a man. You have a pair of lovely lips, and you tend to bite them when you are irritated. Forgive me for noticing." He leaned closer, until the sweet, simple scent of her filled his head and drowned out the sweating bodies on either side. "You are doing it again. To tempt me, perhaps? Or merely to demonstrate your prowess with the act?"

"Probably to keep from blurting out something I shall regret," she huffed.

He looked about the crowded car. It was odd, but the press of bodies suddenly seemed less strangling. His head was beginning to feel clearer, too. Was the brandy finally leaving his system? Or was it because he'd discovered a more enjoyable distraction?

He lifted a hand and gestured toward the mob of people. "No one here knows you, Miss Westmore. Blurt away."

"I think not." She peeked back at him. "Why, I would shock

you senseless with the things I could say. I come from a large family, and my younger brother, Geoffrey, takes great pleasure in bedeviling us all. I've learned to give as well as I get."

He couldn't help it. He laughed out loud.

"What is so amusing?" she asked warily.

"I used to have a sister, Miss Westmore. An independent, outspoken sister. And I assure you, she was capable of the occasional unfeminine expression."

She looked at him curiously. "You *used* to have a sister?"

Thomas sobered, though the urge to make her laugh remained, sharp-edged and wanting. What had made him say that? He rarely spoke about that part of his life, and he didn't know what had brought it out now. Perhaps it had been the unintended detour to Golden Square this morning, stirring painful memories he'd tried to suppress. Or perhaps it was Miss Westmore's easy, affectionate talk of family, reminding him of his own.

This girl reminded him, in small but significant ways, of Josephine. Not in the tragic, fitful way he usually remembered his younger sister, but in more of an elemental way, one that made him smile and made him think of happier times.

He drew a deep breath. "I . . . lost her. Three years ago."

Lost her. That was one way to put it. The truth was far more painful. He rarely talked about Josephine. She was his sister. His responsibility. And he had failed to protect her.

Not that she had given him the time or opportunity to set things to right. The gossip she'd faced had proven too damning, too damaging. Once she'd seen what her condition meant to his own reputation, she'd taken matters into her own hands.

Then again, he'd not been the most dependable—or sober—of potential protectors.

Was it any wonder she'd made such an irrevocable decision? He shook his head, trying to clear away the memories. If

Miss Westmore reminded him in some basic, elemental way of his sister, it was probably because she had a habit of leaping first and explaining herself later.

That, and inciting such a strong urge to try to get her to laugh.

"The point is, she was not afraid to give voice to her thoughts. Your aunt herself was famously outspoken. There is little you might say I would find shocking."

She responded by worrying her bottom lip between her teeth again.

"Go on, then." He pushed his shoulder against hers, the urge to charm her flaring bright beneath his skin. It was almost as though he was coming out of a dark hole, blinking into the sunshine. "I'll even share a few of your aunt's favorites. 'Fiddlesticks.'" He wagged his eyebrows at her, sinking into the old, familiar feeling of being able to tease without worry. "Or, tell me I've got 'gullyfluff' between my ears—that was a particular favorite of Miss E's."

Miss Westmore clapped a gloved hand across her mouth and her shoulders began to shake. For a moment he thought perhaps he had made her cry, to remind her of her recently deceased aunt. But then he realized she was trying very hard not to laugh.

"Come now, you know you want to," he coaxed.

She pulled her hand away from her mouth. "Oh, stuff it, you bloody cocksure bugger."

Thomas choked in surprise. "Well. That was certainly . . ." He reached for an appropriate word. " . . . colorful." A chuckle rose in his throat. Over the course of their acquaintance Miss E had said many outrageous things, but to his recollection the feisty old spinster had never said anything quite like *that*. "You know," he mused, "that might even have made your aunt blush."

In an instant Miss Westmore's cheeks flamed a rosy pink. "Well then, I suggest you remember what I am capable of, the next time you want to tease me," she told him. "I know my lips are not the sort to inspire poetry, Lord Branston. So keep your false flirtations to yourself."

False flirtations? There was nothing false about them. And what was this nonsense about not being the sort to inspire poetry? "Not even a *bawdy* bit of poetry?" he couldn't help but ask. He cleared his throat, searching for a spark of brilliance. "There once was a girl from the city."

She blushed even more deeply, but said nothing.

"It is your turn," he prompted.

After a quick glance to either side, she mumbled, "Who wasn't considered that pretty."

He frowned. Was that how she saw herself? Her mouth was full and wide, and the soft pink hue of her lips was really quite lovely. "But she had a nice smile," he countered.

She raised a brow. "And could curse a fair mile."

This was better. Thomas cracked his knuckles, thinking hard. Inspiration came to him in a flash. "And she had a lovely, fine set of titties."

Her gasp was so loud it bounced off the carriage roof. *"Lord Branston!"*

"Yes?" He tried to sound innocent. "They are. I mean, you *do*." He gestured helplessly in the direction of her bosom. "I couldn't see them yesterday beneath that horrid waistcoat, but today here they are." He knew he was crossing a line of propriety, but for some reason he couldn't bring himself to care. It was almost as though by trying so hard to be irritated with him, she was inviting such a lovely intimacy.

And he'd been lonely for far too long to resist.

She crossed her arms over the generous chest that had inspired such a moving bit of rhyme. It might be properly covered in yellow canary wool and feature a double row of brass buttons marching up the bodice, but *he* knew what lurked beneath.

He was nothing if not imaginative.

He grinned at her, feeling enormously satisfied with himself. "Do you mean to tell me, Miss Westmore, that you'd rather I stare at your lips after all?"

"That is . . . you are . . . *not* being a proper gentleman."

"Am I supposed to be?" He leaned back in his seat. "*You* were the one who called me a bloody cocksure bugger."

"I was trying to shock you," she sputtered.

"A mission well accomplished."

"Lord Branston, I scarcely think—"

"And do you think you might call me Thomas? I prefer that to cocksure bugger." He leaned closer, whispering in her ear. "I'm trying to impress you, you see. I'll not have you thinking I prefer buggery to a proper bedding."

She burst out laughing, and the tips of her ears turned as pink as her cheeks.

"Try it. Thooooo-maaaaas," he said, exaggerating the syllables.

"I couldn't. That is, we aren't . . . that is . . ." She wrestled her laughter under control and then studied him, chewing on her lip. Once again, his eyes felt compelled to linger. "We aren't friends," she finally said. "It wouldn't be proper."

"There is not much about this entire venture I would label as proper," he pointed out. "You are travelling to Cornwall without a companion, and presumably without your father's knowledge. And I don't compose poetry about just *anyone*, you know. Perhaps we could be friends, of a sort. You will call me Thomas, and I might call you Lucy. Or if you prefer, Luuuuuuu-cyyyyyy."

Now, finally, he had her smiling. A broad, beauty of a smile, too.

"I would prefer to be called Miss L," she told him, though she did so with a fair degree of amusement. "If I choose to live at Heathmore Cottage, as my aunt did, I will need a name that fits." She tried it out again. "Miss L." She nodded. "Yes, I rather like the sound of that."

"Miss L, then." He smiled, but her words kindled a faint sense of unease. They were a reminder of her goal here, and his mission, beyond making her smile. The shadow of Heathmorc Cottage sat between them. Still, they needn't face that for at least another day.

And there was no reason they couldn't be friends in the interim.

THE COCKSURE BUGGER—or Thomas, as she was now half-way tempted to think of him—proved a surprisingly charming traveling companion, once he abandoned his scurrilous attempts to buy her property. Outside the window, the English countryside rushed by in a blur, winter fields just starting to turn green, stone bridges and quaint townscapes flashing by.

Inside the cabin, the hours were a similar blur.

Yesterday, when she'd first met him, he'd seemed far too sober and stern. A man without humor, intent on naught but negotiation. It had been easy to imagine she disliked him.

But today Lord Branston seemed different. He tossed off scientific names as though they were supposed to be a part of everyday conversation, and while she'd pretended not to be, she was duly impressed. He'd shown several small kindnesses to complete strangers, and had gamely tried to coax her into eating an apple he didn't have to buy—not that he'd been successful in the gesture, but still, one had to admire the effort. He'd told her ridiculous jokes that made her cheeks burn with laughter. And all during the long train ride, through the mild discomfort of the hard wooden seat and the fussing baby to their left, he kept up a stream of easy conversation, as though it was his mission in life to entertain her in a third class train car.

Had she imagined that all titled gentlemen were like that fop from the coach, the one who'd only come to see her to angle for her dowry? Had she imagined that the sort of men who populated the peerage must all be shallow and dull? Lord Branston was many things, but shallow and dull were not the sort of adjectives that came to mind.

And at present he did not seem to want anything from her but her company.

It was startling to realize she was all too willing to give it.

Any inhibitions Lucy might have initially felt had melted clean away by the time they pulled into the Salisbury station. During dinner at the public room of the inn, she caught herself staring at his mouth more than propriety permitted, fixed on the way the left side rose higher than the other, giving him an impish, crooked smile. And later, when he insisted on walking her to her room, she agreed without the proper degree of hesitation.

Was this merely the latest manifestation of her impulsive nature?

Or was it something deeper, an elemental desire to be admired by a handsome man?

She didn't know. She only knew that as they walked down the narrow hallway of the inn, she couldn't resist taking surreptitious peeks at the man who walked beside her. She'd come to know his profile far too well during the long train ride. He'd been the consummate gentleman all day. Well, except for the poem about her breasts. The truth was, she hadn't really minded. A woman *ought* to have poetry written about her breasts at least once in her life. Aunt E would probably have welcomed such a thing.

And wasn't she supposed to be a scandalous sort of spinster?

But this friendship—or whatever else it was that had been forged between them today—couldn't last. He hadn't mentioned Heathmore again since their first moments on the train, but tomorrow they would board the same mail coach, with the same final destination.

Only, they couldn't both win the prize. She couldn't quite

shake the notion there were things about Heathmore that hadn't been disclosed, secrets her aunt had meant to entrust to her.

Or perhaps that was just her imagination running wild.

Feeling off-balance from all she didn't know—and possibly, from the three glasses of wine she had consumed over dinner—Lucy forgot to object when Lord Branston placed a steadying hand on the small of her back, his touch as tender as a lover's caress. But as they reached the door to her room, she found herself suddenly grateful for the candle she was carrying. She didn't want to be alone in the dark with him if she could help it. She had a fair notion what Aunt E would have done in her situation, thanks to the diary entries she had read.

I might choose to be a spinster, but that doesn't mean I can't kiss a handsome man every now and again.

Aunt E hadn't backed down from a challenge, or a temptation, it seemed.

But who knew what *she* might be tempted to do?

She turned to face him. "Thank you for how solicitous you have been." She breathed in deeply, only to discover the breath was laced with the familiar spiced brandy scent of him. Which was odd, given that she hadn't seen him drink anything at all during dinner.

As if she had summoned him with that indrawn breath, he stepped closer. She jumped, startled by his sudden nearness, and spilled a drop of hot wax on her thumb. "Oh, blast it all," she exclaimed, shaking it.

He picked up her hand, examining the burn. "Now, *that,* at least, is an expression I've heard Miss E use before."

She held her breath as the pad of his finger rubbed gently over hers. "I . . . ah . . . that is, you know an awful lot about the sort of things my aunt used to say."

"I counted her as a friend."

Lucy stared down at the sight of her hand in his, spell-bound. She didn't know whether it was an effect of the wine or the effect of his proximity, but she hoped—prayed, in fact—he might step even closer. She knew she ought to pull her hand away and retreat to the safety of her room. But she didn't. *Couldn't.* She felt . . . reckless. Not an unusual thing, given her nature.

But unusual enough to feel in the presence of a gentleman. She'd never been so acutely aware of her own skin. She'd started out this long, strange day quite convinced she disliked the man. But now her head was spinning and she couldn't sort out which way was up. "Is that the only reason why you are being so kind to me?" she whispered, dragging her gaze up to his face. "Because you were friends with my aunt?"

His smile caught her like a wild swing from the right, crooked and lopsided but still straight as an arrow through her hopeful heart. "If I am being kind, it is not only because I considered your aunt a good friend." He stepped closer, until she was trapped between his large body and her waiting door, her hand still caught up in his. "It is because I would like to be your friend as well, Lucy."

She ought to protest. To correct his presumed right to use her given name. She hadn't agreed to his outrageous proposal in the train.

But there was no denying her name on his lips felt . . . *right.*

She felt as though she was swaying in place. But despite the way her body wanted to lean closer, despite the fuzziness of her thoughts, something wasn't quite right here, and that was the only thing that kept her from dissolving in a boneless puddle on the dirty wood-plank floor. If Lord Branston's mind was truly on the prize of securing Heathmore, he ought to be trying to make her as miserable as possible, not seeing to her every need.

Well, not her *every* need.

There was no denying this moment was stirring thoughts of needs she'd never imagined . . . well . . . *needing*.

She laughed lightly, trying to reassemble her scattered wits. "No matter how kind you are, Lord Branston, I am still not going to sell Heathmore without seeing it first."

"Fair enough." He loosened her hand. "But I maintain hope you might still consider my offer after you've had a proper look. And I would ask that you at least let me be the one to show you Heathmore Cottage. There are things about the property you might miss at first glance."

She had no experience in the matter of dealing with a gentleman who looked at her in this way. The knowledge that—if she wished—she could simply close the small distance between them and stretch up and press her lips against his made her feel light-headed. There was no disapproving parent hovering nearby, no bevy of servants waiting to play chaperone. No matter what she chose to do in this moment, this was *her* decision to make.

She licked her lips. "I'll think on it, my lord."

His head dipped tantalizingly closer. "Come now, can't you even call me Thomas?"

She shook her head. "You've not yet convinced me to overlook the impropriety."

"Haven't I?" He lifted his hand, his fingers lingering near her cheek. She lifted her chin in invitation, only to feel the sharp tug of disappointment as he reached out to tuck a strand of hair behind her ear instead. "You don't strike me as the sort of lady who cares overmuch about propriety."

"I care," she protested.

"Perhaps you care to guard your heart," he corrected, his voice a deep rumble in her ears. "But not because of what people might think."

She drew in a breath. He was wrong. She did care what *some* people thought of her.

She cared about what *he* thought.

"No comment to offer?" His smile returned, slow and spreading this time, but still real enough to make her knees wobble. "I would have thought you might have a smart rejoinder. It seems I am still sorting you out, Lucy Westmore."

"What if I refuse to be sorted into some neat category?" she breathed. "What if I refuse to do the expected thing? I might decide to live at Heathmore Cottage myself, you know."

"You've not yet seen the property. You will change your mind."

"About Heathmore?" she asked huskily. "Or about you?"

His eyes darkened. His hand reached out again, and this time she held her breath until his fingers brushed light as a wish against the delicate skin of her neck, sliding across the pendant she wore, the one Aunt E had sent her. Could he feel the pounding of her pulse, there beneath the pad of his finger? "Perhaps the decision is one and the same," he murmured.

She could feel it in the air, a wicked charge of promise. He was going to touch her. *Kiss her.* She closed her eyes in anticipation.

And then she felt it, the first tentative brush of his lips against hers. She sighed into the experience, heat kindling beneath her skin. His lips were firm but gentle. Warmth spread through her limbs. Oh, but if this was ruin, she welcomed its path.

But almost immediately the tenor of the kiss changed.

Instead of gathering her in his arms, as she'd imagined he might, he took a decided step back. She opened her eyes to find him looking at her as though she were a strange, perplexing creature. *Don't stop*, her heart whispered, though despite her addled judgment, she somehow swallowed the urge to say the words out loud.

Surely there was more to the experience of a woman's first

kiss than *that*. She'd expected fireworks. Singing angels. Or at *least* a case of dyspepsia.

"Well, Miss Westmore." He exhaled loudly, but didn't resume his path toward her easy, assured seduction. "It seems you are rather more experienced in this game of negotiation than I first credited you." He dragged a hand through his already tousled curls, and then his mouth—the mouth that had just touched hers—slid into an easy, crooked smile. "Have you decided to offer yourself as part of the bargain after all?"

She blinked up at him, confused.

He lifted his brows, sliding back into his cocksure ways with the confidence of a professional swindler. His light laughter met her ears with all the subtlety of a branding iron. "You might have just convinced me to offer a solid seven hundred pounds."

All the pleasure his touch had just awakened vanished like a wisp of smoke. Embarrassment bloomed in its place. *Oh, God.*

Oh, bloody, bloody *hell*.

Understanding swooped in, driving its way through the hazy warmth of the wine, and it was brutal. He was offering her more money for Heathmore? Because of a *kiss*? She shrank back against the wall, whatever desire she'd felt drowning against the surge of indignation. She thought back to her fears for the future, the certainty that her Season would be naught but a long parade of suitors, wanting to get their hands on her money. Had she thought Branston was different, then? The opposite of the fop who'd come during calling hours, pretending to be charming and then laughing about his plans when he thought no one could hear?

God, she was stupid. He was exactly the same, wanting to charm her for no reason other than getting his hands on something she possessed.

Where had her wits gone? To hell, apparently. She'd

always considered herself strong, *different* than other girls. She had important things to do with her life, grand causes to pursue. But she felt the slow burn of shame to realize she had just proven she was no better than the usual giggling, empty-headed debutante.

Hadn't she been wondering all day why Lord Branston was being so nice to her? So attentive? Why else would a handsome, titled, wealthy marquess show such attentiveness to someone like her, but to try to change her mind about Heathmore?

"Only seven hundred pounds?" she somehow managed to choke out. "That would be rather unenterprising of me, especially if I am as experienced a negotiator as you just implied. Perhaps, if I threw my maidenhead into the bargain, we might get you up to one thousand?"

His eyes widened. "Your *maidenhead*?"

She lifted herself from the wall, pulling herself together in slow degrees. It wasn't easy, given that the hallway seemed to be spinning. But all was not lost. Perhaps it would be better for him to imagine the kiss was part of her strategy, an intended piece of the negotiations. Better than the truth, which was that she was stupid enough to have begun to trust him.

"Well, a girl like me has so little else to bargain with," she retorted. Why, oh *why* hadn't she followed the advice in Aunt E's diary? Well, she wouldn't make that mistake again. From this point on she would keep her thoughts centered on Heathmore and her legs firmly crossed. She was determined to stay a spinster, by God. And she didn't need a man—especially a man like Lord Branston—to fill her head with thoughts of kisses.

She crossed her arms over her chest. "My titties, you see, have only inspired a bit of poorly formed poetry. I need to bargain with something worth a bit more, don't you think?"

He shifted his weight back on his heels, clearly struggling

to find air, much less the appropriate response. She shook her head, almost disappointed to have silenced him so effectively. After all, it wasn't even the most shocking thing she had ever said. "I am on to your scheme, Lord Branston. You are trying to charm me, apply a little light seduction in the hopes of confusing a silly young spinster into acquiescence."

That, finally, had his expression shifting. *"No."* He shook his head, too vigorously for it to be the truth. "You misunderstand my intentions."

"Do I?" she demanded. Was the man not even going to admit his culpability in the night's ruse? "We were just standing here, having a lovely, *friendly* conversation, when—without invitation—you *touched* me, right here." She tapped a finger against the side of her neck. "And then, to point out the obvious, you kissed me."

He swallowed. "I . . . ah . . . touched you because you've a rash." His voice sounded halfway strangled. He lifted his hand again, motioning this time—no doubt wisely interpreting that another touch might not be as eagerly received. "There, just behind your ear. I noticed it during dinner." His words took a moment to register.

But when they did, Lucy's cheeks burned hotter.

The lobber was claiming he'd only touched her because she had a rash? She lifted a hand to the skin behind her ear, testing the hypothesis, and was almost dismayed when her skin responded with far more than a prickle of awareness. But despite the evidence that in this, at least, he was telling some semblance of the truth, she still didn't believe he was being entirely truthful. How could she when he looked guilty as hell?

And a rash couldn't come *close* to explaining why he had kissed her.

She needed to pay more attention to the advice in her aunt's diary. Aunt E might have had her curiosity roused by the vicar, and consented to a kiss or two, but her aunt had at *least* had enough sense to question the man's motives. She herself had just proven far less wise.

Incensed, she turned and lifted the latch on her door, stumbling her way into her room. Holding up the candle, she peered at her reflection in the washstand mirror. Angry red welts trailed down her neck, just below her right ear.

The evidence that this, at least, was no falsehood did little to soothe her wounded pride.

Perhaps whatever this infirmity was had spread to her brain as well. That might explain why she'd lost her head around this man.

"It looks very much like the sort of rash one sees with *Toxicodendrum radicuns.*" His voice pushed over her shoulder, grating now in its nearness. Lucy whirled around to glare at him. He'd settled a shoulder against the door frame, stopping on the threshold like a proper gentleman.

Only he wasn't a proper gentleman, was he? He'd just proven it.

And she was a stupid, stupid girl.

"What in the bloody blazes is that?" she snarled.

He chuckled—though whether at her predicament or her language, she couldn't be sure. "Poison ivy."

"You've tried to poison me?" she asked incredulously.

"Not me." He shook his head. "And it isn't deadly. But as I said earlier, plants are something of a hobby of mine. It's an exotic plant, from the Americas. Quite beautiful, though its leaves are noxious to touch. It's not common in England, but many university greenhouses and specialty gardens have it. Have you come in contact with any?"

Lucy scratched at her neck. "I . . . no . . . I only work with seedlings for the St. James Orphanage community garden. I can assure you, they are the usual variety of sweet pea."

"Pisum sativum."

She narrowed her eyes, wondering if he was insulting her.

"I beg your pardon?" God, he was just showing off now. She'd never been good at Latin. Her older sister, Clare, was the secretive, scholarly Westmore.

Growing up, Lucy had much preferred to swing from trees, rather than study them.

"It is the scientific name for sweet pea." He rubbed a hand behind his neck. "Sorry. I sometimes forget not everyone shares my interest in botany."

"*Pisum sativum,*" she huffed out, the very words sounding menacing to her ears. Surely a plant with such a terrible-sounding name couldn't be benign. "Well, I've come close to swimming in it this past week." She recalled how many hours she'd spent in the greenhouse, up to her elbows in dirt. "Could *that* have caused this rash?"

He shook his head. "No. Peas are quite safe to touch. I am certain you must have encountered poison ivy somewhere else. Can you think of another instance?"

Lucy turned back to the mirror, running a finger over the offended skin. It had a blistered feel. Where on earth would she have encountered such a thing?

Although, if it was common in university greenhouses . . .

"Geoffrey," she muttered, thinking of the grass-stained letter she had read two days ago, and how after reading it she had tucked her hair behind this very ear. "The bloody bastard."

She'd just been pranked. *Again.*

"Geoffrey is your brother?" he asked from over her shoulder. "The same one who taught you to swear like a sailor?"

"He's something of a professional trickster." Her cheeks felt feverishly hot. Oh, but could this night get any more humiliating?

"You might want to put something on it before it worsens. Would you like me to fetch some grease from the kitchen?" he asked. His voice sounded as if it was laced with concern. But then, he was a scoundrel of the highest order. Pretending to care, hovering over her, entertaining her on the train.

Kissing her in shadowed hallways.

While all the while he was laughing at her rash and keeping his eye on her prize.

Lucy shook her head. "No, I can manage myself, thank you."

"Are you sure there isn't anything I can do?" he pressed. "Distract you, perhaps?" He cleared his throat, and in the reflection of the mirror she could see his mouth curve into a grin. "There once was a very fine neck—"

"No!" She whirled around to face him properly, wincing as the wax from the candle tipped onto her bare skin again. She contemplated snuffing the flame, but then she would be alone in the dark with him, and she'd just proven herself a very bad judge of character. She took a deep breath. "Just go. I would like to be alone now." In fact, she wanted nothing more in this moment than to see the back of him and the door closing behind him.

He spread his hands. "Lucy—" he started.

"Miss L," she countered sharply.

He hesitated. "Miss L, then. If you are bound for bed, please lock the door behind me. You've had a good deal to drink tonight. And a woman traveling alone can't be too careful."

A point he'd well demonstrated, now, hadn't he?

She nodded stiffly, not trusting herself with words. As he pulled the door shut behind him, she stared at the spot where he had just stood, scratching at her neck and trying to remember all the pertinent reasons why Aunt E said she shouldn't trust men.

They lectured women about living on cliffs. They gawked at red ribbons in church.

And oh yes, there was this new piece as well:

They tried to charm young ladies into selling their property.

She lunged toward the door and locked it, as much to secure some distance from him as anyone else. She might have had too many glasses of wine, but at least she'd had the wherewithal to call him out for his actions, and pretend that the kiss had been calculated. She didn't know what his motivations were, or why he wanted Heathmore so much, but a man who paid this sort of close, personal attention to a plain, short-haired spinster like herself had to have an ulterior motive.

And she intended to find out his.

From the Diary of Edith Lucille Westmore
December 26, 1815

It was a Boxing Day to remember.

Is it really so hard for a vicar to admit that a woman—and worse, a scandalously unwed woman—might contribute to the moral and financial needs of the town? I may not be wealthy, but compared to most in Lizard Bay, I have far more than I need.

I only wanted to share some of my good fortune.

Though the role of distributing Christmas boxes has traditionally been managed by the church, this year I prepared several Christmas boxes of my own, as thanks for all the villagers have done for me. For Mr. Jamieson, who faithfully orders my periodicals from London each month, I knitted a lovely set of mittens. For the postmaster, Mr. Bentley, I knitted a warm cap to thank him for always ensuring my mail is delivered promptly, even though my cottage lies so far away from town. Apparently, however, I have stepped on the toes of the bloody Church.

When Reverend Wellsbury saw me coming out of Mr. Jamieson's store, he proceeded to stand in the street and lecture me again about the evils of leading men astray. Well, I can tell you I carried the box and the gift I had prepared for him straight home.

The pompous ass.

What need has a vicar for a length of red ribbon, anyway?

Chapter 10

The coach ride from Salisbury to Lizard Bay proved somewhat less than enjoyable. A week ago Thomas would have been grateful for the silence inside the mail coach. He would have been able to think, to write even, at least on the smoother sections of road. He might have extended his scientific observations on the manuscript he'd been writing, the one he was preparing for the Linnean Society of London describing plant life on the Lizard Bay peninsula.

But after yesterday's laughter-filled train ride, the silence felt awkward, almost painful. He had a notion it was going to take more than a limerick to soften Lucy's hunched shoulders today. She had been withdrawn from the moment she stepped into the public room for breakfast, sitting on the opposite side of the table, avoiding him even when their start was delayed several hours to repair a damaged axle on the mail coach.

They might finally be moving, but now she was sitting stiff as a board on the opposite seat, reading some old book she kept angled away from him, ignoring him as the mail coach careened over Cornwall's rough and tumble roads.

It was galling to sit in such a pointed absence of conversation. He could hear only the creak of springs beneath them and the stutter of the wheels as they scraped the occasional rock, and it had been thus for hours. Yesterday he'd imagined they were making progress. That she'd started to look at him without that pinched expression and clouded veil of suspicion. That they could laugh with each other and be easy friends.

But today the veil was firmly back in place.

Finally, he took it upon himself to say something. *Anything.* "Does your head hurt terribly?"

She looked up, frowning. "I beg your pardon?"

"Your head." He tapped a finger against his forehead. "'Tis the usual casualty of one too many drinks. You had three glasses of wine last night, by my count, and you are being very quiet today. I thought perhaps you weren't feeling well."

She looked back down at her book. "I can't see that it is any of your business to care how many glasses of wine I may have had." She turned a page. "Or whether my head aches this morning. Especially given that yesterday *you* smelled entirely too strongly of brandy."

Her verbal observation landed like a well-aimed arrow. "I . . . that is, I do not usually drink," Thomas ground out.

Not anymore.

"The evidence suggests otherwise." She sounded almost bored, her gaze firmly focused on the page before her. "You smelled like a distillery yesterday morning."

His hands knotted on the seat. "I only meant I understood. If your head ached."

She looked up then, and that was when he realized she was not nearly as bored—or unaffected—as she was pretending. Blue eyes flashed at him across the narrow space of the carriage. "Let us get one thing straight between us. I do not seek your understanding, nor your empathy. We may have exchanged a strategic kiss last night, but you can lay no claim to my health or my feelings. We are only sharing this coach today because you are apparently too much of a spendthrift to have arranged your own private conveyance. If my silence bothers you, perhaps you might want to ride outside with the driver. I know *I* would certainly better enjoy the ride."

He frowned as she turned her pointed attention back to her book. She was miffed because of the kiss last night? He couldn't understand why, when she all but claimed it was calculated.

It hadn't been—at least, not on his part.

He still didn't know what had possessed him. One moment they were locked in an enjoyable bit of banter, and the next his brain had just taken over. No, that wasn't quite right. He might be rusty, but it hadn't been his *brain* in charge of the decision-making process. The experience had shocked him. He'd not kissed a woman in three long years, and he didn't recall the experience being so bloody *vivid*. Was it because he'd been stripped of the haze of drunkenness that had so frequently accompanied him during his courtship of Gabrielle?

Or was it because this woman herself was so different?

Miss Westmore was nothing like his former fiancée. Gabrielle had been coiffed and perfumed, perfectly poised and faintly manipulative. In contrast, Miss Westmore was a wild, rash-covered mess of a thing, her blond hair flying like a halo about her frequently red face. Far from planning her approach, she appeared to lurch from one unplanned disaster to another, climbing out of windows and kissing gentlemen she barely knew.

And yes—no matter her sputtered claims to the contrary, she *had* kissed him back.

He wasn't so rusty he didn't know a willing woman when one kissed him.

He still didn't understand what had made him say those

things in the aftermath of such an indiscretion, to awkwardly tease her about the kiss being part of the negotiations. They'd spent so much of the day locked in laughter that it seemed safer, somehow, to turn it into a joke.

Safer than acknowledging what else was happening.

Yesterday he'd felt . . . well, he'd *felt*. She ignited something in him he hadn't felt in three long years—quite possibly ever—and it went so far beyond the urge to make her laugh. He'd been beyond tempted to take more than that quick, fumbled kiss, to pull her against him, to explore the sweetness of her mouth until she was gasping for more.

But if his body had led him down this thorny path, at least his brain had retained enough sense to end it quickly enough that there were no long-term repercussions. God, he was a cad. She was alone and unprotected, likely for the first time in her life. She'd had too much to drink and likely regretted the memory of their actions now—a notion he understood all too well. So he couldn't take advantage, no matter how much he wanted to.

No matter how much *she* wanted to.

Not that she appeared to want to at the moment.

His gaze lingered on her long, lovely neck, the skin above her serpentine pendant red and angry-looking. "How is your rash today?" he asked, though he could see, plain as day, that it was worse, not better. She continued staring down at the pages of her book, though her fingers drifted tellingly toward her collar. "Did you find a salve for it?" he pressed.

"There is no need." But despite her words, she began to scratch.

Would she not even admit such a basic need? Christ, but she was a tough little thing, stubborn to the point of exhaustion. Cursing beneath his breath, he rapped on the roof of the coach until it began to slow. That finally had her eyes lifting from the pages of whatever she found so fascinating. She shut the book's cover. "What are you doing?"

"Ensuring you don't sit there for the remaining two hours in agony."

"I am fine," she protested as the coach rocked slowly to a stop. "I don't need help, and I *certainly* don't need it from you."

"Is everything all right?" the coachman called down.

Thomas opened the window on his side and leaned out. "Miss Westmore needs to stop at the chemist's shop in Marston," he called up to the driver. "Could we make a detour?"

She opened the window on her side of the coach. "We do *not* need to stop at Marston. Carry on, if you please. We have already endured a late start, and I would like to reach Lizard Bay before nightfall." She pulled her head back inside and glared at him, her fingers clenching over the spine of the book. "If this is some tactic to delay our arrival, it won't work."

Thomas shook his head. Christ, she was as stubborn as her aunt had been. When she deigned to look at him, her chin always seemed to be pointing up. "You do realize we'll arrive too late for a proper visit to Heathmore tonight, don't you? I will be more than happy to show you the property in the morning."

She opened her book again. "Your assistance won't be necessary."

He gritted his teeth as the carriage began to pick up speed. "Do you even know how to get there?"

"I am sure I can find it."

"The property is two miles from town, and is not easy to find." In fact, he'd only discovered the path by accident, stumbling across it during a long, hard walk. Miss E had enjoyed her solitude.

Her eyes flickered toward him. "Does it lie east or west of town, Lord Branston?"

"I thought we had agreed you would call me Thomas."

She ignored his entreaty. "I know it isn't north, that way

lies the ocean. It can't be south either, as I vividly remember the view of the water from the cottage's front door. That means it is either east or west. Which direction do I need to walk from town?"

He glanced down at her boots, which, while halfway sensible, were still of the exquisitely crafted London-street variety. Her yellow wool skirts dragged the filthy floor of the coach, and looked as though they were waiting to tangle about her feet and toss her over the side of a cliff at the slightest provocation. "I don't think I ought to tell you." He shook his head. "You shouldn't attempt it without a guide. As I said, I can show you."

She looked back down at her book. "I will find someone else in Lizard Bay to help me."

"I wouldn't bet on it," he muttered beneath his breath.

Her heated blue gaze flicked back. "What is *that* supposed to mean?"

He exhaled. "The citizens of Lizard Bay are none too fond of Heathmore Cottage at present. They'll not be keen to help you." He thought of how scared young Danny was of the moaning wind. How he'd had trouble finding anyone to manage the repairs on the roof. No, she'd not find a warm reception for her inquiries.

But she'd find that out soon enough on her own.

"Is it because you have poisoned their judgment against me before I've even arrived? That they want *you* to have the property instead of me?" Her voice wobbled. "That's hardly playing fair, Lord Branston. And I can promise you won't be successful."

Thomas sighed. Damn, but she was mulish. He didn't suspect the residents of Lizard Bay cared overmuch who owned Heathmore Cottage, so long as *they* didn't have to set foot on the property. "I just think you are being hasty," he told her. "You've not yet even seen the place."

"I will tonight."

He shook his head. "You can't stay there tonight." Perhaps, when the new roof was finished, she might have a fighting chance. But right now at least half the structure was open to the overhead elements. All she needed was a good storm and she'd be washed off the edge of the cliff. "It is uninhabitable in its present form."

"Oh yes, the rats." She rolled her eyes. "Please, spare me the boring details. I've heard them all already. You'll find I don't scare away that easy. And I refuse to give up my inheritance without a fight, especially to a man who would stoop to such means." She turned, fuming, to her window, holding the book up to her nose.

Stoop? *Means?* What on earth was she talking about?

The fact he had traveled all the way to London to give her a better offer?

Or the fact that last night he had taken wrongful advantage, swooping in for a kiss that he should have first begged permission to take?

The answer might be muddled, but her dismissal was clear. There would be no more questions, no more conversation. Following her example, Thomas turned to his window. But he knew she was there, simmering on the opposite seat. As obstinate as she was, he couldn't help but admire her spirit. But spirit alone wasn't going to save Heathmore, nor make it livable either. She was either naive to the point of stupidity, or she believed he was lying about the cottage's poor condition.

And for the life of him, he couldn't figure out why either should be the case.

LUCY STEPPED DOWN from the coach into the waning light of evening, her feet grateful to finally be touching Cornwall soil.

And by soil, she did mean *soil*.

There were no cobblestone streets to speak of in Lizard Bay. No streets, really, beyond the one on which she was standing.

Well. She clearly wasn't in London anymore.

But as the crisp salt air off the coast filled her lungs, the initial confusion she felt faded. Overhead, against a darkening sky, a trio of gulls somersaulted on the breeze coming in from the ocean, and she felt nearly the same sense of exuberance. She had done it. Survived an eight hour coach ride with Lord Branston, in spite of her lingering anger. She was here.

Well, *nearly* here. There was still the matter of sorting out where Heathmore Cottage actually lay relative to the town.

But surely there was someone here who might help her. After all, her aunt had lived here for over forty years. The diary's pages were full of tales of people Aunt E had known. She *must* have had friends here, people who cared enough about her to mail a package for her after she had died. Lucy knew she just needed to sort out friend from foe and ask for their help.

Behind her, she could hear Lord Branston's voice as he conversed with the coachman, thanking the man for a pleasant ride. She tried to ignore the evidence of his civility. It didn't matter if he was kind to strangers and bought apples on trains. It mattered little whether he remembered to say please and thank you. He wanted Heathmore and was willing to flirt his way to success. That made him the foe in this small drama.

Through the gathering twilight a sea of curious faces started to crowd in around her. It looked as though the entire town was coming out to meet her, spilling out of weathered doors, pressing close. Word seemed to have traveled quickly. Young and old, tattered and well-kempt, their voices melded into a rough-edged dialect she had trouble understanding. They didn't appear to know quite what to do with a visitor.

Well, she knew what to do with them. Her mother's incessant nagging about manners had been good for at least *something* by way of theatrics. She gave them a deep, perfectly executed curtsy, the one she had been practicing her entire life.

An awed hush fell over the crowd.

She straightened, willing her heart to stop thumping so loudly. "Good evening," she said. "Might someone please point me in the direction of Heathmore Cottage?"

The whispers started.

"It's her."

"No it couldn't be. She's dead."

"She's the spitting image."

Before Lucy could speak, a quartet of gangly boys tumbled to the forefront of the crowd. The setting sun reflected off their dirty faces, and she counted at least a dozen missing teeth between them. "Gor," the tallest of them said. "She looks just like old Miss E, don't she?"

"No, she don't," another protested, reaching out a grimy finger to touch her skirts, leaving a smear of dirt behind. "She's got blond hair, not gray."

"Well, maybe Miss E when she was younger, then."

Lucy jumped as her skirts moved. She extracted a filthy hand from her dress pocket. "Excuse me, but I believe a handshake is a more customary form of greeting." The lad's eyes widened, and he twisted out of her grip and darted back to the safety of the pack.

"She even *sounds* like Miss E," the tallest said in awe.

They all peered up at her, their eyes wide. "It's her ghost," the youngest whispered. "She's come back for her lost love, just like I told you."

Lucy felt her lips start to twitch. Ghost? *Lost love?*

What on earth where they talking about? No matter. She knew how to deal with naughty young boys. She'd been raised with Geoffrey, after all.

So she stepped forward, flapping her hands and filling her lungs. *"Boo!"*

As though shot from a cannon, they scattered, shrieking into the twilight. The crowd shifted, too, murmurs rising. Lord Branston's bemused voice floated over her shoulder. "Well, I'm afraid *that's* not going to help your cause."

Lucy turned around. "What do you mean?"

He was standing on the runner of the mail coach, getting her bag down from where it had been lashed to the top. "The boys are usually quite helpful when there's a bit of money in it." He jumped down from the runner, a puff of dust rising up from where his feet connected with the road. "But now you've just gone and scared off the only souls in town besides myself who might have been convinced to show you the way to Heathmore."

She wanted to ignore him but knew it was a battle she was bound to lose, given how her entire body seemed to stretch in awareness whenever he was near. Worse, his words sparked a deeper worry. She reached a hand in her pocket, suddenly suspicious.

Wilson's gold sovereigns—her fallback to return to London—had gone missing.

She turned back to the milling crowd, her heart twisting in mild panic. "Who has charge of those boys?" she demanded. The thought of being stranded in Lizard Bay with no money made her throat feel tight. "One of them has picked my pocket."

A gray-haired woman stepped forward, wringing her hands. "Oh, please don't pay them any mind. They're just the Tanner lot, our local pack of orphans."

"Well, why aren't they confined in an orphanage?" Lucy demanded, confused by the explanation. In London, orphans were secured away in locked buildings, for their own protection and the protection of those they might harass.

"Lizard Bay isn't a large enough town to have a proper orphanage." Lord Branston's voice tapped against her ears, and then he emerged beside her in the settling gloom, setting her bag down in the dust of the street. "The Tanner boys' mother died when the youngest, Danny, was born, and their father was a local fisherman who died at sea just last August. Since then, I'm afraid they've had the run of the town."

Lucy pulled her hand from her empty pocket. Her heart squeezed tight. Good heavens, the oldest boy couldn't have been more than eleven. "But . . . where do they live?"

"Here and about." He nodded toward the gray-haired woman who had stepped forward in their defense. "This is Mrs. Wilkins. She sees to their care and feeding most days." He gestured toward Lucy. "Mrs. Wilkins, may I present Miss Lucy Westmore. Of London."

"Miss *L*," Lucy interjected, miffed that he had taken her introduction out of her own hands. "If you please."

Branston raised his voice to the crowd as though presenting a prize horse at auction. "She's Miss E's niece. Not her ghost." He hesitated, and then his gaze slid hot against her skin. "I can promise you, she's a real enough woman."

Lucy's cheeks heated, remembering how he had kissed her.

He would know, wouldn't he?

As murmurs once again swept the crowd, the gray-haired woman who'd spoken for the boys stepped forward. "Oh, Miss L, we are so happy you have come. You're the spitting image of your aunt, you know." Mrs. Wilkins smiled, stretching wrinkled skin. "Gave us all a fright, stepping down from the coach like that. We'd thought it was her ghost, come back to life." She stepped closer, her hands smoothing over the front on her apron. "I run the boardinghouse in town. I reckon you'll be wanting a room for the night?"

Lucy shook her head. "Er . . . no. Thank you." She was more than a little bothered by the notion of being offered a bed while the orphans were left to roam the streets. "But if I might ask, where do the boys sleep?"

"Here and about," Lord Branston said again, breaking in by way of an answer. "Oftentimes they bed down in the anteroom of the church."

Lucy frowned. "Why does no one look after them?" Her mind was already racing with all the ways she might be able to help. "I would be happy to write to the curators of the St. James Orphanage. These boys should be sent to London, where someone would see to their well-being and their education. 'Tis pitiless to leave them to fend for themselves."

"Oh, miss, please don't do such a thing," Mrs. Wilkins gasped.

Branston just shook his head slowly.

"What is wrong with my idea?" she said, turning on him.

"You can't take them away from the only town they've ever known." He lifted his hand in the direction they had scurried, the closing darkness making it anyone's guess where they had gone. "They were born here. They know every soul in town. Trust me, Lizard Bay looks after its own."

"They don't seem looked after to me," she retorted. "Their faces are dirty, their grammar is deplorable, and they picked my pocket the moment I stepped off the coach. I could take care of them far better than the town has." She clenched her fists. "I *could*."

He stared at her, and that was when Lucy realized she ought to stop talking. It was a vulnerability to give him this insight into her nature. *A peek behind the curtain*, as Aunt E would say. And he'd already proven himself willing to exploit other vulnerabilities.

But instead of scoffing at her—or worse, dismissing her—his jaw softened. "It's a kind offer, Miss L, but we have laws in Lizard Bay about these things. Your aunt personally saw to it the boys were well-cared-for, before her passing. She even paid their school fees." He nodded at her in what might have been grudging approval. "You might think about fulfilling that role yourself, now that you're here."

The anger coiling inside her collapsed. Bugger it all, he could show the most disconcerting kindness at times. Did his voice have to be so compelling? So inviting? But she couldn't let herself believe it. Couldn't let herself *trust* it. He had kissed her, after all, to further his own hand. She felt safer when she was sparring with him.

"You mean *if* I stay, don't you?" she pointed out. "I still have to see Heathmore and determine if I wish to sell it or not, and as you've told me so incessantly, it's nothing but a pile of tumbling-down stones and rat droppings." She picked up her bag and looked down the darkening street. "Now, can anyone here tell me whether I head east or west?"

Once again a murmur ran through the crowd.

Lucy bit her lip. This was proving rather harder than she'd expected. "Surely someone here knows the direction," she called out. If she wasn't mistaken, several townspeople turned around and hurried away. "Will *no one* help me?" she asked, turning in a helpless circle until her gaze landed finally—regrettably—on Lord Branston. "What is the matter with everyone?"

He pulled a hand through his hair. "As I said during the coach ride, they are none too fond of the place, especially at night. Besides, it's too late to safely visit Heathmore today. A good night's sleep and a clear head will be the least you need to get you there. For tonight I'd suggest you go with Mrs. Wilkins."

Lucy dug in her heels, and not only because thanks to the loss of her sovereigns she could scarcely afford another night in a rented bed. "I really must insist—"

"You've eschewed my offer of help, and that's within your rights," he interrupted. "But Mrs. Wilkins has offered *her* help, and I'd suggest you take it. She's a living to make, and visitors to Lizard Bay are scarce at present. Moreover, you are exhausted and I can tell the rash on your neck is bedeviling you a good bit." His voice softened, and she felt an almost instinctive melting in her spine. "So why don't you put that charitable spirit to good use and purchase a room for the night?"

Lucy lifted her chin, trying to hold her glare through the shadows. No matter her bravado, she didn't exactly relish the thought of stumbling off through the darkening night. Save the light from a few oil lanterns spilling through the windows that fronted Lizard Bay's only street, the night was threatening in earnest now. It almost made her miss London's gaslit streets.

Almost, but not quite.

It was then she realized it was so dark she could no longer see the color of Lord Branston's eyes. She knew they were hazel, of course, having wasted far too many hours yesterday staring up into them—a fact she'd made sure to remedy during the coach ride today.

"Fine," she huffed, turning her back on him so she didn't have to see his lopsided smile. She nodded stiffly at Mrs. Wilkins. "I suppose it wouldn't hurt to spend *one* night in town." And she supposed it didn't matter either whether she spent her last few shillings on a room or kept them as a safeguard. It wasn't as though she really needed the money to return to London. Wilson had promised to try to delay her discovery as long as he could, but once her father realized she was gone, she didn't doubt he would follow behind, determined to fetch her back. She intended to be fully ensconced in her house by then.

Chained to a table leg, if need be.

"Oh, I am ever so glad you decided to stay with me." Mrs. Wilkins took her by one arm and began to lead her toward one of the houses that lined the street. "Your aunt stayed here with me in town the past two years, you know. I charge five shillings a night for a proper bed, and it includes meals. Laundry is extra, if you'd like it."

Nodding helplessly in response to the woman's chatter, Lucy peered over her shoulder. Lord Branston was disappearing into the darkness, without so much a good-bye. *Infuriating man.* He was the only person she knew in Lizard Bay, and yet he was taking the first opportunity to slip away with nary a clue as to where she might find him.

"Do you know where Lord Branston is going?" she interrupted.

"Oh, on toward home, I suspect."

"Home?" A flare of anger unfurled as they made their way up onto the sagging porch and stepped through the front door of the boardinghouse. "Do you mean to say he is going to Heathmore without me?"

"Oh, no. He has his own house, just outside of town." Mrs. Wilkins clucked in apparent sympathy. "It's strange, I say. It's large enough for twenty, but he keeps mostly to himself, and keeps no servants to speak of. Brings his laundry to me for washing, but makes his own meals and such. 'Tis unnatural for a man to prefer to be alone. Well, except for the vicar. *He* lives alone. Of course, he'd got God, hasn't he?" Mrs. Wilkins tugged Lucy down a hallway and gestured to a threadbare parlor that lay to their right. "Here's where we take tea in the afternoons, two o'clock sharp." She waved a hand vaguely to the left. "And there's breakfast at eight here in the dining room. Now, we've a lovely bed abovestairs, but we've a room on the bottom as well. Your aunt preferred the bottom, on account of her knees, which bothered her on rainy days. Do you have a preference?"

But Lucy's mind was gone, drifting away to the more pertinent question at hand. Lord Branston had his own house, if Mrs. Wilkin's gossip could be trusted. A large one, too.

So why in the blazes was he trying to take hers?

From the Diary of Edith Lucille Westmore
July 1, 1816

Never trust a vicar further than you can throw him.

Once again, Reverend Wellsbury has proven himself imminently untrustworthy. When the newly married Mrs. Wilkins confided in me that her husband had flown into a rage and beaten her for no greater transgression than breaking the eggs, I did what any self-respecting spinster would do. I poisoned the man's pudding.

Now, I am not saying I intended to do Mr. Wilkins harm. Not permanent harm, at any rate. But for some reason, Reverend Wellsbury chose that day to visit the Wilkins residence. Two bites of that pudding and the vicar spent a fortnight in the privy. I felt terrible, of course. Visited him in his sickbed, even offered him an apology. But the man's arrogance knows no bounds. He told me he had intended to give Mr. Wilkins a lecture on how to be a better husband and that I had ruined everything. Moreover, he informed me he can manage the souls of this parish without my interference, thank you very much.

Well, I told him a man who beats his wife deserves more by way of punishment than a bloody sermon.

And then I offered him some more pudding.

Chapter 11

*E*ight o'clock the next morning saw Lucy up, dressed in her gold wool walking gown, and ready for battle. She'd fallen asleep quickly the night before, the second volume of her aunt's diary open across her chest, two nearly sleepless nights catching up with her.

She had awakened at dawn with the rash on her neck itching like the devil. It was *almost* enough to make her regret refusing Lord Branston's offer to stop yesterday at the chemist's in Marston. But not enough to make her admit it out loud.

Try as she might, she couldn't shake him from her thoughts. She kept reliving the kiss in her mind, picking the experience apart, trying to examine its various pieces. In doing so, she'd reached a more muddled conclusion than the one she'd leaped to two nights ago. Yesterday, in the coach, he seemed truly hurt at her determination to avoid speaking to him. Either he was trying to earn back her trust, in order to further his own goals, or she'd misinterpreted something about their interaction in the hallway. Had she overreacted to his comments in the aftermath of the kiss? It was clear a strong sense of humor lurked beneath Lord Branston's crooked smile, given his propensity for terrible limericks. Had he been trying, perhaps, to lighten the mood, rather than truly meaning to accuse her of negotiating a better price?

With some much-needed sleep to untangle her thoughts, she was no longer quite as sure.

But whether he was an upstanding citizen or a plotting blackguard, the truth was, she didn't know whom to trust. Lord Branston might be the closest thing she had to an acquaintance here in Lizard Bay, but with his actions in Salisbury, he'd given her far more reason to distrust him than not. Until she saw Heathmore with her own eyes and sorted out the secrets Aunt E had hinted about in the letter, she intended to keep her options close and her putative enemies at arm's length.

As she opened the door from her room and prepared to head downstairs for breakfast, she half imagined she heard the blasted man's voice rumbling up from the first floor. Her mind insisted on conjuring a mental picture of that compelling, crooked grin.

Determined to see him—if only to once again have the pleasure of refusing his offer of assistance—Lucy hurried down the dark stairs. As she reached the bottom, she tripped over something and pitched shoulder first against the wall with a loud *oomph*. She glared down at the floorboards, wondering what she had stumbled upon. A fluffy gray cat stared back up at her from the threadbare runner, its yellow eyes blinking soulfully. Its fur was matted with burrs, as though it had no one to brush it out.

Well, that someone wasn't going to be her. *Orphans* were her specialty.

Orphans and felons.

She wasn't going to get involved with cats.

"Shoo," she muttered, then glanced down the first floor hallway, straining for a glimpse of Lord Branston's broad shoulders. She was almost disappointed to find no evidence of the man anywhere in sight. Had she dreamed she'd heard his voice? It hadn't been the only thing she'd dreamed about him either. The man had thoroughly crept beneath her skin, and somehow crept into her dreams as well. Disconcerted by the direction of her thoughts, she waved her hand at the cat. "Shoo!" she said again, louder now.

The cat didn't "shoo."

Instead, it stood up and began to wind its way around her ankles.

"Stop that." She stepped over it, only to encounter another cat waiting just beyond, this one an orange and black calico. As she approached, it yawned, and then it, too, began to rub its face against her skirts.

She skirted the edge of the wall until she finally was able to step into the dining room. She could smell toast and eggs and tea, as if breakfast had started hours ago. Her mouth was already watering. But as she turned toward the table, she discovered a rather rude shock.

To start, breakfast appeared to be over.

And second, there were cats everywhere.

Four stood on chairs, stretching high on hind legs, snatching bits of coddled egg off china plates. She counted five on the dining table, lapping from saucers of cream. At least two were rolling about under the table playing—although Lucy allowed they might have also been mating.

Who could tell, in this melee?

And in the middle of it all stood Mrs. Wilkins, a smile on her wrinkled face.

"Have I missed breakfast?" Lucy asked. She was sure that last night the woman had said eight.

"Oh, no, you are right on time." The older woman picked up an empty saucer. "'Tis just feeding time is all." She motioned Lucy in with her chin. "Come on in and I will get you a plate." She began to bustle about, waiting on the rest of the animals.

"Are these all yours?" Lucy asked as she approached the table. Bits of cat hair and fluff rolled across its surface, making her stomach turn.

"Of a fashion." Mrs. Wilkins nodded toward a brown tabby, rather more rotund than the rest and sitting in the center of the table washing his face with one paw. "Only Peter here is truly mine. The rest used to live down by the wharf, eating the castoffs of the day's catch. But fishing's been a bit off lately, and the poor souls need someone to look after them." She clucked in concern. "They keep multiplying, though. Two of them have litters of kittens, at present."

Lucy picked up a cat from one of the chairs and then sat down herself before another stealthy creature could claim it. "Let me see if I understand the way things are done in Lizard Bay," she mused, settling a napkin on her lap. "Orphans must sleep by themselves in the church, but you open your house to the town's strays?"

Mrs. Wilkins chuckled. "Oh, I offered a roof to those boys, right enough. But the Tanners are tough little nuts. Don't like the idea of charity. And between you and me, I suspect they like to sleep in the church because they can run up and down the aisles at night and make all the racket they want." She ran a gnarled hand along Peter's back, making the cat's tail arch high in the air. "And you'll have to get up a mite earlier to see *them*. The boys come by nigh on seven o'clock every morning." She gestured to the table. "This here is just what's left over from their breakfast. Lord Branston came by to collect them for school about ten minutes ago, as he does most mornings. He's the only one who can convince young Danny to go half the time. He practically had to drag the lad along today."

"Oh." Lucy blinked. So she *had* heard Lord Branston. Despite her determination to steer clear, she couldn't help but feel a bit disappointed she had missed him. "Why did Danny not want to go to school today?"

"I believe it was because of long division."

Lucy smiled at the evidence that, if nothing else, the orphans of Lizard Bay were getting a proper—if unappreciated—education. "Well, I suppose I can understand the sentiment. I preferred to run up and down church aisles over mathematics myself." She accepted the cup of tea Mrs. Wilkins handed her and offered the proprietress a wry smile. "But those boys will have need of *some* math skills if they continue on the illustrious route to thievery."

Mrs. Wilkins chuckled. "I am not sure they teach that at university."

Lucy blinked. "University?"

"Lord Branston has pledged to pay for each of the lads to go eventually." She nodded approvingly. "Lizard Bay's first graduates, they'd be. And what a sight that would be." Her mouth firmed. "But to qualify, they need to commit themselves to a proper round of study now. The older lads seem willing. But young Danny's been a bit harder to convince."

Lucy leaned back in her chair, stunned. Had she really heard correctly? The town's unruly, unkempt orphans were being groomed for higher education? And moreover, the blackguard Branston had pledged to pay their way?

"He asked after you, you know."

Lucy's gaze jerked up to meet the old woman's, still trying to sort through the incongruous images of the man as simultaneous philanthropist and scoundrel. "Danny?"

"No, Lord Branston."

"Did he?" Lucy's cheeks heated.

Mrs. Wilkins nodded. "Told me to tell him if you seemed to need any help."

"I don't need help from Lord Branston," Lucy replied, though her heart kicked over with the knowledge he'd asked after her.

"He asked me to give you this." Mrs. Wilkins placed

two gold sovereigns down on the table beside her. "And to convey his apologies on behalf of young Ethan."

Lucy stared down at the coins, swallowing. "Which one is Ethan?"

"The second to youngest. Apparently the lad confessed his crime this morning, and so Lord Branston covered the cost of the theft out of his own pocket."

Lucy exhaled slowly. Did this mean she was now in Lord Branston's debt? Or was it young Ethan who carried that cross? And blast it all, did Branston have to be so . . . so . . . damnably pleasant? Aunt E had said in her diary that men weren't to be trusted, but how was she supposed to maintain her resolve in the face of such infuriating *niceness*?

"That was rather kind of him," she admitted reluctantly.

Her stomach chose that moment to grumble.

Nothing quiet and demure about that.

"Oh, you poor dear." Mrs. Wilkins bustled to fill a plate from the sideboard. "You missed dinner last night, arriving so late. You must be starving. I hope you like sausage. They are a local variety and were your aunt's favorite." Her forehead wrinkled. "Well, except for that period a few years ago when Miss E decided to form the Lizard Bay Vegetarian Society." She shook her head. "Never did take on the way your aunt had hoped."

Lucy slid the coins into her dress pocket, grinning in spite of herself. That, at least, had a familiar ring to it. "There was a time when I refused to eat meat as well," she admitted, accepting the plate Mrs. Wilkins passed her. "I was convinced of the need to save all the animals of London."

"Why, you sound just like Miss E." Mrs. Wilkins scooped up a black and white cat that had begun to circle Lucy's plate in anticipation of its spoils. "She had a big heart where animals were concerned. People, too, I suppose. Feeding the cats from the wharf was her idea."

Lucy picked up her fork, feeling a tug of something that might have been nostalgia. "I didn't know my aunt very well. I last saw her when I was six years old." She thought of the next two volumes of her aunt's diaries, tucked in her bag abovestairs. She wasn't anywhere close to the end, but the pages she'd progressed through were offering more fascinating glimpses into her aunt's secret life. "I've only got bits and pieces that I've . . . er . . . heard."

Mrs. Wilkins bustled about, collecting dishes and warming up to her gossip. "Well, Miss E was a handful, I'll tell you. No one else like her, from London to Marston. She wasn't beautiful in the usual way, mind you, but she had a way of warming men's hearts right up whenever she walked into a room."

Lucy looked up, startled at the notion that beauty and attraction needn't be linked. "Do I really remind you of her?"

"Well now, let's see." Mrs. Wilkins put her hands on her hips. "There's your hair, of course. A bit shorter than most women wear it. Miss E was fond of the modern styles herself."

Lucy lifted a hand to her short, rebellious strands. "It . . . er . . . isn't really a style—"

Mrs. Wilkins laughed. "When you stepped off that coach without a maid in hand or even a proper chaperone, that was our next clue. Miss E valued her independence. Tell me, child, how much trouble do you usually get up to?"

Lucy's cheeks heated, thinking of all the trouble her letter-writing campaign to prisoners had caused back at home. "More than enough."

The older woman nodded in apparent approval. "Your aunt stirred up trouble wherever she went, too. The Vegetarian Society was only one of the causes she tried to introduce here in Lizard Bay. Before that there was the Fisherman's Wives' Relief Fund." She began to count on her fingers.

"The Christian Ladies' Temperance Society." She chuckled. "She created that one for Lord Branston, back in 1850. Made him join as the sole member." She counted another finger. "Oh, and the Safe Orphans Act of 1852."

"My aunt passed an *act*?" Lucy asked, incredulous. "I thought only Parliament could do that."

"Oh, here in Lizard Bay, we see to our own rules and laws. Miss E didn't think Parliament's laws regarding orphans were good enough. She was always going on and on about those idiots up in London." She began to bustle about again, clearing more dishes and cats from the table. "She wanted more protection for the Tanner lads, and so after their father died, she convinced us all to agree to her notion that every single person in town was responsible for the care, feeding, and moral upbringing of the rascals. Made us sign a paper and everything."

Lucy laughed, enchanted by the notion of her aunt's industry. Given her own unproductive experience with trying to evince a governmental change in the conditions for London's prisoners, she didn't doubt her aunt's method was probably far more effective than the usual way of going about it. "It sounds as though my aunt was fond of good causes."

Mrs. Wilkins nodded. "She was kind, that way. To nearly everyone. Well, except for the vicar. Never did understand the animosity between those two." She waved off a trio of cats that had somehow made their way back onto the table. "I would have done anything for Miss E, you know. 'Twas *her* money that set me up in this posting house, after Mr. Wilkins passed on."

Lucy sobered, remembering the entry she'd read in her aunt's diary as she drifted off to sleep last night. "Er . . . if I might ask, Mrs. Wilkins . . . what did your husband pass from?"

Please don't say pudding.

"Oh, it was the blood poisoning that took him. Five years

ago, I'd say. He was a fair enough husband, after a bit of a rocky start." Mrs. Wilkins began to move about again, collecting dishes and sweeping the never-ending sea of cats from the table. "Miss E saw to that, too. Showed him the right way to treat a lady the first year we were married, and what could happen to a man who forgot it." She nodded approvingly. "All the men in town took notice. The women of Lizard Bay will forever owe her a great debt."

Lucy breathed a sigh of relief. She would have hated to destroy her aunt's journals, especially given that she hadn't even finished them yet, but she supposed she would have done it if she needed to destroy evidence of a murder.

She was a bit in awe of what her aunt had accomplished with a bit of poisoned pudding. She thought of the other diary entries she had read, and tried to imagine how different Lizard Bay might be today if her aunt hadn't ridden into town, once upon a time. It sounded as though Aunt E had touched the lives of most of the town's residents, turning some of those lives upside down, lifting others out of despair.

Lucy was reminded, then, of all the faces who had gathered close yesterday when she stepped off the coach. No one had offered to help her find Heathmore yesterday evening, but perhaps she hadn't found the right person yet. *Somewhere* in this town there were people in Aunt E's debt, people who might be convinced to help the woman's niece. Someone, after all, must have helped her aunt by mailing the package after Aunt E had died.

And surely there was someone in this town who would help her, too.

"Mrs. Wilkins," she said slowly. "May I ask you a question?" When the older woman nodded, she plowed on. "It sounds as though you were good friends with my aunt."

Mrs. Wilkins beamed. "Oh, I was."

"Did you perchance mail a package on her behalf?" Lucy

gestured with her hands. "It was about this big, and wrapped in brown paper. It had to have been posted after her death."

"Oh no, she didn't have time to ask me to do anything like that. She wasn't sick for long, you know. Just woke up one morning with chest pains." Mrs. Wilkins collected another plate. "We barely had time to call the vicar to come and see her, and then she was gone by evening. I've a theory on that, you know. She was a good woman, and I think her big heart must have plain tuckered out from all that worrying over everyone else." Her wrinkled face softened. "We all miss her. The town isn't the same without her. We've been talking about what we might do to honor her. A monument of some sort, placed in the center of town."

Lucy bit her lip. She'd not known Aunt E very well when she was growing up, but she was beginning to get a stronger sense of the woman. And though she hadn't mourned properly when news had come of her aunt's death, a part of her was mourning the loss of Aunt E now.

"Mrs. Wilkins . . . may I ask you for a favor?"

"Of course. Anything for Miss E's niece."

"I had thought to inspect Heathmore Cottage this morning. Would you perchance be willing to show me where it is?"

Mrs. Wilkins froze, a plate in each hand. "Oh, no." She shook her head, setting gray curls bouncing. "Not after what happened the last time."

Lucy frowned at the woman's theatrics. "Whyever not?"

"Lord Branston hired me on to wash the windows." Mrs. Wilkins set the plates down and clasped a hand to her heart, her gnarled fingers curled in fear. "But Miss E's spirit pestered me something awful. Moaning and carrying on. Warning me to stay away. It's not safe."

Lucy gritted her teeth. So, Lord Branston was tied up in all this talk of ghosts, was he? Just when she'd begun to reconsider her doubts, too. She felt oddly disappointed.

Mrs. Wilkins fixed Lucy with a stern look. "And you

shouldn't go up there either. There's haints about up there on the cliff, and hidden dangers, too. It's much better to stay down here in town. The vicar was always worried about Miss E living alone up there. Why, you would have thought it was the Lord's own war, the way those two carried on about it. He was pleased when she finally moved down to town."

"Haints?" Lucy scoffed. Surely Mrs. Wilkins didn't believe that nonsense from the orphans. "I don't believe in ghosts, Mrs. Wilkins. And my aunt left me the property for a reason. She must have imagined I would want to visit."

Mrs. Wilkins looked doubtful. "Better to sell it to Lord Branston, I should think. In fact, everyone in Lizard Bay thought you already had."

Lucy shook her head. "No. I've not sold it yet." And she'd come to make sure she wasn't swindled into it, hadn't she? "But I do need to sort out what it's worth before I make that decision. Is there someone else in town who might be willing to show me the property?" she pressed. "What about Reverend Wellsbury?" According to her aunt's diary, he well knew the way. And surely a *vicar* didn't believe in ghosts.

Mrs. Wilkins picked up the plates again. "Oh, I wouldn't ask him, dear. He and Miss E didn't get along, and you seem rather cut from the same cloth as your aunt." She headed for the kitchen door, dodging a pair of cats as she went. "Best to just potter around Lizard Bay," she called over her shoulder. "And remember, there's tea at two."

Since my arrival in Lizard Bay, Mr. Jamieson has continued to offer me his hand in marriage. But it's clear he's not the right man for me. He has no idea what to do with a strong-willed woman. Or a dog, for that matter.

I've told him over and over again it is too cold to leave his dog tied out of doors. I'd hoped the regard he held for me might encourage him to action, but as I headed home yesterday after the weekly meeting of the Fisherman's Wives Relief Society, I saw the poor thing shivering outside in the snow again.

It was then that I decided to teach Mr. Jamieson a lesson he wouldn't soon forget.

Despite the weather, it didn't take much to convince him to meet me outdoors. He even obligingly shrugged out of his coat and dropped his trousers. I still can't believe he let me tie him up. Apparently, the grocer is the sort of man who appreciates a woman who sews red ribbons on her petticoats and can tie a good knot. Oh, the look on his face when I blew him a kiss and walked away. But I wasn't entirely heartless.

I gave him a blanket, and I untied him after three hours.

Mr. Jamieson hasn't asked me to marry him again. But his dog lives in the house now. Sleeps on an embroidered pillow, to hear the gossip.

I'd consider that a knot well-tied.

Chapter 12

*B*y late afternoon Lucy had learned the meaning of Mrs. Wilkins's word "potter."

It meant do nothing productive, despite one's best efforts.

She'd been up and down Lizard Bay's single street no less than a half-dozen times, trailed by a gaggle of caterwauling cats who had decided she was either Miss E in the flesh or a suitable substitute for their adoration. The few townspeople she'd met were quick to greet her with a smile or a nod. When she initiated a conversation, several proved willing to share amusing—and sometimes downright scandalous—anecdotes about her aunt. But to a one, when Lucy's inquiries turned toward finding Heathmore Cottage, they shook their heads and hurried away. After what seemed like her hundredth refusal, she wanted to scream.

Worse, her sense of worry—always honed and ready for a good cause—was starting to simmer. Something felt . . . *wrong*. On the surface, Lizard Bay appeared to be a charming coastal town of a few hundred or so people, built up slowly over hundreds of years until it had settled firmly into the small, comfortable space permitted by the surrounding cliffs. But in the harsher light of day, Lucy was beginning to realize the town appeared to be in some trouble.

For a start, many of the townspeople she passed had a worried, haggard look, as though finding a way to make ends meet was beginning to wear them down.

And for another, there seemed to be little evidence of industry.

She counted a butcher's shop, a posting house, the grocer's, Mrs. Wilkins's boardinghouse, and a schoolhouse—where presumably young Danny was squirming in his seat, suffering through his math lesson. Up on a small rise sat a small stone church, no doubt where the infamous Reverend Wellsbury attempted to save lost souls and determined spinsters.

But where was the backbone of the town, the main business that fed those other establishments?

There was a small wharf where, presumably, baskets of herring were supposed to be unloaded. She counted the fishing boats—three of them, in total, all tied to the posts. But she could see no evidence of a bustling fishing trade, and when she ventured out onto the dock and looked down into the water, the only fish she'd seen were floating on top, grotesque and bloated.

But as curious as it all was, she couldn't take the time to sort through the mystery. Time was marching by and she felt its loss keenly. At some point her absence from Cardwell House would be discovered and her father would presume where she had gone and come to haul her back.

It was nearly enough to tempt her to set out on her own, directions and escorts be damned. But despite her rising frustration, she wasn't a fool. She'd seen enough from the mail coach window to know the moors were vast, endless stretches of grass and rock.

And she hadn't yet tried *everyone* who might be convinced to help her.

As she headed toward a store whose sign identified it as the grocer's, her mind drifted toward the latest diary entry she'd read. If Mr. Jamieson, the town grocer, had once fancied Aunt E, perhaps he might have a soft heart where the woman's niece was concerned. And if he proved reticent, well now, she had a bit of blackmail material at her disposal, didn't she?

As they had all day, the wharf cats followed her, their tails high in the air. "Shoo," she muttered outside the grocer's, flapping her hands. "I don't have any more sausage."

They sat down and meowed up at her, their pitiful cries softening her heart. Oh, damn the wily beasts and their Pied Piper theatrics. It was as though they knew—and were determined to exploit—her weakness. She sighed. "Although, I suppose I could ask inside."

A small bell tinkled on the door as Lucy stepped into the store. She was immediately struck by the dueling scents of licorice—which she attributed to the glass jar of candy on the counter—and unwashed dog—which she attributed to the large, gray-faced hound lounging in a patch of sunlight just inside the door. Given the passage of time, it could not possibly be the same dog Aunt E had mentioned in her diary. But the evidence was irrefutable. It seemed that Mr. Jamieson's revised notions of pet care had stuck all these years.

She crouched down, running a hand beneath the dog's ears. The dog pushed its warm, wet nose against her hand. "I'm not Miss E," she laughed. "But no doubt you owe her a great debt, given how comfortable you look in the sunlight."

The dog's tail thumped on the floor.

Smiling, she stood up and turned toward the counter. It was a neat, spare shop, made even more so because the shelves were nearly empty. A small rotund man was staring at her from behind the counter, his gray beard sprouting at odd angles from his cheeks.

"Mr. Jamieson?" she asked, taking a step toward him.

"It's t-true then," he stammered. "Miss E's—"

"Niece," Lucy inserted firmly, then took a step closer. If she heard the word "ghost" one more time today, she was going to strangle someone. "My name is Miss L." She reached the counter and placed her hands on the top. "And I would know *you* anywhere."

"How . . ." Jamieson swallowed. "That is, how do you know me?"

Lucy bit her lip to hold in a giggle. Hanging on the wall just beyond the grocer's head was a length of rope for sale, and her gaze insisted on drifting in its direction.

He began to squirm. "Your aunt didn't say anything about me to you, did she?"

At his look of near-panic, Lucy relented, knowing there was no way she could leverage the information she knew against him. The poor sweet man looked as though he might piss his pants. She shook her head. "No. I scarcely knew my aunt, Mr. Jamieson. I hadn't seen her since I was six years old." She pointed toward the door she'd just come through. "It is just that your name is on the sign outside, above the door."

"Oh." He straightened, looking relieved. "Well." He tugged his old-fashioned smock down over his round frame. "I am sure if you had known her, you would know that I admired Miss E."

Lucy's lips curved upward. "Yes, I have no doubt of it. The whole town seems to hold her in high stead."

"Most of the town. Between you and me, the vicar was always a bit hard-headed about her. Never did understand what lay at the heart of their quarrel."

Lucy hesitated, but she'd come for a reason, and even if blackmail wasn't part of her plans, she still needed to ask. "My aunt left me Heathmore Cottage. Perhaps you've heard?" At his nod, she pushed on. "Well, I need to inspect my property. Do you know of someone who might be able to escort me to see it?"

He shook his head. "I never went up there myself, mind you. Your aunt made it quite clear she valued her privacy, and didn't welcome suitors traipsing about her property."

"Ah." Lucy smiled. "Were you a suitor, then?"

"Oh, no." He looked alarmed by the notion. "Not for a lack of trying, mind you. We all were a little in love with Miss E. But I knew better than to cross her. You'll not find many in town who know the way to Heathmore."

Lucy stifled a groan. Finding a person who both admired her aunt and was capable of showing her to the cottage was proving damnably difficult. "But if you never went up there," she asked, "how did she get groceries and such?"

"We had a man who made those deliveries, but he moved to Marston last year. Not many could make it carrying a load. Oh, it's a terrible path. Steep and rocky. Dangerous, too."

Lucy frowned. That sounded less than promising. "But . . . if the road is so terrible, how was the house even built?" she pressed.

"There *used* to be a road back to town, once upon a time. But after she moved in, Miss E let it all grow over. She preferred to walk down to town, you see, and never kept a horse. Something about objecting to harnessing the poor creatures and forcing them to labor at our bequest." His whiskers twitched at the memory. "You know, you might ask the Tanner lads. They know the way, and they'll be in here soon." As though struck by inspiration, he reached in the candy jar on the counter and drew her out a piece. "Speaking of the boys, you might want to claim a piece before they get here."

Lucy stared at his palm, still sorting through the notion that despite being somewhat intimately acquainted with her aunt, Mr. Jamieson didn't even know the way to Aunt E's house. "How did you know I liked licorice?"

"I didn't." He looked sheepish. "It is just that your aunt

enjoyed a bit, every now and again, and you seem so much like her. I always kept it stocked for her."

"It is kind of you, but I really shouldn't," Lucy said, thinking of the precious coins she had left. She shook her head. "I need to save my money."

"Oh, 'tis already bought and paid for. Miss E ordered it up from London every few months but left it here so she wouldn't eat too much at once. This is what is left from her last order, God rest her soul."

"Oh." Lucy smiled, relenting. "Well then, I suppose I might have just one." She accepted the piece of candy and placed it on her tongue, sighing at the pleasure of its melting sweetness.

Mr. Jamieson chuckled. "Your aunt had a sweet tooth, too. She always rewarded the Tanner lads with a piece when their school day was done. It will be a shame when this order's all gone." He checked a pocket watch. "The boys should be here in just a minute now. One of my favorite parts of the day. Those rascals are a handful, but they are sweet boys who need our help." He slipped the watch back into his apron pocket and put the top back on the jar of candy. "I'd heard you'd come to town, but when you walked through that door and I saw it with my own eyes, I could hardly believe it. Have you come to collect your aunt's snuff, perchance?"

Lucy choked on her candy. "I beg your pardon?"

He ducked behind the counter and came up holding a small tin. "Miss E ordered it from London every month. Refused to buy it out of Marston. Hated that town something awful." He shook his head at the memory. "She claimed Marston was ruining Lizard Bay's economy." He placed the tin on the counter and regarded it sadly. "She never did pick up her last order."

Lucy eyed the snuff tin with curiosity. "I am afraid I never developed the habit."

"Oh." He frowned. "I don't know what I am going to do with it, then. No one else in town can afford the five shillings it costs, except Lord Branston, and he's been a teetotaler ever since Miss E shook out his hide and set him on the straight and narrow path."

"Lord Branston? A teetotaler?" Lucy scoffed, remembering how he had smelled like brandy that day on the train. She'd like to forget how she'd taken secret, covetous sniffs of him, but she suspected she was bound to keep remembering. The bloody man had been burned onto her brain. "Surely you jest."

But Jamieson shook his head, all seriousness. "No spirits. No snuff either. Not for a couple of years now." He looked forlorn. "I suppose I will just be out the money, then."

Lucy considered again the two precious sovereigns tucked in her reticule. She shouldn't spend them, given they were all she had left in the world. But she couldn't stand to think of Mr. Jamieson suffering a financial hardship on her account. Neither could she imagine going back out and facing her expectant feline friends empty-handed. They were liable to follow her back to Mrs. Wilkins's house if she did, and then she'd be forced to share her dinner.

She reached into her purse and pulled out one of the precious sovereigns, placing it on the counter. "I suppose I can give the snuff a try, just this once. And do you perchance have any salve?" She scratched at her neck, cursing Geoffrey and his pranks. "I'd like to buy some fish for the wharf cats as well."

Mr. Jamieson began to wrap the tin up in brown paper. "I am afraid we don't have any salve. Items like that have to be ordered from Marston, and they take a few days to get here. And there's been no fishing here for months."

"Isn't Lizard Bay supposed to be a fishing town?"

He shook his head. "The fish have all gone up coast, or died."

Lucy tried to puzzle it out. Why would a fishing village—one that had clearly been here for many generations—suddenly have no more fish? Jamieson might depend on the townspeople for his living, but they depended on fish for theirs. She eyed the empty shelves with fresh understanding. It wouldn't make sense to stock them if no one could afford to buy the goods.

"But . . . what do people do instead?"

"Some folks have already moved away, looking for better opportunities. Some have even gone up to Marston. Your aunt was livid over it." Jamieson leaned across the counter and beckoned her closer, as though eager to impart a bit of gossip. "Miss E was determined to fix matters, too, you know. She had grand plans and wasn't going to let Marston have the last say in Lizard Bay's future. She told us we couldn't depend on fishing and her forever." His face fell. "Turns out she was right on both fronts."

The bell on the shop's door tinkled. But even before she heard the exuberant voices of the Tanner boys, she felt a telltale shiver roll pleasantly up the base of her spine. Lord Branston had not even said a word, and yet she was already as aware of his presence as if he'd trumpeted his arrival. Blast it all, but was it possible that in spite of her resolve to have nothing to do with him, she was even more aware of the man than before?

Heart thumping, she swung around to face them.

But was it even the same man?

In London, he'd scarcely stood out for anything but his handsome face. He'd worn the requisite checked wool trousers and silk waistcoat of any town gentleman. But it seemed he shed that skin here in Lizard Bay. Today he was at ease, smiling, and dressed in a loose-fitting frockcoat and flannel brown trousers, unusual only in how ordinary they looked. He was lacking a collar entirely, and instead of a necktie wore an old scarf looped about his neck.

Had she ever seen a gentleman look so . . . *useful*?

Lord Branston stood back and let the boys surge forward, their school books and lunch pails swinging. The boys converged on the counter, their hands grappling with the licorice jar.

"Watch it, Charles!"

"Leave some for me, Ethan!"

As they each fought for their fair share, she watched Lord Branston. As it stupidly insisted on doing at every coveted sight of him, her heart wobbled a bit in her chest. He looked at ease—not only more so than he had in London, but even during the long journey to Lizard Bay. He carried an old leather satchel over his shoulder that appeared to be bulging with secrets, and his jaw looked unshaven. The dark stubble made her wonder what it would feel like to run her finger along it. But she wasn't going to get close enough to do such a foolhardy thing.

She tried to be irritated with him, in his easy, carefree appearance. He was a marquess, for heaven's sake. Could the man not employ the services of a valet?

Or be bothered to put on a hat?

His auburn hair was wildly awry, as though he'd spent the entire day out of doors. That gave her pause. She hadn't seen him about town—not that she'd admit to looking for the man. But given that Lizard Bay only had the single street, she couldn't help but wonder just where he passed his hours all day, only to emerge looking so delectable.

Their cheeks full, the boys began to move away from the counter. They parted like the Red Sea and came back again to surround her.

"It's Miss E's ghost!" crowed the one who had extracted the sovereigns from her pocket last night.

The youngest—Danny, she recalled—elbowed his brother. "Lord Branston said we wasn't to tease her like that anymore, Ethan." He sucked on his candy, and looked up at her with hollowed cheeks. "Besides," he said with a knowing air. "Miss E's ghost don't live here in town. She lives up at Heathmore." He snickered. "Not that any of you are brave enough to know it."

Lucy lifted a questioning brow in Lord Branston's direction. He stared back. She felt again that shiver of awareness, no doubt because his attention was focused so inappropriately on her, and not at *all* another reason. She fit a purposeful frown to her lips. "Have you been spreading more tales of ghosts then, Lord Branston?"

"I don't know why I'd need to." He shrugged. "The town will believe what it wants."

"Mm hmm." Lucy reached behind her and collected the paper-wrapped tin of snuff. She hefted the weight of it in her hand. She needed something more substantial if she was going to put a dent in that man's cocky grin. And she probably ought to set a better example for the young boys. God knew she'd never been able to aim worth a shite.

So instead of hurling it at his smiling face, she put the tin of snuff in her reticule and pulled out her last sovereign instead. Holding the coin up, she flashed it temptingly at the lads. "No matter what untruths Lord Branston has told you, Miss E is not a ghost. Now, which of you boys might like to earn a bit of money? I need a guide to Heathmore Cottage."

HE'D GIVE HER this: she was a persistent thing. And it was proving an enjoyable experience, watching her try to turn the tide of local opinion. He suspected Miss E would have been proud of her niece and what she was trying to do. The elderly spinster had been a woman who admired persistence and backbone, in all their various forms.

But persistence alone wasn't going to get Lucy Westmore to Heathmore Cottage.

And if she continued to refuse his offers of help, she deserved whatever misery her backbone brought her.

He watched the boys, waiting to see what they would do. Danny was the most likely choice to take her money, given that he'd been the only one of the four brave enough to bring the letter up a week and a half ago. But Danny was looking down at his shoes, shuffling them in near agony. A properly earned sovereign was an unheard-of luxury, but it seemed fear had a way of paralyzing even the neediest of feet.

If one of the boys did accept, Thomas knew he would have to go with them. The lads knew the way, of course, but the path would be complicated to navigate in heavy skirts. And *her* skirts were an atrocious, bell-shaped thing, stuffed from beneath with crinolines that probably weighed close to a stone. No doubt she'd need help to pull herself over rocks and such, and to make sure she didn't break that long, lovely neck.

And it wouldn't be a hardship to feel the slip of her hand in his own.

But it seemed such wild, fanciful notions were not to be. As though they were a single organism, the boys came to a joint conclusion and escaped through the door, chattering about ghosts and haints and the like.

"I am sorry about that," he offered, shaking his head.

"Somehow I doubt it." She shoved the coin back into her reticule. "Things seem to have a way of going to hell around you, Lord Branston, and I suspect that's exactly what you intend," she added, then turned back to the counter and offered the grocer a thin smile. "Thank you for everything, Mr. Jamieson. It was nice speaking with you."

"'Tis my pleasure, Miss L. I hope you find someone soon who might show you the way to Heathmore." He glanced Thomas's way, a confused slant to his brow. "Have you . . . ah . . . asked Lord Branston? He knows the way quite well."

"No, thank you." She gave a haughty sniff. "I prefer to find someone else to help, someone who doesn't expect something in return." She gathered her skirts in one hand

and pushed past him, stepping over the hound and leaving the scent of licorice in her wake.

Mr. Jamieson winked at him. "She sounds just like Miss E, doesn't she?"

Thomas offered the grocer a bemused shrug and shook his head. "Seems a bit more determined, if you ask me."

"More determined than Miss E?" Jamieson scratched his chin. "Heaven help us all."

Not wanting to let her escape without offering a word of explanation—or an apology, if need be—Thomas shoved his hands in his pockets and followed her outside. He spied her a hundred feet distant, walking away from the store, her back rigid as she stepped over a pair of adoring wharf cats.

"I really am sorry about the boys, you know," he called out. He headed toward her, relieved to see her stop, at least. "They should have been more polite in their refusal. That wasn't well done of them. Miss E was planning to work with them on their manners."

She turned to face him. "They'd not have refused in the first place if their minds hadn't been poisoned to the idea from the start." She lifted one hand to extend the shade of her bonnet and stared up at the edge of the cliff that ran along top edge of the town. "Your hand in that matter does you no credit."

Hand? What on earth was she talking about? And the way she was eyeing the top edge of the cliff made him uneasy. So far it seemed like she'd stuck to town in her efforts to uncover the path to Heathmore, proving herself smart enough to recognize the danger that awaited her in the surrounding cliffs. Surely she wouldn't try to strike out on her own?

Then again, she'd struck out for Cornwall on her own, hadn't she?

"Tell me, Miss Westmore," he said slowly. "What is it you think I've done?"

"One would think a marquess had better things to do

with his time than tell ghost stories to small, impressionable boys."

"I've not told them anything of the sort. In fact, I've encouraged them to stop spreading such tales. And they don't think of me that way here." He hesitated. "You shouldn't either. In Lizard Bay, I am not the Marquess of Branston. I am just a man." He took a step forward.

And she was just a woman.

A woman, in fact, who made his blood stir, even when she was spitting mad at him.

"Not a marquess?" She continued to scan the upper cliffs even as she scoffed at him. "As though you can shove the title in a drawer and forget about it? You might be able to pretend such nonsense, but I can't. Nothing about you makes sense." She lowered her hand and gave him a disdainful glance. "Apparently you've a grand manor just outside of town, and yet you are determined buy my little house. Willing, even, to stoop to disrespectful means to do so. Why are you hiding away in a little town like Lizard Bay, anyway? Don't you have a seat in the bloody House of Lords you could be putting to good use?"

"I'm not hiding." In spite of his rising confusion, his lips twitched at her language. Did she trot it out just for him, or did it flow off her tongue like butter? "I just don't like London very much," he admitted. Too many memories.

And too many of those very ghosts she was accusing him of conjuring.

"Well *I* don't like useless gentleman, particularly ones who squander their potential political influence by hiding away in fishing towns."

"I don't have any political influence," he answered.

"And whose fault is that? You do realize you are entirely Radical in your views, don't you?" At his look of surprise, she sighed in exasperation and threw up her hands. "Surely you have *some* view of politics."

Thomas blinked. "I . . . ah . . . I hadn't really thought of it." Mainly because since he'd gained his majority, he had either been lost in a bottle, playing at a betrothal, or . . .

Damn it all . . .

Hiding in Cornwall.

She rolled her eyes. "Honestly, Lord Branston, did you really think the study of botany was going to properly prepare you for the responsibilities of your position?"

Her words stung, as she had likely intended them to. It was very nearly an accusation that he had been selfish in his choice of studies, and part of the problem was that perhaps it was true. He'd certainly been selfish in not considering the impact his absence would have on his sister. And then, in the years following university, when he floated through London's social scene in a drunken haze, he'd never once considered answering that summons from the Crown, never stopped to consider if he ought to be doing something else with his life. Was it because he'd been orphaned at such a young age, with no firm sense of the expectations of the position?

Or had he rejected the notion because he was sure he would only muck it up, the way he'd mucked up his life?

He cleared his throat. "My . . . ah . . . parents died when I was eleven. I wasn't old enough to take my father's seat then, and I suppose it never occurred to me to do so later, when I reached my majority." He had told himself that so many times he wasn't even sure now whether or not it was the truth. But it *sounded* like the truth.

And it was preferable to admitting his failures.

"I am sorry for your loss," she told him. But she didn't *sound* sorry. In fact, her eyes flashed at him, nearly silver in the sunlight. "But there is a good deal happening right now in London with Lord Aberdeen as prime minister. If you would but take your seat in the House of Lords and put some of your good instincts to wider purpose, you might influence the lives of thousands of orphans, not just four. You might even be able to do more. Improve the lives of women, for example. Change the laws so they might keep their property after they are married, or retain their children if they must leave brutal husbands."

He stared at her, feeling more than a little lost at sea. She thought he had good instincts?

And when had this become about *him*?

She stared back. "But no, you're too important for such matters, it seems. *You* seem more content to hide away here, making sure one young man doesn't play truant." She looked away and tugged at the edges of her gloves, the very picture of a dismissal. "Now, if you'll excuse me, I don't have time for idle chitchat, Lord Branston. I've a cottage to find."

He stepped in front of her. Damn it all, but how could she see through his black heart and know just how to poke at him? If there was a measure of guilt to be found in his self-imposed isolation, in the panic he felt at the thought of returning to live in London, she had surely just found it. He'd known his choices of the past three years were cowardly at best, selfish at worst.

He'd just never had anyone—not even the outspoken Miss E—call him out for it.

"This isn't about my empty seat in the House of Lords." He shook his head, trying to steer his thoughts back to center. "It's about your determination to reach Heathmore. Why are you wasting your time traipsing this dusty street, asking everyone you meet for help? As I have repeatedly offered, I am more than willing to show you the property myself."

"And as *I've* repeatedly said, I prefer to find someone else to help me. Either that, or find it on my own."

Thomas knew he shouldn't. He shouldn't even be standing here talking with her, much less touching her. His last disastrous touch had led to the kiss that brought him to all of *this*. But as though it had a mind and imagination of its own, his hand reached out to curve over her arm. Her spine remained stiff and unyielding. Her skin, though—that was soft, as soft as he remembered. He recalled how pliant her hand had felt in his own, there at the inn in Salisbury, when she burned her thumb on the hot wax and he'd taken it up in his. He wanted desperately to go back to that place, however dangerous the sentiment was.

"Promise me," he said, softening his voice, "that you won't attempt it without a guide."

"I see you have continued in this habit of touching women without their leave," she told him, though she didn't pull away.

"I assure you, it's an entirely new phenomenon, one that only seems to occur around you." He tugged until she thumped up against him, both of them breathing harder now. "Promise me, Lucy. The cliffs are dangerous. You could easily be killed."

Her lower lip slid between her teeth, causing him to suck in a breath. "I owe you no promises, Lord Branston." She hesitated. "But rest assured I have no intention of purposefully meeting my demise." Her lips firmed. "Because then you'd have Heathmore without a fight."

He wanted to point out that was hardly a reassurance she wouldn't do something stupid and find herself dead by accident, but he somehow held his tongue. He could feel the energy humming in her where his hand curved over her skin. She might not be setting off on her own yet, but she was poised to do *something*, that was assured. "Why are you being so stubborn about this?" he asked.

"Why are *you* being so persistent?" she countered, but he couldn't help but notice she wasn't trying to twist out of his grasp. If anything, he felt the merest loosening of her spine, a melting response that told him she, too, felt this queer, electric pull between them. "I can't help but think you aren't telling me the whole truth about Heathmore."

"I've told you no lies," he said, though his conscience scratched at him, reminding him that a falsehood and an omission of the full truth could be argued as shades of the same transgression. He stared down at the wide, well-shaped mouth that somehow—despite being attached to a spinster who insisted on saying the most outrageous things—tempted him beyond reason. She smelled of licorice and sunshine, and he wanted to know if she tasted the same way.

He licked his lips. "You can trust me, Lucy. I am not lying to you."

She pulled away, out of his grip. "I *can't* trust you. I can't even trust you to use the name I have asked you to." She took a firm step away from him. "My name is Miss L. Not Miss Westmore, and *certainly* not Lucy. And a woman like me can't be too careful."

"What do you mean, a woman like you?" he asked.

"I know how you see me. How everyone sees me. An easy target. A woman who ought to be grateful for an ounce of a handsome gentleman's attention."

He shook his head, surprised at her admission, and more than a little confused. "That isn't how I see you at all." No, quite the contrary. He saw her as determined. Decidedly *un*grateful.

And utterly, entirely desirable, despite her sharp edges.

"Miss L," he said, being sure to emphasize the words, "you are the farthest thing from an easy target. In fact, if a suitor's arrows were drawn, I suspect they'd go flying in the exact opposite direction. You've a way of pushing people away, even people who have your best interests in mind. You might try trusting others, on occasion." He paused, remembering how Miss E had helped him, even when he'd initially resisted the offer of assistance. He'd needed a shove to be convinced to give up the bottle, and Miss E had been all too happy to provide it in the form of a little blackmail. "You'll find," he said ruefully, "that life sometimes requires an outside hand. And beyond how I or anyone else sees you, I would imagine, in the end, it only matters how you see yourself."

She threw up her hands, her reticule swinging wildly about one wrist. "How, exactly, am I supposed to see myself? When I look in the mirror, I see someone who is supposed to be perfectly happy with her lot in life, pleased to have drawn the short straw of the sexes. I see someone who is expected to be thrilled at the ridiculous circus of a Season being pressed upon her, eager to give her dowry to a complete stranger. I see someone who is expected to change herself, her thoughts, her *life*, to become nothing more than what a man would make her." She lowered her arms and drew a deep breath, bowing her head as she exhaled. "Well, that may be what is expected," she said bitterly, "but that's not me, Lord Branston. It will never *be* me."

He stared down at her then, remembering how Lord Cardwell had once claimed his daughter was looking forward to the coming Season.

The man hadn't known his sister very well.

And apparently he didn't know his daughter either.

"Lucy," he said softly. "Not every man expects a woman to change to suit him. You can trust me on that."

She laughed, a rueful sound. "Don't you see?" She shook her head. "That's just the sort of thing an untrustworthy man would say. So save your breath, Lord Branston." She drew a deep breath. "I've better uses for mine."

From the Diary of Edith Lucille Westmore
July 15, 1820

I'd hoped all this talk of marriage might finally subside. After all, I'm a spinster by choice, no matter Reverend Wellsbury's thunderous objections from the pulpit.

But after successfully putting Mr. Jamieson's hopes to rest, it seems Mr. Bentley has stepped up his own peculiar notion of courtship.

It started with the roses. The bloody things started appearing—freshly cut—on the steps of Heathmore Cottage every morning. Never mind that I hate roses. There is only one man in town with rosebushes, and while Mr. Bentley would make someone else a fine husband, he doesn't make my heart flutter in anticipation of seeing him on Sundays, or tempt me to sew red ribbons on my petticoats. When I pulled him aside after church to try to explain we must only be friends, Reverend Wellsbury scowled terribly at us, as though he thinks I might be trying to poison the postmaster of Lizard Bay.

Or worse, trying to seduce him.

Well, I have no intention of seducing Mr. Bentley. Quite the opposite, in fact. When he didn't take the hint, I took the necessary step of ordering a supply of fireworks from London. Then, I waited up one night, and when I saw Mr. Bentley sneaking through the rocks, I lit the fuse and plugged my ears. The poor sweet man screamed like a baby. His hearing's been a bit off ever since, which I regret, but I believe he understands how things must be between us now.

The roses have finally stopped, thank goodness.

Now if only Reverend Wellsbury's scowls would stop as well . . .

Chapter 13

On Friday morning Lucy rose early and hurried through her morning ablutions before the sun was even slipping through the lace curtains of her window. She buttoned herself back into her tired gold walking gown, wincing at the layer of dust now coating the hem of her skirts. If she stayed, she needed to sort out what to do about laundry.

But she hadn't the faintest clue how to start.

So she tore down the stairs in her rumpled gown, scattering cats and hairpins in her wake. She refused to question her motives for rising at such an early hour.

She was in Cornwall—country hours applied.

And an early start was surely advisable, given the importance of succeeding in her mission today.

Her father could appear at any moment, and that meant there was no time to lose. She'd shown remarkable restraint so far, waiting to find someone to help her. Today she would find *someone* in this town who would show her the way to Heathmore.

And by someone, of course, she meant anyone who *wasn't* Lord Branston.

But that didn't mean she couldn't happily catch a peek of him before she started her day.

She didn't quite understand this strange attraction where he was concerned. She was supposed to hate him. Had more or less *told* him she hated him. And still she was rising at dawn, earlier than necessary, simply because she wanted to catch a glimpse of him.

She tumbled into a melee of a breakfast, boys and cats intermingling in a rush of eggs and buttered toast. Mrs. Wilkins was bustling about like a busy shepherdess, but when she saw Lucy she beamed. "Ooooh, you're up early today." She pulled out a chair. "Come sit down and entertain the boys. Young Danny was just threatening to play truant, and Lord Branston was explaining why that was a poor idea."

Lucy caught her breath to see Branston sitting at the far end of the long table. Much as he had yesterday, he looked anything but a gentleman. In his loose frockcoat and collarless shirt, he looked closer to a field laborer than a marquess. Would anyone in London be caught dead at the breakfast table in anything less than a starched collar and necktie?

And would she rise so early to see any of them?

She willed her pulse to settle into only a mildly exuberant rhythm as she settled herself into the chair Mrs. Wilkins had pulled out. "Truant, hmmm?" She smiled at Danny, who was looking down at his plate, his bright red hair falling over his eyes. She remembered that Branston was ostensibly trying to convince Danny to study so he might eventually have a chance at qualifying for more advanced schooling. "And what does Lord Branston have to say about that?"

Danny made a sour face. "He says I need more practice with my ciphers."

Lucy laughed as Mrs. Wilkins sat a plate down in front of her with one hand and scooped up a cat with the other. "It seems to me that an enterprising young man such as yourself could only benefit from a strong start in the mathematical sciences. Thievery is all well and good, but if you can't count your spoils, what good is the skill?"

"'Twasn't me who stole your money, that was Ethan." Danny pouted. "But that's what Lord Branston says, too."

"Really?" Lucy risked another covetous glance at the man who had pulled her so early from bed this morning with nothing more than the hope of crossing his path. He saluted her with a raised brow in return. "Well, Lord Branston is an educated man." Her cheeks heated. "Studied botany in school, useful skill that it is. He can tell you the names of any plant you want, even the poisonous ones. You might want to listen to him."

Over the edge of his cup, Lord Branston's grin was slow, sure, and spreading. "Does that mean you will listen to me as well?" he asked down the barrel of the table.

Lucy shook her head. "I already know my ciphers, Lord Branston. So you shouldn't bet on it."

"Oh, I wouldn't." His eyes crinkled, daring her to commit all matter of folly. "Impossible wagers were never my style, Miss L."

Danny squirmed in his chair. "It's just that I *hate* math. I'd much rather go walking on the moors. But Lord Branston said he won't take me today." He scowled. "Says I belong in the schoolroom, where I can learn something more practical than botany."

Lucy regarded Lord Branston curiously. Walks on the moors? That was interesting. And a bit confusing. His leather satchel—suspiciously thinner than it had been yesterday—was slung in wait over the high back of his chair. She thought back on her chance meeting with him yesterday, when he'd looked so tousled and windblown, and how she had wondered where he passed his day.

Just what was Lord Branston up to?

And what did it have to do with Heathmore?

As though he could read her mind, he set down his cup and stood up, slinging the satchel's strap across one broad shoulder. "Time to go then, boys. We mustn't be late."

The boys began gulping down the last bits of breakfast, then picked up the lunch pails that Mrs. Wilkins handed out. As Danny stood up and began to trudge toward his fate, Lucy motioned him closer, buttoning up the boy's faded jacket and cuffing him on the chin when she was done. "Can I tell you a secret?"

Danny nodded morosely.

She leaned toward his ear. "My brother hates math, too, and *he's* going to be a viscount. So you're in good company."

Danny jerked a finger toward Lord Branston. "Yes, but *he's* a marquess. You have to listen to a marquess. Everyone says so."

Lucy looked down the table, wishing the man didn't make her stomach churn so pleasantly, wishing she could just trust him enough to believe his offer of assistance held no ulterior motives. "Well *I* don't have to listen to him," she told Danny. "And once you've learned your ciphers, you won't have to either."

As the boys and their mentor trooped out to start their day, Mrs. Wilkins approached to gather the empty plates. "Now, what was all that business about?" she chided in her gentle way. "It almost sounds as though you don't like Lord Branston. How could that be? The man charmed the very rust off your aunt's iron will. She thought a good deal of him."

Lucy shrugged, picking up her fork. "It isn't that I don't like him. I don't *trust* him."

"Whyever not?" Mrs. Wilkins asked, sounding perplexed. "Has he done something wrong?"

"What *hasn't* he done wrong?" Lucy replied, thinking of yesterday's conversation in the street. Though, there hadn't been anything *wrong* about that, per se. Her distrust stemmed more from the way he flirted with her in Salisbury, when all along he'd had an ulterior motive. But she couldn't very well claim the man had kissed her and then stopped himself from taking additional liberties—that would scarcely bolster her argument of untrustworthiness.

Lucy leaned forward, her chin resting on one hand. "It's just . . . don't you find it strange? That he's here, in Lizard Bay? He's a marquess. He's supposed to be managing estates and passing bills. Or if not that, gallivanting about London and frequenting gaming hells. Instead, he's hiding away on the outskirts of a little coastal town."

"I don't think he's hiding, dear. He's *healing*. Some family tragedy."

"Do you mean his sister's death?" Lucy asked, remembering the conversation on the train. "That was three years ago. Surely he's past mourning now."

"I am afraid it goes a bit deeper than that." Mrs. Wilkins looked around, as though suspicious of lurking gossips, then pulled out a chair and sat down. "When Lord Branston first came to Lizard Bay, he told us all his sister had died. Miss E subscribed to the gossip rags from London, and *she* read that his sister had died in childbirth, though she was scandalously unwed. But Miss E had her own opinion on the matter. She wondered if his sister might have actually taken her own life." She shook her head sadly. "Such a terrible misfortune, whichever way it happened. It seems a man might need more than the usual amount of time to recover from something like that."

Lucy bit her lip, feeling ashamed of her petty remarks. She couldn't imagine losing one of her siblings in such a terrible way. She remembered what Branston had said on the train about his sister. *I lost her.* It sounded as though that may have been a euphemism, at best.

"So you might want to go easy on him, hmmm?" Mrs. Wilkins stood up and began to stack the boys' dirty plates on the sideboard. "Now, before you head out for the day, I thought you might like to take a look in Miss E's room, look through her things. I've a box of curiosities that by rights should belong to you."

Lucy stood up, eager to step away from the table and the sad knowledge that had just been imparted there. She didn't want to think of Lord Branston with sympathy, and she suspected he wouldn't want her to think of him that way either. "Thank you, I would enjoy taking a look."

"Her room was second to the left on the lower hallway." Mrs. Wilkins motioned with her chin. "Go on. I'll come and show you after I've put these dishes on to soak."

Lucy made her way down the hallway, stepping over a pair of cats rolling about the floor. She lifted the latch on the indicated doorway but then stopped, her fingers hesitant. After all, this was the room where her aunt had lived during the last two years of her life.

The room where her aunt had died.

She was learning so much about Aunt E here in Lizard Bay, though it seemed each new layer she uncovered only added to her confusion rather than sharpening her understanding. But she would never sort it out standing in the hallway, so she gathered her courage and stepped inside.

The room echoed with a heavy silence. A patchwork quilt lay across the simple bed, slightly rumpled, as though her aunt had just stepped out for a moment. Dust motes rode small, invisible currents of wind, and they stirred more vigorously as she stepped inside. These things she had expected.

The mess, however, caught her off guard.

There were journals and newspapers stacked floor-to-hip. Hundreds of them, at least two decades worth of accumulated pages. Lucy turned in a circle, taking it all in.

Well. It seemed her aunt may have subscribed to more than just the gossip rags.

Mrs. Wilkins appeared beside her and began clucking her

remorse. "Ooooh, it's dusty in here. I haven't had time to clean properly since she died, God rest her soul, and she wouldn't let me clean when she lived here. Said she preferred her privacy."

"Were these all my aunt's?" Lucy asked, running a finger across one stack of periodicals.

"Oh yes, she loved to read." Mrs. Wilkins bent over at the waist, her generous rear waggling. When she came up, she held out a wooden box. "Here you are. It's not much," she said as Lucy took it. "Just odds and ends, but I know these were dear to her." With a sad smile, she turned to go. "Well, I'll leave you to it. Just close the door when you are done. Wouldn't want the cats to get in here."

And that was how Lucy came to find herself alone, sitting cross-legged on a dusty floor as she went through the contents of the box. Lifting each piece out, she tried to match the objects to the diary entries she had read. A pressed flower caught her eye—one of Mr. Bentley's famous roses, no doubt. A bit of frayed rope that made her giggle and clap a hand over her mouth.

And length of red ribbon, faded with age. That one made her frown.

Finally, at the bottom of the box, a cloth-wrapped object caught her eye. A set of fragile glass horses appeared as she carefully peeled away the edges of fabric. She hadn't properly cried when she'd first learned of Aunt E's passing, but there was no mistaking the welling of tears in her eyes now. She caught her sob in one hand.

She *remembered* these horses.

Remembered, too, some stolen, faint memory of her aunt. It was hazy, but she could almost feel her aunt place one of the fragile horses in her hand, cautioning her to be careful but not scolding her, not even when she almost dropped it. She'd forgotten so much of that short, shining visit when she had been six years old . . .

But it was clear, in the keeping of these figurines, her aunt never had. Lucy vowed, then, not to forget. And not to give up either. Aunt E had left her Heathmore for a reason.

And she needed to honor those wishes.

THE AFTERNOON BROUGHT rain clouds and a rising wind out of the east. But the surly weather couldn't dampen Thomas's mood. He grinned in anticipation as he tapped the soil off his boots at Mrs. Wilkins's front door. Friday afternoons were when the town's more prominent residents gathered in her parlor for a cup of tea and a spot of politics. He enjoyed these meetings, though they'd been less lively since Miss E's passing.

But the fact that it was Friday afternoon wasn't the only cause of his high spirits.

Lucy—or, Miss L, as she had insisted he call her—was still in town. The villagers were buzzing with the gossip. She'd spent the day tromping up and down Main Street again, talking to everyone who would listen. But for all her bluster and bravado, he'd heard from old Jamieson that she had still not coerced anyone into showing her the way to Heathmore Cottage.

Not that he was surprised by her lack of success. The town was now quite terrified of the place—a fact he'd discovered when he tried to get the roofer to finish the roof this morning. Apparently, Miss Westmore's remarkably similar appearance to a younger Miss E had only stirred the gossip-prone bunch on to higher superstition, and no one was willing to return to finish the job. But despite his lack of success on that front, it was a step he was determined to complete, even if he had to go to Marston to hire workers, and even if he ended up losing the property in the end. After all, it was *his* fault the cottage was missing a roof, because he'd prematurely removed the old, moldy thatching in the first place.

She shouldn't have to bear the brunt of his mistake.

Still, she was going to be in a foul mood, one he suspected might even make the hellish coach ride he'd endured two days ago seem like a Sunday stroll. A better man would let her enjoy her tea and her sulk in peace. But Friday afternoon tea at Mrs. Wilkins's house was one of the few social pleasures to be had in Lizard Bay.

He'd be damned if he let an ill-tempered spinster chase him away from *his* town.

And if his feet were moving forward now out of a desire to see her, well now, that was just something he would be sure to keep to himself.

He stepped inside, shaking the first patter of raindrops from his hair, and made his way into the parlor. Had the room always seemed so small? Or was it just that she filled it so completely? It hardly mattered that the room also contained Reverend Wellsbury, Mr. Jamieson, and the postmaster, Mr. Bentley. All he could see was her.

Her gold walking gown bore the brunt of four days of wrinkles, and her short blond hair was a wild halo about her cheeks. But the evidence of her dishabille wasn't what made the grin on his lips stretch wider. She was standing in one corner talking to Mr. Bentley and holding a calico cat. She looked as though she belonged here.

As though she might want to *stay*.

Odd, how that notion made his chest tighten in hope. She was meddlesome and annoying and refused to consider even the most reasonable of offers. So why should he want such a thing? Everything would be so much easier if she just agreed to sell him the property and returned to London. But seeing her here waiting on afternoon tea made him wonder if she might consider a future here in Lizard Bay. And not only that, a *real* future, where she was as much a participant in the saving of Heathmore as she was an observer.

To achieve that, he needed to show her the property's secrets. And he couldn't do that until she trusted him.

She spared him a quick glance as he stepped toward her, then swung her attention back to the postmaster. "Mr. Bentley," she said, offering the man a dazzling smile, "I've been meaning to ask, do you remember mailing a package for my aunt after she died?"

"Eh?" the postmaster asked, cupping a hand around one gnarled ear.

"A package?" She tried again, gesturing with one hand while balancing the cat in the other. "About the size of a stack of books?"

Bentley looked perplexed. "Hooks, did you say? Might try down at the wharf."

"No, *books*." Her face began to turn red. "They were wrapped in brown paper."

"Town hater?"

"No, *brown*. Paper."

Thomas stepped closer, trying unsuccessfully to temper his grin. "Old Bentley's hearing has about given up the ghost." He lowered his satchel down on a nearby table. "He can usually muddle along with a little help, but I suspect it is your accent that has him flummoxed. Your words have too much London polish to them. I could help translate, if you like."

She turned to face him, her face growing redder still. "Speaking of ghosts . . ." She sat the calico cat down on the floor. It stared balefully up at her, as though there was nowhere in the world it would rather be than in her arms. It was uncomfortable for Thomas to realize he knew how the cat felt. "I've spoken to everyone in town, and it seems you've achieved your goal, Lord Branston. No one in Lizard Bay is willing to help me, on account of Heathmore's reputed ghost."

"I did not start that rumor. And as I've repeatedly explained, *I* am willing to help you."

She lifted her hand to scratch her neck. "I'd rather pluck

out my eyelashes than accept your help, thank you very much."

Thomas nodded sagely. "There once was a girl without lashes . . ."

Old Bentley stirred to life, as though he had finally latched onto something his hearing could understand. "Lashes?" He glanced between them, his rheumy eyes wide with interest. "Surely you don't mean to *flog* the girl, Branston."

Thomas burst out laughing, then pulled the small tin he'd brought out of his pocket. He held it out to her, flat against his palm. "Who was always covered in rashes."

"My rash is better now, thank you very much," she protested. And then promptly scratched at her collar again.

He shook his head in mock disappointment. "She was known to sometimes lie . . ."

"Lord Branston, *you* are the one who is spreading lies—"

"And we hope she won't die . . ."

Her eyes narrowed. "You said poison ivy wasn't dangerous!"

"But she'll regret it if she won't use his mashes."

"That doesn't even make sense." She pursed her lips. "Or sound grammatically correct."

"I was reaching for that last bit, I'll admit." Seeing that she was determined to be stubborn, he took the lid off the tin and held it out again. "I've brought you some mashed goldenseal. *Hydrastis canadensis.* American natives use it for a variety of medicinal purposes."

"More poisonous plants from America?" She made no move to take it. "I think not."

"It's not poisonous." He dipped a finger in the mixture and rubbed some on his own wrist. "See? Some people even drink extracts made from it."

"Where did you get it?" She put her hands on her hips. "Mr. Jamieson said all special orders had to be brought from Marston."

Mrs. Wilkins chose that moment to bustle in carrying a tea tray, the china cups rattling with each step. But Thomas was too locked on this brewing confrontation of wills to turn and offer the kindly woman a proper greeting. "And how would you know that if you didn't ask him for a salve you claim to not need?" he asked archly. When Lucy glowered at him, he chuckled. "You simply can't admit I might be right, can you? There was a reason why I asked the coach driver to stop in Marston. Lizard Bay has little by way of sophisticated comforts. Fortunately, I keep a small greenhouse. This is from my personal collection of plants."

"No, thank you." But her protest sounded weaker.

He held out his palm farther. "You'll feel better," he coaxed.

"I'll feel better knowing I haven't accepted your help."

He laughed out loud at that, though her comment also had him shaking his head. "Christ, but you are stubborn. I can't help but question whether I'm going about it all wrong, trying to charm you into compliance."

Her chin lifted. "So you *do* admit you are trying to charm me."

That gave him pause. No, he hadn't been trying to purposefully charm her. Something in their exchanges just brought it out of him, until he was knee-deep in an ill-advised flirtation, trying whatever he could to make her laugh. He knew it wasn't logical. He knew it wasn't *advisable*. But that didn't mean he could be diverted from the path.

"If I am, it seems I am failing miserably." He stepped closer. "I wonder . . ." he murmured, "if I am going about it all wrong, offering my help, waiting for you to come around. What might a dare do, I wonder, instead of another tedious offer of help?"

Old Bentley, who was still standing beside them, began to laugh, his cackle echoing through the room. "You want to ride the mare?"

Thomas shook his head, not taking his eyes off Lucy. "No, Mr. Bentley, a 'dare.' "

"Looks like more of a filly to me." Bentley slapped a hand on his thigh, and then began to shuffle toward the tea service. "Young people these days," he wheezed, shaking his head in high humor. "Never know what they are going to say."

From the Diary of Edith Lucille Westmore
February 10, 1823

I find myself spending more and more time in Lizard Bay. It seems as though I have finally begun to earn the respect of the town. They have even invited me to join the town council . . . the only vote against my participation came from Reverend Wellsbury (oh, the shock of it!), who claimed it went against the natural order of things to have a woman involved in politics. Of course, Mrs. Wilkins is a member of the town council, so that argument scarcely holds water.

It seems the man has still not forgiven me for the Pudding Incident.

Or does it stem, perhaps, from the Boxing Day Debacle?

He accused me quite publicly of being a trouble-maker, the sort of spinster who preys on innocent men and spends her nights plotting their demise. Innocent—ha! I was halfway tempted to flash my red ribbon at him. Whatever the source of this odd, simmering feud between us, one would think a vicar could find his way to forgiveness, but apparently the man holds an everlasting grudge. Fortunately, he was overruled by Mr. Bentley, though one has to wonder if that is because the postmaster didn't properly hear the question.

As the newest member of the Lizard Bay town council, I vow I shall do my best to improve the lives of the people who live here. And if I stay up at night thinking of ways to annoy Reverend Wellsbury, that's nobody's business but my own.

Chapter 14

Despite the rush of heat in her cheeks at old Bentley's words, Lucy found herself tempted. By the salve, by the offer of help . . .

But most of all, by Lord Branston.

Thomas. Her mouth might be insisting on using given names, but her thoughts were less circumspect. Despite her resolve to keep him at an arm's distance, he had burrowed his way beneath her skin like poison ivy, with his offers of help and his reasonable, practical gifts.

She glanced around the room, at the other town citizens who had all—to a one—refused to help her reach Heathmore. Well, except for Reverend Wellsbury. She'd not asked him. In fact, she'd roundly avoided him, turning in the complete opposite direction when he tried to engage her on the street earlier in the day. She felt no need to speak with him—after all, she rather knew where the vicar stood on the matter of spinsters living alone on cliffs, didn't she?

She glanced back at Lord Branston, who was still standing with the tin in his palm, that familiar, crooked grin on his face. She needed to remember what was at stake. It didn't matter that his smile made her pulse thrum in her veins, or that he alone in this room was offering to help her. She needed to remind herself that this man was very likely the cause of the delay she was experiencing, with his carefully placed rumors of ghosts and the like. She knew next to nothing about him, how he spent his days. He might have taken a few orphans under his wing and he might possess a smile to melt hearts, but that didn't make a man trustworthy.

Take his satchel, for instance. This morning it had looked empty, but now it was sitting on a side table, bulging with interesting shapes. That went against everything she knew and expected of someone in his position. He was a marquess, not a schoolmaster. He was either supposed to be staid and quiet, sitting in a desk chair, shuffling through papers, or young and salacious, stumbling out of gaming hells with a whore on each arm.

He defied categorization. She couldn't—*shouldn't*—trust him.

Even if she was more than halfway toward wanting to.

Mrs. Wilkins clapped her hands. "Let's take our seats, if you please!"

Lucy moved toward the nearest chair, grateful for an excuse to put some distance between her thoughts and the man. Slowly, the gentlemen took their seats, sauntering or shuffling as age and spirit dictated.

Lord Branston, of course, was the lone saunterer.

And chose the seat closest to hers.

Lucy breathed in, praying for patience. Unfortunately, the breath only ensured that she inhaled the unique scent that seemed to cling to him and always sent her head—and her heart—spinning. As Mrs. Wilkins began to fiddle with the delicate china cups on the tray, he leaned toward her, making her squirm in anticipation. "At the risk of unsheathing your claws, why are you here this afternoon anyway?" His gaze lingered overlong. "I imagined you would still be beating the bushes, trying to find someone to take you to Heathmore."

"Mrs. Wilkins told me the town would discuss a memorial for my aunt today," she said, reaching for a believable half-truth. "It seemed appropriate to be a part of that conversation." She hesitated. "I will resume my efforts to reach Heathmore when tea is over."

"You might let me guide you there, you know. I promise I only want to see you safely delivered there and back. Your aunt would have wanted me to help you."

"I regretfully must decline." She shook her head but allowed a smile to bloom. "As we've already established, I need my eyelashes, Lord Branston."

His sudden bark of laughter made her insides stir pleasantly. It made her want to bask a moment in the warmth of his obvious pleasure, which was an odd thing to think about someone she was supposed to dislike. Unfortunately, one of the cats milling about her feet had other ideas for basking. It jumped in her lap just as Mrs. Wilkins handed her a full cup of tea.

"They seem to be multiplying," she groaned, trying to balance the cup over the animal's back. And was it her imagination, or was another one trying to sharpen its claws on her stockings?

Her words earned another bark of laughter from Lord Branston. "Yes, cats tend to do that."

"Then why does the town let them mix?" she asked, jiggling her thighs until the cat finally jumped off, sulking its way to steadier accommodations. She looked up to realize everyone was staring at her, from Mrs. Wilkins to the postmaster.

"Did she say tricks?" Bentley asked.

Mrs. Wilkins eyed her with curiosity. "What would you suggest we do, Miss L?"

"Well, it's not that different than London Society." Lucy

gestured to two cats on the floor, one clearly male, the other clearly not. "Why not separate the sexes? Or keep them tightly chaperoned? Females indoors, males outside. They'd cause less trouble that way and I suspect you'd have far less litters of kittens."

"Did she say sex?" Bentley asked, cupping an interested hand to his ear.

"No, sexes, Bentley, *sexes*. Plural." Mrs. Wilkins tapped a finger to her lips. "That sounds just like one of the ideas Miss E was always coming up with, dear. She had a brilliant head for seeing the solution to a problem."

Lucy flushed. "Well, it just seems logical."

"It won't work, though," Lord Branston interjected mildly.

Lucy glared at him. "Why not? Believe you me, the archaic system of keeping a female cloistered until a mate is chosen for them is an age-old process. Invented by aristocratic males, no less."

He shook his head. "Males and females intent on mischief will always find their way to trouble. They'll sneak through windows, dart through doors. Anything to get to where their instincts take them."

"And how would you know that?" she challenged. "Do you like to sneak through windows yourself, Lord Branston?"

He smiled, and *bugger it all*, it was that lazy slide of a smile that sent her insides stirring and her determination to remain unaffected crumbling to dust. "No," he drawled. "But I recall that *you* do."

Lucy squirmed in her seat, wishing she'd never told him such a thing. Then again, he'd coaxed a good deal of intimate conversation from her that day on the train. Disconcerted, she looked around at the little ragtag group seated in a circle around the tea table. The current topic was far too close to real life for comfort. And that meant a change in topic was needed.

"Well, besides Lizard Bay's problem with multiplying

cats, what do you usually talk about during afternoon tea?" she asked the small group with forced brightness. "Two o'clock is a bit earlier than we take tea in London."

"We take tea early because we are sometimes here for several hours," Mrs. Wilkins told her, passing a cup to Mr. Jamieson.

Lucy's fingers tightened around the handle of her cup. "I beg your pardon?"

Branston leaned toward her. "Friday tea is where the serious business of the town is discussed." He gestured toward the postmaster. "Mr. Bentley is the mayor, but as you can see, his hearing makes things difficult, so Mr. Jamieson serves as his deputy. On the fourth Friday of each month, they serve together as justice of the peace for the parish. Those days usually run even longer. Last month we heard a case about stolen chickens, and the session went three hours past supper."

Lucy blinked at them. Chickens? *Supper?* "Which Friday of the month is today?" she asked weakly.

Branston smirked. "It's the fourth. We'll be here for several hours at least."

Lucy set her cup firmly down on the side table. "Oh, for the love of God."

"Did she say she loves cod?" Bentley asked, perking up.

"No, *God*." Old Jamieson's whiskers quivered with amusement,

"It is only . . . I mean . . . I had hoped to reach Heathmore Cottage today." She bit her lip, thinking of the two days she had already lost trying to be sensible about it and find herself a guide. Surely by now her father had reached Salisbury.

And that meant she was running out of time.

"Can we not make this go a little faster?" Lucy looked around, panic making her bold. "Or pick a different day to hear cases?"

"Impossible." Reverend Wellsbury shook his head. "Any

change of date requires a majority vote *and* two weeks notice." He frowned. "We've established the rules for good reason. Miss E was always trying to thwart them, too."

Lucy glared at the vicar. No wonder Aunt E didn't like the man. He appeared close to seventy, with thick gray hair and a perpetually downturned mouth. She supposed he might have once been handsome, but all she could see when she looked at him were the damning words in her aunt's diary. She forced herself to smile, feeling anything but charming. "Perhaps that is because the rules are stupid, Reverend Wellsbury."

Jamieson's sides began to shake with suppressed laughter. "Oh, ho! What a spitfire! It's just like Miss E was back, isn't it?" And then they were all dissolving into chuckles—even the vicar—the memory of Miss E alive and well in the small room.

When their amusement finally died down, the vicar turned to Mrs. Wilkins. "Well, rules or no, I think we ought to spend a little time having a serious discussion," he said, accepting the cup the woman handed him.

"Are you referring to Miss E's memorial?" Mrs. Wilkins poured another cup. "I was thinking a rosebush, planted in the center of town."

"My aunt hated roses," Lucy interjected.

"She did?" Mrs. Wilkins looked at her, perplexed. "But how would you know that? I thought you said you scarcely knew your aunt."

Lucy spared a glance at Mr. Bentley, who looked blissfully unaware of the conversation, bless his poor, addled ears. It seemed like this was a secret Aunt E had taken to her grave. "Er . . . she . . . ah . . . wrote of her preferences. In her annual Christmas card," Lucy improvised.

But Reverend Wellsbury shook his head. "There will be time enough to discuss a fitting tribute later. I mean, we should talk about the town's future."

"How can we talk about the town's future now that Miss E is gone?" Jamieson asked balefully. "*She* was the one who had all the grand ideas." He looked down at his hands. "It doesn't seem the same without her here."

"I know, Mr. Jamieson." The vicar's voice softened. "But to be perfectly frank, Lizard Bay's economy has been faltering for years, and despite her efforts, Miss E hadn't come close to solving our problems yet. Her scheme to have a cooperative town chicken coop and sell the eggs to Marston was well-intentioned but poorly executed."

"Why didn't it work?" Lucy asked, looking up. It was curious, but he almost sounded approving of her aunt's plan.

"Well, for one, the Tanner lads kept stealing the chickens and selling them," Mrs. Wilkins bemoaned. "That was the case we heard last month. They were sentenced to a month's worth of extra mathematics at school."

Lucy bit her lip in a smile. That certainly explained Danny's plans for truancy.

"Also, the eggs all broke when we tried to cart them to Marston," Reverend Wellsbury explained. "The road is terribly rutted and we can't afford to repair it. But with the loss of fishing, we need to find *some* sort of alternative industry to support our town's residents. And we all know the ground around here has never supported much by way of farming."

"There's tin mining up the coast near Marston," Mrs. Wilkins said, passing a full cup of tea to the postmaster.

"Shining'?" Bentley asked.

"No, *mining.*" Mrs. Wilkins turned to Lord Branston. "You are always poking about up on the moors, collecting rocks and plants and such. Have you seen anything promising up there, something that might help the town? There have been rumors in the past of tin deposits."

"I've seen nothing to speak of." Lord Branston paused. "And even if there was tin here, it would not necessarily mean improvements for the town."

"But wouldn't an industry like that provide a significant boost to the town's economy?" Lucy pointed out, thinking of Mr. Jamieson's nearly empty store shelves. "There would be workers for the mine. They would need dry goods. New roads for transportation." She realized they were all looking at her again, and her cheeks heated. "It seems more sustainable than chickens and broken eggs, anyway," she mumbled.

"It's a bit more complicated than that." Lord Branston's gaze seemed heavy. Assessing. "If the tin were found on private land, the town would need to purchase it first."

Mrs. Wilkins poured her own cup. "Well, you've been saying for some time you would like to find something sustainable to invest in here in Lizard Bay, Lord Branston. If we found a rich deposit, you could buy the land and help fund a mining operation."

Lucy couldn't help the smirk that made its way onto her face. "What an interesting idea, Mrs. Wilkins. By my understanding, Lord Branston is quite eager to toss his money away. Why, did you know he has over seven hundred pounds he is just *itching* to invest in a piece of property?"

He scowled at her. "Just because there is tin on a piece of land doesn't mean the person would be willing to sell." His gaze felt hot against her skin. "Some people, you see, can be rather stubborn about things like that." His eyes shifted to meet the larger group's attention. "It is said a mine is a hole anywhere in the world with at least one Cornishman at the bottom of it—the industry tends to benefit the wealthy off the backs of the poor. Hardly the leg up Lizard Bay needs. And we mustn't forget the tin mining operation near Marston very likely polluted the river, which is why the fishing along the coast has been off of late. Do we really want to take advantage of our citizens and despoil Lizard Bay's natural beauty, destroy what makes it special, just to earn a few shillings?"

"I rather think it would bring in more than a few shillings," Lucy grumbled, though she could admit—to herself, at least—that his argument made a good deal of sense. If mining had poisoned their water and destroyed the fishing opportunities, it sounded as though they needed to give it a little more consideration. And the thought that the citizens of the little town might be hurt by such an operation was difficult to swallow.

"Lord Branston is right," the vicar said. "If there is tin to be found around Lizard Bay, we must take care not to leap to hasty decisions. After all, the Lord creates temptations, as surely as he creates opportunity. He placed Eve in the Garden of Eden for a reason. To know which is the right choice requires prayer and careful thought."

Lucy had to school herself not to roll her eyes. Though the first part of the vicar's speech seemed rational enough, it was the latter part that stuck in her craw. She was reminded, then, of the red ribbon Aunt E had written about, the one she'd sewn on her knickers. She thought of how Reverend Wellsbury had suspected her aunt of trying to seduce all the men in town, when in reality she was forced to deflect their pestering advances.

And she felt the heat rise in her cheeks.

"How do you know Adam didn't deserve his fate?" she asked, taking a not-so-innocent sip of her tea. "After all, men are not to be trusted." She bared her teeth neatly over the rim over her cup. "Or so I've heard my aunt say."

Reverend Wellsbury's face reddened.

A mischievous part of her wanted to keep needling him—to honor her aunt's legacy, if not to vex the almighty hell out of him. But she held her tongue. She didn't have time for an argument. Something niggled at her, something important. The town was in trouble, and normally this was just the sort of thing that would send her mind spinning with all the ways she might help.

But this wasn't an ordinary tea: these people truly intended to sit here for hours, talking about tin and chickens and the reproductive vices of the town's cats.

What was she *doing* here, balancing a cup of tea on her lap while the minutes marched by? It had been three days since she left London, and her father was very likely en route now, coming to fetch her home. She'd been as patient as she knew how to be, but the discussion of a memorial to honor her aunt had clearly been curtailed in favor of other business.

This was all too much.

They might need to sit here and discuss town politics, but by God *she* didn't.

She stood up. The gentlemen clambered to their feet as well, though poor old Bentley had to be poked until he saw she was standing. "Where are you going, dear?" Mrs. Wilkins set her cup down on the table. "We're just getting started, and Reverend Wellsbury was, I am sure, going to lead us in a moment's prayer before we discuss any more town business." She shot him a superior look. "Rules, you know."

Lucy took a step toward the door. "Unless that prayer is for my safe travels, I am afraid I'll have to decline."

"Eh?" Bentley said, cupping a hand to his ear. "Something wrong with her spine?"

"No, my spine is fine, Mr. Bentley. I just need to get to Heathmore. And if no one in this room will help me find it, I am afraid I will need to get there by myself." She nodded to Mrs. Wilkins, whose look of worry had shifted to more of a look of horror. "Thank you for your kindness, Mrs. Wilkins, and for tea. I think a memorial in my aunt's memory sounds like a lovely notion, as long as it isn't roses." She stepped over a black and white cat that had begun to wind his way around her legs. "It was nice to meet you all."

"We can't let her go alone," she heard Mrs. Wilkins hiss to the group.

But Lucy was already slipping through the door, her

mouth stretching to a smile. *Finally.* She was taking matters into her own hands, doing something besides wearing out the soles of her boots pacing the town's only street. It might be foolish to attempt it without a proper guide, but she'd tried to be sensible and that hadn't worked. Now it was time to act. And truly, with the threat of her father's arrival looming ever closer, she was far past the point of caution.

So she dashed upstairs and grabbed her bag, which had been sitting—packed and ready—since eight o'clock yesterday morning. She flew back down the steps, exhilaration coursing through her. But just as she reached the front door, a shadow loomed in the hallway, blocking her way. The size of it alone was enough to cause her to catch her breath, but the breadth of those shoulders identified the body to whom that shadow belonged all too well.

She pushed past Lord Branston, jolted by the way that slight contact made her skin sing with awareness. "I believe we established that I don't require your help."

"Perhaps I intend to follow you, not offer my aid."

"Follow me?" she scoffed. "It seems more like you are stalking me. I understand there are dangerous cliffs about." She glared over her shoulder. "Perhaps you mean to push me to my death so your plans to acquire Heathmore may continue unimpeded?"

"Well, just so you put on a coat before I push you to this mythical death." He lifted his coat from a peg on the wall. "It's raining."

She hesitated. It hadn't been raining earlier, when she wasted hours pacing Lizard Bay's dusty street. But he didn't *look* as though he was lying. His own coat was a heavy oilskin thing. She nodded grudgingly. "All right." She dug through her bag and pulled out a light shawl, the only cover she'd brought with her from London.

"Don't you have anything heavier?"

"Don't you have other people to bother?" she retorted,

resenting the question as much for its accuracy as the fact it had come from Lord Branston's mouth. She *should* have brought a heavier cloak with her, and a parasol besides. Her nose was still pink from yesterday's walk up and down the street. But she'd been in such a hurry to leave London without discovery that she'd not put the proper thought into packing.

Not that she felt compelled to admit such a thing out loud.

Shrugging on the bit of lace that passed as a shawl in London drawing rooms—but which she suspected fell woefully short here in Cornwall—she jerked open the door and stamped her way out onto the porch. Immediately, she was struck by a thin curtain of mist. She breathed in, the usual tang of salt air now muddled by the scent of fresh rain and wet earth.

Well, he might be a bounder and a spreader of nefarious gossip, but he hadn't been exaggerating about the rain.

As if in agreement, the rain picked up, drumming harder on the roof of the narrow porch. Unable to back down now, she pulled the shawl tighter about her shoulders and stepped off the front steps. Turning to the right, she went a good hundred yards down the muddying street before glancing over her shoulder.

Lord Branston was standing in the middle of the road, his arms crossed across his chest, rain already coating his bare head.

"You decided not to follow me after all?" she challenged, though a part of her felt deflated by the thought that perhaps he meant to watch her traipse off alone through the rain.

He shook his head, and she could hear his long-suffering sigh. "No. Not in *that* direction, at any rate. Heathmore lies to the east, not the west." He gestured for her to retrace her steps. "Come along, then. Might as well find the perfect cliff to toss you over."

It is exhausting always being right. Well, perhaps not always right.

There was that time I kissed the vicar . . .

That lapse in judgment has been firmly rectified today. You see, I voted against Reverend Wellsbury's proposal to build a proper road to Marston and he stormed out of our town meeting in a great, manly snit. He suspects I cast such a vote only to be argumentative. I don't deny that after he left I lodged a vigorous and well-constructed argument against his plan. But I had my reasons, and they were not only to needle him.

Marston, I feel, is enjoying the wrong sort of progress. It is growing quickly, a mining town of the worst variety. There are regular fights in the street, and a young man was knifed in front of the gin house, just last week. A better road would carry our citizens to Marston for work, not the other way around. I am in firm agreement we need to collectively consider Lizard Bay's future, but I think we need to consider measures that preserve the character and charm and— yes, anonymity—of this little town that has become my refuge and my life.

Reverend Wellsbury needs to learn to trust my

judgment. I am neither a brainless, helpless female nor a cunning, plotting seductress. Honestly, the myriad ways he views me are becoming quite comical, as though I am multiple women wrapped up in a plain spinster's body. I am more than willing to work with him . . .

As long as he admits I am right.

Chapter 15

*H*e'd been joking, of course. About the cliff.

But still, Thomas was surprised when she trudged her way back. She stopped in front of him, her lower lip caught between her teeth. The sight of it made him feel better about this foolhardy decision to go traipsing off in the rain. At least she was *thinking* about things.

He was beginning to get a sense she didn't always before she tossed herself in the direction of her impulses.

"Lord Branston, I . . ." She hesitated, seemingly on the cusp of an apology, but then seemed to settle into a decision. "I suppose I am stuck with you, given that no one else in this town can be bothered to help. If you are inclined to visit Heathmore on this fine afternoon, I suppose it would be all right for me to accompany you."

Thomas bit back a chuckle, imagining that was about as close to an admission of error or an expression of thanks as he was likely to get where this woman was concerned. "You are welcome."

She looked away from him. She looked damp. A little lost, shivering in the worsening rain. And so damned desirable he wanted to pull her into his arms and kiss away the rain-drops clinging to her skin.

But he wasn't going to do anything about that. He finally—*finally*—had her trusting him enough to accept his offer of help. He wasn't going to destroy that with another ill-timed kiss, however tempting the thought.

More than anything, he wanted to show her why Heath-more was so special. To show her its hidden secrets and see the wonder on her face when she realized the potential to be found in the land. Given her interest in helping orphans and fixing the town's stray cat population, he had a feeling she might champion this cause if it was presented in the right way. She seemed to latch onto good causes the way the be-leaguered cats of Lizard Bay latched onto free meals. If she cared enough for the place and the town to stay, perhaps the land would be safe in her hands after all. But first he had to get her there.

He steered them east, out of town. A good, hard tramp was an excellent way to take his mind off the dilemma this woman posed, and he knew from experience that one lay ahead of them now. Lizard Bay had originally been founded as a small fishing village near the mouth of the Helford River, and it was sheltered on three sides by crumbling cliffs. The town's geography, however, had been its ultimate downfall, the tight rocks ensuring the town's architecture never expanded much past a single street and a few hundred hearty souls. Besides the single road leading in, there were perhaps a dozen foot and cart paths, scattered among the rocks, leading to a few homes and other secret places.

They began to climb one of those foot paths, the twisting, rocky path a series of mad switchbacks that always left him puffing, no matter how fit he was.

On sunny days the climb could be spectacular, with breathtaking ocean views and the dizzying acrobatics of the jackdaws that nested in the cliff face as entertainment. But today the jackdaws were more sensibly hunkered down in their nests. The path was shrouded in fog, and with the curtain of rain to contend with, he didn't dare take his eyes off the path for a second, or else risk slipping on wet rocks and loose earth.

"How did you know which path to take?" she asked, panting along behind him, dragging her bag with her. "They don't appear to be marked."

"No," he answered. "They once were, mind you. When I came here three years ago, there were still a few old directional signs left." He glanced back at her and stopped, realizing she was almost soaked through. Her shawl was scarcely the right sort of armor for a Cornwall rain, but he suspected she would only refuse his help if he offered his own coat, given that she had already twice refused his offer to carry her bag. "The salt air tends to weather the wood, and they don't last more than a few years. You just get to know the right path after a while."

"Well, there's your new industry for the town," she said, stopping beside him and wiping a strand of wet hair out of her eyes. "Directional signs." She set her bag down in the mud. "It's perfect. You'll need a constant supply. Perhaps you can even sell them to the almighty Marston." She made a face. "I swear, that town needs its comeuppance. Did they really poison your fish?"

He chuckled, remembering how Miss E used to harbor a similar opinion against the nearest town, always resenting how Marston had flourished while the residents of Lizard Bay struggled to make ends meet. "I am sure the Marston Mining Company would deny it if asked. And while directional signs are a good idea, you are forgetting one important thing."

"Oh?"

He lifted a hand to the high edge of the cliff, beyond which waited an expanse of grass and rock. "No trees. We'd have to buy the lumber for the signs from—"

She held up her hand. "Don't say it."

"Marston," he finished, his grin spreading higher.

She nodded. "All right, then," she said worrying her lower lip. "We'll have to just keep thinking about what other sort of industry might help Lizard Bay."

Thomas stared down at the sight of those neat white teeth against the pink curve of her lip. Damn, but it made him want to kiss her. Taste those lips again. What would she do if he took the invitation she probably didn't even realize she offered? Kissing her three days ago had proven a heady, unique experience. She was different than any woman he'd ever known. She appeared to approach everything in life with unrestrained passion, leaping first and asking questions later. And he couldn't help but admire that sort of spirit.

Her determination to reach Heathmore—no matter the distance, no matter, even, the miserable weather—was a perfect example. She was a reckless counterpart to his own scripted isolation, and a part of him envied her that freedom. The most unplanned thing *he* had ever done was flee London three years ago. That wasn't passionate or courageous, it had been cowardly. He'd just run—charged, really—seeking solace from the tattered remnants of what had once been a promising life. And then, once he reached Cornwall, he'd fallen into a defined, pitiable pattern of grief and isolation. For some reason, this woman made him want to loosen his hold on that increasingly distant part of his life.

She looked up, shielding her eyes from the rain. "How much higher do we need to climb?"

"Oh, I don't think the cliff face itself is higher than a thousand feet."

"That doesn't sound so bad."

"But with the switchbacks, it's another half mile of upward climbing on this path, then we take a hard right and have another mile and a half over rough terrain, on to Heathmore."

The smile slid off her face. "Another half mile? Of *climbing*?"

He nodded.

"But . . . however did my aunt manage it?"

"She was a tough thing, though I doubt she would have attempted it in the rain. She seemed to do all right, at least for the first year I lived here. But she moved down to town two years ago. She said she missed her daily dose of bickering with Reverend Wellsbury and wanted to be able to pester him all the time, but I suspect the climb became too much for her knees." He shrugged out of his oilskin coat, wrapping it around her shoulders. He held his breath, waiting for her to throw the garment back at him. Instead, she lowered her chin and breathed in, long and slow. He could almost imagine the war waging inside that fair head.

Should she or shouldn't she?

Well, he wasn't going to ask.

In a similarly surreptitious manner, he picked up her bag and slung it over one shoulder, opposite his satchel. He turned back up the path, welcoming the heaviness of the bag and the feel of the rain as it began to soak through his frockcoat, because that meant she was protected from those annoyances. After a moment he heard the hard scramble of her boots against the loose rocks. He paused, waiting for her to catch up, trying to imagine how difficult it was to attempt something like this in wet skirts. He was quite sure *he* wouldn't have attempted it.

"Well, if you truly want Heathmore for yourself, you are going to need to find a new way to do me in, Lord Branston," she panted.

"Oh?" he asked around his smile. He reached out his hand—no words, just a quiet, blind offer of assistance that she was free to take or leave according to her own whims.

He was rewarded for his patience by the clasp of her gloved hand in his.

"That's right," she said. "Because I refuse to be tossed off a cliff if you are going to force me to climb it first."

DESPITE HIS TEASING threats, he hadn't paused to toss her over once they reached the top.

In fact, he'd kept her quite close to his side, helping her up here, pulling her over there.

She had not had the breath to refuse his help, choosing instead to concentrate on the necessary task of not breaking her own neck. She slipped several times, saved only by the steady, reassuring pull of his hands. She regretted, now, the stubbornness that had brought them out in such foul weather. It was clear that she was endangering them both. But he didn't offer a word of criticism, just kept moving, solid and steady, in the direction she'd asked to go.

Eventually, they passed a white brick lighthouse, its rhythmic swirl of light and horn hardly piercing the deepening fog. She was tempted to stop, collect her breath. But he didn't slow down, just moved on, the trail becoming something more precarious now, little more than a goat path.

Not that she'd seen any goats.

In fact, after another half hour of walking, it occurred to Lucy that she hadn't seen *any* signs of life since the lighthouse. A single word came to mind when she considered how to describe the fog-covered vista, and that was "barren." As she stared out at the alien landscape, it occurred to her that her father had been right about at least one thing: the land up here appeared to be little more than useless heath and bog. To their right lay the ocean, and to their left lay what seemed to be miles and miles of stony ground and waterlogged grasslands, glimpses of loneliness snatched through the occasional break in the fog.

"In case you were wondering, we are on the outer edges of Heathmore's grounds now," Branston offered.

Lucy squinted into the swirling mist, wishing she had waited for a better day, wishing for even a small, twisted tree she might count on for a landmark. She didn't see anything that looked familiar. In point of fact, she didn't remember *anything* about this harrowing journey, though her six-year-old legs must have traipsed this treacherous path, once upon a time. A sense of uncertainty settled in her heart as she stared out at the foreign vista.

What had she gotten herself into?

"You look disappointed."

"It is just that the word 'grounds' implies something a bit more . . . well . . . grander." She turned in a small circle, looking for some glimpse of life. "I remember it rather differently. Fields of flowers and butterflies." Then again, she'd been six. What was she supposed to remember, lethal, rain-slick paths where one wrong step could send you plummeting to your death? "Does nothing grow up here besides rocks?"

He shrugged. "That depends on your perspective. This is a peculiar piece of land. The Lizard Bay peninsula is the only place in England with this type of geography. The soil along this stretch of coast is too alkaline for traditional crops. But that doesn't mean nothing will grow." He cast a hand toward the fog-shrouded side of the path. "It is hard to see at present, but there are many examples of unusual plant life here." He paused. "More than you can imagine, rare and beautiful. Whoever has the care of Heathmore has care of them."

Lucy looked again, trying to blink away her prejudices. She didn't see how it involved any care at all: it was wild and vast, quite independent of any human hand. She felt a catch in her throat as she considered this all belonged to her now, the rocks and grass and even the fog.

But she suspected she was going to have a hell of a time growing a vegetable garden.

"The cottage is only few hundred yards farther." He pointed to a distant outcropping of rock. "Just through there."

She peered through the curtain of mist. Why was her stomach skittering? She *couldn't* be nervous. She was almost there, nearly at the end of this mad crusade that had all but consumed her the last few weeks. She ought to be sprinting down the path. But for some reason, her nerves were jumping. What would she find beyond those rocks? Her future, bright and shining and perfect? Or a reality she didn't want to face?

She trudged the last few steps, grateful for the weight of the borrowed oilskin about her shoulders. The gesture had been kind—kinder than she deserved, given that it was her own stubbornness that had them out in this weather. But for Lord Branston, such kindness seemed to be commonplace. Just ahead she could see his shoulders flex and twist as he stepped over rocks and obstacles, the delineation of firm muscles outlined by the wet frockcoat, plastered against his skin. Though she was quite sure Aunt E would be appalled by the direction of her thoughts, she was rather grateful to be following.

Otherwise, she'd miss the view.

Finally, Lord Branston circled around from behind, his hand gentle against the small of her back. "There you are, then," he said, pointing through a break in the rocks. "Your first sight of Heathmore Cottage."

Lucy stepped forward, staring at this house her aunt had bequeathed her. Fears of gaping holes and sagging roofs were shoved to one side as she took in the whitewashed stone walls and the gleam of new, wet slate on the roof. It appeared to have once been a crofter's cottage, two stories and solidly built. In the waning light it looked safe and warm and altogether inviting. She glanced back at him. "Uninhabitable? It looks rather well-tended to me."

"Yes, well, there's been a bit of work put into it since your aunt's passing."

"Which you had neither permission nor the right to do," she reminded him archly. She turned back to her cottage and strode toward it until she was running a hand over the damp stones, stones that now belonged to her. Her lungs squeezed tight to feel the solid promise of them.

"The repairs aren't finished yet." His voice pushed from behind. "It's been slow going, bringing the slate up the path one bundle at a time. If you plan to keep it, you'll need to be prepared to invest a bit more in its upkeep."

A frisson of irritation curled through her. "I don't know what you mean, Lord Branston. The house looks quite livable to me." She pursed her lips and held out her hand. "May I have my bag, please?"

He handed it over. It was heavier than she remembered. She probably ought to thank him for carrying it so far. But somehow the realization that his descriptions of the cottage's state of disrepair were more falsehood than truth made the gratitude shrivel a bit on her tongue.

She moved toward the front door, wanting to see if a similar state of falsehood waited inside. Opening her wet bag, she drew out the key she'd carried all the way from London. She slid it into the lock and tried to turn it. Nothing happened. She jiggled it. Took it out and tried again. "Is there a trick of some kind?"

"No. It has a new lock."

She turned to face him, her hands clenching. "You've locked me out of my own house?"

He held out his hand, a different key lying flat against his palm. "We had to break the latch initially to get in. I thought it safer to repair it than leave it open to vandals."

She took the new key, examining it with a sense of increasing annoyance. Unlike the key that had come mailed in the brown paper package, this one was new and shiny.

Full of fresh promise.

And not at all the one that had become her talisman.

From the Diary of Edith Lucille Westmore
April 3, 1826

It is said (by Reverend Wellsbury) that women change their minds more frequently than the weather. How, then, do you explain the nearly constant nature of our feud? After the Great Marston Road Debate of 1825, the vicar and I reached a rocky state of equilibrium. Reverend Wellsbury would propose an action, and I would vote it down. Or else I would come up with a brilliant idea, and he would work behind my back to convince the townspeople to take the opposite view. The two of us have tied up town politics in a vitriolic standstill, and I am not proud to admit that perhaps we have both given our personal differences free rein and not always considered the betterment of the town.

Something has to change. We can't continue this way, or poor Lizard Bay will suffer the consequences. But I'm not leaving.

And I hear there may be a position opening up for a new vicar up in Marston . . .

Chapter 16

Thomas stepped inside the cottage and wiped his feet on the rag carpet by the door. Over the past two weeks, he'd spent countless hours here, consumed by the cottage's never-ending list of repairs. Three years ago, when Aunt E still lived here, she'd always welcomed him into the small parlor, sitting him down in one of her ancient, creaking chairs, asking him what he'd found during the day's walk. He'd shared his secrets—willingly or not.

But Lucy didn't seem interested in sharing any secrets. She set down her bag and stood in the middle of the room, stripping off her gloves one finger at a time. She turned in a slow circle, and he could see her gaze skitter across the trio of beleaguered chairs and the old settee, its upholstered cushion lopsided and sun-faded. He leaned one shoulder against the wall as she completed her perusal, his satchel heavy about his shoulder. It might not be much to look at, but he was rather proud of the parlor's state of cleanliness.

After all, he'd dusted the furniture himself.

"I don't remember any of this." She chewed on her lower lip as though it held answers the room couldn't give her. "My memory of it seems . . . I don't know. Larger." She sighed, looking around again. "Then again, I was only six years old."

Thomas thought of how much Miss E had loved the small crofter's cottage, even with all its cramped corners and old, dilapidated furniture. There were four rooms in total, a sitting room and kitchen on the bottom floor, and two bedrooms on top. Small by London standards, but it had been more than large enough for Miss E.

He shook his head, a bit disappointed by the girl's lack of enthusiasm. "If you had visited your aunt more often, perhaps your memories would be clearer," he replied.

She cut him a sharp glance. "I may not have known my aunt through frequent visits, but do not presume I know nothing of her, or of this house. She sent us a Christmas card every year." She hesitated. "And she left me her diaries."

"Ah. I had wondered how you knew she hated roses."

She blinked at him. "You mean . . . *you* knew about the roses? And Mr. Bentley?"

Thomas nodded. In her old age, Miss E had been a chatty thing, prone to the occasional bout of dementia. As someone who spent time with her, he was bound to collect odd bits and pieces of her history. He hadn't known Miss E kept a diary, but it didn't surprise him. She had been a fiercely bookish sort of spinster with a lot of lonely hours to fill.

"But why would my aunt tell you something so . . . so . . . personal?" In the room's muted light, Lucy's eyes seemed huge.

"I reckon she was glad for the chance to simply talk to someone." He crossed his arms. "I suspect she was a little lonely, living by herself all the way up here." He hesitated. "And I predict you will be as well."

Her eyes narrowed. "My aunt *chose* to live here, by herself. She could have visited us in London anytime she wanted." She took a step toward the fireplace and ran a finger along the empty mantel. "And I am not completely without memories, you know. I remember a set of glass figurines she kept here. A pair of horses. She took them down for me to play with." Her voice deepened. "I nearly broke one of them, but she didn't scold me."

Thomas's shoulders softened. Now *that* sounded like Miss E. The woman might have been quick to snap at Reverend Wellsbury, but she had an imminent store of patience for mischievous young children.

Lucy turned to face him, taking a deep breath. "The house looks quite clean, Lord Branston. So much for the stories about the rats."

He shook his head. "I didn't lie about that."

"I was given to believe the place was filthy. That it was all but falling down."

"I've pulled out the parlor furniture and cleaned and dusted." His defense echoed fitfully through the small room. He could well imagine how it looked, but she was leaping to a conclusion she didn't understand. "But there are other rooms still waiting for a proper cleaning. I've had trouble finding anyone to come up and help, of late."

"Because they knew the place didn't belong to you?" Her voice was sharper now.

"No, because they think it is haunted."

She rolled her eyes. "This talk of ghosts again." She took a step toward him. "Lord Branston, I've heard quite enough. The evidence speaks for itself. You were untruthful about the condition of this house, no doubt to try to convince me to sell it to you sight unseen."

"I didn't —"

"*And* you have lied to the people of Lizard Bay, stirring stories of ghosts and the like, no doubt so they wouldn't offer you a challenge."

His spread his hands, growing a bit angry himself. Was she truly so blind that she couldn't see how hard he was trying to help her? "I have offered to pay more than the house's actual value—"

"But not at first. Your initial offer was far too low."

He gritted his teeth. She had him there. But he hadn't wanted to rouse suspicion as to the property's true value. Not with so much at stake, and not when he'd still believed her an empty-headed debutante. "I will pay you whatever you think the property is worth."

"That's a generous offer." But her voice echoed with doubt. She took a step toward him, cocking her head. "But such generosity only rouses my suspicions more. Why do you want Heathmore so badly you would at first try to purchase it for a blind pittance, only to now offer whatever I might ask? What hidden value does it have to you?"

There was enough truth in her musings to make him swallow. But he wanted to show her. To explain his thinking. "If you would just let me show you—"

"Show me what?" she interrupted, shaking her head. "Can you conjure a house full of rats now? Wave a magic wand and turn the place filthy again? I don't trust you, Lord Branston." There was a moment of painful hesitation, and then she sighed. "And I can admit to being disappointed that my lack of faith seems well-founded." She shrugged out of the oilskin. "Thank you for showing me the way here, but I no longer require your assistance." She tossed the coat toward him. "I'll thank you to leave now."

He caught it with an awkward hand, droplets of water flying here and yon. She wanted him to leave? Oh, *bugger it all*. There she went, leaping in without thinking again. He recognized the sharp tilt of her chin. She'd looked much the same yesterday afternoon when they sparred on the street. He widened his own stance. "Absolutely not. I am not leaving you here alone."

"The choice does not lie with you." She pointed toward the door. "Please, go now."

Thomas tried to find a calming tone, something to ease the rising redness in her face. "Lucy. You are cold and wet and not thinking clearly." He'd meant to soothe her. Soften the tightness of her jaw. But instead his words seemed more like a match touched to tinder.

"Oh, for the love of bloody *Christ,* would people stop telling me I am not thinking clearly!" she exploded, throwing her hands up in the air. "First my father, then my sister Lydia, and now you. Why must my thoughts be muddied, simply because they don't agree with yours?"

Thomas gritted his teeth. *Right, then.* Perhaps a soothing tone had been the wrong tactic to take. "Well then, don't be foolish," he said next. "The path was dangerous enough in daylight. If we delay returning until dark, it could well prove lethal."

Her face turned a bright red. "Foolish, am I? I have breasts, I suppose, which makes me capable of nothing more than a touch of hysteria every now and again. Well, if you are so afraid of the dark, best get started back. I will not be returning to Lizard Bay tonight."

Not even the mention of her breasts could cool his rising ire. Damn it, but would she not listen to reason? He knew she was smart—smart enough and brave enough to find her way to Cornwall, against all odds. She'd waited for two long days to try and locate a guide, so she at least understood the risks of being alone. So why was she insisting on doing something so dangerous now, without stopping to think it through? Was it because the house was not as large or grand as she remembered and she was battling the sting of her pride?

Or was it because she felt like he was still trying to somehow force her hand?

"You can't stay in a house like this," Thomas protested. "It isn't safe."

"Because I'm a woman?" She threw her hands up in the air again. "You sound just like Reverend Wellsbury. I *have* to stay in a house like this. I don't have a choice. I can't afford to stay in town another night, and unlike you, I don't have entailed property at my disposal or an income I can depend on."

Thomas scowled at her. Was she truly so blind to the privilege she enjoyed? "You toss out excuses rather easily, but need I point out your father is a viscount? Yesterday you mentioned a dowry. Shall I guess the amount? Five thousand?" At her scowl of annoyance, he pressed on. "Ten thousand?" He knew he had her when she began to bite her lip. "Admit it, Lucy. You are scarcely the impoverished chit you are claiming to be."

Her hands gripped the fabric of her skirts. "If you think a woman's dowry is her own," she ground out, "then you are delusional. It will only be delivered into the hands of a husband, a fact my father has made more than clear. And given my plain appearance and contrary notions about life and love and everything in between, any man who offers for me will most assuredly only be interested in putting his hands on my dowry." She drew a ragged breath. "Not on *me*."

A strange, telling silence descended. He wondered if she even realized just how much she had revealed. She'd been claiming from the day he met her that she didn't want to marry, that she intended to be a spinster like her aunt, but this confession suggested a deeper, underlying doubt. And not only a doubt in men and their intentions: a doubt in herself.

His eyes lingered on cheeks flushed pink with agitation, the rise and fall of those lovely breasts. Christ above. *Plain?* Was that really how she saw herself? Had she any notion of how she looked at the moment, her wet dress molded to her curves?

Her chin tilted even higher. "So no, Lord Branston. I am not going with you, and I have no intention of selling this property. You can't imagine what Heathmore represents to me."

"Then tell me," he said, more quietly now. "Convince me

why I should leave off. Tell me you can handle this house, manage its repairs and upkeep. Promise me you won't sell it, and I will walk away and leave you in peace."

"Heathmore means my freedom. Independence." She choked on a sob and charged at him, her hands making hard contact against his chest. "A life where I don't ever have to marry, a life I would make on my own terms, not dictated by my parents or a husband."

He stood firm, letting her abuse him. "I understand such a sentiment more than you think." Something of her panic, her resolve, reminded him of another young woman, once upon a time. "My sister—"

"You *don't* understand." She pushed again, and this time he yielded, stumbling back toward the open front door. "I *can't* muddle through life the way my father expects me to, and I can't be what my mother would make me!" She was shouting now, nearly shaking the rafters. "I can't face the Season they have planned for me or marry a perfect, titled stranger just because it is the 'done' thing! God knows I have tried through the years, but that is a shoe *that will not fit*. My aunt wanted me to have Heathmore because she knew from a single, childhood visit that I was different, that I would never fit into a life someone else made me. And I can't sell the house she intended as my salvation."

Now, finally, they were getting into the heart of the matter. She was determined, he'd give her that. But had she really thought this through? She was fixated on a path she knew nothing about, nothing beyond the hazy image she held of Miss E as a saintly do-gooder and a kindly aunt. But he'd known Miss E well enough to recognize the restlessness that lay inside her. The woman had never been content. Always floating from project to mad project as if she were trying to fill some endless hole in her life. Always searching for something: company, grand causes, something to ease that ache in her heart.

"I can understand a need to make your own life," he said, wincing as another hard shove knocked against his chest, pushing him ever backward. "But are you meant to be alone in that future?"

"Yes," she said, panting now. "My aunt did it. *You* live alone, to hear Mrs. Wilkins tell it."

"Yes. I live alone. And that is why you should listen to me when I say you should reconsider your plan."

"You'd like that, wouldn't you?" she spat. "To force me to sell Heathmore, and run back to London with my tail tucked between my legs."

"Damn it, this isn't about Heathmore! It's about *you*."

She stopped, her eyes wide with surprise, her chest heaving. "Of course it's about Heathmore."

"I mean it, Lucy." He shook his head. "Do not rush into a decision like this." He dragged a hand through his damp hair, needing to make her understand. "Do you know what it means to be truly, completely alone?" he demanded. "Sitting in a room for hours—for *years*—with naught but the crack of a fire in your ears? To feel the weight of your own thoughts, second-guessing every decision you ever made, every person you ever disappointed, until you think you might go mad from it?" He threw up his hands. "Your aunt understood it. *I* understand it. It isn't for the faint of heart, Lucy. You can trust me on that."

There was a long, awkward moment of silence. She stared at him.

He stared back.

"How can I *trust* you?" she whispered, her eyes welling with tears. "I can't even trust you to use my name properly, much less tell me the truth." Her voice was a catch in her throat now, and the sound made him want to reach for her. "My name is Miss L now, not Lucy." She gave a new, hard shove, and suddenly he was standing outside the door. "And I can't trust *anyone*."

LUCY SHOVED THE door closed and turned the shiny new key in the lock.

Her heart was thumping with emotion—emotion that, admittedly, had little to do with Heathmore Cottage. Oh, God. Oh, *bugger it all.* Had she really just confessed to Lord Branston she was afraid a husband would not want to touch her?

And more to the point . . . was it true?

Until that moment, she hadn't realized just how much of her obsession with this house and her fears for the Season were tied up in her own confused feelings about her future. She had claimed—loudly and often—that she didn't want to ever marry, that she wanted to be a spinster and live life by her own rules, the way her aunt had. But in that mad, miserable moment when she choked it all out to Lord Branston, it had all become clear.

It wasn't that she didn't want a husband, as she had been claiming.

It was that she wanted that husband to want *her.*

And that, she realized with a sudden sob, was the crux of everything. She clapped a hand over her mouth, trying to hold it in. *That* was why she didn't want a Season, why the thought of setting up a spinster's house in a crofter's cottage in Cornwall held such appeal.

But if the thought of a loveless marriage frightened her, she was also scared to find herself eventually wanting things like children, a desire to share her world and her worry with someone other than felons and orphans. Would she feel empty without them, the way Lord Branston implied she would? She was suddenly frightened she would never be happy, no matter which decision she made.

She swiped at her traitorous eyes and stalked to the front window. Brushing aside a faded curtain, she peered out. He was shrugging on the oilskin she had thrown at him. It had smelled of him when he draped it around her shoulders on their walk up. She had closed her eyes when he'd done it, breathing him in, trying to believe he wanted the best for her.

But that was just wishful thinking, it seemed.

There were too many reasons to distrust him.

In the drizzle, she could see him offer one last glance toward the door. He took a hesitant step away, then another, until his damp, dark head disappeared through the rocks. How long she stood there, she couldn't say, but eventually her emotions began to calm and her tears to dry. With it, the chill of the house began to seep through her clothes. She pulled the wet shawl off her shoulders and turned to face the room she had just fought so hard to win. Already the shadows were lengthening, and not only because of the dreary day.

It was starting to get late.

And it was definitely getting colder.

As she knelt in front of the parlor's fireplace and sorted through how she might start a fire, she realized with dismay she didn't know how. Much like laundry, she'd never even considered learning how to do it. Could she really be stymied by such a basic, primal skill?

Give her a pen and paper and she could change the world, but start a fire? She hadn't a bloody clue.

She searched her memory. How did the servants light fires at Cardwell House? They seemed to always be carrying around buckets of embers. That implied that new fires were started from old ones. But there was no fire in this place. No scent of smoke either, suggesting there hadn't been a fire in a very long time.

And bloody hell. Even if she found a match, there didn't appear to be any wood.

"Don't panic, Lucy," she muttered into the ominous silence of the house. "You just need to look around." She stumbled into the next room, determined to search every nook and cranny for matches and wood. But things seemed even less encouraging here. She was standing in a kitchen, with a wobbly old table and a few chairs. Dust coated the table, and the floor crunched menacingly under her boot, two years of dirt and neglect impossible to ignore. There was no stove to speak of but she saw a cooking hearth that appeared to be stuffed with hay or dried grass. She sniffed, searching for evidence of a recent fire, but all she received was a nose full of ammonia for her trouble.

Worse, something rustled in the grass.

Oh God, oh God, oh God.

Lucy turned and ran out of the kitchen, slamming the door behind her and breathing hard. She hadn't believed it, not really. She'd thought her father and Lord Branston must have made that part of the story up, like a twisted fairy tale meant to keep children from wandering into the woods. But stories didn't rustle about in the grass, nor urinate in hearths either.

She placed a trembling hand over her heart.

She wasn't the Westmore sibling who was terrified of rats. She *wasn't.*

And as long as the dreadful beasts stayed on their side of the house, everything would be fine.

She somehow pulled herself together, her wet skirts dragging the floor and leaving a dirty smear behind her. She knew she needed to get dry, but how could she in the insistent damp of the place? She fumbled out of her skirts and bodice, laying them across the back of a chair. But she soon discovered that dry clothes were going to be in as short supply as firewood: everything in her bag was soaked through. Even the snuff she'd bought from Mr. Jamieson was clumped inside its tin. "Right then," she muttered, squaring her shoulders. "Surely there is *something* dry to wear in this house." A blanket, perhaps. Or a curtain.

She would find it, even if it meant braving . . . She shuddered.

No, if it meant braving the rats, she'd rather stay cold and damp, thank you very much.

Shivering in her damp chemise, Lucy armed herself with an old moth-eaten broom and completed a cursory inspection of the rest of the house, her trepidation rising with each new discovery. She found the half-finished roof and the rain-slick floors that lay beneath. The rotting floorboards in the upstairs bedrooms. And the closet full of old, musty linens, which had at first caused a hopeful leap of her heart, only to have those hopes curdle as she realized the cotton had all been chewed through by rats.

Through it all, the outside light grew dimmer through the windows, until finally she had to make her way back to the parlor by feel rather than by sight.

She was cold. Wet. Hungry.

Wrong.

The realization formed slowly, growing teeth along with the night. With it came an acute embarrassment. She sank to the floor, her face in her hands. Lord Branston had warned her the repairs weren't finished. Her own inspection had just confirmed the worst: everything he had said about Heathmore was true.

Oh, damn her indomitable pride, and damn her compulsive nature besides.

She'd known the cottage was miles from town, and now the sheer isolation of Heathmore began to close in. She couldn't make her way back down that treacherous, slippery path tonight without a light to guide her. She wasn't sure she could do it even *with* a light in hand.

She'd never felt so alone in all her life. She thought of her family, back in London, and the bustle and efficiency of Cardwell House. Oh, but she had taken that life for granted. Lord Branston had been right when he claimed she was spoiled. She'd imagined she hated the wealth surrounding her, when in reality she hadn't realized how fortunate she was.

Was *this* what Lydia meant that day when her sister implied that she was naive to the ways of the world? She looked around the small room, with its simple furniture and unlit hearth. If Lydia were here, she would probably know how to start a fire.

Hell, Lydia would probably know how to catch a rat and turn it into dinner.

But all she herself knew how to do, really, was write letters to prisoners.

She blinked back tears as she thought of the grand causes she had supported in London, and how her father always tolerated them with a bemused shake of his head. They *did* seem like petty diversions now, compared to the reality of life. She'd devoted herself to them for the wrong reasons, wanting to feel important, rather than wanting to help as an honest expression of gratitude for all she had.

What had she been *thinking*, charging so blindly to Cornwall, so ill-prepared for it all? And just how had Aunt E done it, managed to live here, all by herself? How had she found firewood, in a landscape barren of trees? How had she fetched water, and cooked without a stove? It was far too dark to read her aunt's diary for clues, and so far she'd uncovered no details in her reading that pointed to the day-to-day workings of Aunt E's life.

She thought of the pages she had read, the vivid descriptions of her aunt's adventures. In point of fact, Aunt E hadn't written much about her life here at Heathmore Cottage at all. Instead, she'd written—nearly incessantly—about the people of Lizard Bay.

Was Lord Branston right? Was it possible her aunt hadn't been as content a spinster as her diaries implied?

At that moment, an eerie moaning sound reached through the cottage walls to find her ears. *Whooooooo. Whooooooo.*

"Who is there?" She sat up, her heart clawing a hole in her chest.

Whoooooo.

Her mind summoned Mrs. Wilkins's earlier warning

about ghosts and magnified it tenfold. She didn't believe in ghosts. But something rustled in the darkness to her left.

And, oh God, that sound came from *inside* the house, not out of doors.

What if . . . what if the vandals Lord Branston had mentioned were staying here after all? Her imagination took hold then and went further.

Vandals wielding knives.

Or worse . . . *vandals wielding rats.*

The rustling came again, louder now. Something brushed by her leg, and she opened her mouth in a long, terrified scream.

Oh God, oh God, oh God.

She was a victim of her own stupidity, bound to stay in this house tonight, or die trying.

And it was beginning to look as though dying was a distinct possibility.

Living alone on the edge of a cliff is not for the faint of heart.

Sometimes, especially when the season shifts, the wind moans terribly, reminding you that warmer homes and warmer beds await in town below. I shudder to think of the coming winter, when I will be confined to Heathmore by ice on the path more often than not. I would move to Lizard Bay in a heartbeat if the bloody vicar wasn't still there, his smugly handsome face glaring down at me from the pulpit. But moving to town for the winter would be akin to admitting Reverend Wellsbury was right.

And I would rather die than ever admit a thing like that.

Chapter 17

*T*he bloody girl was going to die.

At the sound of her scream, Thomas launched himself out of the shelter of the rock where he'd been hunkered down, resolved to a miserable, sleepless night. As he sprinted toward the dark house, he cursed out loud. There was no wisp of smoke curling from the chimney, no glimmer of light in any window. She was going to break her goddamned neck, puttering about that treacherous house with no lamp.

And it was going to be his fault for bringing her here.

The moaning wind battered its way through his oilskin, but not even the thought of his warm, dry manor on the west side of town was enough to deter him from reaching her. She was trapped inside the cottage, cold and terrified and impossibly naive.

And that meant he couldn't yet leave.

Thomas threw his shoulder against the front door, cursing his foresight in repairing it so well. As his body made impact, she screamed again. He slammed his shoulder against the door again, then again. Finally, the weathered wood splintered around the new lock, and then he was tumbling inside, blinking, ready to defend her to the death.

There was another shrill scream, followed by a foul curse that would make a sailor blush, and then an acrid cloud of cloves and tobacco enveloped him.

He twirled into the darkness, grappling for both air and understanding.

It smelled like . . . snuff.

More specifically, it smelled like Miss E's snuff.

Bloody hell, what was going on?

Choking, he dropped to his knees, clawing his throat for relief. The snuff assault was followed by a blow that seemed to come out of nowhere.

Whack.

His head jerked backward against the scratch of straw against his cheek. "What the devil?" he managed to choke out. He searched through the murky darkness until his gaze landed on a white ghost of a girl. Lucy was wielding a broom in both hands, brandishing it like a sword.

And she was dressed in little more than a dream.

He coughed long and hard, doubling over, then lifted his hands in a gesture of surrender, forcing his eyes to keep to the prescribed path of her huge eyes and pale face, rather than the rounded, full shape of her breasts beneath her slip. "Lucy," he croaked out, "it's me."

The broom lowered. "Thomas?" came her agonized whisper.

He nodded, the sound of his name sounding like heaven on her lips, no matter that her voice was strained with terror. He climbed awkwardly to his feet. So much for defending her to the death. He'd barely managed to survive his own entrance. He glanced around the dark room for evidence of whatever had sent her to arm herself with a tin of snuff and a broom.

"Do you . . . ah . . . need my help?"

He half expected her to fly into a rage at the question. At the evidence he was still here, despite her order to leave.

Instead, she flew into his arms.

He caught her up as the broom fell to the floor with a loud clatter. His eyes and nose were still burning, but his arms proved entirely capable of closing about her quaking body. He'd seen this woman angry on more occasions than he could count. He'd seen her square her shoulders, stronger than any soldier. He'd seen her skin warmed by candlelight, that tempting mouth begging for a kiss. But he'd never seen her so . . . vulnerable.

"You came," she sobbed, her hands clutching at his oil-skin.

"I never really left," he admitted. She was trembling—shivering so hard, in fact, her teeth were chattering. He forced his arms to loosen, though it was a battle to get them to follow orders, given the screaming knowledge that she was dressed in nearly nothing.

"I . . . I don't know why you are here." Her breath hitched, and he could feel her warm tears soaking through his frock-coat. "I don't deserve it, given how foolish I have been. But I am so, so glad of it."

Though his eyes were still stinging from the snuff, Thomas smiled above her head. *Well.* He had finally received a word of thanks from this sharp-tongued girl. But instead of feeling self-satisfied, guilt crept in. She wasn't aware of all his motives regarding Heathmore yet.

And apparently she wasn't aware of the very inappropriate direction of his thoughts.

He cleared his throat, still smelling snuff with every breath. "Well, you armed yourself admirably. I am not sure you need my help after all. You seem capable of handling yourself in the event of vandals."

"I'm not so worried about the vandals," she said, shaking against him.

His hand crept up to the nape of her neck, brushing the short, damp strands of hair aside until his fingers touched skin. Christ, but she was cold. "What, then?" he asked, lowering his hands. He began to briskly rub her arms, shoulder to elbow. "What has you so frightened you needed to whack me with a broom?"

She buried her face against his chest but didn't pull away. "Didn't you hear it?"

"The wind?"

"The ghost."

His hands stilled. "There's no ghost, Lucy. No matter the superstitions of the townspeople, 'tis only the wind, as I've always said. It blows hard on this part of the coast."

She pressed tightly against him. "Well, *something* ran across my leg."

"Ah." Understanding settled into the cracks of his thinking. "You've met the rats, I see."

She breathed in and out, then pulled back, her eyes meeting his through the darkness. "If they insist on living here, too, I am afraid we aren't going to get along."

In spite of himself—and in spite of the absolutely not humorous feel of her in his arms—he chuckled. "Then you'll just have to bring up some cats from town. If you brought the males, I suspect you might even solve two problems at once."

She pulled back and offered him a hesitant smile, though in the dark it was difficult to see anything beyond the blinding, transparent whiteness of her chemise. "You are being so kind. Kinder than I deserve. But the presumption I can fix this with a few cats . . ." She glanced around the dark room. "You were right. The parlor might be clean and put to rights, but the rest of Heathmore isn't what I expected. I . . . I am not sure I am meant to keep it after all."

That plucked at his conscience. He ought to be glad to hear her say it, given all that was at stake. But after the terrible row where she had shoved him outside, after all the shouted accusations, he felt as though he understood better now what drove her. She was searching for a handhold, a peg on which she could hang her future. Something to define her, beyond what Society expected of her. She wanted someone to love her, to share her life, but she wanted to be able to trust that person.

He could understand the need. And because he understood, he found himself wanting to help. Even at his own expense, and even if it meant losing this worthy fight.

Somehow, he held out hope it might yet become her worthy fight as well.

He offered her his hand. "Well, you've not given it a proper chance yet. The cottage has its own charms, in the daylight." When she hesitantly placed her hand in his, he tugged her toward the kitchen. "Come on, then. Let's get a fire started."

SHE WATCHED AS he lit a candle, using a match he pulled from a tin in the kitchen cupboard. The flickering light made Lucy feel marginally better, but it was his sure, solid movements that calmed her the most. He pulled a kettle down from the same cupboard, then filled it with water from a rusty pump she'd missed on her first frantic inspection of the kitchen.

"There's a well?" she asked, feeling sheepish.

"Yes, a nice deep one. You'll be glad of it come summer. Some of the villagers have shallow wells that run dry in the warmer months and flood in the spring."

Lucy bit her lip. She wasn't at all sure she was going to be here come summer. The truth was, she wasn't sure she was going to be here tomorrow. The reality of what she was facing here was sobering. It wasn't only the rats. The sheer physicality of the experience overwhelmed her. She didn't know how to make a fire. She couldn't dry her clothes, much less know how to wash them. She'd imagined inheriting a cottage in Cornwall would be a simple thing.

But this was no ordinary cottage, and nothing was as simple as it seemed.

And her hesitation wasn't only about feeling woefully underprepared for the business of taking proper care of herself. She could learn how to do laundry, if need be. Build a fire, given time and the proper tools. But in the time she had spent in the echoing silence of this house, she discovered a very important fact about herself, one she was not sure she had understood before. She didn't like solitude. Already, she could feel herself missing London. She missed her family and the warm, well-run house full of servants who cared for her.

Missed her parents, even her blustering father.

And she missed, especially, Lydia.

The thought of living here at Heathmore, alone, and never seeing family or friends, was untenable. Everyone in Lizard Bay presumed she was just like her aunt, but Lucy was beginning to suspect she was not nearly as brave.

Thomas gathered two china cups and a tin full of tea. "Let's do this in the other fireplace," he murmured, balancing the items in both hands. "The rats still have the run of this one." He moved smoothly and methodically, as if it was an ordinary thing for a marquess to make a spot of tea. The man might be a peer, but it was clear he knew what he was doing around a kitchen.

The house seemed slightly less terrifying now that the candle's light touched the corners and she had someone else here with her, but there was still the moaning wind to contend with, seeping between small cracks beneath the window frames.

She stayed close by his side as they made their way back to the parlor.

"Hold this, please." He handed her the candle and set the kettle down beside the fireplace. "Will you be all right until I return?"

"Where are you going?" She shivered. Surely he didn't mean to give her a single guttering candle and a cold tea-kettle and then tuck himself back to town?

"To the shed out back. I thought we might sleep in the parlor tonight, given that it is the only room that has been properly cleaned. But I need to start a fire to get you warm." His eyes swept over her. "And get your clothes dry." He swallowed. "As quickly as possible."

"There's a shed?" she moaned out loud, embarrassed to have not known that. It was another reminder she knew close to nothing about this property she had inherited, and less than that, even, about how to take care of herself here. "And how can there be wood? There are no trees within two miles."

"We burn peat in our fireplaces here." He cocked his head, looking impossibly handsome in the candlelight. "Unless you would like to burn some of the furniture instead?" He grinned. "We could start with the dining table. It has a wobble on its right side, one I haven't been able to fix. But we might want to hold off breaking it apart for firewood until we've had breakfast in the morning."

Her stomach churned. He planned to spend the night here with her. And apparently eat breakfast in the morning. *For her safety*, she told herself. It was clearly too dangerous to go back down the path tonight, given the foul weather. She forced a smile. "If there is dry fuel somewhere, by all means, carry on."

So he brought in two armfuls of peat logs, then shrugged out of his oilskin and frockcoat and crouched in front of the fireplace in his shirtsleeves. She watched as he laid the fire, the dark bricks of peat propped in a pyramid and a handful of straw on the bottom. He took his time, showing her how to do it, patiently waiting for her to assemble some of the pieces herself. "Starting the initial fire is the hard part," he explained, holding the candle to the straw. "Once it is started, you shouldn't let a fire go completely out, just stir the hot ashes back to life and add fresh kindling."

It took a few moments for the flame to take hold. The peat

gave off a smoky, acrid smell, quite different than the coal fires she was used to in London. But fire was fire, and when the orange flames began to lick through the darkness, she breathed a sigh of relief.

"Where did you learn to do all this?" she asked, sitting down cross-legged in front of the fire in the vain hope it might help her stockings dry faster.

"Not Eton." He chuckled as he put the kettle on the grate, then rocked back on his heels and dusted off his hands. "Nor university either. In London, I had scores of servants to do this sort of thing." His eyes met hers. "Your aunt showed me how, actually."

"My aunt?" Lucy echoed.

"I arrived in Cornwall imminently ill-suited for the environment. Tea was something that had always been brought to me by servants, and I had no idea how to go about the mechanics of it. Whisky was far more convenient to pour, and I made a habit of pouring it early and often." He sat down himself, one leg stretched out, the other bent lazily at the knee. "Miss E recognized a fellow Londoner set adrift, having once been in my shoes. She also disapproved of spirits, in all its forms. So after she punched me, she showed me how to make tea."

Lucy choked on her surprise. "She *punched* you?"

"Well, she'd honed her instincts for self-preservation, I guess, living up here alone all those years." He stared into the flames. "I stumbled across her property during a long walk, quite by accident, mind you, and she punched me in the eye for trespassing."

Her gaze lingered over his strong profile, the curve of his cheek below his eye, where Aunt E's fist must have struck him. "I am sure you deserved it."

"Probably." He leaned forward and busied himself with their meager place settings, fiddling with her cup, not quite looking at her. "Looking back on the man I was, I could almost punch myself. I still don't know what she saw in me to prompt her to try to help. I wasn't good company. I'd . . . well, I'd dealt poorly with the loss of my sister and a broken betrothal."

"You were engaged?" Somehow, in all their flirtations, in all their arguments, it had never occurred to her to question his seeming lack of attachment. But she *should* have considered it. An unmarried man of his unique persuasion would be considered quite a catch on the marriage market—whether it be London's or Lizard Bay's.

He nodded. "For a time. Miss Highton broke off our engagement at my sister's wake."

Lucy sucked in a breath. "That's . . . *terrible.*"

"She had her reasons." He pulled the kettle off the grate and added a measure of tea leaves. "I was unfit to be anyone's husband at the time."

"I rather think you'd make a brilliant husband," Lucy protested. She laughed. "A wife would never want for tea."

He offered her a thin smile. "Well, I was rather different back then. Useless, really. I'd spent four years studying plants and rocks, only to discover that sort of knowledge provided no advantage for someone in my position. I should have studied other things as well, as you enthusiastically pointed out yesterday."

Lucy flushed. "Sorry."

"No, you were right." His smile faltered. "After university, I didn't know what to do with myself. I was a bloody marquess, not the botanist I wished to be, and I truly had no idea what that meant. I drifted through London and fell in with the wrong sort of crowd, friends who spent their nights bent over bottles instead of books. So I was drunk that day Miss Highton left me. Drunk, too, the day I met your aunt." His head moved slowly, side to side. "I had no business traipsing about the moors like that. It was a wonder I didn't fall off the cliff."

Lucy winced to hear the raw pain in his voice. She thought back to how he'd smelled faintly of brandy, three days ago on the train. She hated to . . . but she needed to ask.

"Are you still tempted by such vices?"

He stared straight ahead. "I thought I'd gotten over all of that. Three years, after all, is a long time to go without a drink. But the trip to London proved me wrong. I was so . . . *angry.* Everything I saw reminded me of her." He pulled a hand across his face. "I've been telling myself I stayed here in Cornwall because I didn't like London, but now I can't help but think staying away has simply been an excuse to avoid facing my fears." He lowered his hand to stare again into the fire. "To avoid facing *her,* and what she might think of me now."

Lucy's stomach contracted. It sounded as though he was still a little bit in love with the silly girl who had left him, even after she'd treated him so callously.

God, men were stupid.

"If you ask me, you shouldn't think of her at all," she told him. "Miss Highton should have stood by you, not left you. She should have helped you the way my aunt did. If someone really cares for you, they stay." She hesitated, thinking of how he'd not gone back to town, even when she'd ordered him to. "No matter what."

His head jerked up, and she gamely met his gaze.

Heat crackled across the space between them, heat that had nothing to do with the crackling fire or the warming kettle. She swallowed, her gaze lingering on the sensual curve of his mouth, the compelling little quirk on one side.

And then the kettle began to whistle, making Lucy jump.

The moment slid by. He poured tea into her cup, then his own, the picture of gentlemanly behavior—if one over-looked the fact that she was unmarried and he was wearing little more than a damp shirt and trousers. "There's no sugar, I'm afraid," he said.

"I am simply happy to have it hot," she assured him, accepting the cup he offered. She took a gulp, wincing as the hot black tea burned her tongue. "Damn it!" she gasped, choking for air. She rocked backward, wishing now for a sliver of ice.

Thomas laughed, and then blew gently across the surface of his own cup. "As impatient as Miss E, I see. She was forever burning her tongue."

In spite of the pain, Lucy laughed, too. "Yes, well, I have trouble believing she would have been quite as impatient tonight as I have been." She cupped her palm around the cup, waiting for it to cool. She thought of how terribly she'd acted earlier. Screaming at this man who was now pouring her tea. Shoving him out the door into the rain.

Putting both their lives in peril.

She looked down at her teacup, swallowing. "Knowing my aunt, she would have had the foresight to tie you up here, just to make sure she had a handy accomplice to start her fire."

"Ah. So her diary mentioned the incident with Mr. Jamieson, I take it?"

Lucy looked up in surprise. "Has she told you *all* her secrets?"

He shrugged. "She seemed to trust me, for some reason."

A notion struck her. If he'd been something of a confidant to her aunt, was it possible he knew about the package? "Thomas," she began, surprised to realize how comfortable his given name was beginning to feel on her lips. "Did you perchance mail a package for my aunt after she died?"

"No." He shook his head. "I would have, of course. It would have been the least I could do, after all she did for me. But she didn't ask me to do anything of that sort."

"Oh." Lucy felt disappointed. "It's just that . . . well, you seem to know an awful lot about my aunt." She looked back down at her cup. "It doesn't seem fair that you knew her better than I did."

There was a drawn-out moment of silence, where the crackling fire held sway. Finally, he sighed. "I am sorry for what I said earlier, about not visiting her enough." She looked up to discover he was watching her intently. "That was not kind of me."

"Yes, well, I should not have said those things about you yesterday either." She offered him a tentative smile. "I only said it to hurt you, and I regret it now. I know all too well how disastrous the outcome may be when you are forced to do something you are not ready for."

"You only stated the truth." he said. His jaw hardened. "I *should* take my seat in the House of Lords. You've made me think, perhaps, that I have been neglecting my duties. That staying away from London so long has carried a price I hadn't considered."

She took a sip, grateful that the tea was cooler now. "Well, I should have visited my aunt instead of expecting her to come to London. But after my father inherited the title, all contact with her ceased, and I gradually began to think of her as someone who didn't care." She frowned. "I still can't understand why she didn't just come to London. She could have made an effort to know *me*. But she never did. We only got a card from her, once a year at Christmas."

There was a cramped moment of silence, punctuated by the pop and crackle of the flames. "I don't know why either, but I do know Miss E cared about you," he said slowly. "She told me several times how much she wished she could know you better. But if I know anything about your aunt," he added, "she had her reasons for staying in Lizard Bay, and for staying away from you."

"Perhaps. But whatever they were, I haven't uncovered them yet in her diaries."

He turned back to the fire, staring at the flames. "These diaries you speak of . . . did she write anything in there about me? Or Heathmore Cottage?"

"I haven't finished reading them yet," Lucy admitted. "So far I am only up to . . ." She closed her eyes, trying to remember. "Eighteen twenty-seven." She opened her eyes to find him watching her. "Why, are you afraid my aunt will tell me all about your public drunkenness? Or your fiancée's stupidity?" she teased. "I already know all those things."

He shook his head, his mouth spreading in a rueful smile. "No. I am afraid she will tell you all the rest."

From the Diary of Edith Lucille Westmore
May 2, 1828

Today I did the unthinkable. I voted with the vicar, instead of against him.

I know . . . it was something I had sworn to never do. But the man had a brilliant idea, and I couldn't see thwarting him, just to continue making a point.

You see, Reverend Wellsbury proposed a lending library for Lizard Bay.

I have long ordered diversionary reading material from London. It gets lonely, living by oneself, and reading is one of the few pleasures that helps soften Heathmore's solitude. I have a habit of loaning my copies to some of the women in Lizard Bay when I have finished reading them, hoping to improve their narrow view of the world. You could have scraped me off the floor when Reverend Wellsbury praised my generosity—publicly, no less!—and suggested a more orderly approach, identifying new periodicals to add, such as The Illustrated London News.

Am I grateful? I don't know that I would call it that.

But I definitely feel a curious thawing where Reverend Wellsbury is concerned.

Chapter 18

All too soon the tea was gone, and the conversation drifted toward a comfortable trickle. Thomas placed his cup down on the hearth. He still couldn't believe he had shared so much of his life's story with this woman.

Far more than he had intended, though he thought he'd covered the slip well enough.

She had an almost uncanny way of drawing it out of him. Her aunt had been possessed of a similar skill, and was perhaps the only other person who'd known these bits and pieces of his life. In this very parlor Miss E had extracted the secrets from his drunken, bumbling self like a master spy, and then promised to never tell—*if* he threw out the bottle and maintained a proper foothold on the straight and narrow path.

He'd done it, too. It might have been blackmail, but there was far too much at stake back in London to risk not complying with her terms. He'd imagined—*hoped*—those secrets had been carried to the grave with Miss E. But if the diaries Lucy held told all, things were not going to be as simple as he'd presumed.

He stood up, wiping his hands on his trousers, wincing to realize how damp he still was. "I suppose we should prepare ourselves to dry out as best we can." He added another peat log to the fire and stirred the ashes until the flames leaped high. Then he motioned for her to help, and together they pushed the old sofa closer to the grate, angling it so it captured most of the heat given off by the fire. "There you are," he said, rubbing his hands. "Your bed awaits, my lady."

Damn it all if she didn't bite her lip. Parts of his body that ought to have known better insisted on taking notice. "Where will you stay?" she asked.

He could tell what she was thinking. They were alone.

He was cold and wet, too.

And they had forged a truce in the past hour, if not something more substantial.

Worse, his mind *wanted* her thoughts to wander there. Her drying chemise might be losing a bit of its transparency, but when she'd stood up and put a shoulder against the sofa, her tantalizing curves had been revealed to his far-too-eager gaze.

Christ, but she was perfect. Lushly fashioned, with full, rounded breasts and a sweet parabola of hip shifting temptingly beneath the thin white cotton. He still couldn't believe he'd ever thought her a boy. But just because she had kissed him at the inn in Salisbury and thrown herself, trembling, in his arms tonight did not mean she had abandoned all propriety.

She might be a walking, talking scandal, but she was also an innocent. Despite the lingering glances she cast his way, despite, even, the way she had leaned toward him when they were talking by the fire, the slight distance she kept from him now told him the direction of her thoughts far better than her words.

Sitting down, he pushed against the upholstered seat, as though testing the solidity of it. At least this particular item of furniture had been properly cleaned. "It *is* a rather large sofa," he teased. "I don't doubt that two people could comfortably sleep here, if the circumstances warranted." Her cheeks turned red, and he relented. "But as I am nothing if not a gentleman, I will happily sleep on the floor." He grinned at her. "Don't worry. I will be but an arm's length away if you need me to save you from the rats."

She sat down on the far edge of the sofa, keeping several feet between them. But the cushion tilted, tempting him to slide toward her.

"Do you want me to leave while you dress for the night?" Thomas stood up and shrugged out of his damp shirt and draped it across the back of the sofa, where it might have a prayer of drying by morning. His trousers would stay on—for modesty's sake, if not sanity's.

"I don't have anything dry to wear," she admitted, looking down at her hands. "Everything in my bag is soaked through."

"You mean you weren't dressed this way on purpose to greet me?" he teased, lowering himself onto the floor. The redness in her cheeks deepened. Which of course only made him laugh. He watched as she fumbled her hair into two short braids—the left side of which promptly unraveled again. She abandoned the effort to scratch at her neck.

"Is the rash still bothering you?" he asked unhelpfully. The skin of her neck below her ear was nearly as red as her cheeks, and against the stark white of her chemise, it drew the eye nearly as effectively as her other barely covered parts. But he asked because he wanted to see if they'd at least progressed to truth.

"Yes." She sighed. "How long does this terrible scourge last?"

"A few days. You are nearly at the end of it."

"It doesn't feel like the end is near."

He patted his trouser pocket. "You have only to ask."

"Lord Branston—"

"Ah, ah, ah." He wagged a finger. "Thomas, if you would."

Her lips flattened. "Thomas, then. I might like some of that salve, if you still have it."

"You didn't say please."

He heard an audible grinding of teeth in reply.

"But as I know good manners are difficult for you, I have supplied the phrase with my imagination, so there is no need to exert yourself." He stood up and sat down next to her, pulling out the tin. "Now, then. You might want to lay back."

She stretched out on the sofa and pulled her short hair to one side, baring her long, lovely neck. As he stared down at the tempting image she presented, Thomas swallowed. Christ, what was he thinking? What was he *doing*? He could just let her put the salve on herself. It would certainly be the safer choice. But some stubborn part of him insisted on accepting—*taking*—the honor. After all, he'd fought hard to earn the privilege.

But as he touched her skin and a soft moan escaped her lips, he realized how stupid such thoughts were. Had he naively imagined the salve might be a sort of peace offering? A means to pave the way to an easier friendship?

It was proving instead to be the match to a fuse.

He dipped his fingers beneath the delicate ribbon of necklace she wore, the serpentine charm winking up at him like a promise. Who needed a fire when the simple act of touching her threatened to set off sparks? As the salve warmed on her skin and slipped over his fingers, Thomas began to learn the true meaning of the phrase "trapped in hell." Because holy God, he wanted this woman. Wanted her like he'd never wanted anything—or anyone—in his life.

Wanted her more than he wanted to save Heathmore.

More than a bottle of whisky.

It might not have been the most honorable thing he'd ever done, but his fingers insisted on staying to ensure a very thorough job. After all, he was being permitted to touch her now with impunity, though the gesture paled in comparison to what his fingers really wanted to do to her.

Who knew whether this might be his last—his only—chance?

Finally, she shifted on the sofa, pulling her knees up and slipping her hands beneath her cheek. "Thank you," she told him, her eyes drifting closed.

Thomas put the cap back on the tin and laid it down beside her. "In case it begins to bother you again in the night." He pulled his oilskin from the back of the sofa and placed it down over her, laying his palm against her cheek. "Sweet dreams, Lucy."

She cracked open one eye. "Not bloody likely."

"Don't worry. The ghosts shall stay outside, and the fire will keep any rats at bay."

Both eyes flickered open. "I'm not worried about *them*," she whispered. "I know you will protect me."

He hesitated, his hand lingering over the soft curve of her cheek.

Christ, but she was lovely. *Lovely, lovely, lovely.*

He was an educated man. A peer of the realm, though it was too easy in Cornwall to forget it. He knew the names of over a thousand plants—the English *and* the Latin. And she had reduced him to mentally chanting a single, wholly inadequate, two-syllable word over and over again in his mind. "If you know I will protect you, then what worries you?" he asked.

She sighed, and in the gentle lift of her chest he felt it, the same coiled frustration he felt himself. She closed her eyes, as though seeking courage. "I don't know who's going to protect you from me."

SHE DIDN'T KNOW what had made her say such a thing.

And worse, she didn't know what he thought of her for saying it.

It was brazen. Not at all the sort of thing a proper lady should say.

Well, she *wasn't* a proper lady, was she? Wasn't even trying to pretend to be one. She was herself, and nothing else.

And he would either appreciate her for it or not.

She squeezed her eyes shut and waited to see what he would make of her confession. So much of their relationship had been built on manufactured mistrust that to utter such a stark truth now felt nothing less than earth-shattering. She'd presumed the worst of him from the start, even when he'd tried his best to explain. Presumed his interest in Heathmore—and her—was based only on selfish motives. Aunt E's diary had spurred her on, perhaps, to adopt such a strong degree of skepticism where men and her inheritance were concerned.

But by the things he knew, it was clear her aunt had trusted him. He'd proven himself a gentleman—and a patient one at that.

Gratitude thickened her throat as she considered all he had done.

Oh, but she had misjudged this man. Worse, she had misjudged herself. She'd presumed she couldn't stir a man's romantic interest. That she wasn't *meant* to, being fashioned instead for more spinsterly things, such as improving the lives of orphans. Or felons.

Or cats.

But need those qualities be mutually exclusive? In this moment, she could nearly believe that in his eyes she was more than a plain, short-haired miss.

More than a shrill, outspoken harpy.

More than a lonely, unlovable spinster.

"What are you planning to do to me, then?" His voice was husky, deeper than she'd ever heard it. It sent her head spinning in glad circles.

She opened her eyes and pushed herself up on the sofa until they were only inches apart. In her mind she counted all the times he had previously touched her. That night at the inn, when she had burned her thumb and he picked up her hand to inspect it. Their disastrous kiss, which had led to so much mistrust. Yesterday, on the street, when she'd felt the electric pull of his hand on her arm. And most recently, that sweet, seductive touch, there against her neck.

But it was a collection of small moments, not nearly enough.

She could smell the salve he had rubbed on her skin. It had already started to do miraculous things by way of relieving her discomfort. As she breathed in the sweet, pungent scent, along with the sharper underlying fragrance of snuff, she felt a spreading warmth in her stomach that had nothing to do with hot tea or peat fires.

This time *she* was the one who pressed her lips against his, taking the kiss she sought instead of waiting for it to come. He held still, his breath indrawn, as though unsure of what she meant to do but afraid of breaking the spell.

But the spell was stronger this time. So, too, was her desire.

She knew this man better now. Knew his history, his faults, his innate, maddening goodness.

He would not harm her.

But damn it, wouldn't he *kiss* her?

He held himself still, a cautious recipient, rather than an active participant. It was a kiss of the tumbling dare variety, one that was snatched in the moment and could go in five different directions. But the blasted man needed to choose which direction he would take it.

And so to help him along, she lifted her hands and clasped them behind his neck, daring him to resist. She slid her tongue along the seam of his lips, begging him to indulge in the sort of kiss she'd imagined.

Dreamed of.

And finally, he chose. He opened his mouth and his tongue swept inside her, tasting of tea and warmth and everything right. He gave a low, guttural groan, and she could feel his restraint slip away. And then they were tumbling down a path of promise, each dragging the other along for the journey.

She couldn't think of anything beyond this single point of pleasure where their lips met. She didn't know where this was heading, hadn't thought much beyond the need to feel his mouth on her own. But as she blindly pressed against him, only wanting more, it became clear the sort of kiss she'd imagined had been fashioned far short of the reality he was delivering.

She felt him *everywhere*.

In her mouth, the sweep of his tongue possessive against hers.

In her arms, which pulled him closer, seeking the friction of skin against skin.

And in her core, which swirled in a slow, liquid circle as his mouth moved over hers.

And still the path diverged from the expected. He lowered her, slowly, back onto the sofa, but didn't break off the kiss, moving instead to stretch out beside her, their limbs tangling, breaths melding. "God, what you do to me, Lucy," he muttered against her mouth, making her heart leap in happiness, because it was so closely the echo of how he made her feel.

If their first kiss had been something to forget, this one was destined to be remembered. She was panting now, wanting to climb inside his skin. His hand crept up to knead her breast, and her body shuddered at the wanton feel of his fingers there, only the thinnest layer of cotton between them. "Your breasts," he murmured, "are perfection."

And in that moment she could almost believe it was true.

His mouth left hers, and for a moment she nearly cried out an objection, but then she was biting her lip because he'd only left to blaze a trail of hot, wet kisses down her chin, tumbling over to her chest, and finally, then . . . *yes* . . . to settle around one firm nipple, drawing the cotton-clad bit of her into his mouth. Shaking with sensation, Lucy sank back against the sofa, turning herself over to this. To *him*. Whatever he wanted he could have.

Whatever he sought from her was his.

Be it her body, her house, she didn't care, as long as he didn't stop.

"Touch me," she begged. "I . . . I want more."

She could feel his body shake with suppressed laughter, his breath hot and welcome against her breast. She didn't take offense, the way she once might have. She understood now that he was a man who sought humor, that laughter was a sign of his own pleasure. She was pleasing him, somehow. And that made her want more still.

He lifted his head, his lips a wicked curve, his eyes a glittering storm. A rush of cool air hit her thigh, and she only just barely registered her chemise was sliding upward, aided by a helpful hand. And then she felt the brush of his hand on the newly exposed skin, a searing touch and yet far too gentle, there against her inner thigh.

"Here?" he asked, his words nearly a groan.

"Yes," she gasped. "There."

He duly lingered a moment, his fingers sweeping against her trembling limbs. But then he was shaking his head. "Oh, I don't think you want me to just stay there," came his low-throated chuckle. And then his hand was moving upward, swirling in lazy, frantic circles. Ahead of his path, her skin warmed in anticipation, then blazed in approval as his fingers met their mark.

And still, higher and higher he went.

"Thomas," she gasped as his hand brushed against the most achingly intimate part of her. "I think . . . yes . . . *there*," she gasped, her hips bucking off the sofa, her thighs clenched in surprise. His fingers swirled over that place he somehow knew, though Lucy herself hadn't the slightest clue what made that spot different. His fingers lingered there, slipping along that pleasure point with a pointed assurance. She felt the most amazing sensation coiling in her, like the harbinger of an electrical storm, the air snapping with fever. Her legs fell open, practically insisting on it in reaction to such a wicked, warm feeling. He could not mistake the invitation she was issuing, though she wasn't sure she understood it herself.

The truth was, she didn't know what she wanted.

She only knew she didn't want him to stop.

And yet . . . even with that pointed invitation, she could feel him start to withdraw. His touch against her core became gentler. His mouth tipped downward, his smile faltering.

And then he was pulling away, sitting up to smooth a trembling hand across her chemise, pulling it down into proper place. "I . . . I am sorry. We can't do this, Lucy."

She struggled to her elbows, feeling the familiar burn of embarrassment, though it was a softer cousin to the acute edge of humiliation she'd felt back at the inn. "I want to. Truly."

But he shook his head. "There are potential consequences to letting our passion run away with us. I can't let you take the risk, not outside of marriage. And as you seem to be a rather determined sort of spinster . . ." His voice trailed off and he offered her a thin, strained smile, his jaw tense with a question he seemed to not quite know how to ask. "I don't suppose you might consider more than just an offer for Heathmore?"

She sucked in a breath. "Are . . . are you proposing?"

"Yes." At her stunned silence, he shook his head. "Maybe." He swung his legs over the side of the sofa, sinking his head into his hands. "I don't know." The war being waged in his head was written clearly in the line of his shoulders.

She ought to be offended that he felt he must offer for her

now, when it was clearly such a difficult thing for him to do, and when he had so recently mentioned his regrets over his fiancée. It was a fumbled farce of a proposal, but despite its poor delivery, his words still made Lucy hesitate and actually consider the possibility. And that, perhaps, was what surprised her the most. Even more than the surprise of the proposal itself.

She'd publicly sworn she would never marry. She still believed such an institution served only to bind and restrict women. She'd seen the effects of an unhappy marriage firsthand, in her parent's own strained, unfaithful model. She'd seen the more devastating examples, too, in the haunted eyes and bruised faces of the women who too often dropped their children at the St. James Orphanage. And her own aunt had resorted to poisoning a friend's husband, all to make a point against the sort of violence men wielded all too readily against wives.

But she'd had at least one positive example of marriage in her life as well. Her sister Clare was married, and quite happily so. She could see now there were benefits to be had.

More kisses, for one thing. She wouldn't mind a few more of *those*.

Worse, she could almost—*almost*—believe this man wanted her. Wanted her just as she was, not as the sort of woman Society expected her to be. He didn't have to do any of this. He'd delivered her an aching pleasure, meted out in slow, tortuous degrees. Touched her reverently, as though there was something between more portentous between them than a tumbling down cottage or a ten thousand pound dowry.

But was it real? That was the question, and to believe it took an uncertain leap of faith, one she was not at all sure she could manage. She felt nervous. Possibly even afraid. To agree to his offer would mean giving her body, her dowry, her soul to another human being, one that, in spite of the pleasure he kindled beneath her skin, might—in the end—only be interested in her dowry. Or worse, her property.

That seemed an awfully big sacrifice just to get him to kiss her properly again.

"Thomas," she said, reaching out a hand to cup his face. "It was only a kiss." Though that was not exactly true. She could almost imagine she still felt his touch, there where her skin burned beneath the damp cotton. Where would he have taken her, if only his gentlemanly senses hadn't gotten the best of him? "A kiss *I* started this time, no less. Nothing to bemoan or regret."

"It was more than a kiss to me."

His hoarse voice tore at her resolve, weakening it but not quite breaking it. His proposal and all the fear that accompanied it made her breath feel knotted in her lungs.

That meant—*had* to mean—that it was the wrong decision. Didn't it?

She reached out and kissed him again, gently, once, on the lips, her mouth closed. And then she pulled away to meet his hazel eyes. "Still, I would not consider another sort of offer. I have no intention of marrying, as I've long said." She tipped her forehead against his. "But that does not mean I do not hold you in the highest regard."

He nodded, swallowing hard.

She tugged him down beside her and pulled the oilskin over them both. "You were right, I think. There is room on the sofa for two, if the circumstances warrant." She closed her eyes with a tired yawn. If there were to be no more kisses, no more breathless moans, at least they could both be dry. "And these are unusual circumstances, are they not?" she mumbled sleepily.

He didn't answer.

But thankfully, neither did he leave.

From the Diary of Edith Lucille Westmore
July 20, 1829

There is something about waking up to the promise of a new day that makes the world seem right. Heathmore might be lonely, but it is glorious on a summer morning, the moors bursting with color and bird life. I often try to take morning walks during this time of the year, and truly, I've never seen flowers like these anywhere else in England.

I like to think Heathmore is misunderstood. A spinster of a cottage, with its hidden secrets and slightly sagging roof and stiff, upturned chin, bravely facing the wind.

Like me, it is starting to feel a bit old and creaky.

But like me, I have to believe there is strength below its crusty surface.

Chapter 19

Thomas jolted awake, his arms full of soft, feminine flesh. Lucy was pressed against him, one arm draped over his chest, her body rising and falling in a peaceful rhythm. His body was more than a little enthusiastic about the discovery.

His heart, however, was conflicted.

She'd refused his offer of marriage, but then pulled him down to sleep beside her.

Christ, but could she be a more confusing mix of emotions?

He scrubbed a hand across his face. How long had they slept? The peat fire had burned down to little more than ashes, and a faint, gray-pink light flooded the room through the windows, signaling the approach of dawn and the end of the stormy weather. He looked down at her cheek where it nestled against his bare chest, following its subtle curves and hollows in the predawn shadows. The oilskin had slipped off during the night, leaving a smooth pale shoulder bared to his gaze. She looked utterly disheveled, her hair a wild golden tangle about her peaceful face. He ought to get up. Fetch more fuel, stir up some breakfast.

But he didn't want to shatter the spell.

God, but she was beautiful. The sort of woman a man would happily wake up to every morning, if given the chance. He breathed in, inhaling the warm, familiar scent of her. The novelty of waking up next to a woman was not lost on him.

The impossibility of waking up next to *this* woman nearly was.

It felt . . . right.

He had no more eloquent word for it than that. He wanted to lie like this for hours. He wanted to wake her with kisses, pull her chemise up higher until he reached greater treasures. He wanted to protect her. To push her to reconsider his offer of marriage. Show her the potential benefits to be found in such a union, instead of simply posing the question.

But he knew it was an illusion. The dream of a lifetime, dangled just out of reach.

Last night he'd nearly lost his head over this woman, and she very nearly lost her innocence. It had taken every bit of willpower in his bones—and some, no doubt, provided by divine intervention—to halt their reckless path. He'd offered her marriage, and not because he felt compelled to do so by Society's dictates. After all, no one had witnessed her compromise, and he stopped himself before anything truly regrettable happened.

He'd offered her marriage because he wanted *more*.

More breath sighs, more mind-robbing kisses. More, more, *more*.

And he might be a man with his share of personal regrets, but his history—and his sister's tragic example, as well—had shaped him into the man he was. He was not someone who could compromise an innocent and leave her to deal with the consequences. He was no longer a randy young peer, stumbling about clubs and bawdy houses, ignoring his responsibilities.

For both of them, *more* needed to mean marriage.

But last night she'd made her intentions clear.

I have no intention of marrying, she told him.

Which meant she'd enjoyed their kiss but had no notion of following the proper path to where those kisses ought to lead. And if there was one thing he'd learned about Lucy in the short time he'd known her, it was that you tried to force her hand at your own—and the world's—peril.

He shifted, trying not to wake her. But it turned out she slept like the dead, which was a good thing, considering the degree of calisthenics it required to extricate himself from their tangled sleeping arrangement. Finally, he was free of her sleepy hold and shrugging into his dry shirt. He watched her as he fumbled with his cuffs, feeling at once protective and helpless at the sight of her. One pale leg was curved upward and her chemise had rucked up around her hips, giving him a hint of garter ties and expensive silk stockings, wholly unsuitable for cliff-top trekking through Cornwall. Did she understand the dangerous game they played? The consequences of casually dabbling in desire?

And yet . . . his interest in her was more than carnal. More than casual. How long had it been since he'd felt such human contact? It felt as though he had been waiting for this his entire life. But she wasn't his to protect if she didn't want to be.

Neither, in fact, was Heathmore Cottage.

Aside from the question of funds, she would be an entirely capable mistress for Heathmore. In the course of the last few days, he'd seen the unusual strength in her, the kindness and even the patience she showed to Lizard Bay's grizzled, eccentric residents. She might have kissed him madly, but he'd also seen her apply that same unfettered passion toward trying to solve the problems of the world around her.

He smiled to himself. Had Miss E somehow known all along her niece was the right choice to protect Heathmore?

He supposed he hadn't trusted either of them enough to know their own minds. And that was a mistake he needed to correct.

He scribbled Lucy a note with paper from his satchel, then replaced the oilskin over her sleeping shoulders and tucked the letter where she would be sure to find it.

Then he turned toward the door, picking up his satchel and slinging it across one shoulder. Perhaps, if her heart was in the right place, Heathmore's future might actually be safe in her hands. And he could start, he supposed, by showing her some of it.

LUCY WOKE SLOWLY, her face turned toward the cold hearth. For a moment she hovered on the edge of uncertainty, unsure of where she was.

She breathed in, catching the dueling scents of musty air and snuff. The fire was out and sunlight flooded the floorboards beneath the parlor window. She was at Heathmore Cottage, the knowledge of which sent her heart jumping in a glad little rhythm.

But just *what* she was doing at Heathmore was something she still needed to sort through.

She stretched, testing her limbs, sorting through the acute silence of the house. The rats, it seemed, had scurried back to their daybeds. The ghosts, too, had retreated, the unearthly moaning sound having been tempered by the dawn.

Both good things, she could allow.

But where on earth was Thomas?

She placed a hand on the cushion beside her. The fabric was not warm, suggesting he must have left some time before. Her cheeks heated as she recalled the kiss from last night and the proposal that had accompanied it.

Had he awakened to regrets, and then left because she had refused him? But how could she have reacted differently? She couldn't think of marriage and imagine herself in anything besides a sort of prison. Bedlam itself could scarcely strip a woman's freedom, her choices, any more effectively. And in spite of his inarguably honorable proposal, it was clear the man was still tormented by thoughts of his former fiancée.

She couldn't help but feel a burn of jealousy at the thought.

She closed her eyes with a soft, confused sigh, only to realize that something was poking her neck. She sat up, fumbling at her neckline. Her hand closed over a folded piece of paper.

Sitting up, she unfolded it.

> I trust you've had a good sleep, given that you proved nearly impossible to wake. I will be back shortly. Stay inside, if you would. I have something important to show you when I return.
> —Branston

Warmth spread through her. He'd not left after all. And though his signature was impersonal, the notion that he had something important to show her sparked her curiosity. But he expected her to stay inside, did he?

Silly man, to expect she might be the sort of woman to follow orders.

She dressed hurriedly, though she supposed the sentiment of modesty was a bit odd when his *mouth* had been on her *breast* last night. Next, she shoved the sofa back to its proper position, though it took a good deal of nondemure ladylike cursing and grunting to move the heavy item back into place.

"There, now," she said, collecting the cups from the hearth and carrying them toward the kitchen. "No evidence of indiscretion to be had."

Although the memory lingered.

So, too, did her smile.

But as she stepped into the kitchen and took it in properly in daylight, her smile faded. The parlor might be put to rights, but the kitchen was still a mess. The cupboards were all but bare, and several of the cabinet doors were hanging by their hinges. The pump, while functional, was rusty, and wouldn't budge for her when she tried to get a bit of water from it to wash the cups.

She set the unwashed cups down and faced reality. Her empty pockets were a problem she couldn't precisely ignore, but they weren't even the worst of it. She had no idea how she was going to deal with the reality of owning a falling down house, but neither did she know even the most basic facts about how to take care of herself.

Take her walking gown, for instance. She'd been wearing it since she left London because she'd not known how to properly pack, much less tackle the terrifying chore of laundry. She flushed, recalling how last night she'd not even known how to start a fire or heat water for tea. And her rumbling stomach told her she had no idea how to fill her belly this morning either.

Perhaps she should accept Thomas's offer to buy the property and return to London.

It might truly be the best—the *only*—option available to her.

It would hurt to lose Heathmore and this connection to her aunt. She felt as though she was slowly discovering who Aunt E had been, through the diary entries and the memories of Lizard Bay's residents, but the fact was, even if she sold the property, she would still have those. It would hurt, too, to return to London and face her mother and the tatters of the Season she had ruined. But it would hurt more, she suspected, to be the one responsible for destroying the cottage her aunt had loved.

And she would surely destroy it, out of financial neglect and stupidity, if nothing else.

Thomas, at least, could afford to invest in its upkeep, though she still didn't quite understand *why* he wanted it so much.

She drifted back to the parlor and looked up at the hint of new slate peeking through the rafters. It scarcely mattered why he wanted it, she supposed, only that he did. She needed to stop distrusting his motives and put her faith in the man he'd shown her he was.

The man who'd patiently waited for her to come around and accept his offer of help.

The man who'd held himself back last night from her impulsive dash toward wantonness.

The man who'd offered her *marriage*, instead of heartbreak.

It was clear he cared about this house. The parlor gleamed with spit and polish, and the evidence of what he'd try to do by way of external repairs was impressive. The half-finished roof must have cost several hundred pounds of slate alone.

Opening the front door, she stepped outside, intending to get a better look at the half-finished roof and sort out whether she had a prayer of being able to fix it herself. But as she looked out over a glittering green ocean, the view from the front door made her forget her reason for going outside.

She gasped out loud. This . . . *this,* finally, she remembered.

A memory rushed in, of holding her aunt's hand and stepping out into a glorious morning. She remembered staring agape at the ocean, and Aunt E squeezing her hand and warning her to hold on tight so as not to tumble over the edge of the cliff. Together they'd hunted for eggs along the scrub grass, hens scattering in the wake of their treasure hunt, loudly clucking their consternation. The descendants of those half-wild hens looked warily at her now, peeking out from the narrow curtain of grass and reed.

Suddenly realizing where she might find breakfast— though still having no idea how to actually go about preparing it—Lucy stepped closer to the edge, shielding her eyes against the glint of sun off the water down below. She stopped near the edge and looked out, awed to silence, the eggs forgotten.

Well. Had she just been wondering why Thomas might want the cottage so much? She supposed he could desire the place for the view.

Who wouldn't?

The fog had lifted during the night, and the horizon line was as sharp as a surgeon's blade. Blue-green water and froth-tipped waves stretched out to that line. The sky was the sort of blue that made her blink, a sky so clear it was as though she'd never seen its like. Then again, she lived in London—she very liked *hadn't* seen its like, not since she was six years old.

She breathed in deeply, wishing Thomas were there with her, to share the moment. The beauty of the morning and the pleasure of the memory made her want to reach for him. What was it about the man that had her mind turning in directions it never had before?

She felt something odd then, a subtle shifting of the ground beneath her feet. She took a step backward, and her heart bunched—pounding—against her ribs. She'd been warned that the cliff was dangerous, and though she'd rolled her eyes, she hadn't precisely ignored the warnings. She'd been careful, after all, to stop several feet from the edge.

Apparently, the edge had other ideas.

As the earth dissolved beneath her, she out threw her hands, screaming, seeking purchase against something. *Anything.* But her nails clawed naught but mud and rocks. The ground was sliding, tumbling away, and then she was, too, skirts tangling about her ankles, her arms flailing against the air.

And then she slid over the edge toward the sharp rocks below.

From the Diary of Edith Lucille Westmore
January 5, 1830

Sometimes, I am my own worst enemy.

When I first arrived in Cornwall, I was determined to preserve my solitude. Letting the road to town grow over seemed like a good idea at the time, but now I can't help but wonder if I have cut off the arm to the very lifeblood that sustains me. It's been a long, lonely winter and it's scarcely half over. It has snowed for a week straight, and the icy path has kept me confined to my house and away from the warmth and companionship to be found in town.

This morning, I stood on the edge of the cliff and screamed, as loud as I could, just to see if my voice would reach town. But no one came.

Either they can't hear me . . .

Or I've led them to believe I don't care.

Chapter 20

The cottage was just rounding into sight when Thomas heard Lucy's scream.

Immediately, he felt that rush of panic that can only come from knowing you have failed someone you were charged to protect.

He'd felt that way only twice before. Once, when his sister had shown up on his doorstep, frightened and very noticeably pregnant. And then again at her funeral wake, facing the unimaginable loss of her even as he drunkenly questioned her choices that had brought about the necessity of a closed casket.

He'd *known* the cliff side was unstable, especially with all the rain last night.

And if he'd hurt Lucy with his neglect, he'd never forgive himself.

He tore toward the house, his satchel slapping against his thighs. He could see the raw earth, the new jagged rim, and knew instinctively what had happened, damn her adventurous heart. She'd wandered too close to the water-logged edge and it had given way. He began tossing up prayers for a miracle to a God who'd rarely answered his entreaties these past three years.

Damn it all, why hadn't he been more specific in his note? *Stay inside*, he'd told her.

Stupid, stupid, to not tell the girl *why* she ought to heed his warning.

"Lucy!" he shouted, his feet sliding on the wet ground, his voice a hoarse knot of terror. "Can you hear me?"

A feeble voice reached up toward him. "I . . . I am all right." She sounded winded. Frightened.

But whole.

This time the words he muttered to God were words of thanks. He skidded to a halt several feet from the edge and lowered himself to the ground, fearing what was left might shift again. Sliding forward on his hands and knees, he inched forward, trying to distribute his weight so as not to create undue pressure points on the fragile earth. Peering over the edge, he exhaled in relief to realize she had landed on a shelf of rock, some twenty feet or so below.

She was standing still as a dormouse, her arms tucked tight against her, a blue backdrop of sky reminding him just how dangerous a position she was still in.

"Are you injured?" he called down.

She peered up at him, her face white as a bedsheet, blond hair flying about her dirt-smudged cheeks. "Not badly. A few scrapes. I do not doubt I shall be sore tomorrow." She gestured to the ledge beneath her feet. "Can you get me out?"

"Wait here. Don't move, not even an *inch*."

She pursed her lips. "You don't have to be so short with me."

"Christ above, Lucy, there was a very good reason I told you to stay inside, and there is a very good reason I don't want you to move an inch now!" And that was because he feared she was an inch—or less—away from sending the whole bloody cliff sliding into the surf below and snapping her stubborn little neck.

Battling back panic, he sprinted toward the cottage and returned with a length of rope from the peat shed. Holding his breath, he threw it down. The rough fibers snagged on jagged bits of soil, but it slithered down to gather at her feet. Thank God the ledge was closer to the top of the cliff than the bottom. "Tie it around your waist," he instructed. That way, if the worst happened she would at least be caught before she tumbled to her death.

She did as he asked, and he was relieved to see she at least knew how to tie a knot.

Miss E would be proud, his mind unhelpfully supplied.

Yes, well, Miss E had known better than to get too close to the edge.

He carefully climbed to his feet and widened his stance. The earth seemed to be holding. Exhaling in relief, he tried to pull her up. But the girl was solidly built, and the rope's friction against the edge of earth was worrisome, sawing against the tenuous new rim. He cursed beneath his breath as bits of mud rained down. He didn't know how fragile the remaining earth was, and he didn't want to risk another landslide.

"See if you can climb up," he called down, tying the rope about one shoulder and trying to hold it away from the edge. "Do it the way a sailor would, your feet knotting in the rope. Keep your body away from the cliff," he instructed.

She tried, he'd give her that, but he could see it wasn't going to work. Her skirts kept tangling treacherously about her ankles, and despite several attempts, she only made it a foot or so up the rope before her grip slackened and she slid back down again. Worse, the shower of rocks and mud raining down intensified, making his gut tighten in worry.

"Take off your skirts and corset," he directed, cursing beneath his breath.

She frowned. "If you are trying to charm me—"

"Lucy!" he growled.

"All right." She grinned, the gesture looking out of place against the stark whiteness of her face. "No need to shout." Her smile was probably meant to reassure him, but her voice trembled a bit, quite ruining the effect.

She untied the rope—making his stomach clench for the half minute's vulnerability—and pulled off her heavy clothing and corset, leaving them bunched on the ground. Then she retied the rope and tried to climb up again, this time in her chemise. She got a little farther without the burden of all that fabric, but once again made it only a few feet before sliding back down. "I . . . I am afraid it's not going to work." She shook her head. "I'm not the most athletic of souls." Her pale face mooned up at him. "You should know I can't throw worth a shite either."

In spite of the fear he felt, he somehow forced a hollow chuckle. "Oh, I don't know. Your aim last night showed remarkable promise." He could still smell the snuff on his hair and clothing. "And didn't you say you climbed out of a window to get to Cornwall?"

She grimaced. "Yes, well, that wasn't done very gracefully. I usually do these things wearing trousers, you know."

That, finally, brought a real smile to his face. "Do you want me to take off my trousers and toss them down to you?" he teased, even as he tried to sort out another way to bring her up. If he climbed down, he could boost her from beneath. Carry her up one-handed, if he had to.

He'd go down, and willingly, but would the ledge hold them both? She had a rope tied about her. At least *she* would be saved if the worst happened.

"No." He heard her puff of laughter. "You'll need your trousers on when you explain to the authorities how I came to toss *myself* over the cliff." Despite her attempt at humor, she blinked up at him, her lower lip trembling. He focused on that small evidence of fear, feeling glad for it. If she was frightened, it meant she at least understood the precariousness of the situation. "Perhaps you should go to town and find some other people who might help?" she asked.

He shook his head. "Too risky." He didn't add that only the oldest, most stubborn souls still lived Lizard Bay. Those who could still earn an honest wage had moved to Marston when the fishing industry had collapsed. There wasn't anyone left in town with the strength to pull a rope. But that explanation would only frighten her more. Some hundred or so feet below lay a rocky coast. He could see the rocks lying in wait, sharp as an axe blade, eager to greet objects falling from above.

He would not, under any circumstances, head back to town and leave her in such danger.

Sorting through his options, he settled on the only way he could see even a glimmer of success. He wrapped the top end of the rope around a large jutting rock that rested a dozen feet back from the new edge of the cliff. His knowledge of geology told him it was very likely part of a larger underground constellation of granite, and given the barren nature of the landscape, it was the closest thing to an anchor he was likely to find.

But that didn't mean it wouldn't prove false if the entire cliff went tumbling down.

With the rope as secure as he could make it, he began to lower himself, one careful hand at a time, until finally he was putting one foot down gingerly, then the other. He exhaled slowly as the ledge held. In a second she was plastered against him, his hands full of soft, trembling skin, his nose filling with the scent of her.

"I . . . I can't believe you came down for me," she gasped.

"How could you believe I wouldn't?" He lowered his lips to her wild halo of hair. Christ, what this woman did to him. Tied him up in knots, then shook him back out. "I would do anything for you, Lucy."

She pulled back, blinking up at him with a tremulous

smile. "Well. It seems you've proven once and for all you don't have plans to kill me."

He frowned. "You weren't really serious with that nonsense yesterday about tossing you over the cliff, were you?"

She shook her head. "No. I was only trying to vex you."

"Ah." His lips twitched, even as his mind turned itself over to the problem of how he was going to get them out. "A mission you've accomplished all too well this morning."

She stilled. "I am sorry."

"No regrets, Miss Westmore. And no apologies either. It's not your style." He looked up, assessing the twenty foot climb that awaited them. A short enough distance, one he could make easily on his own. With his arms full of Lucy, however, it was going to be a bit trickier. Though he kept one wary hand on the rope and one on her, the ground seemed reassuringly steady beneath their feet. And from this new lower vantage point, he could see the earth had slid cleanly away from the cliff, leaving a wall of newly exposed rock.

"It seems solid enough," she murmured beside him, echoing his thoughts.

"Yes, it appears to be granite," he murmured, though the thick, telltale white veins running through the bedrock were something else entirely. He winced as he took them in, his knowledge of the geology of the land far too sharp.

Well. That was *one* of Heathmore's secrets that was hidden no more.

But he would deal with that later.

For now, he had a spinster to save.

He pulled her against his chest, one arm wrapped firmly around her, the other still clutching the rope. Given the fact that the remaining bit of cliff seemed made of rock, he could see now that they were probably safe enough from further calamity.

But that didn't mean he couldn't keep her close as his own skin.

Just in case, his brain tried to whisper. But it wasn't the entire truth. He wanted her close for reasons more selfish than her mere safety.

"Thomas," she whispered, blinking up at him, but not trying to extract herself from his grip. If anything, it felt as though she burrowed closer. "What are you waiting for? We *do* need to sort out how we are going to get us both back up."

"In a moment," he growled, lowering his head. "First, a token. I've played the hero today. It's customary to offer a kiss."

He claimed her mouth fiercely, savoring the small gasp of surprise and pleasure that escaped her lips. He pulled her flush against him, welcoming the heave of her breasts against his chest. There was no time for murmured pleasantries or acquiescence, no time for second-guessing or planned seductions. He was driven by the same demons that had brought him down that rope: grab whatever piece of her he could, for as long as she would let him, and don't look back. And through the addled haze of desire, he could see she wasn't resisting in the slightest.

Finally, he pulled back, his breath an absolute tangle in his lungs. But he didn't loosen his grip. Could she feel the pounding of his heart, there where their bodies met? It felt absolutely right to kiss this woman on the edge of a catastrophe, the ocean in their ears and the Cornwall sunshine beating down on them. As he stared down into her dirt-smudged face, realization sank in. He was meant to marry this woman. He'd never felt so sure about anything in his life.

But feeling right and *being* right were not at all the same thing.

And he couldn't quite shake the worry that she might yet resist, for no reason other than sheer stubbornness.

LUCY OPENED HER eyes as she tried in vain to catch her breath.

Good heavens. What had just happened?

She pulled in a great lungful of air, but did not pull away from Thomas. Her lips still burned from the feel of his mouth on hers, bruising and promising all at the same time. This had been yet another sort of kiss, far different than the last two they had shared. And more than the kiss, she could feel the unmistakable ridge of flesh pressed tight against her belly.

Suffice it to say, she'd never once imagined herself the sort of girl who might inspire such . . . *chivalry.*

She pressed closer, welcoming the evidence of his desire. He might still be tormented by thoughts of his broken betrothal, but it was clear he wanted her.

Wanted *her,* short-haired Lucy Westmore, vociferous spinster and climber of trees.

Even as her pulse bounded with the thrill of such knowledge—even as the thought of where they stood made her head spin—Lucy realized with a start she wasn't afraid. She felt an unshakable faith in the way his arms held her, as though he wouldn't let go until their feet were back on solid ground. The realization of what that meant began to seep through the pleasure of the drugging kiss he had just delivered.

She trusted him.

And not only trusted that he would save her from a fall. She trusted he was here for the right reasons, that he had her—and Heathmore's—best interests at heart.

She stared up at him in wonder. His eyes were some shade of the soil, rich brown and green, inviting her back. "Thomas." She framed his face in her hands, running her fingers across his jaw, reveling in the contrasts to be found there. "I am so, so sorry I ever doubted you."

"Lucy—"

She pressed a finger against his lips. "You have been honest with me from the start, and I didn't appreciate it for the gift that it was. There was no reason, none whatsoever, for me to have distrusted you as I did. I have been contrary and presumptuous and naive, but I would be honest with you now. You are an honorable man. You have risked your life to save me." She hesitated. "And if you would promise to take proper care of my aunt's cottage, I can think of no one to whom I would rather sell Heathmore."

He stiffened. "There is no need to make a hasty decision. You haven't seen the remainder of the property yet in daylight. You may decide you don't need to sell it at all."

She shook her head, knowing it was the truth. "I can't afford the property. It doesn't matter how much I want it, I can't continue the repairs you have started. I believe you will be a good steward of the trust I would place in you."

His arm tightened around her. "We could continue those repairs together."

"Thomas. Be serious." She batted him on the arm. "You can't continue to spend money on a house someone else owns."

"I *am* being serious. Marry me, Lucy. It would solve everything."

She caught her breath, more than halfway tempted to just say yes and be damned the consequences. And not because she'd spent the night wrapped in his arms, or because he presented such a ready solution to the dilemma of what she was going to do about Heathmore.

It was because of how he made her feel.

Before she'd met Thomas, she never imagined feeling this way. Never *once* imagined her future to be shaped as one half of a pair.

Never once imagined someone she cared about might offer for her.

Last night, when he proposed so awkwardly, she'd worried that he only offered out of some misplaced sense of honor. Worse, she'd frightened herself by actually considering it.

She could imagine no worse scenario than finding herself trapped in a marriage where only *she* felt such things.

She was far more confused on that front this morning, after seeing him climb down to rescue her. He cared for her. He *must*. But once again her breath felt knotted in her lungs.

What did that mean? Did it mean she was bound for a different path, or just that she lacked the imagination to see the potential in the road he offered? Aunt E's words—the very first entry in the diary—echoed in her head.

A wife belongs to her husband.

But a woman alone belongs to herself.

Lucy had always imagined her life would be spent focusing on grand causes, changing the world one unjust practice at a time. But a body couldn't do that if they were bound in marriage to another. She placed her hands against his chest, pushing him back an inch, seeking space to breathe and think.

His jaw hardened. "Is this to be another set of negotiations, then?"

She shook her head. She felt confused, and the temptation of his arm around her middle wasn't helping unmuddle matters in the slightest. "I . . . I just need to think on it."

And she couldn't do *that* when she was sighing contentedly in his arms.

She took another step away, and then another. Why did it feel as though she were going in the entirely wrong direction?

"Lucy, be careful," he warned.

Suddenly, she was wobbling. She cried out in fear.

But he was there beside her, his hand closing over her arm. He hauled her back against his chest, his arms closing tight. She pressed her face against his shirt, smelling cloves and tobacco, feeling the solid thump of heart and muscle and promise beneath her cheek.

"Can't you see?" he growled in her ear. "It is going to be the death of me if I can't be the one to keep you out of trouble."

She closed her eyes, savoring the feel of him, even as his words kindled a deeper uncertainty. Damn it, now he'd saved her life *twice*.

How could she be thinking to repay that debt with disappointment?

"Lucy!"

The voice pushed down at them from twenty feet above. Her eyes snapped open to see her father's face, peering over the edge.

She'd been expecting him to come, of course. The fear that her father would show up was part of what had pushed her these past few days to reach Heathmore as soon as possible. But there was an unanswered question hanging in the balance.

And she couldn't help but wish she had a few more minutes to think.

"Are you hurt?" Her father's voice had shifted. Anger churned beneath his curt tone. He looked like hell, his hat askew, dark smudges of exhaustion below his eyes. She was used to seeing her father mad, having caused such reactions frequently enough over the years.

But she'd never seen him look quite *this* angry.

"I am fine, Father," she called up, trying to extricate herself from Thomas's tight grip. But as she braced herself for the expected tirade and lecture, Lucy realized something odd. Her father wasn't glowering at *her*, though she inarguably deserved it.

He was glowering at the man standing beside her.

The man who was all that stood between her and the bottom of the cliff.

"I'll thank you to take your hands off my daughter, Lord Branston," he snarled.

Lucy could feel Thomas's fingers tighten over her arm. "With all due respect, Lord Cardwell, I don't think that's a very good idea."

The distinctive sound of a hammer cocking cut through the air. Lucy caught the gleam of metal in her father's hand, the barrel of a revolver pointing straight at Thomas's chest.

"No!" she screamed, suddenly realizing just what sort of picture this little scene painted.

She was wearing her chemise.

Her dress was bunched on the ground.

And she was tied up with a rope and plastered against his chest.

Oh, God.

"Lucy," her father said, his voice hoarse. The barrel lowered, aimed somewhere now in the vicinity of Thomas's upper trouser area. "Has the bastard touched you?"

She hesitated, shocked at her father's ferocious display of protectiveness. And unfortunately, the answer to that question wasn't exactly a resounding no. But the explanation was going to take more than a few mumbled seconds, and she wasn't sure her tongue was working properly at the moment, tied up as it was in fear and surprise.

"Then I hope you've a second in this town who will stand up with you, Lord Branston," her father snarled, raising the barrel again, this time to point toward Thomas's head. "Because you're going to need one."

From the Diary of Edith Lucille Westmore
November 14, 1830

Is there anything lonelier than a life built entirely of secrets?

No one here knows me, not really. Oh, they know who I have become, but not who I was once. Even my name is a secret, one I have zealously guarded from the day I arrived in Lizard Bay. Through the years, I have taken such care that no one in town suspects my connections in London. If they knew I was Lord Cardwell's daughter, who knew what might happen?

Worse, Heathmore hides secrets of its own. I must confess, as my money wears thin I wonder if I might need to consider a more mercenary approach to the property. I cannot live on good intentions and fresh air, and I've no more jewels to sell. Yet such a choice would destroy the very life I have built. Worse, I'd have to sign my true name on a contract, and solicitors would be involved. There would be no hiding my connections then.

And then, of course, there is the biggest secret of all, the one that carries me down to town so often, particularly on Fridays and Sundays. The one I refuse to confess, even in my diary. Because putting words down on paper would be admitting I have been wrong, all these years. And a lady never admits she is wrong.

Chapter 21

*T*homas raised his hands, though he was loath to let Lucy go.

It didn't make him happy to relinquish his hold. After all, there were two dangers they were facing. One was obvious, aiming down at them above the cliff. The other was waiting below, the sharp rocks eager to claim their first victim.

"Father, give me a chance to explain," Lucy twitched beside him, her agitation palpable. "There is to be no duel. I absolutely forbid it. And put the damn gun away. You know you can't shoot the side of a building in broad daylight."

The barrel slowly lowered. The sound of the hammer uncocking had Thomas breathing a sigh of relief. It seemed the girl even cursed around her father, a fact that ought to make him smile. But this was not the time to give into such an impulse. In terms of explanations, he was curious what Lucy had in mind, because the truth was rather likely to send that barrel pointing again at his head

"We need to get her to safety," he called up to Lord Cardwell. "Can you haul the rope up while I push her up from beneath?"

Lucy turned to him, shaking her head. "I want you to go up first. I'm safe enough with the rope tied about my waist."

"No!" Thomas growled. In that moment, he heard, as well, Cardwell's nearly simultaneous echo. Thomas looked up at her father, his irritation with the man easing somewhat. It was hard to be annoyed with Lord Cardwell when it was clear he loved his daughter and was concerned with her safety.

"Lucy, you must come first." Cardwell's voice was hoarse with worry. "I insist upon it."

Lucy put her hands on her hips. "Do you promise you won't shoot him once I am up?"

Cardwell's mouth turned down in a frown. "I . . . er . . ."

A snarl of irritation escaped those lovely lips. "Throw the revolver over the edge."

Cardwell's face reddened. "Now Lucy, be reasonable . . ."

Thomas winced. If he learned one thing in the week since he'd met her, it was that telling this woman to be reasonable was an entirely stupid thing to do.

"No, *you* are the one who needs to be reasonable." She took a step toward the edge and pointed to the empty space beyond. "I mean it, Father. I am not playacting here. This isn't one of Geoffrey's pranks. And the longer you wait, the longer it will take to hear my explanation."

There was a muttered oath, and then the revolver came sailing down. The sound of metal on stone clattered up from below.

"I knew that would work," she whispered, offering Thomas a cheeky smile. She squared her shoulders and nodded. "Right, then. Up I go."

This time her progress was solid. With Thomas working from below, boosting her bum against his shoulder, and her father hauling the rope from the top, she half climbed, half hung, until she was being pulled over the edge and her face was peering down at him beside her father's.

Thomas smiled up, relieved to see her safe. And then it was his turn, his progress sure and swift as he went up the rope, hand over hand, welcoming the burn of the rope fibers against his sweating palms. It was only after he reached the top that he realized the obvious.

Damn it all, but Lucy's skirts and corset were still on the ledge below.

"Well?" Cardwell crossed his arms, his frown deepening as his gaze shifted between them. "I think I have been more than patient." His gaze hardened on Thomas. "And I would have you know that my gun may be gone, but I still have a knife in my possession."

Lucy waved a hand in the air. "There is no need to resort to threats. It is really quite innocent."

Her father's eyes narrowed. "It doesn't *look* innocent."

She gestured toward the cottage. "Well, it all started with the rats."

"The rats?" her father echoed with disbelief. "Have they chewed off your skirts, then?"

"Actually, I should probably go further back." She began to collect the rope, coiling it about her arm and shoulder. She seemed outwardly unruffled, but Thomas had come to know her these past few days. He could tell by the way her teeth were gnawing her lower lip that she was thinking, hard and fast. "Lord Branston escorted me here yesterday to see Heathmore, and I fell off the cliff while . . . er . . . inspecting the property."

"That scarcely explains how he came to be down there with you *today*." Cardwell's gaze turned back to him, and Thomas felt the burn of a father's ire. "Or how your skirts came to be removed."

"It is all very simple." She reached the end of the rope. "My skirts were in the way."

"In the way of *what*?"

At her father's enraged growl, she took a step toward the

rock where the rope was still tied and began to tug on it. "You know, this is really knotted quite tightly," she said. "Do we have anything we might cut it off with?"

With a growl of frustration, her father pulled a wicked-looking blade from his coat pocket and handed it over.

"Thank you." She cut the rope free and then promptly sent the knife sailing over the edge of the cliff as well.

"Lucy!" Her father's voice was now as hopelessly knotted as the rope had just been.

Any meekness in her manner vanished along with the knife. "Well, I can't bloody well think of a proper explanation when you are shouting at me and waving a weapon about!"

"I wasn't waving it about!"

"Well, you were threatening to! And proving quite the idiot about it, too."

"Young lady, you will not speak to me that way—"

"I'm not a young lady! I am twenty-one years old!"

Thomas stepped between them, raising his hands in a bid for peace. Or quiet. *Something* beyond shouts and accusations. They both fell abruptly silent.

"May I have a chance to explain?" he asked tersely. They nodded, their faces matching shades of red. He turned to Cardwell, determined to erase the censure he saw on the man's face, to make him see his daughter the way he himself did: brave and resilient and unwavering in her desire to set things right. "You should be proud of your daughter, sir."

He looked unconvinced. "I should?"

Thomas nodded. "She has proven herself a shrewd negotiator. She sensed from the start something wasn't right about my offer for the property."

"Not right?" Cardwell echoed, looking more confused than angry now.

"I tried to convince her to sell me Heathmore for less than it was worth, and she insisted on coming to conduct a proper inspection of the property so she could determine its true value."

Cardwell blinked. "She . . . ah . . . she did?"

"She drives a hard bargain, too. Has me up to one thousand pounds."

Cardwell's eyes bulged in his head. He looked at his daughter, his mouth open in surprise. "She does?"

But Lucy was glaring at him, no doubt remembering that moment in Salisbury when she'd choked out the outrageous amount. "If you recall," she said tightly, "I did not agree to the terms of that particular offer."

"I would gladly give you my name," Thomas said bluntly.

"I don't want your name. I have a perfectly good name," came her strangled response. "Why do men always think women want a new *name*?"

"Lord Cardwell." Thomas turned, prepared to ask the man for his daughter's hand in marriage—a proper proposal, done right. He knew she cared for him. Could feel in his bones the rightness of them together. But Cardwell wasn't listening. Instead, he was scratching his head, standing by the rock where the rope had just been tied. Thomas saw him run a hand across its white-marbled surface, heard him muttering under his breath.

"Lord Cardwell?" Thomas called, trying to pull his attention back to the matter at hand.

But the man was striding away now, shaking his head. He peered over the edge of what remained of the cliff, then turned back around, his face red with anger. "Well *done*, Lucy."

She stared at her father, her mouth open. "I . . . ah . . . thank you?"

"I didn't see it at first." Cardwell pointed a finger at Thomas. "But *you* did, brilliant girl. He's tried to swindle us!"

Thomas felt a knot begin to grow at the pit of his stomach.

"Don't you mean he's tried to swindle *me*?" Lucy asked archly.

Missing her point, Cardwell pointed back to the newly exposed cliff face. "I missed it before, during my first visit. I was too upset over Edith's death, and I didn't understand why she would leave Heathmore to you when it seemed all but worthless. But damn it all, there's *tin* on this property, isn't there?" His voice rose in volume and his finger came back to stab the air in Thomas's direction. "You, sir, have tried to steal my daughter's inheritance!"

The knot in his stomach began to tighten. In fact, it began to feel a bit like a noose, particularly when Lucy turned troubled blue eyes in his direction.

"Lucy, I can explain."

"Is this what you meant in your note? What you wanted to show me this morning?" she whispered, her voice anguished. "That there is tin on the property?"

Thomas hesitated. It would be so easy to lie. To nod and play along.

But he had given her far too many omissions of the truth already. And so he shook his head. "No. I had planned to show you something else." Anything, in fact, but this. He gestured to the moors, to the wild barren fields that stretched out above the cottage. "I wanted to show you what lay on the grounds." At her look of confusion, he stooped down and fumbled in the satchel on the ground, bringing out a fistful of heath—wilted, now, in all the excitement and delay. "I wanted to show you this."

There was a strained moment of silence, where only the wind and the ocean held sway as she stared down at his hand. "You wanted to show me *grass*?" she finally whispered.

He stifled a growl, frustrated beyond reason at the awkwardness of the conversation, one he had no hope of remedying in the moment. "Not grass. Heath. A flower, actually."

"It doesn't look like a flower."

"It flowers later, in summer. The point is, it is indescribably rare." From the satchel he pulled out the rock he'd dug up this morning, its green and gray dirt-crusted surface hiding its potential beauty a little *too* well. "There is this, as well."

Her lips firmed. "A rock?"

"Not just a rock. Lizardite." He gestured toward her neck. "It can be fashioned into serpentine, like the necklace around your neck."

Her brow puckered and her fingers drifted toward the pendant.

"I know it doesn't look the same," he said hurriedly. "Not yet. It has to be polished first. But it is part of the rare geology of this peninsula, found nowhere else in England. And there is more, if you would let me show you."

He could tell, by her lengthening frown, that she didn't understand. Either that or she didn't care to try. The problem was, you couldn't *tell* someone something like this. You needed to show them, needed time to explain how rare and precious and *important* such things were.

But time was something she didn't appear to be willing to give him.

"You wanted to show me flowers and rocks," she said flatly. She straightened her shoulders and looked him in the eye, her dirt-smudged face stiff with disappointment. "Well then, that makes me very sorry I pitched my father's pistol and knife over that cliff, Lord Branston."

LUCY'S THOUGHTS TUMBLED ungracefully about in her skull.

Tin. It would need to be mined. Refined. Presumably, the entire cliff might need to be dug out. Possibly even the entirety of the property. She hadn't a clue as to its value, but she suspected it was something more significant than one thousand pounds.

With or without her maidenhead.

Her father was standing beside her, glaring at Thomas every bit as fiercely as she was. As though he was *proud* of her. She had little enough experience with the notion, but in the shadow of what appeared to be Thomas's overwhelming betrayal, she wanted to lean toward that now. It was perhaps the only thing holding her together. One pull and it might all unravel.

"I would ask you to leave now, Lord Branston," she choked out, even as she had to school her mouth to skip over his given name. Had she felt humiliated that day at the inn, when she'd first imagined his interest had been feigned to tempt her to sell Heathmore? That experience was a pale cousin of the mortification she felt now.

"Lucy—" he began.

"You lied to me," she ground out. "Lied to the town, too. There is tin here, perhaps enough even to save Lizard Bay from its slow, steady slide toward nothingness." He'd tried to steal it, and for what? To hide it away, never to be disclosed? Or was he trying to acquire the property so he alone would be poised to benefit, at the expense of everyone else?

Because that, after all, was what he'd gain in the marriage he'd been pursuing.

Her body. Her soul.

Her goddamned property.

"Lucy, please." Thomas's voice was strained. "Give me a chance to show you what I am talking about. The heath and the lizardite are only part of it. There is more of value to Heathmore than you think. And a mining operation will not be the boon to the town you think it will be. It would destroy what makes this part of the coast unique."

The sound of her name on his lips and the hoarsely uttered "please" nearly undid her resolve. She could almost— *almost*—believe he was sincere.

But she shook her head. "You had plenty of chances to show me already," she pointed out, thinking of the long minutes they had stood on that narrow slice of ledge, minutes where he'd distracted her with a heart-stopping kiss instead of discussing the fact that the entire cliff face was riddled with veins of tin. "And if I were you, I'd go quickly." She held up one arm. "After all, I still have a rope."

His jaw hardened. "You are bloody stubborn, you know that?"

She raised her chin. "So I've been told."

He looked in her father's direction, as though he was seeking help from that quarter. Stupid man, to think he would find a kinder reception there. Ten minutes ago she was all that had stood between her father's pistol and his bollocks.

"I believe my daughter asked you to leave, Branston," her father said, crossing his arms. "You are fortunate I don't call the magistrate."

In spite of herself, Lucy rolled her eyes. As if old Bentley—the town's magistrate and mayor—could hear an explanation like this and think they were talking about anything other than "sin."

Thomas's gaze swung back to her. "I won't give up on this," he told her, his words like heavy weights, aimed squarely at her heart. "I won't give up on *us*, Lucy. And when you've had a moment to think on it, when you decide you want to see the rest of it, you have only to ask me to show you." Then, with a curt nod, he left, striding down the path that led back to town.

She stood, silent, watching him go.

"Well then. Good riddance, I say." Her father came up to stand beside her, his hand settling on her shoulder. "It seems like we might want to seek some other offers for Heathmore."

She nodded, trying not to care that he continued to say "we" instead of "you."

"I could make some inquiries in Marston before we go back to London," he offered.

Lucy grimaced. *London.* The word sounded foreign to her ears. She thought of all that waited her there. Balls and gowns and useless, endless parties. Mother, and her interminable frowns. "All right," she said, not knowing what else to do.

She was so bloody confused. She was usually quick to leap to action, to fix whatever problem loomed large, but in this, she wasn't sure how to proceed. "But I do not want to sell Heathmore, not without knowing all my options," she warned.

Her father's fingers tightened on her shoulder, but his face softened as he nodded down at her. "Of course, Lucy, I am sorry for not trusting your judgment before. I don't approve of the fact you ran away and left without even a note, but I can see you had reason to come here. You saved us from a tremendous mistake."

She exhaled, the praise feeling awkward to her ears. So, too, did the word "us." Hadn't she saved *herself* from the mistake? At least Thomas had respected the fact this was her decision to make—even if he'd hidden some of the facts from her.

"I would like to stay in Lizard Bay while you place those inquiries." She hesitated. "Mrs. Wilkins has been telling me stories about Aunt E." And the thought of going to Marston, the town her aunt had hated so much, made her feel nearly as ill as the thought of Thomas's betrayal. She held up a hand as her father opened his mouth. "And before you go on about my needing a chaperone, I would remind you I came here without one."

After a moment, her father nodded. "All right. As long as you stay with Mrs. Wilkins and don't wander too far afield." He hesitated. "I want you to know I am proud of you, Lucy. You've a solid head on your shoulders. Your brother could learn a thing or two from you."

"Thank you." She stared down at the ground, feeling miserable, rather than pleased. How long had she wanted such affirmation? It seemed nearly her whole life.

But at what cost had she earned it?

Her gaze fell on the satchel that Thomas had left behind. It was a sign of how upset he was that he'd forgotten it. The bulging sides made her wonder if the contents might contain samples of tin and rock, collected from her property and spirited away for analysis. But when she picked it up and peered inside, she saw only an odd mix of plants, their roots carefully bundled in cloth and twine. A few more lizardite rocks, their green mottled hue scarcely recognizable as the same rock in the pendant about her throat. And, near the bottom, dirt-smudged but unmistakable, a thick sheath of papers, addressed to the Linnean Society of London.

She caught her breath at the utter lack of evidence for his nefariousness.

Plants. Rocks.

Oh, God. The man was obsessed with nature. How many unintelligible scientific names had he quoted to her in the course of their brief but memorable acquaintance? Worse, holding the satchel now reminded her of how he'd carried both his own bag and hers up the wet path last night. And this morning, when he'd pulled out the bunch of heath, drooping and wilted . . .

How could he be so kindly in one moment and scheming in the next? She didn't know, but the answers weren't going to fall out of the sky.

Perhaps, though, they might fall out of her aunt's diaries.

She glanced back toward the cottage, where the volumes were still tucked inside her bag—the very bag *he* had carried up here for her. Had Aunt E known about the tin on the property, and held opinions of her own on the right way to proceed? Lucy was scarcely halfway through the third volume. Any clues must be buried in the later passages. The morning had uncovered one dramatic secret, one she wished she'd known earlier.

Could more be waiting?

"I need to fetch my bag before we go," she mused, looking down to realize with horror she was standing out of doors in only her chemise and stockings. "And put on my spare dress," she said in a rush, wincing at the thought of how this must all look to her father. She might be a scandalous spinster, but she didn't relish the thought of strolling back to Lizard Bay dressed like this. "It's in the house."

"You stayed here last night?" her father asked, looking suddenly a little less proud of her. "With *him*?"

"Nothing inappropriate occurred. We were trapped by the weather." A partial truth, perhaps. Last night had been . . . well, in the harsher light of morning, perhaps the right word might be "confusing." She sighed, staring down the path that had just swallowed him.

Never trust a vicar farther than you can throw him, Aunt E had written.

Apparently, one shouldn't trust a marquess either.

But at what point did she need to begin to trust herself?

Though it is hard to admit out loud, there are times when I miss my family. I miss the sound of voices, a house full of people. I miss my brother, and even Father, with his blustering, forceful views on the place of women.

Perhaps I am simply waxing nostalgic. It isn't that I hold any regrets. But for better or worse, the lending library and its new periodicals have shifted my awareness of London and the things I left behind. The Illustrated London News has proven a particular source of comfort and despair, and I find myself eagerly searching for some word of my family. Yesterday, I found it.

A birth announcement for Miss Lucille Westmore. My brother's child.

And apparently my namesake.

In nearly twenty years I've not been brave enough to send a note to Father, fearing that despite the passage of time, he might still swoop down onto Cornwall and try to force me into an asylum. But my brother . . . there is an avenue to forgiveness I had not previously considered. Perhaps a congratulatory note on the birth of my niece might not be out of order.

And oh, to eventually be able to see my niece, to hold her in my arms . . . that would be the sweetest of impossible dreams

Chapter 22

"I've brought you a letter, Miss L."

At the sound of the boyish voice hovering at the doorway, Lucy looked up from her aunt's diary. Welcoming the distraction of some conversation and the chance to rest her eyes, she smiled at the lad and motioned him in. Danny skipped into Mrs. Wilkins's shabby parlor, his right hand already held palm out, seeking recompense. A pair of scrawny cats curled around his legs, meowing a welcome. Her pulse began to thump more forcefully inside her skin when she saw the letter in his left hand.

Could it be from Thomas?

It had been two days since that awful confrontation on top of the cliff. Two days since Father had headed for Marston. She had started the fourth volume of her aunt's diaries this morning, and her eyes ached from the strain of trying to decipher the increasingly unintelligible print of her aunt's arthritic hand. But it had also been two days of misery, long, restless hours when she'd spent far too much time thinking about a handsome auburn-haired marquess, wrestling with the memory of every word, every touch, ever exchanged between them.

She'd been left more confused than ever.

Far from providing the clues she sought, Aunt E's third volume had rambled on for a good three hundred pages, filled with bits of daily life and nostalgic wanderings of an aging mind. Lucy had read all about the cautious reconciliation between her aunt and Father. She'd read about her own visit as a child, and her father's provision of a quarterly stipend, a gesture that had apparently granted her aunt the ability to delay any hard decisions about selling her property. She'd read about her father's eventual acquisition of the title, and the invitation he'd issued to Aunt E to come and live with them in London, provided she take pains to "hide" her past to protect the children. And she'd read about her aunt's despair to realize that reestablishing a proper relationship with her family was contingent on leaving the town she loved, and worse, pretending to be someone other than she was.

Lucy could no longer blame Aunt E for choosing to stay. She could see, through her aunt's written words, the choice had been a difficult one, a decision borne out of love and a desire to protect her nieces and nephew, not neglect. But though Lucy now felt she understood her aunt's choices far better, she was still no closer to understanding her aunt's wishes on the matter of what to do about Heathmore.

And disappointingly, she hadn't read anything yet about Thomas either. Lucy knew she shouldn't want to read about him. She shouldn't want to *think* about him.

But she did, almost constantly.

How could she not? Everyone in Lizard Bay was talking about Heathmore and the discovery of tin, and that, in turn, made her think about *him*. The excitement in town had grown to a fever's pitch, the trouble with ghosts forgotten. Jamieson's store was buzzing with locals wanting to know if the rumors were true. Poor old Bentley had to have it explained to him no less than four times. And on Sunday,

Reverend Wellsbury had lectured them all on the dangers of temptation—using the example of Eve in the Garden of Eden again.

As if it wasn't Eve who had lost everything in that whole sordid tale.

Lucy had tried—in vain—to remind herself of Thomas's betrayal. But in truth, she was no longer sure her hasty conclusions regarding his motives held merit. He had rescued her. Saved her life. Her hand lifted to her neck, her fingers pressing against the delicate skin there. Far from poisoning her, he'd done the opposite: her rash was now completely healed. Neither could she reconcile the contents of his satchel with a man bent on gaining a financial advantage. He scarcely lived the life of a man bent on magnifying his wealth.

She thought of the papers she had seen in his bag, addressed to the Linnean Society of London. He collected *plants*, for heaven's sake, not samples of tin. He had been Lizard Bay's most outspoken opponent of a tin mining operation, and he spent his days seeing to the care and well-being of a quartet of unruly orphans. And by outward appearances, Danny and his brothers were clearly doing well under his tutelage.

She smiled at the boy, who was standing beside her in an almost mannerly fashion. Aunt E would have been proud. Closing the diary, she patted the sofa beside her.

Danny skipped forward, the scent of licorice clinging to him like an aura.

She breathed it in, realizing, then, that school must be out for the day. She must have read longer than she'd thought. It surprised her to realize how much she knew about the workings of the little town, how much she had absorbed in only a few short days. In spite of herself, she glanced toward the door, hoping to catch sight of a broad-shouldered shadow, or hear a hint of his voice, out in the hallway. But there was naught but an empty doorway and the ring of disappointment in her ears.

"Do you know who sent the letter?" she asked as the boy settled himself beside her, happily kicking his feet. She tucked the diary into the folds of her skirts. Not that she imagined one of the Tanner boys might ever be tempted to steal an actual *book*, but better not to take the chance.

Danny shook his head, his cheeks full of licorice. "No. But Mr. Bentley said to bring it, straightaway. It came on the mail coach."

Frustration settled in her stomach. Thomas wouldn't mail a letter, not when he could just hand it to the boy. She pulled one of her few remaining coins from her pocket and handed it to Danny, then took up the letter, staring down at it. The handwriting was her father's, the emblem on the red wax seal her family's own crest. She ought to be excited to see it, given that it likely contained news on the value of her property.

Yet, her fingers hesitated.

"Ain't you going to read it?" Danny asked, sucking his candy. "The schoolmaster makes me read out loud, all the time. Lord Branston, too." He made a face. "Says it is even more important than mathematics."

In spite of her uncertainty, she smiled at him. "I hate to say it, but I am afraid Lord Branston is correct on the matter of reading." Danny just sighed, rolling the licorice around in his mouth. Lucy handed him the letter. "Why don't you read it to me?" His sour look made her laugh. "I might be convinced to double your tip if you do."

That had him sitting up straighter. He swallowed his candy, tore open the wax seal, and cleared his voice in a way only a mischievous eight-year-old could, though it made Lucy wince to realize that—to her mother, at least—she probably sounded very much the same way.

"'Dear Lucy.'" His eyes widened up at her. "Gor! Is that your real name, Miss L?"

She nodded. "Go on."

" 'I've met with great . . .' " His nose wrinkled. "What's this word?" He pointed to the page.

Lucy glanced over. "Success."

" 'I've met great *success* in Marston. I gained an audience with the Marston Mining Corporation, and they would like to come and inspect the property. It is likely worth at least one hundred times what Lord Branston offered, so it seems you have some important decisions to make. I must consult with a . . .' " He pointed again.

"Solicitor," Lucy prompted. "You really do read very well, Danny." And the lad was only eight years old. Perhaps Thomas's hopes for university for the young scamp weren't entirely unfounded.

" 'I must consult with solicitor first, but will return with an inspector on Tuesday, and we can return to London thereafter.' " Danny lowered the letter, his eyes wide. "What did Lord Branston offer?" he asked in a hushed tone.

Lucy considered her response. Probably best not to mention the offer of one thousand pounds. *That* would require more explanation than she was comfortable delivering to an eight-year-old. "He's offered me seven hundred pounds to buy Heathmore Cottage," she conceded, remembered the last solid offer between them.

His eyes grew round. "Gor! That's . . . that's . . ." His nose wrinkled again. "Seven thousand pounds?"

She nodded, the amount making her feel ill instead of glad. When it had been only a few hundred pounds at stake, the potential for a misstep hadn't seemed as great. But now Marston Mining Corporation was coming to inspect the property? Wasn't that the company that had poisoned Lizard Bay's fish? "See?" she murmured. "Ciphers can come in handy."

But her mind wasn't on ciphers. Bugger it all, she was

going back to London tomorrow. Part of her was glad. She desperately wanted to see Lydia, to tell her every grand thing that had happened on this mad lark.

But a part of her—a stubborn, insistent part—wanted to stay in Lizard Bay.

"I'll say! That's a lot of money to count!" Danny jumped to his feet, his face dissolving into the largest grin she'd ever seen. The boy held out his palm. "I think you might want to do more than just double my tip, Miss L," he crowed. "Seems like you can afford it."

Lucy smiled as she gave him the last coins left over from Wilson's generous loan. He skidded around Mrs. Wilkins, who was coming through the door with a tea service in her hands, and eagerly dashed for the door.

"It's two o'clock!" Mrs. Wilkins said, setting the tray down. "Time for tea." She glanced back toward the door. "Did Danny give you the letter he brought?"

Lucy nodded, staring at the steaming teapot. Thank heavens it was a Monday, not a Friday. She didn't know if she could face the notion of having the entire town crowd into Mrs. Wilkins's parlor, discussing what to do about the tin and Lizard Bay's future.

A shadow fell across the doorway, and she looked up, her treacherous heart once again leaping in hope. But it wasn't Thomas. It was only the vicar, his white collar like a stick to the eye. Her heart sank. She may not have read much about Thomas yet in her aunt's diary, but she'd read *quite* a bit about Reverend Wellsbury. It was exhausting to read about the constant bickering that came from two determined shepherds trying to steer the same flock of sheep.

Yesterday, though Aunt E was no longer alive to defend herself, the vicar had stood at his pulpit and spoken of Eve as though she was solely responsible for the woes of the world. Lucy had sat in the front pew, seething. But today he didn't look ready to deliver a sermon. He stood quietly in the doorway, his hands clasped in front of him. "Do you mind if I join you for tea?"

"Are you sure tea won't provide too much of a temptation?" Lucy retorted.

"Oh, hush now," Mrs. Wilkins scolded. She smiled in the vicar's direction. "You are welcome to join us, Reverend Wellsbury. It will be just like old times, when Miss E was still with us." She sat down and began to pour the first cup, only to cluck in annoyance as a cat leaped into her lap.

"Here, let me." Lucy scooped up the tabby and held him in her own lap. If she was going to be forced to bear the vicar's company during tea, she'd prefer a feline buffer, thank you very much. She stroked her hand down the cat's back, urging it to settle. She'd become far more accustomed to cats in the past few days, but it was clear that in Lizard Bay, at least, they were still a problem that needed solving.

And while she might be terrible at solving her *own* problems, solving the problems faced by others was her specialty.

"You know," she mused as she accepted her cup, balancing it over the purring cat's back, "you are welcome to take all the male cats up to Heathmore. Separate the sexes, as we discussed." She glanced down at the purring animal. "There is plenty up there for them to eat. And now that I've seen it with my own eyes, I have to admit Heathmore could use a good deratting."

"It's a nice thought." Mrs. Wilkins passed the vicar his cup. "But I would think you wouldn't need to worry about the rats, when the mining starts. The cottage will need to be torn down once the excavations begin in earnest."

Lucy choked around the mouthful of tea she'd just taken. Tear down Aunt E's house? The thought made her throat close tight. "I beg your pardon?"

"Well, the only thing holding the poor house up is that cliff." Mrs. Wilkins shrugged. "If that goes, everything on top must go as well. And really, the entire property will be trampled by equipment and horses. They'll need to open the road back up that leads to town, I suspect." She poured her own cup. "It's curious we never knew about the property's value. Miss E never said a word about the tin, God rest her soul. Then again, she valued her privacy and loved the land. Loved the townspeople, too. Probably she thought it was for the best to keep it a secret."

"She always thought she knew better than everyone else." Reverend Wellsbury shook his head. "One might have thought she'd at least have put it to the parish committee."

Lucy set her cup down on the table beside the sofa, then placed the cat on the floor, needing a free lap to think. "She didn't love *everyone* in Lizard Bay," she pointed out. "It was my aunt's property. *Her* decision. She didn't need to discuss it with anyone."

Reverend Wellsbury's jaw hardened. She almost felt guilty for needling him in this manner. But if he continued to use his Sunday pulpit to besmear Aunt E's memory, she wasn't going to quibble over the moral dilemma of pointing out the obvious.

"If she'd not been so set on remaining a spinster," the vicar said slowly, "Miss E might have had a husband to share such an important decision with."

Lucy gritted her teeth. "She didn't want a husband."

"Nonetheless, she led some in Lizard Bay on quite a merry chase."

"That's a lie." Lucy picked up the diary from where it lay in the folds of her skirts and waved it about. "I've read her diaries, Reverend Wellsbury. Several gentlemen offered for her, but she never seduced *anyone*. Yes, she was outspoken, but being outspoken is not a sin. So instead of lecturing the town about Eve, you might want to spend a sermon or two asking the Lord's forgiveness for doubting my aunt, all those years."

Instead of rising to her bait, he gave a gusty sigh. "I didn't say she seduced anyone, Miss L. I said she led them on a merry chase. She led *me* on a merry chase. That's a distinction of some importance." He set his own cup down and paused, as though praying for patience. "I am glad to see you received the diaries I mailed for your aunt."

Lucy reared backward on the settee, stunned to silence. Her fingers curled over the edge of the last diary. Surely she'd heard wrong. "You? *You* sent the package?"

He nodded. "She asked me to, that day she died."

Lucy lifted a trembling hand to her mouth. "I . . . I don't understand." She glanced toward Mrs. Wilkins, seeking guidance, but the woman was as slack-jawed as she was. Her gaze slid back to the vicar. Everyone in town said the pair hated each other.

Had she somehow heard incorrectly?

The vicar's gaze settled on the pendant about her throat and he smiled sadly, shaking his head. "I've tried to seek you out since you arrived, to talk to you about your aunt, but it's clear you've been avoiding me. Sunday's lecture was intended to be a reminder of the temptations of money, not the temptations of love. Everyone in town is going on about tin as though it alone is God's solution to our problems. But I suspect Lizard Bay needs a gentler form of industry, if my opinion is at all welcome in the mix. The town is fragile enough without bowing to the weight of an unseemly industry like that." He inclined his head. "Your aunt felt much the same way."

Lucy gaped at him, feeling as though someone had kicked her feet out from under her. "But my aunt hated you. You hated each other. You disagreed about everything." She blinked at him, confusion clouding her vision and very likely her judgment. "*Didn't* you?"

"We disagreed on some matters, yes. That is not at all the same as hate." He frowned as he stood up. "I am sorry. I can tell my presence here is disturbing you. I'd hope to get to know you better, you see. It is clear you have a good deal of her strength."

He took a step toward the door, but paused on the threshold, his mouth turned down. "You may not wish to speak to me, but I would leave you with this, Miss L. Your aunt regretted some of her choices as the good Lord called her home, and I suspect her diaries reflect some of that. God has gifted us with the ability to share our lives with others, and it is a gift we should not take lightly. Otherwise, we might find ourselves at the end of our lives, regretting the path we chose." Then, offering one final nod toward Mrs. Wilkins, he walked away, his white collar disappearing down the hallway.

"Well," Mrs. Wilkins said, blinking in confusion. "That was certainly . . . *different.* I've never heard the vicar talk about your aunt that way before. As though he admired her. As though he . . ." Her words trailed off, steeped with astonishment.

Lucy's head helpfully supplied the rest. *As though he loved her.*

Over the years, had Reverend Wellsbury somehow become something more to her aunt than a thorn in her side? It seemed she was missing a few pieces to this maddening puzzle.

And that meant she needed to finish reading the bloody diaries.

From the Diary of Edith Lucille Westmore
August 16, 1850

In my increasing age and wisdom, I have become adept at seeing a problem and knowing immediately how to help. Or, as Reverend Wellsbury likes to grumble, to meddle in things that shouldn't concern me.

But when Lord Branston arrived in Lizard Bay, it was clear I was facing my most challenging case yet. He has led us all to believe a failed betrothal lies at the heart of his self-destruction. But last night, swaying on his feet in my parlor, Lord Branston drunkenly confessed the truth of it. His sister's death was no ordinary death, it seems. If the facts come out publicly, the scandal would be ruinous. His sister must have been desperate to resort to such a scheme. And I can't help but think Lord Branston is a man worth saving, to permit his sister to make such a decision for herself, even when the keeping of it so obviously haunts him.

So, I've a secret to keep now. And I will take it to my grave . . .

But only, I think, if Lord Branston agrees to give up the bottle.

Chapter 23

*L*ucy closed her aunt's diary and lifted a hand to rub her stiff neck. She had read through the night, and *still* she was not quite at the end of the last volume. She'd finally reached the part about Thomas, but far from proving a source of enlightenment on what to do with Heathmore, it seemed to leave the question as a yawning, open thing.

Beside her bed, the candle was guttering, molten wax pooling against the candlestick, the spent wick needing to be trimmed. Father was coming today, along with the inspector from the Marston Mining Corporation. And unfortunately, she felt as confused as ever.

She pulled back her bedclothes and glanced out the window, seeing only the blackness that was so characteristic of a Cornwall night. If her aunt's diaries formed a puzzle, it seemed some of the pieces still refused to fit. Mrs. Wilkins claimed Thomas's sister had taken her own life, and Aunt E's diary passage seemed to confirm it.

Was *this* what haunted him, why he was hiding in Cornwall, why his seat in the House of Lords was sitting empty and unused? If he'd not been able to stop his sister from committing such an act, did he perchance feel guilty for the outcome?

And how did that all tie in to Heathmore and his interest in the property? She still didn't understand what lay at the heart of Thomas's offers or why he'd chosen not to disclose all the facts, but he claimed he had an explanation and she'd refused to listen.

The answer did not appear to be waiting in her aunt's last diary.

And that meant she needed to see him, to *listen* to him, before it was too late.

Hurriedly, she pulled on her boots, not even bothering with stockings. Slipping her shawl over her night dress, she snatched up Thomas's satchel, spilling some of the contents in the process. But she couldn't take the time to clean it all up now that her decision was made. She stumbled down the stairs, tripping over a sleeping cat in her hurry.

Despite the panicked push of her pulse, as she turned the key in the front door lock and stepped out onto the porch, she stopped dead still. What was she *doing* tearing off into the night her nightclothes? She hadn't any notion where Thomas lived, only the general direction in which he had disappeared that first night in town. Once again she was charging into the unknown, not giving herself time to think.

Except . . . that wasn't exactly true.

This time, the trouble was that she had thought it all through too much. She'd gone about this all wrong, and as a result had let the opportunity to trust him slip through her hands, time and time again. She'd wrongly presumed her aunt's diaries were full of advice, guidance she was meant to follow. But she'd been ignoring her own instincts all along.

Her instincts told her Thomas was honorable, even if the evidence seemed to point against it. And therein lay the problem.

It wasn't only that she needed to trust him. She needed to trust herself. Moreover, she needed to be true to herself, rather than what her mother or Aunt E's diaries would make her. She was neither a tittering debutante nor a scowling spinster.

She was simply herself.

And she needed to stop trying to be someone else.

Lucy stared out into the black night, cursing fate and God and anything else she might reasonably credit with her situation. But most of all, she cursed herself, for her lack of faith. *She* was to blame for the fact she was standing out of doors, tears pooling in her eyes, her future sliding out of her desperate grasp.

And then she saw it. A distant light, cutting through the night, but growing larger and warmer and steadily closer. She considered reaching out a hand to try to touch it. Considered, too, opening her mouth to scream. After all, she had no notion of what waited at the other end of that swelling light. But instead she watched, mesmerized, until it took the shape of a lantern held high. Thomas emerged from the shadows, his face so dear her knees felt like buckling.

"You came," she whispered. *Again.*

It seemed he was always coming to save her.

Even from herself.

"I came," he affirmed, his voice hoarse. The light sent shadows swirling across his face, but she could see the hollows beneath his eyes, the evidence that he, too, had spent a sleepless night.

"Why?" she whispered.

He hesitated. "Danny told me about the letter that came today."

A week ago uncertainty might have pushed her to accuse him of coming to offer her seven thousand and *one* pounds for Heathmore Cottage, to come out ahead of the offer mentioned in her father's letter. But not now.

"You heard I was returning to London," she said softly.

He nodded. "Is it true?"

"Yes. We leave today." It was a conflicted truth. Part of her wanted very much to return to London, to see her family again. Her bag was sitting upstairs at the foot of her bed, already packed in anticipation of this fact.

But another part of her—the same part that had sent her dashing into the night—wanted to stay right here, on the dark street, with this man.

"I waited for you," he told her. "To come to me. To ask me to show you what I meant about Heathmore being worth more than you knew. But then, with morning approaching and still no sign of you . . . I thought perhaps that waiting anymore was a stupid thing to do."

She shook her head, hiding a smile. "You are not the stupid one in this scenario, Thomas. I am, for not giving you a chance to show me three days ago."

He offered her the lantern. "Do you trust me?"

A question of some portent. And one for which she finally had an answer. "Yes." She took the lantern and offered him the satchel in return. "With all my heart."

His smile was like dawn breaking, though that was still at least two hours away. "Then follow me," he told her, motioning for her to follow.

THEY WALKED, HAND in hand, pulse against pulse, steadily upward in silence.

She seemed content to go where he would take her, and the wonder of that kept his feet steady on the rocky path. The past three days had been some of the hardest of his life, and there were quite a few worst days in his past to compare them to. He'd nearly come to see her a dozen times, wanting to explain himself, knowing he had, in some respects, failed her.

He'd known about the tin, although he hadn't known what

a rich vein ran beneath the cliff, not until the earth had given way to reveal it. But he'd certainly suspected it. The rocks above the cliff were a mixture of serpentinite and granite, littered with streaks of white tin. Telltale geology, one a man of scientific persuasion couldn't miss.

But he should have shown Lucy the tin from the start and trusted that she was capable of making her own decision on the disposition of the property.

They passed the lighthouse, its bulbous, obscene light swinging wide, and he realized he could just see a hint of the coming dawn, the thinnest of lines stretching across the horizon. He tugged harder, hurrying her along. They couldn't do this properly this close to the lighthouse.

Too much light and too much sound.

Finally, after another twenty minutes of walking, he stopped. Cocking his ear, he listened. It took a moment, but he caught it on the edge of the wind, a rustling of life in the grass, the faintest quiver of birdsong. This was it. The perfect place—and the perfect time—to show her.

He lowered himself to the ground.

"We are stopping?" Lucy asked through the darkness, though she willingly dropped to her knees beside him. "The cottage is a half mile farther, isn't it?"

"You've already seen the cottage. I've a mind to show you something else about your land." He pulled off his boots. "You might want to get comfortable. We are going to be here an hour, at least."

He expected questions. A staunchly worded objection.

After all, such exchanges had characterized so much of their acquaintance to date.

But instead of arguing, she handed him the lantern and began to take off her boots. He stretched back on his elbows and watched her work, admiring the wild sway of her short hair as it caught the lamplight. She was dressed in some filmy white thing that covered her from neck to toe, but its color caught the light from the lantern and tossed it back defiantly toward the darkness. He couldn't take his eyes from her.

Finally, when she had her bare feet tucked up under her and her boots safely stowed beside his, he smiled. "Are you ready?"

She nodded. Closed her eyes and leaned toward him.

As though she was anticipating a kiss.

He was tempted. Hell, he was beyond tempted. She looked so sweet, so expectant in the lamplight, he wanted to tip her back onto the soft grass and show her something else entirely. He wanted to make love to her, to uncover each cotton-wrapped piece of her and kiss her until she was soft and sighing beneath him. But there was never going to be another moment, a different time. She was returning to London today.

So he held himself away from the pretty invitation she offered, opened the door of the lantern and blew out the flame. In an instant they were surrounded by darkness, the faint glow of the horizon a poor substitute for the lantern's strength.

"Am I to presume you are trying to show me how dark it is?" she asked dryly.

"Shhh," he whispered. He could feel her beside him, the air between them humming with want and other more potent things. He could hear it now, the calls and trills of the birds hiding in the brush growing stronger and more enthusiastic.

"Are you telling me what to do?" she asked archly, but amusement feathered her words.

"I would never be so foolish as to presume I had the right to do that. I am merely encouraging you to consider my request. I want you to see the sunrise."

"But . . . shouldn't we be angled toward the ocean for that?"

He lifted a finger to his lips, though he doubted she could see it yet, as his own eyes were still adjusting to the shock of darkness. "You claimed to trust me. Now you must prove it. Let your eyes and ears go. Watch . . . and listen."

She fell quiet, but she leaned into him, huddling, perhaps, for warmth. The chill of the night began to creep in now that they were still, and he gathered her closer, tucking her thin shawl about her shoulders. He felt it then, her hand, fumbling through the darkness.

It burrowed into his and he obligingly held on tight.

All around them the symphony of birdsong was growing louder now, a hundred different birds, each announcing the coming of the day. The darkness was shifting, the colors of the moors beginning to take shape, pink and gold and umber. He felt her hand tighten against his and heard her breath catch in wonder. "What is happening?" she whispered.

"Sunrise," he said simply.

"The sun comes up in London, too." He heard her swallow. "But it bloody well doesn't look or sound like *this*."

"No." He chuckled, in spite of his resolve to stay quiet. "This is known as the dawn chorus. Birds do it all over the world. But civilization has a way of ruining it. Now *shhhh*."

They sat for a good half hour, until the light overtook the dark and the air began to warm around them. At some point he stopped watching the meadow and began to watch her instead. He'd experienced this morning sunrise more times than he could count, but given her pending departure, this might very well be the last time he could watch *her*.

And to his mind, she made a far more compelling subject for observation.

Her eyes were wider than he'd ever seen them, sparkling with excitement in the muted light of morning. Her generous mouth was open, as though surprise had caught her and forgotten to loosen its hold. She was watching the meadow as though it was the most beautiful thing she had ever seen, but there was more than just beauty at stake.

There was *life*.

And as rich as it was, it was fragile. Thomas knew every bird species in this field, each family of plant that called this rare peninsula home. He'd trekked the entire coast and recorded hours of observations, meticulously writing the arguments for the preservation of this acreage, knowing that once it was lost, there was no reclaiming it.

A bird landed on a piece of shrub not five feet away, and he heard her gasp of pleasure. The chorus was growing quieter now, as the fickle creatures began to turn their attention away from the sun and toward the task of finding breakfast. This bird, in particular, appeared to think they might be the ones to provide him with it. It cocked its glossy black head, studying them, and then jumped down, hopping closer.

"What kind of bird is this?" she whispered, breaking the silence. She reached out a hand and the bird let her come as close as a half foot before it let out a shrill squawk of objection from its red beak and flew away to safer quarters.

"Pyrrhocorax pyrrhocorax."

She turned her head toward him. "Are you sure you are a marquess? Because honestly, you sound more like one of Geoffrey's sour-faced Latin tutors."

In spite of himself, he chuckled. "The Latin names are a manner of classifying organisms based on a system created by Linnaeus."

"Well, that's all well and good," she laughed, "but Linnaeus isn't here. What would an ordinary person call it?"

"That was a Cornish chough."

"Tell me more." When he hesitated, she pulled her hand from his and shifted her entire body to face him, her chin upturned. "Isn't this why you brought me here?" She lifted a hand to the landscape she was now missing. "So you can explain it all?"

He nodded, wanting to tell her, but also not wanting to spoil the moment. Would she understand? He didn't know if she would appreciate it as he did, but he had been wrong to try to wrest the decision away from her, from the start. "The Cornish chough is a bird that makes its home here on the Lizard Bay peninsula. But they are declining in numbers, due in part to the mining operations up and down the coast."

"Are they bound to suffer the same fate as the fish?" Lucy asked with a frown.

"I am afraid so."

She loosened a frustrated sigh. "Oh, the bloody Marston Mining Corporation." She glanced toward his satchel. "And what about the flowers you tried to give me on Saturday? Are they in danger too?"

"Cornish heath."

"No Latin?"

"It hasn't been named yet because no one knows about it. It is a unique variety, different than any I've ever seen. And yes, they are in danger, too. This is the only place it grows, in all of Britain, and if my suspicions are correct, on all of earth." He gestured toward the sun-drenched meadow. "You can't imagine the rarity of the land you hold, Lucy. Heathmore has created an entire world of its own, with its strange soil and unusual geology. I've cataloged over two dozen different species of fauna and flora, each unique to this part of the coast. I don't know how many more species are left to be discovered. Hundreds, possibly." He breathed in, thinking of the proposal he had drafted. "I've a paper for the Linnean Society of London, outlining my findings. I don't know if it will be enough to generate the sort of interest we need to save Lizard Bay. But I *do* know that if the land is turned over to the Marston Mining Corporation, it will be lost forever."

"Oh, bugger it *all*," she whispered softly.

"I can envision a pilgrimage of naturalists and enthusiasts from all over the world. An industry, of sorts, for poor beleaguered Lizard Bay and even Mrs. Wilkins's boardinghouse. I was prepared to invest in such a scheme, to offer

Heathmore Cottage—free of rent—as a naturalist's retreat, for scientists to come and study this part of the coast. That is why I had devoted so much effort to repairing the cottage."

She blinked up at him. "You would invest in this, but not tin mining?"

"Lizard Bay is important to me. To *all* of us. I would willingly put my own funds behind something that might make the town flourish. I understand, though, that this isn't my choice. I won't submit the paper I have written to the Linnean Society, not if you do not wish me to. The property belongs to you. The decision does as well."

He waited, his chest tighter than a noose, to hear what she would say to his proposal.

"Why does it all mean so much to you?" came her agonized whisper. "Some people would look at this and see only an ugly, useless piece of land, a bit of grass and rock. But you . . . you look at it and see beauty. Potential."

He inclined his head, his gaze wanting to linger on the lovely curve of her cheek. "I don't know why I see it so differently, only that I do." He reached out a hand and brushed a strand of blond hair from her eyes, tucking it behind her ear. In some ways, he supposed, it was not that different from how he looked at her. She saw herself as a plain spinster, but he looked at her and saw the good, the potential, and yes, the beauty.

She was so damn beautiful she took his breath away.

"But it does not matter what I see. The choice of what to do with Heathmore is not mine to make, and I was wrong to try to buy it without showing you this from the start. The decision is yours, Lucy. It should have always been. And no matter the decision you make, I will honor it."

Her mouth rounded in surprise. "You would risk losing it?"

"If I've learned but one thing in my life, it's that it's no small thing to lose something so rare. To fail to protect something you love." He hesitated, thinking that in some ways this was proving less difficult than he'd imagined. "But sometimes the choice does not lie with you."

There was a moment's pause. "Is that why you were trying so hard to protect this piece of land?" Her voice hushed. "Because of your sister?"

He sucked in a breath. "You know?"

She nodded. "I finally reached eighteen fifty in Aunt E's diary."

Thomas reached out again, picking up her hand and turning it over in his. If she knew, there was little he could do to change it. And a part of him was glad she knew.

He wanted her to know this about him. He wanted her to know *everything* about him.

And he wanted to know everything about her as well.

But to do that, he needed to do more than unlock her secrets.

He needed to unlock her heart.

Chapter 24

*L*ucy stared at this man who had become so inexplicably dear to her that he made the rest of the morning—wondrous though it was—fall away. When had his profile become so familiar? She felt as though she knew every angle, every plane, of his face. He'd shown her an amazing world this morning—*his* world, the one he dreamed of protecting. But even more importantly, he'd shown her his hopes for its future, all cards on the table, no more bluffs between them.

And then he'd left the choice in her hands.

"Thomas," she whispered.

"Yes?"

"Would you kiss me?"

He smiled, and it was a slow, spreading, *wicked* smile, a smile that sent one edge of his mouth a little higher than the other and her stomach twisting in pleasure.

"You didn't say please," he said, but his voice had gone hoarse and deep.

"Please." She was rewarded for her honesty by the sight of his mouth lowering toward hers. Unlike the last kiss they'd

shared, this time he was punishing in his slowness. An agonizing inch at a time, he closed the space between them like
a man at leisure.

But she had never been good at waiting.

She looped her arms about his neck and pulled him into
her until their noses bumped and their mouths found the
right mark, and the feel of his lips on hers outstripped the
anticipation. She gasped in pleasure as his mouth claimed
hers. That noise, finally, seemed to unleash the predator she
sensed lurking beneath the gentlemanly surface. His kiss
turned from tender to demanding, and she welcomed the
shift.

She kissed him openly. *Honestly.* Kissed him as though
her world was ending and she might never get another
chance. Kissed him as he eased her back onto the grass and
stretched out beside her, their tongues dancing in a rhythm
that sent shivers up her spine and her thoughts racing in
more mischievous directions.

She turned herself over to it, trusting him to know her own
mind better than she knew it herself. She was rewarded for
that trust when his kiss turned playful, just as she thought
she might shrink from the intensity of it. His mouth gentled,
his teeth nipping at her lower lip, his moan of pleasure a
perfect echo of her own want.

"Thomas," she gasped as his mouth left hers to land,
warm and wet and achingly welcome, against her neck. She
arched up, tipping back her head, her eyes open to the pink-
tinged sky above them. "I . . . I think I am wearing too many
clothes."

He ran a possessive palm down the length of her torso,
torturing her with its slow, relentless path southward. "How
would you like me to rectify that misfortune?" His hand
trailed lower, down one calf, until his fingers were teasing
the very edge of her nightdress.

She held her breath in anticipation.

"Would you recommend I do this?" he asked, lifting the hem a few inches. He lowered his head to press a kiss against one bare calf, his mouth warm and full of promise. "Or perhaps this, instead?" He lifted the hem higher, grazing her thighs. He lowered his head there, too, his mouth and tongue swirling against skin, dangerously close and yet so far from where her body and imagination screamed he might yet go.

She thrashed her head, her lungs feeling too constricted to breathe as he eased the hem upward, ever more slowly, to bare her most private secrets to his gaze. He hesitated there, his indrawn breath louder, even, than the thundering of her heart.

"Holy God," he whispered. "You are so, so beautiful." He reached out a hand and touched her, swirling a finger against that spot he'd discovered the night they'd spent at Heathmore. His touch sent her nerves twisting in pleasure until Lucy moaned out loud, wanting him to move on and yet wanting him to linger.

He swept the nightdress higher still, pressing kisses against her belly now, moving upward with slow, lascivious intent, until she was lifting her arms above her head and he was sweeping the confounding cotton aside, tossing it away. He loomed over her, staring down, his breath coming in hard pants. Behind his head the sun had shifted from pink to gold, casting his face in shadows. It made him appear hewn from stone, an almost-stranger, but the knowledge that this was *Thomas* softened the impact of her nudity.

She waited, unembarrassed, for him to take off his own clothes.

Instead, he fell upon her body like a starving man. "Beautiful," he groaned out loud, his mouth against her breast, and then he was drawing her nipple into his mouth and suckling with the sweetest, gentlest pressure. She closed her eyes, the feeling of his tongue against her breast almost unbearable. He moved to the other breast, his hands sliding across skin, kneading and pulling. All the while, he murmured to her, groaning as if he took his own pleasure from hers.

But as wonderful as it was, it wasn't enough.

She wanted to feel his body against hers, without the inconvenience of wool and cotton.

As his mouth came back to greet hers for a long, bruising kiss, she tore at the buttons of his coat. "You, next," she gasped against his lips.

He sat up and shifted slowly out of his frockcoat, one arm at a time. For heaven's sake, did the man never hurry? She lifted herself up and helped herself to the buttons of his waistcoat, then plucked at the scarf about his neck and pulled his shirt over his head. "You are too slow," she said, batting his hands away. But then there was a woolen undervest to contend with, and that stymied her for several long seconds. "Bugger it all, why do men wear so many clothes?" she muttered, making him chuckle. When she finally reached skin, she nearly groaned with relief.

For a moment she just stared at the sight of him, his bare chest gleaming in the morning sun. That night in the cottage, she'd averted her eyes from his shirtless form, but this morning an entire team of horses couldn't have dragged her gaze away. He was magnificently made, his chest a series of planes and ridges, so the opposite of her own soft curves she was tempted to question if they were the same species. There was a faint pattern of hair, glinting red, but it thinned and darkened as it arrowed downward, disappearing into the waistband of his trousers.

She ran a fingertip down his rib cage, enjoying the turnabout as he drew in a startled breath, sending his musculature into even starker relief. She leaned forward and pressed her mouth against his chest. He tasted of soap. Of salt. Of *Thomas.*

And so she kissed him there, again. Ran her tongue along those ridges and planes, marveling at the coiled strength she sensed beneath his skin. Flattened her palm against his hard abdomen, enjoying, too, the quiver of muscles there.

She discovered the sort of wild, wanton joy to be found in giving pleasure, instead of only receiving it. Because there was no doubt at all she was enjoying this, every bit as much as he was. Her breathing was every bit as fast, her limbs every bit as weak. The wonder of that made her want to slow down, relish the moment.

Perhaps he was onto something with his slowness.

As she returned to kiss him, full on the mouth, she lowered her hands, down, down, past the band of his trousers. "Next these," she murmured against his mouth.

He stilled and shook his head. "Lucy, I don't think that is a wise idea."

Her hand slid lower, to the long, hard length of him beneath the wool. "I would beg you, then, to stop thinking."

His hand stilled over hers, halting her progress. "Lucy—" he warned, panting with the effort of holding back. "Do you trust me?"

She blinked in surprise. "You know I do." She would not be here, now, *naked*, touching him so intimately, if she did not trust him with her very life.

"Then trust me when I say we cannot do this. Not this way." His voice sounded close to breaking. "I cannot let you risk that sort of ruin," he went on, shaking his head. "I will not be the sort of man who fails to protect you, however much I want you in this moment."

"But . . . I want you, too," she protested. And she wanted to feel him stretched out next to her, skin on skin, until they were both out of breath and far too gone to care about consequences.

But she understood, in some way, what he meant. She'd read enough in her aunt's diary to know this piece of his history. He'd seen his sister's fall from grace, and so she knew there was honor—not rejection—lurking in the shadows of his refusal. He was fashioned as a protector. Had proven himself a determined one, too. Time after time he'd held himself back from what she'd offered, when a lesser man might have tupped her against the wall of the inn.

Or, on the sofa in the cottage.

Or, in this lovely, wild meadow, the rising sun laughing down on them.

"Can't we . . . just once?" she asked, biting her lip.

"Even once is too great a risk." He reared back and pulled a hand through his hair, as though seeking an answer to the dilemma she posed. As she groaned in frustration, his hazel eyes slid back to hers. One side of his mouth quirked upward, transforming him in an instant from protector to rogue. "But perchance there are other ways . . ."

"What other ways?" she asked, even as her more devilish side told her no, thank you very much, she really *did* want his trousers off.

"Lay back," he told her. "And close your eyes."

She did as he asked. She felt the long sweep of his hands across her body. Imagined she might next feel his mouth, warm against the underside of her breast.

But this time his mouth touched her somewhere else.

Somewhere *impossible*.

And despite the fact her eyes were squeezed shut, she knew it was definitely the touch of his mouth. She could feel the gentle scrape of his whiskers against her thighs, feel the warm heat of his breath as he kissed her there. She gasped out loud and lifted a knuckle to her lips, trying to draw a proper breath. She'd never heard of such a thing, could not believe he meant to do it.

And yet she couldn't summon the proper words to beg him to stop.

She bucked against the feelings, her hips and thoughts helpless against the pleasure he was kindling in a very extraordinary place. How could his mouth on that one small spot stir such feelings elsewhere? She seemed to feel him everywhere. In her core, beneath her skin. It was as though he was lighting a fire inside her, patiently laying the bricks, kindling the flames until they leaped, high and sure. She felt as though her bones were melting against that sure heat, pooling in a wanton heap as he worked, gently, on that most vulnerable part of her body.

And then she was flying.

Figuratively speaking.

It was a sensation very close to how she had felt when the earth crumbled beneath her, a sense of weightlessness, and a certainty that something unchangeable was about to happen. She slid over the edge of this new, strange cliff, flailing and panic and a rush of blood to her lungs. Only this time instead of fear, there was the most glorious feeling accompanying the fall, as though every inch of her body had been thrummed to the point of breaking and then loosened, like an arrow. And oh, how she flew.

It stretched out for a long, glorious, insensible moment.

And then she was landing, safely on her back, clouds spinning above her, one singular thought in her head.

Bugger it all, she wasn't quite sure what had just happened.

But she was *quite* sure she was going to want it to happen more than once.

THOMAS SETTLED BESIDE her, gathering her into his arms.

To have seen her that way, stretched out beneath the sun, her hair flying wild about her face and her skin flushed pink with pleasure, had been the rarest of gifts. But now she looked sleepy and satisfied, and he felt the sharp arc of possessiveness to know he had been the one to put that look on her face.

Her head tipped back against his bare chest, and as her breathing gradually settled into a more tenable rhythm, her hand crept up to twine in his. How long they lay there, he couldn't say. They drifted a long moment, lost in the low, happy buzz of the meadow, the insects and birds going about their lives as though something momentous had not just taken place here.

Thomas would have liked to linger. Hell, he would have *liked* to do it again.

But the sun was climbing in the sky and they had already tarried longer than he'd intended. He pressed a kiss to her hair. Though he'd left her well-satisfied, his own lack of relief was waging a stern protest. His heart might be enjoying this continued bit of tenderness, but the knowledge that there was a very naked, very willing woman in his arms was not at all conducive to the cause of wrestling his body back under control.

"It's getting late. We should probably go back soon," he said, shifting his body to relieve the tightness in his groin.

"Just a few more minutes," she sighed, burrowing her naked body deeper into his arms. "I don't want to go back to London quite yet."

Thomas's fingers tightened. Her words startled him, somehow. She still intended to go back to London, despite all that had passed between them? He could scarcely breathe. She seemed so at ease here, with the serpentine stone glinting about her bare neck, her body nestled against his. He'd thought she would want to stay. He'd imagined, perhaps . . .

Well, that was the problem with imagining.

So often one was disappointed when reality prevailed.

He was selfish enough to hope she might yet change her mind. Nearly selfish enough to stay here, his arms holding her close, keeping the lurking world at bay. But he wasn't so selfish as to presume he had the right to make that decision for her.

"Your skin is starting to burn in the sun," he pointed out. Already, he could see parts of her starting to turn pink.

Though he hated to do it, he sat up and tugged her night-dress over her head, pulling it down over the body he had just so thoroughly pleasured. As the last inch of fair skin disappeared beneath the hem, he swallowed. Well, that was that. She was covered back up, hidden away. Untouchable once more.

But oh, what a pleasurable interlude it had been.

"What time do you think it is?" she asked as Thomas worked to try to remove some of the bits of grass and twigs from her hair.

"Perhaps eight o'clock. I would guess you've missed breakfast," he admitted. "And that means your father will be here soon. Lizard Bay is only an hour's coach ride from Marston. If he intends to start for Salisbury today, he'll want to get an early start."

She responded with a sleepy pout, but she let him put her boots on her feet and pull her up. Thomas brushed off her night dress, the sea grass clinging to the white cotton the way he wanted to cling to her. It had taken every bit of self-possession not to take what she had so sweetly offered. But much like Heathmore, he knew he couldn't pressure her on this. The choice, when—and if—it came, needed to be hers.

He had shown her a taste of passion, but her virtue remained intact. He was rather proud of himself on that front. He'd kept her safe. There were no dire consequences in her future.

If only he could be half as sure of his own.

The walk back to Lizard Bay seemed to take only half as much time as it should, no doubt because he was dreading the return. They'd left under cover of darkness, but now the sun was rising higher overhead, and so he stopped her at the edge of town.

"I think it's best if we part here," he said, pulling the edges of her shawl closer about her shoulders. "I believe it is in both our best interests for me not to walk you into town in your nightclothes and deposit you on the front steps of Mrs. Wilkins's boardinghouse."

She arched a brow. "Because the town loves its gossip?"

He shook his head, smiling. "No, because your father loves *you*." He wasn't afraid if the whole of Lizard Bay knew how he felt about this woman. But Lord Cardwell had made his opinion of him all too clear down the barrel of a pistol. Lord knew what the man might do if his daughter showed up looking like this with her hand twined in his, a dreamy smile on her face and grass in her hair.

"I can handle my father."

"Yes. But I don't want our appearance together to force his hand on this. I want it to be your choice, not your father's."

"Do you refer to my choice about Heathmore?" she asked, blinking in confusion.

He stared down at her sunburned cheeks, not wanting to walk away just yet. He'd given her all the facts but didn't know what she intended to do. It wasn't his place to ask. She might decide to sell the property. Or she might decide to keep Heathmore whole. Either decision might keep her in Lizard Bay, which was an outcome he was selfish enough to want, even if one of those choices meant the destruction of the town. But harder still was the thought that she might still choose to leave with her father today, and he would be forced to watch the dust chase her coach to London.

"No, I mean the choice about us. Whether we are talking about Heathmore or about marriage, I want you to know I don't believe there is a set of right or wrong answers. The decision is yours, and no one has the right to force you to make one or the other." He hesitated. "I remain quite serious in my offer of marriage. It is not dependent on the outcome of your decision regarding Heathmore."

Her eyes widened. "Thomas—"

"I would want to marry you even if you decide to sell the property."

"But . . . how can you mean that? If I sold it . . . destroyed its natural beauty . . . Heathmore means so much to you . . ."

He reached out a hand to cup her cheek. "Can't you see?" he told her, his fingers wanting to linger far longer than was prudent, given the high march of the overhead sun and the imminent arrival of her father. "You mean more to me than any of it. I love you, Lucy. My heart has been yours since that day on the train. Possibly even that day in your father's drawing room. You surprised the hell out of me. You still do."

"Thomas," she said, shaking her head. "You are everything that is good and strong and *right*. But you don't have to, just because we . . . because you . . . What I am trying to say is—"

He lifted a finger to her lips, stilling her voice. "I am not only telling you this because of that either," he said. "Nothing happened between us that could be formally classified as ruin. A physician's examination, if it came to that, would confirm you are untouched." He smiled as her cheeks flamed pink. "It wasn't even that scandalous, certainly not for a spinster as wild-hearted as *you*. And I am not asking for your decision right now."

He hesitated. "I understand you are not sure if you want to marry, that you consider spinsterhood to be some kind of badge of honor. But I am not some nameless, faceless stranger on a ballroom floor, angling for your dowry and wanting to change you. I *love* you. Just the way you are. And if you ever find that you are ready to consider marriage, I only ask . . ." He thought back to their very first conversation, that day in a London drawing room. "I only ask that you give me right of first refusal."

"Oh." She blinked, as though the question stung her eyes. For a moment he worried she might toss back the same witty retort she'd given him the first time.

I would not depend on it, my lord.

Instead, she drew in a deep breath and smiled slowly, as

though inspiration had been found in that indrawn breath of air. "I think I can promise you that."

His chest loosened. It wasn't a yes. Not even close. She hadn't told him she loved him, though he'd bared his heart neatly enough for her.

But neither was it a no.

That was a stark improvement over where he'd feared they were yesterday.

So he leaned down and kissed her. She kissed him back, her hands tangling in his coat, then finally broke off, panting up at him, eyes wide.

"Farewell, Lucy." He turned to go.

"Wait!"

His feet stopped all too readily, his pulse a mad thing in his veins. Did she mean to accept his proposal? But no, as he turned around, he could she was biting her lip. She glanced down the street, toward the boardinghouse waiting in the distance. "Will you come with me today?"

"To speak to your father?" He chuckled. "I am not sure that is the wisest of ideas without a formal betrothal between us."

"No, I mean come with me back to London." She stepped forward to grab his hand, squeezing. "Come with me. Come with *us*."

He shook his head, shocked by the request. "You know I cannot do that."

"Of course you can." She looked hurt. "I would explain things to my father. Don't worry about him. He's all bluster and scarcely ever bites."

"It's not that." Thomas pulled his hand free, the pressure of London feeling like a weight on his chest. "I *can't*, Lucy. Think of all that is at stake."

"Do you mean you can't come to London now?" she asked slowly, as though understanding was taking slow, painful root. "Or ever?"

His silence, apparently, was answer enough.

She pursed her lips. "Do you mean to say your proposal of marriage is not contingent on my decision regarding Heathmore, but it *is* contingent on the fact we must always live here, in Lizard Bay?" Her eyes narrowed. "That seems a rather selfish viewpoint. What about your seat in the House of Lords? What about my *family*? I know I may have put on a brave front coming here, but in truth I am very close to them. I can't imagine being gone from them so long."

Thomas wanted to growl in frustration. This was not the conversation he had imagined having in this moment, and certainly not the place he would have picked for it. Were they really standing in the middle of Lizard Bay's only street having a public argument about where they might live if she ever consented to marry him?

Although . . . the fact they were having an argument at all meant she was actually considering his proposal, so he reined in his objections and shook his head.

"I can't risk it. Surely you can see why."

"No, quite frankly. I *can't* see why." She put her hands on her hips, her shawl slipping off one shoulder. "For heaven's sake, it's been three years, Thomas. Surely this business with your sister has settled now. Trust me, people have a way of forgetting the gossip. Why, four years ago my sister Clare was publicly shamed, a scandal to be covered up. That's part of the reason my Season was delayed as long as it was. But already people have forgotten, and she is quite happily married now."

He shook his head. "For Christ's sake, Lucy, it is more complicated than that. Now that you've read your aunt's diary, now that you know about my sister, I'd hope you might understand why I can't live in London. My sister is a strong woman. A *good* woman, no matter what others might say about her. I don't want to hurt her again."

She gaped at him. *"Again?"*

And that was when he realized that perhaps she didn't know the whole of it after all.

From the Diary of Edith Lucille Westmore
March 4, 1851

Not all grand causes have happy outcomes, but in this, I think, I shall count myself a success. Lord Branston has made great strides toward sobriety. Of course, I threatened Mr. Jamieson with bodily harm if he didn't stop stocking whisky in his store. Reverend Wellsbury even joined the cause by watering down the wine in the parish Eucharist cup.

I suppose I might grant them both a tiny bit of claim to my success.

But most of it, I think, lies in Lord Branston's own hands.

He is a good man, and as I watch him struggle to come to terms with his sister's choice, I am reminded, in some ways, of my own situation. Distancing myself from the family I love is a decision I wrestle with nearly every day. I could never have been the sort of aunt they expected me to be, and I didn't want to taint my innocent nieces and nephew with the weight of my scandal. Did I make the right choice? It is hard to know.

But I hope, someday, they might understand that I did it out of love.

To know that Lord Branston feels a similarly protective instinct toward his sister nearly restores my faith in men.

Chapter 25

*L*ucy lifted a trembling hand to her mouth. "Your sister . . . is *alive*?" As she stared up at him, she thought of all the conversations she'd ever had with Thomas about his sister.

He had said he "lost" her. That he missed her.

As Lucy sorted through the words, the specific phrases, she realized he'd never once said his sister was actually dead.

He frowned. "Didn't the diary reveal that piece of it?"

She shook her head. "It only mentioned a secret." She felt as though the street were spinning beneath her feet. "I thought, perhaps, that Aunt E meant you'd confessed your sister had taken her own life." But she could see now it was so much more than that. Aunt E must not have wanted to betray such a vital trust, not even in her own diary.

His jaw hardened. "No. My sister only pretended to take her own life."

Lucy blinked, trying to clear away the fog of confusion. No wonder her aunt had believed in Thomas so strongly, had trusted him so implicitly. He'd kept his sister's confidence,

even when it cost him a betrothal, even when it forced him
to leave London far behind.

"I am glad you know." His voice deepened. "But now that
you do, what will you do with the knowledge?"

She looked up, startled. Once again he was leaving the
choice in her hands. Not trying to pressure her or steer her in
a particular direction. She swallowed the lump of gratitude
in her throat, the answer instantaneous in her mind. "It is not
my place to tell such a secret."

"Thank you." His voice was scarcely louder than her own,
but the words might as well have been shouted, so fiercely
did he say them. "If it becomes known . . . well, suffice it to
say, Josephine would lose any small measure of respect she's
gained in the last three years."

Lucy placed a hand on her stomach, still reeling from the
surprise of it all. "If I may ask . . . why did she do it? *How?*"

"As to the 'hows' of it, the usual way, I would imagine.
I'd left her behind in the country when I came to London,
imagining her safe from harm and perpetually fifteen. She
was only eighteen, not even out yet, when she found herself
with child. So she came to London, thinking I would be able
to help her. But instead of the capable older brother she remembered, she found *me* instead."

Lucy blinked up at him. "I don't understand."

"I was drunk when she arrived, and drunk most of those
hours thereafter. I was barely able to take care of myself. I
suppose Josephine felt she had no other choice."

"But . . . did she even think of what it might do to you?"

"I half suspect she did it *for* me." He shook his head.
"When it became clear the gossip was going to be ruinous,
she decided it would be easier for me to have everyone think
she was well and truly gone." He exhaled, his fingers curling
to fists. "She was so, so certain of her path. I know it sounds
like a terrible choice," he added, "but you can't imagine how
cruel the whispers were."

Lucy thought back to her older sister Clare's experience with the ton, and its myriad examples of cruelty. She thought, too, of the dread she herself had felt for the Season she'd fled. "I think I can imagine," she said dryly.

"She was only three years old when our mother died. I imagine her decision had something to do with that. She wanted something more, something better, for her own child. At least now she can live with some measure of respectability, pretending to be a widow."

Lucy nodded. She could understand his sister's choice. She was nothing if not sympathetic to the plight of women whose choices in life were limited by fate and Society, and who chose, instead, to take matters into their own hands. In some ways it was brilliant. There was no need to hide. No need for his sister to pretend to be something she was not.

But there was still the matter of Thomas. *He* was still hiding, it seemed.

And that made her want to help.

"I think," she said slowly, "that your sister did what she needed to do, and there is no shame in that." She lifted a hand to the little town, where it sat, quietly waiting. "But how did *you* end up here in Lizard Bay?" She swallowed the rest of it.

And why are you still here?

"Our family's holdings included a house here in Lizard Bay. It was a place we'd never visited, and where no one knew us. I'd originally considered it as a home where Josephine could come and raise her child. But she didn't want to leave London." He smiled grimly. "So I left instead. I was afraid that if I stayed, I would want to see her, and that might give her away. By coming here . . . and by *staying* here, at least I can protect her now."

The echo of pain in his voice told her far more than his words did. He had loved his sister. He loved her still.

Lucy leaned forward and placed a hand against his cheek.

"Thomas," she whispered. "No matter what you've been telling yourself these past three years, you *did* protect her. In some ways, you protected her better than if you had stood firm and insisted she follow a more expected path. You respected her choice, even at your own expense." She lifted her other hand to the opposite cheek, framing his face, hoping he could see the truth reflected in her eyes. "I can see why my aunt felt you were worth saving."

THOMAS WANTED TO anchor himself in her gaze, to the promise he saw there and the hope he heard in her voice. He felt as though he was drowning, his lungs exhausted from the hard slog of trying to keep his head above water for three long years.

"I failed her," he said, shaking his head. He pulled Lucy's hands away, feeling undeserving of such a gentle touch. "You didn't know me then. I was no one my sister could depend on, even though she'd come to me, asking for help."

He could still remember how shamefully he'd reacted to Josephine's tearful confession, demanding to know who had done it to her, threatening to kill the man. He'd been drunk when she arrived on his doorstep, but could one ever really be drunk enough in those circumstances? She poured out her heart to him, and he'd only been capable of pouring himself another glass.

"She never told me who was responsible, only that she was an equally culpable party. I tried to convince her to marry someone expedient, a second son desperate enough to overlook her circumstances. Anyone I could find, I didn't care who it was. But I was wrong to suggest that of her." He could see that now. He hadn't counted on his sister's quiet strength.

Or the lengths to which she was willing to go to protect her child.

A quiet touch came on his arm. "Thomas, she will forgive you."

He looked down at this woman, who somehow, despite

all good logic, trusted him. "How could she? You didn't know me then, how hard and callous I could be when I was drinking." The thought of all that the whisky had taken from him over the years made him feel quite sick to his stomach. Christ, was he even the same person now?

"You've changed, then, for the better," Lucy said. "You are strong enough to stay away from something that hurts you and those you love. Surely it is time for you to go back and visit your sister now," she added, squeezing his arm. "Three years is a long time to stay away from family." She hesitated. "And there is more than enough room for you to come with us in the coach today."

He could see what she was trying to do, could see the way her eyes shone at the thought of orchestrating this heart-felt, tear-stained reunion. She was trying—wanting—to fix this, but she really didn't understand. He wasn't ready.

Wasn't anywhere *close* to ready.

He shook his head. "I am the brother who failed her. She'll not want to see me."

"My own brother tried to *poison* me, and I would want to see him."

In spite of the gravity of their conversation, Thomas's lips tipped up. He had a feeling her brother was going to pay dearly in that eventual exchange. "I appreciate your ideas Lucy, truly I do. But this isn't some grand cause that can be fixed so easily. The truth is . . . I *did* try to see her, last week in London. I had my cab drive by her town house and I caught a glimpse of her through a window." He looked up at the sky. "She looked . . . content. It appears she has finally found happiness." His gaze lowered again to meet hers. "I don't want to risk knocking on her door and destroying that."

"Shouldn't that decision be *hers* to make?"

He exhaled slowly. "I can't see a way to do it safely. What if someone recognized me? What if, by association, someone recognized *her*?"

"Well, I don't recommend you charge in waving a flag or holding a sign. You could wear a disguise, or pretend to be a family friend." She smiled, but he could see it was strained, not the full, open smile he was used to. "Perhaps you could try to buy her house. You have some practice in that, after all."

He pondered it. Christ above, he actually *considered* it. Could he go to London, knock on that door, and actually tell Josephine he was sorry? Could he look at his sister and small niece without feeling as though he had failed them?

She reached out and took up his hands, holding them in her own. "I can see this is a decision you must make in your own time, Thomas. But know this. You are presuming your niece would be happier growing up without knowing you. I am not sure that is true. Maybe now is not the right time, but someday, won't she deserve to know who she is, where she came from? Won't she deserve to know the truth of her grandparents, and her wonderful, stupid uncle?"

He frowned. "How can I be wonderful *and* stupid?"

"The two are not necessarily mutually exclusive qualities." She sighed. "The point is, I understand this is a decision you are wrestling with. My aunt stayed away from London, presumably to protect me, but oh, how I wish she'd made a different choice. All I have of her now is her diary." Her hand drifted to the serpentine pendant about her neck. "A bit of jewelry, a pair of glass horses. Far too few memories. I can't help but wish she'd have let *me* make the choice whether or not to know her, because now I'll never know how brilliant she actually was, beyond what the townspeople of Lizard Bay tell me."

Thomas swallowed. "I can't go to London, Lucy. Not right now."

"Then I am going to miss you," she said sadly, stepping forward and pressing a quick, sweet kiss to his lips.

And then she turned toward town.

Regrets are a hard fact of life.

My life has been long and ostensibly full. I've friends and grand causes to keep me busy. A set of diaries to chronicle my adventures, and a lovely— albeit distant—family back in London. But I have not been as brave as I should have been.

And that is what I regret most of all.

Lately, as my body grows weaker and my mind sifts through forty years of decisions, I find myself questioning too many of them. Did I make the right choice for my family, isolating myself in Cornwall to protect their reputation? I do not know. I only know I regularly scan the London Times, eager for any whiff of news, however small and unimportant.

And on the matter of spinsterhood . . . did I make the right choice for me? This, too, I do not know. I only know that my life, since moving to town, has seemed fuller. Richer. I see Reverend Wellsbury nearly every day now, and it makes me wonder if that, too, is a loss I will always regret. But a lady never admits she is wrong.

She holds her head up and pretends it is all as she planned.

Chapter 26

As Lucy slipped into the front door of Mrs. Wilkins's boardinghouse, she heard her father's voice, shouting in the parlor.

"What do you *mean* you don't know where she is? I left her here with the express understanding you would be watching her closely, Mrs. Wilkins. She's a young woman whose reputation is already hanging by a thread. She needs to be chaperoned!"

Wincing, Lucy glanced down her grass-stained night rail. Her father had come early. Or else she had returned too late. Thomas had been right, it seemed.

Already, she missed him. Already, she wanted to run back to him, loop her arms about his neck and pull him down for another bone-melting kiss. Already, she wanted to tell him that *yes*, please, she would marry him, and they should hurry up and post the bans this Sunday in the little church on top of the hill.

But it was too late. He'd said he couldn't come to London, and she knew, in spite of all that had happened, that she needed to spend at least *part* of her life in the city. Lydia was in London. Her sister Clare and her growing brood. Nieces and nephews and family. Thomas had said his good-byes, and she had said her piece.

There was naught to do but wait for him to come to his senses.

And try not to anger her father any further.

"I am on a very tight schedule," came a man's voice she didn't recognize. "The Marston Mining Corporation receives many inquiries, and I don't like having my time wasted."

"Let us give her ten more minutes," came her father's strained voice. "I can show you the property without her, if it comes down to it."

Lucy gasped out loud. Oh, God. Oh, *bugger it all*.

She'd forgotten about the inspector from the Marston Mining Corporation.

She slipped past the parlor, dread making her feet fly up the stairs and over more cats than she could count. In her room, she yanked off her nightdress and pulled on her one remaining gown, her fingers skating across the mother-of-pearl buttons. A quick glance in the mirror confirmed the worst: there were twigs and grass in her hair, and her nose was a helpless sort of pink. Well, it scarcely mattered what she looked like. Her future was hanging in the balance.

She could brush her hair later.

As she turned toward the door, the toe of her boot kicked something hard. It rolled away, off the carpet, rattling onto the hardwood floor. Bending down, she picked it up, turning it over in her hand. It was the lizardite rock from Thomas's satchel, apparently dropped in her haste this morning. She looked further, to the papers that had fallen out and were now scattered across the floor. His proposal for the Linnean Society of London. So much hope, so much work in those pages. But she couldn't take the time to clean it up now. Perhaps later . . .

Only, later, she was going to London.

She swallowed against the surge of panic that wanted to wash over her, and dashed back down the stairs, her fingers closing over the stone in her hand. She burst into the parlor just as her father was stepping toward the door.

"Wait!"

"Lucy, *there* you are! Are you all right?" her father exclaimed, striding toward her. Mrs. Wilkins stood to one side, wringing her hands with worry. Farther afield, a bearded gentleman stood by the fireplace, consulting a pocket watch.

"Oh, thank goodness you are back." Mrs. Wilkins clucked, placing a gnarled hand across her chest. "I'd thought perhaps the haints had taken you."

Beads of sweat had popped up on her father's forehead, and he mopped them with a handkerchief. "God's teeth, child, I was worried sick when we arrived this morning and Mrs. Wilkins said she had no idea where you had gone." He frowned and reached out a hand, plucking a piece of grass from her hair. "What is this?"

Lucy's cheeks heated. "It's just a bit of grass from the moors. I went out to inspect the property one last time." She glanced toward the man from the Marston Mining Corporation. "I am sorry. I didn't mean to inconvenience anyone." Her hand tightened around the stone, wishing for some of its resiliency. "But now that I am here, why don't we all sit down and discuss matters?"

"Young lady," the bearded gentleman said, snapping his watch shut and placing it in his coat pocket. "We are nearly an hour behind schedule as it is. Let us be on our way to see the property."

Lucy glared at the man. The embarrassment of her dishabille paled against the distaste she felt in *his* appearance. The man's suit was worsted wool, and his pocket watch was etched silver. He was clearly well-paid, and likely quite good at his job. She thought of the unspoiled beauty Thomas had shown her this morning, and how the Marston Mining Corporation would happily destroy all of it without a second thought.

The inspector seemed unconcerned by the enormity of the choice in her hands.

She, at least, was wrestling with the decision.

Thomas had truly made her feel as though the decision was hers, and she felt no pressure beyond her own conscience for the direction she ought to go. Seven thousand pounds was a tremendous sum of money to forego. It was far more than she needed to ensure her independence. More than she needed to secure a future, on her own terms.

But greed had never been a part of who she was.

She lifted her chin. "I am very sorry to have you come all this way," she told the inspector, "but I won't be showing you the property today."

The inspector's face darkened. He looked pointedly at her father. "I am afraid I don't understand, Lord Cardwell. You said I might see a sample of the rock."

"Now Lucy," her father coaxed. "There is no harm in at least letting him inspect it. We'll need to know the property's value if we are going to make an educated decision."

Lucy exhaled slowly. "Not *we*, Father. *Me*. It is my opinion. My decision. My property."

Her father blinked. "I . . . that is to say . . . I did not mean . . ."

"You once said I had a good head on my shoulders. You need to trust me to use it now," Lucy warned softly. She turned to face the inspector. Although she was still confused on the matter of what to do with the property, she knew she couldn't stomach the idea of selling Heathmore to the Marston Mining Corporation, not even for seventy thousand pounds. Her aunt may not have made her wishes known in the pages of her diary, but it was clear she had loved Lizard Bay and sought every chance to fix the little town.

Every chance, that was, except the one thing that would likely destroy it instead.

Lucy held out her hand, the green rock resting against her open palm. "There's no need to visit Heathmore today, because I've brought a sample of the rock in question back with me."

The inspector plucked the stone from her hand. "What is this?" He frowned. "It's nothing but a bit of lizardite."

"Oh?" said Lucy innocently. "Do you mean to say it isn't tin after all?" She placed a hand against her chest. "But I thought it must be tin. There's so *much* of it on the property. I simply presumed—"

"Do you mean to say you dragged me all the way here for this?" The inspector scowled in her father's direction. "This rock is useless. *Worse* than useless."

Her father frowned but miraculously held his tongue.

Lucy retrieved the rock from the inspector's hand, her fingers curling protectively around its rough edges. It wasn't useless. Not to her. And keeping Heathmore's secrets out of the hands of the Marston Mining Corporation was a cause that came closer to priceless, in her estimation. "Oh, dear." She sighed dramatically. "I feel so *silly* to have wasted your time."

"As well you should," the inspector snapped, already heading for the door.

Lucy waited until the man's mutterings about wasted time and featherbrained chits faded away, until, even, she heard the front door slam. Then, unable to face the questions she saw in her father's eyes, she gave a curt nod. "I will just go upstairs and pack, then."

She climbed the stairs, fighting back tears as she stepped into her rented room. She shoved her grass-stained nightdress into her bag, then laid the small rock and her aunt's diaries carefully on top. Then, sinking to her knees, she started to shuffle the papers that had fallen out of Thomas's satchel into a neat pile.

Touching them reminded her, too much, of touching him.

The tears that had begun on the stairs fell harder then, threatening to soak the pages. She wiped a sleeve across her eyes, not wanting to damage the delicate paper. They were painstakingly written, his neat handwriting outlining his findings, the language stilted and formal. She thought of his hopes for the area, of his plans to use Heathmore Cottage as a naturalist's retreat. It was a fine idea, but she couldn't imagine it would be enough to save an entire dying town. Because Lizard Bay *was* dying.

It was in every bit as much danger as the Cornish chough.

And while she may have just saved Heathmore's natural beauty from an unscrupulous mining operation, she hadn't exactly come up with a way to save the town yet. It needed something more tenable. Sustainable. After all, nature was fickle. It was not something to hang an entire town's future upon.

A knock came at the door. "Lucy?"

She wiped her eyes more thoroughly. "Come in, Father."

The door opened and her father stepped in, his hat in his hands. She studied him from where she was kneeling on the floor. He looked nervous, though she couldn't sort out why. She was the one who didn't know how to explain herself here. How did one justify giving up such a fortune? The thought that her father might consider her mad for making such a decision gave her pause. She'd come here, after all, because she feared he might be considering such a dire thing.

But that fear didn't come close to changing her mind.

"I see you are packing." He nodded, as though trying to convince himself of her sanity. "The coach I hired in Marston is waiting just outside. No sense delaying our return to London now that the inspector has gone." He reached out and picked up her valise, holding it in front of him like a shield. "Your mother and Lydia miss you terribly."

Lucy stood up, clutching the papers in front of her as

though they might provide a bit of defense. Why did she always feel as though she was at odds with her father? She'd once wanted nothing more than his approval, but as the years rolled on, that approval had become so much harder to win. Or perhaps it was that she had become more fiercely determined to be herself, rather than what he expected?

She pondered that a moment. It had taken Thomas's unquestioning acceptance of who she was—grand causes and all—to understand that she was not some misfit, needing to change.

Thomas liked her—*loved* her—just the way she was.

And . . . *oh, God.* She could see it then, what this terrible, gaping hole in her chest was. Why it hurt so much to consider getting on that coach without him. She loved him, too.

But was love enough, given all he needed to overcome to make a proper life with her?

"I am ready," she whispered, grasping the papers in one hand. If only Thomas was as well.

Her father stepped to one side as she brushed past him. "Lucy," she heard him sigh. "Will you stop for one second and talk to me? I don't know why we always seem to be at such odds."

She stopped with one hand on the stair rail and looked back over her shoulder. "I am not trying to be quarrelsome, Father. I am just being . . . well, *me.*"

"Yes, well." Her father's voice softened. "The decision you have made about Heathmore . . . are you very sure of it?"

"I am."

"Does this have anything to do with Lord Branston?" He frowned. "Or the fact there is a good deal of grass in your hair?"

Lucy's cheeks heated. She lifted a hand to her tangle of hair. Her fingers danced over bits of twigs and the like, the evidence both comforting and damning. "Perhaps."

He bristled. "Do you want me to speak to him? I've another pistol in the coach."

"No. And if I have grass in my hair, you must know it is by my own choice." She permitted herself a thin smile. "If I have changed my mind about selling Heathmore, it is only because he has shown me the truth, and then left the choice in my own hands."

"As long as he's kept his hands to himself," her father growled.

Lucy sighed. No, Thomas hadn't kept his hands to himself. And she hadn't wanted him to either.

"Just tell me why," her father pressed. "Why give up such a potential fortune?"

"Because there are some things in life more important than money." Lucy thought of the sunrise, and all Thomas had shown her. "I don't know what I will do with the property, but I do know I do not wish to exploit it, especially to a company like that. Aunt E considered protecting this town one of her grand causes, and I do as well. There is no harm in letting the cottage and the property sit untouched for a while as I sort out what to do about it."

"Your aunt was involved in this?" Her father frowned. "I might have known. You are so much like my sister, it frightens me sometimes. I still don't know what she wanted, what made her happy, what made her *stay* here." His voice broke with emotion. "And despite it all, you have grown up to be just like her."

Lucy swung around to face him more fully, her fingers tightening about the papers she still held. "Is it really such a terrible thing that we are so much alike?"

Because if it was, it was far too late to fix.

"I . . . that is—" He broke off, seeming unsure of his answer.

"Aunt E chose to stay here to protect our family against the gossip she feared stirring." Lucy hesitated. "She loved me, you know. She loved *you,* in her own eccentric way. Family was important to her, though she didn't always show it. She felt she couldn't come to London because of the danger her eccentricity posed to us, but you never came back to visit her. Why? What harm would there have been in letting me know her?" Lucy stepping toward her father. "Why not send me to her? And why, when you learned she had left me Heathmore, were you so dead set against me even coming to see the property?"

Her father's throat bobbed as he swallowed. "I suppose I feared you might decide to stay here, as she did." His voice broke with emotion. "All those years, with no word from her, not knowing what had happened, or if she was even alive. And then to discover she was here, only to then scarcely ever see her again . . . Lucy, can't you see? I don't want to lose you. It would break my heart to only receive a single card from you at Christmas."

Lucy stared at her father. *Oh God.*

Oh, *bugger it all.*

Was this what their awkward feud was about? He didn't want to *lose* her?

With a small, fierce cry, she moved into her father's arms. "But you would never lose me," she protested, her throat thick with emotion. "I *am* returning to London."

Even though the thought of it made her want to cry.

His arms tightened around her until she was breathing in the familiar scent of tobacco and peppermint, the scents of her childhood. Above her head, he gave a shuddering sigh. "I love you, Lucy. I only want your happiness. And if keeping Heathmore Cottage makes you happy, I shall have to find a way to accept that. Just . . . don't disappear. Not without a word, as my sister did."

"I won't," she promised, pulling back with a tremulous smile. "I'm not *exactly* like Aunt E, you know. I am not at all sure I want to live in a falling-down cottage in Cornwall. I've come to appreciate a few things in life that I had previously taken for granted on this trip."

Things like laundry, and warm fires that didn't go out, and kindly, aging servants who looked out for her, even when she forgot to look out for herself.

And kisses. She had definitely come to appreciate kisses.

Her mind tripped to Thomas's proposal and how tempted she was to accept it. No, she wasn't like her aunt. Aunt E would rather tie someone up or light a fuse than even *consider* the possibility of marriage. But in spite of the pages and pages of guidance warning against it in her aunt's diaries, marriage had shifted to something more possible in Lucy's mind.

"But you should know," she told her father through her slow-blooming smile, "I may want to come back to Lizard Bay and visit on occasion."

He smiled back. "Well. You *are* of an age to make your own decisions."

"Oh there you two are," came Mrs. Wilkins's voice. She appeared at the bottom of the stairs, motioning them down. "Come on, then. I've stirred up Mr. Jamieson and Mr. Bentley to see you properly off to London."

Lucy looped her arm through her father's, as much to find an anchor as to show her affection. But as they stepped out onto the front porch into the bright sunshine, her knees threatened to buckle to see the small crowd that had gathered to see them off.

She wanted to go back to London, and yet she didn't.

Lizard Bay had become very dear these past few days, and she was going to miss each and every face in this crowd. And if *he* was here, watching her with that crooked, compelling grin, she knew there was no way in hell her feet were going to carry her into that coach.

Not unless he was there to help her up into it and climb in behind her.

She craned her neck, searching, but there was no sign of him. And the realization, then, settled over her like a wet, heavy blanket. Thomas wasn't coming to stop her. He wasn't coming to *join* her. Tears welled up in her eyes.

"Don't cry, Miss L," Mrs. Wilkins said, patting her back. "We'll miss you, too, child."

Lucy sniffed as Jamieson slipped a handful of licorice into her hand. "To hold you over until you return," he said, whiskers twitching.

She moved on to the postmaster, who looked a little lost. "Good-bye, Mr. Bentley," she said, wiping her eyes.

"They said you were aggrieved," he said, looking confused.

Behind her, Mrs. Wilkins raised her voice. "No, I said she must *leave*, Bentley."

Lucy smiled through her tears, realizing, suddenly, how much she was going to miss this place. How was she to properly manage a life when her heart lay in two very disparate places? She held out the sheath of papers that had spilled from Thomas's satchel, her fingers trembling against the edges. "May I beg a favor, Mr. Bentley? Would you please give these to Lord Branston? They do not belong to me."

"Eh?" He cupped a hand behind his ear. "You want a song?"

She shook her head. "No, *belong*." She pressed the pages into the postmaster's hands. "Remember, give them to Lord Branston. He needs them most."

And hopefully, with this gesture, he would see she was delivering the decision back into his hands.

THOMAS RETURNED TO his lonely house and tossed his lonely satchel onto his lonely table.

It fell awkwardly, the contents spilling. A handful of wilted plants and a few lizardite rocks fell out, the stones rolling noisily across the table. He stared at the mess, his brain slowly registering the obvious. His proposal was missing. Not that it mattered anyway.

It wasn't his decision. It never had been.

His gaze landed on the clock that sat on his mantel. It was a quarter past noon. Had it really only been a few hours since he'd held her in his arms? Kissed that wide, laughing mouth, and other secret places, the very act of loving her so right, so heartfelt, he felt as though it had been his future spread out before him?

And now she was on a coach to Salisbury, bound with all due haste for London.

Christ, but what had he done?

Or rather, what *hadn't* he done?

Lucy had invited him to come with her and he'd hesitated. No, that wasn't quite the truth. He'd refused. It had been an automatic response, borne of three years of practice. But had he done so to protect his sister, or because he was afraid of how Lucy might see him there?

After all, he *had* gone to London. Just last week.

But therein, he suspected, lay the problem.

His last trip to London had been disastrous. He'd succumbed to the temptation of the bottle far too easily, and the glimpse he caught of his sister had left him more haunted than relieved. But it wasn't the thought of his sister that had him tied up in knots now.

It was the thought of Lucy.

What if she saw him as he used to be, out of control and angry with the world?

There was so much more at stake now that he knew he loved her.

A knock on the front door startled him from his thoughts. Surely he'd heard wrong. He hadn't heard a knock on his front door in . . . well, forever. Everyone in town understood his need for solitude and respected those boundaries.

Everyone, that was . . . except Lucy. She was not a woman who respected boundaries.

And God, how he loved her for it.

He charged to the front foyer and pulled open the door, only to choke back a snarl of disappointment as he realized it was only the vicar standing on his doorstep.

"Good afternoon, Lord Branston."

"Reverend Wellsbury. I am afraid now is not a good time."

"No, I can see it is not. And that is why I really must speak to you about a matter of grave importance."

Thomas swiped a weary hand across his face, knowing he was being rude, not sure if he cared enough to correct it. Finally, he offered a grudging nod. "All right. Come in, then." He stepped aside, motioning the vicar in. "What brings you here?"

And why couldn't it have been her, instead?

"A mistake, I hope," the vicar informed him, stepping into the foyer. He looked around. "Good heavens, boy, where is your bag? Do you want to throw it all away?"

Thomas gaped at him. "I beg your pardon?"

The vicar drew himself taller. "You let Miss L return to London without you."

Understanding dawned. "She wanted to go."

"Bollocks, boy."

Thomas stared at the man. Had the reverend just said . . . ?

"I'll say it again. *Bollocks*." Reverend Wellsbury began to pace. "Bollocks to your pride, to hers, to all of it. Pride is a terrible sin, particularly when it suffocates love. I don't care what she's done or where she's gone. The only thing that matters now is what you will do. Do you think love is so plentiful, so easy, that you might ever expect to love another the way you love her?"

"But . . . how did you know?"

"That you loved her? I have eyes in my head, don't I? I can see the way you look at her, and the way she looks at you. I recognize the signs because I can look back and see them in myself. You *love* her. And yet, you are letting her go?" He shook his head, disgusted. "I let my pride get in the way of forty years of potential happiness. A life I might have shared, if only I'd seen fit to bend a little, at the start. And I see it all happening again. Well, bollocks to that."

"Er . . . should you be saying that word?" Thomas asked uneasily.

"Because I'm a man of God?" The reverend rolled his eyes. "Well, I'm a man first, and I'm saying it for her. It's what Miss E would have said. And she'd also want me to say this as well: don't wait too long to make this decision. Not as *we* did."

Thomas blinked, beginning, finally, to understand. He'd long suspected an attraction between the pair, however much they seemed to deny it. There was too much anticipation in their exchanges. Miss E had actually seemed to look *forward* to church on Sundays—an odd reaction, considering how she all too predictably heckled the sermons.

"Reverend Wellsbury," he sighed. "I appreciate you coming, and you should know, I *want* to go. To follow her. And yes, I love her. So much it hurts to breathe around her. But . . . if I go to London, I may prove myself unworthy of her. And then I shall have even less than a chance of changing her mind."

"Bollocks to that as well. Miss E had faith in you, you know. Not only that you would stay sober, but that you were a good man. But if you stay here, you will prove her wrong." The vicar's mouth, finally, began to stretch into a smile. "And you and I both know, Miss E was *never* wrong."

Diary of Edith Lucille Westmore
April 2, 1853

Stubbornness, I'll allow, is one of my most significant flaws. Even now I am stubbornly resisting my body's weakness. Some say your life should flash before your eyes as your last breath draws near, but in truth, I see only the life I hadn't the courage to live.

I would like to say I have no regrets.

But a lady shouldn't lie—even to herself.

When he heard I was ill, Reverend Wellsbury came to hear my confession, and oh, what a confession it was. His confession, not mine. He held my hand and told me he has loved me for nigh on forty years. Moreover, he asked me to marry him and gave me the most beautiful serpentine necklace as a token of his love. I declare, if I'd known a little infirmity was the key to unlocking this truce, I might have pretended to be dying decades ago.

But I am not pretending now. Whether we have days or hours left, I will make them count. I accepted his proposal, and gladly. And if I could reach out to my younger self and offer a bit of advice . . . I would encourage myself to listen to my heart a little more and my pride a little less.

A life well-loved is a life well-lived.

Even if that realization comes nearly too late.

*C*hapter 27

*L*ucy closed the cracked leather cover of Aunt E's final journal and leaned back against the seat of the Cardwell coach as it carried them away from the train station. Tears blurred her eyes, and her hand crept up to tangle with the serpentine pendant she still wore about her neck. A token of love nearly lost.

At least she understood its significance now.

No matter how she might wish it, there were no more pages to read. The date of the final entry in the last of her aunt's diaries was the date of her aunt's death.

Outside, the chaotic streets of London were giving way to the order of Mayfair, which meant Cardwell House would soon be looming into view. But she was too distracted by her aunt's final words to focus on her homecoming. To read her aunt's dying revelation felt like the cruelest of jokes. Was this why Aunt E had asked Reverend Wellsbury to send her the diaries? Her aunt had not, after all, actually been able to reach back in time and give her younger self the advice she'd longed to.

But perhaps Aunt E had realized she could still offer that advice to her niece.

And the advice imparted in that final page . . . it changed everything. Lucy had imagined she was following her aunt's guidance, holding herself apart from love, a determined spinster to the end. But the truth was, she had missed Thomas from the moment the wheels of the coach began to roll away from Lizard Bay. She should have tried again to convince him to come to London.

Should have accepted his proposal and lived wherever fate dictated.

Should have told him she loved him in return.

Should have, should have, should have.

Aunt E's life was made entirely of that regretful refrain, it seemed. But what refrain would best describe her own life?

And was it too late to change?

"I know your mother will be pleased to have you back," her father said beside her, by way of making conversation. "She's been frantic with worry, trying to sort out how to keep the London gossips from catching wind of your little adventure."

Lucy wiped a quick hand across her eyes and sighed. *Her mother was worried.* Over her safety, or over the embarrassment of a missing daughter? After all, the Season had already started, and she had gone missing for the first crucial week, when impressions were best made and flirtations established. In all likelihood, her mother was livid beneath that purported worry.

Finally, the cab was slowing, a footman helping her down. The polished marble steps of Cardwell House seemed to go on for miles. But before she could climb them, the front door burst open and Lydia came tearing down the steps.

"Oh, you *beast*," her sister cried, wrapping her arms around Lucy and shaking with emotion. "I can't believe you left without saying a word! But I am so, so glad you are back. I've missed you terribly." She pulled back, her blue eyes shining. "I want to hear everything about your adventure. Did you really go to a town called Lizard Bay? It sounds quite odd."

Lucy shook her head, smiling. "It isn't odd. It is lovely." And in truth, she was already missing it. But she could scarcely explain before apologies were made. "Can you forgive me for not telling you I was leaving?" She looked beyond Lydia's shoulder to see her mother step out onto the front steps as well. She winced to see her mother's rigid posture, her fixed smile. "Can you *both* forgive me?" she asked, louder now. "I . . . I'm sorry I destroyed the Season you worked so hard to plan, Mother."

"There is nothing to forgive." Lydia's voice rang firmly, and she glanced over her shoulder at Lucy's mother. "And nothing has been lost. We conspired a way to cover for you." She turned back, a delicate blush staining her cheeks. "I . . . I may have gone to two balls and a musicale this week, pretending to be you."

"What?" Lucy gasped. She looked between Lydia and her mother in astonishment. She could imagine why Lydia had agreed to do it. Her sister had long dreamed of a grand come-out. But to have her mother concoct such a charade . . .

Wasn't a lady always supposed to tell the truth?

"Well, you both look so much alike, dear," her mother offered, her smile softening to more of an apology. "And she had done such a good job during calling hours . . ."

"And I *wanted* to do it," Lydia chimed in, her cheeks still pink. "I danced nearly every dance, and drank ratafia and lemonade, and met the most handsome gentleman." She sighed dreamily. "I am grateful for the experience, actually."

"I had already accepted these invitations for you before you disappeared," Mother went on, coming down the stairs now to give Lucy a hug of her own. "The gossip would have been immense. It seemed the most logical and least embarrassing thing to do until we found you."

"You mean . . . my Season isn't ruined?" Lucy somehow managed to whisper against her mother's embrace. The thought made dread pool in her stomach.

Her mother straightened and smiled gratefully in Lydia's direction. "Far from it. Your sister did brilliantly. She's even attracted the attention of a nice viscount who might do well for you. I think you will be well set up to go on with the rest of the Season. The Duchess of Pembroke's ball is tomorrow, where we can make the switch. Best do it now, before people catch on." Her hand crept up to touch Lucy's hair. "Provided, of course, we can do something about this."

Lucy frowned. She didn't want a nice viscount. She *wanted* an auburn-haired marquess. Thomas had made her feel beautiful, as though she was the only woman in a room. In the *world*. But she had a notion that on a London dance floor, she was going stand out in a more obtrusive way.

Her mother's hand fell away. "You are frowning. Do you mind so terribly? We couldn't see another way forward without claiming an illness, and we didn't want to give anyone the impression of infirmity." She shook her head. "I still can't sort out how Wilson thought you were locked in your room all that time. And then, when Lydia's initial appearance worked so well, it just seemed natural enough to go on . . ." Her voice trailed off, no doubt on account of the look on Lucy's face. Her mother cleared her throat, a wholly unladylike sound. "Well, should you choose to not go through with it, then we'll come up with a more fitting exit from the Season." Her lips tipped downward. "Perhaps we can have you sprain your ankle. Call in Dr. Merial, spread the word about. It worked well enough for your sister Clare."

Lucy shook her head, not wanting to foster any greater deception. It was already going to be difficult enough to keep it all straight. "I will go, at least for tomorrow." She didn't know how long she could stay in London, given that her heart was already urging her back to Lizard Bay. But for now, what harm would there be in paying this penance? Surely she could suffer through an awkward waltz or two, play the dutiful daughter, for a few days.

Provided, that was, anyone wanted to dance with her.

Suddenly, a sprained ankle seemed like a smashing good idea.

Her mother's gaze fell lower, to Lucy's neck. "What a lovely necklace you are wearing," she exclaimed, tilting her head. "I've never seen it before." Her mother reached out to touch the pendant, turning it over thoughtfully. "Beautiful, really, especially against your blond hair."

Lucy's hand crept up to covetously cover the stone. "It belonged to Aunt E."

"Hmmm." Her mother's hand fell away. "Well, she may have been eccentric, but your Aunt E clearly had excellent taste in jewelry."

Lucy remembered, then, her mother's opinion of the woman. It was an opinion Lucy had once wrongly harbored herself. But Aunt E wasn't mad, or thoughtless, or uncaring either. She was simply who she was, and Lucy would always treasure the bits and pieces she'd learned of her aunt's life. "I would like to wear my necklace tomorrow night," she said impulsively, lifting her chin. "For good luck." The unspoken warning hung in the air. She would go to the ball . . . but she would do so on her own terms.

Her mother considered it a moment. "I can't see any harm in that. Just do not let people know where it came from. I would hate for anyone to suspect you've been in Cornwall this past week."

Geoffrey chose that moment to step out of the front door and tumble down the steps. His blond hair was rumpled and he looked as though he'd just been roused from bed despite the fact that it was approaching dinnertime. The scent of stale cheroots and gin clung to him like a miasma. Good heavens. The boy was only seventeen.

When had gin and cheroots and sleeping until evening become a part of his daily diet?

"There you are, sis!" A shit-eating grin split his face. "I hope you know I am missing a good deal of fun at university on your behalf."

Lucy's eyes narrowed. Her rash might be better, thank you very much, but her temper was anything but. "What are *you* doing here?" Her hands came up to settle on her hips. "Come to put poison ivy in all of our beds?"

His eyes crinkled. "Come on, don't snarl at me so, it was only a little bit of fun. No harm done. And someone needed to help Lydia make a grand splash during her debut. Or rather, during *your* debut." He shrugged. "Who better than someone who is practically a professional jokester?"

"He's been a big help," Lydia interjected. "He introduced me to several of his friends."

"Mother summoned me to make sure it was as believable as possible. And we've done a ripping good job of it, if I do say so myself." Geoffrey's grin widened as his gaze swept over her rumpled appearance. "Good God. You look a little rough around the edges, sis. Then again, I suppose you *have* been staying in a rat-infested cottage. Bring any back for us?"

Lucy huffed out a breath. Leave it to Geoffrey to say *she* looked rough around the edges, when his own appearance practically screamed he'd been frequenting a gin house. "As a matter of fact . . ." She put her hand in the pocket of her skirt. "I've brought you something from Cornwall."

The cocky smile slid off his face.

She pretended to hurl something at him.

Damned if he didn't shriek like a girl, slapping at his chest, his face gone white.

"Idiot," she laughed. "I'm not afraid of rats. And I'm a bloody *lady*."

"I AM GLAD to have you safely back, Miss Lucy."

Lucy glanced up from her self-appointed role pacing the drawing room carpet to see Wilson's broad, familiar face. He was standing at attention, his gleaming silver tray balanced precisely in his gloved hand.

In spite of her worry, the sight of him warmed her heart.

"It is good to be back," she lied. "Thank you for keeping my secret for so long. Your loan was much appreciated." She hesitated, trying to sort through her debts. She owed Wilson more than she could ever properly repay. Those extra days he had given her were just enough time to reach Heathmore Cottage and fall madly, deeply in love. "I promise I will pay you back when Father resumes my pin money."

"It was a gift, Miss Lucy, not a loan." He shook his head gently. "I was pleased to do it."

She swallowed, gratitude thickening her voice. "I understand Mother didn't realize I was gone for several days at least."

"There was much shrieking when Lady Cardwell finally discovered you were missing." A smile twitched at the corners of Wilson's mouth. "Loud, *unladylike* shrieking. You would have enjoyed hearing her screams, I suspect. But if I may ask . . . I understand you've a ball to attend in only a few hours. One would imagine you will need to preserve your strength for dancing. Why are you pacing a hole in the carpet instead?"

She looked down. "I am not looking forward to tonight's ball," she admitted.

Or the one after that, or the one thereafter.

Something about tonight's ball and all the expectations it carried made her want to toss up her luncheon into the nearest potted plant. She had promised her mother she would attend tonight's, at least. To smile and dance and pretend all was well. Lydia had worked hard to give her this opportunity, and she didn't want to let her sister down. But it felt wrong to be forced to go through the motions of pretending to be carefree and available, when her heart was so clearly tied up in Thomas.

"Ah." The butler frowned. "Am I to presume, then, that you are not open to receiving a visitor either?"

Lucy winced. "If it is Lydia's viscount, I think not." In fact, the thought of facing the man tonight made her stomach churn a vigorous protest.

"It is not a viscount." Wilson paused dramatically, then stepped forward and extended his silver salver. "It is, in fact, a marquess."

It took a moment to sort through the butler's words, but when they registered, her eyes flew to the card presented there, the black ink stark against the white vellum.

The Marquess of Branston

Lucy suddenly felt as though she had run the length of Oxford Street and back, her heart pounding and her face burning. He had come. To London.

For *her*.

With a small, glad cry, she lifted her skirts.

"Er . . . Miss Lucy . . ." Something in Wilson's voice made her still. "He did not come to the front door. He is at the *scullery* door."

That made her blink, but only for a second. No doubt Thomas was being cautious of her father's propensity to wave pistols about.

She dashed down the hallway and burst through the kitchen doors. Yanking open the scullery door, she nearly launched herself into his arms.

Except . . . it wasn't quite the Thomas she remembered from Cornwall.

Oh, the important parts were all there. Familiar hazel eyes seemed to scrape against her skin with a raw hunger she understood all too well, given that the very same emotion was coursing through her. His mouth was still quirked higher on one side, a rakish, lopsided grin that pulled her heart right up alongside it. But the clothing . . . now, that was a different matter entirely. She stepped back to properly take him in, her gaze tripping across his checked wool trousers, the embroidered waistcoat, the gleaming top hat. He was wearing his London costume, again, having shed the achingly familiar skin of his Cornwall clothing.

Which only made his appearance at the scullery door all the more confusing.

"Why have you come to the scullery entrance?" she asked dubiously. "You look a bit ridiculous standing here, as if you've come to deliver the fish."

"Ridiculous, am I?" He lifted a brow as he twirled a silver-tipped walking cane. "Strange words, coming from a lady who first met me dressed like a boy."

She sniffed the air suspiciously. "Are you drunk?"

"No." His eyes met hers, deadly serious. "I've not even been tempted to have a drink since my train arrived, which has been a revelation in and of itself." He looked down at his clothing, and finally a sheepish smile broke through. "Although I am beginning to suspect a man would have to be either a fool or desperate to dress this way sober. I've come straight from the train. And I've come to the scullery entrance because I wanted to keep news of my arrival quiet." He hesitated, just enough. "I've come to see my sister, you see."

Lucy knew she ought to be glad. But instead of giving a little leap of gladness, her heart stubbornly insisted on feeling a little hurt instead.

He'd come to London to see his sister. Not to see her.

Still, he was here, wasn't he? At *her* scullery door. There was something in that, even if it wasn't the dramatic, sweeping declaration of love she had hoped for.

"Will you come with me?" he asked.

She caught her breath. "I . . . I am afraid I can't tonight." Oh, she wanted to. But his timing was to rot. "I'm to attend the Duchess of Pembroke's annual ball in just a few hours. I promised my mother I would go, and I've a good deal of disappointment to make up for, apparently." And she needed to do a proper job of it, too, or else *all* their reputations would be ruined.

"This will only take an hour or two. You will be back in plenty of time."

Lucy bit her lip. She wanted to say yes. She *wanted* to say yes to an entire host of things. But was she to serve as a crutch for this mad adventure, or had he issued the invitation for more honorable reasons? "Why?" she whispered. "Why do you want me to come with you?"

"I want you to meet her. In truth, I've wanted you to meet her from the start."

Lucy could feel herself wavering. She suspected she might go anywhere with this man. "Thomas, I am glad you want to see your sister, truly I am. But if I may ask . . . why are you dressed like this?"

He glanced down. "I was trying to be subtle. I thought my usual clothing from Cornwall might cause more attention on the streets of London."

"Subtle?" Lucy snorted. "I am quite sure the pattern on that waistcoat has never been called anything of the sort. Are those really embroidered cherubs?"

His smile seemed to stretch across his face. "Yes. Trappings of my previous time in London, I'm afraid. A gentleman ought not to visit the tailor's when he is drunk." He hesitated, his smile hanging on the edge of falling away. "I suppose I do look a bit ridiculous. What do you suggest, then? I want to see Josephine, but I am worried my appearance may attract undue attention. I don't want people to see me knocking on her door and guess the ruse."

"Well then, you need a proper disguise, not a waistcoat

with cherubs." She thought back to their first meeting, in the drawing room that fateful day when he'd come to increase his offer for Heathmore. She'd been dressed as a boy, and it had taken more than a second glance to set things straight. She motioned him inside. "Come on, then. I need to get you upstairs without the servants seeing you."

"Why, Miss Westmore." His gaze trailed warmly down her body, making the fine hairs on the back of her neck sing to attention. "Are you intending to have your way with me?"

Lucy's laugh slid right out of her, like a bird bursting into song. "I intend to have my way with your wardrobe." She smiled up at him. "And *someone* is going to have teach you how to walk properly in skirts."

Chapter 28

Thomas lowered his hand from the knocker and stared up at the front of the red brick town house. Behind him the sound of shod hooves rang out on the cobblestones, fair notice that the hackney they'd hired out of Mayfair was leaving—and along with it, any notion to quit this lark. He ran a finger beneath the stranglehold of his high lace collar. Lucy had gamely pilfered through the dregs of her wardrobe and dressed him as though he was a china doll: petticoats, corset, bodice, skirts. He was even wearing stockings, the whisper of silk against his legs a poor promise of comfort, given they were already showing a tendency to sag about his ankles.

Christ above, how did women *do* this?

Lucy stood beside him, loose-limbed and easy, far more comfortable in her boy's clothing than he felt in his dress. She'd laughingly insisted he needed a chaperone, and then proceeded to step into a bloody pair of trousers.

Not that he blamed her. It turned out that wearing skirts was not for the faint of heart.

A hand burrowed into his. He looked down to see Lucy's

fingers twine with his, and his chest tightened. God, he loved this woman. She was brave and courageous and daring and mad, and all those things combined in him as a rush of affection and lust.

And what a pair they made, she in her trousers and he in . . .

Well, suffice it to say, his Hessians did not match his lace collar.

"Are you nervous?" she asked, squeezing his hand. Her blue eyes met his, open and honest beneath the slouched brim of her hat. Her hair was poking out in a hundred different angles, as though she was a blond porcupine. He'd never seen a more beautiful sight.

He smiled. "No," he said, honestly. Perhaps it was because his head felt almost violently clear, focused on the task at hand instead of the bottle. Or perhaps it was the anticipation of introducing his sister to the woman standing beside him. He was heading into this with a clear head and a hopeful heart. And no matter the outcome, he was at least going to try.

The door opened and a mob-capped maid peeked out. "May I 'elp you?"

Behind the servant a pleasant foyer loomed, and from deeper in the house he could hear the awkward notes of a pianoforte, seemingly plunked at random. It sounded a bit as though someone were trying to murder a piano, and instead only succeeded in maiming it.

Thomas pulled out his card. "Please tell your mistress Lord Branston is here. We would like to see Mrs. Smythe."

The maid's eyes trailed down his clothing. "Did you say . . . 'lord'?"

Bloody hell. He'd forgotten he was wearing skirts. And pretending to be someone else.

Lucy, thank God, sprang to action. "*I* am Lord Branston," she corrected, her voice artificially gruff. "And Mrs. Smythe will want to see us."

The maid looked doubtful, but she motioned them in. The sound of mismatched piano notes grew louder as they were led down a hallway, and then they emerged into an airy drawing room. In one corner a pianoforte was in use, explaining the racket he'd heard in the hallway. A small child—little more than a toddler, really—was seated on a piano bench that was far too big for her, her legs kicking industriously in the air as she pounded on the keys. A woman sat to one side, her chin in her hand, eyes closed shut in a well-defined wince.

The maid left him standing by the doorway and went to whisper something in her mistress's ear. The woman looked up, her beautiful face pale with surprise.

She stayed the child's fingers with a quick hand. "Thomas?" she whispered as the last note awkward trailed off. Her eyes tugged toward him in confusion.

He nodded, his shoulders tense.

Would Josephine be happy to see him? Angry? It had been three years, after all.

But then she was standing up in a rush of heavy silk, stumbling toward him, her eyes bright with tears. And then, unbelievably, he was being folded into her arms.

After a long, wonderful moment she pulled back, framing his face with her hands. "Oh, you terribly wicked man, why are you dressed this way, and why didn't you tell me you were coming?" she demanded, laughing and crying all at the same time.

"I didn't want anyone to recognize me. And I wasn't sure of my reception," he admitted.

"You are *always* welcome here," she said, almost fiercely. Her hands tightened against his cheeks, as though to punish him for thinking such a thing. He took the moment of silence to study her. He was more than a little surprised by the changes time had wrought—the fullness about her cheeks, the way her eyes crinkled when she laughed. She was scarcely recognizable as the child she had once been. Her hair had darkened with motherhood, her figure grown more generous. She was still beautiful. Still Josephine, through and through. Just . . . older. Wiser, perhaps. It was good—if startling—to see.

Her hands fell away. "Why have you come?" A slight frown formed on the edges of her lips. "I feel certain it isn't merely for a social call, not when you've stayed away for three years."

"I was finally forced to see reason." He glanced back at Lucy, who was waiting patiently to one side. She might be dressed like a boy at present, but he knew the kind, generous heart that lurked beneath those boy's togs, and he was proud to present this woman to his sister. "Josephine, may I present Miss Lucy Westmore."

"Ah." Josephine's voice sounded amused. Her eyes swept Lucy's clothing and came back to rest on her face. "I am beginning to understand, I think."

Lucy stepped forward. "Do not worry. Your secret is safe with me." Her cheeks pinked up and she gestured to her trousers. "Clearly, I have a few secrets of my own."

Josephine tilted her head, studying Lucy with interest. "I don't know what you've done to my brother to get him to finally come and visit me, but whatever it is, you have my undying thanks. I've missed him, terribly."

"Oh, it wasn't all me. I merely pointed out to him that men could be both stupid and wonderful at the same time." Lucy laughed. "He did the rest on his own." She hesitated before adding, "Though it took him bloody long enough."

Josephine's smile stretched higher. "I can see we are going to get along brilliantly, Miss Westmore."

A tug came on his coat. Thomas looked down. A bright face peered up at him, hazel eyes, framed by light auburn hair. "Who are you?" came the tiny voice attached to the small, beautiful creature.

A lump formed in his throat. Christ, but his niece looked just like Josephine had, once upon a time. His mind cartwheeled backward. His sister hadn't been much older than this when their parents died. "Er . . ." He hesitated, then glanced helplessly back at his sister, unsure of what—if anything—she had told her daughter about him.

God knew, the rest of the world had been kept in the dark.

"He's your uncle, Ellie." Josephine put a hand on the child's head, caressing the curls. "Can't you see? He's got the same color eyes you do."

The girl scrunched her nose. "He's not very pretty."

Thomas laughed out loud at that. "No, I don't suppose I am."

Despite the child's pronouncement, her eyes were bright and curious. She looked up at him as though it was the most natural thing to have one's long-lost uncle show up wearing skirts. Then again, she likely still lived in a world of make-believe. He probably could have shown up on a winged horse and been met with the same acceptance.

His niece cocked her head. "Eddie next door has an uncle who takes him to sail boats on the water at Hyde Park. *You've* never taken me to sail a boat," she accused.

Josephine laughed softly. "He lives in Cornwall, duck. You haven't seen him since shortly after you were born, so you don't remember him."

The lump in Thomas's throat grew larger and he had no chance of swallowing it away.

No. The girl didn't remember him, and he ought to be ashamed of that fact. "But I remember you," he told her solemnly, lowering himself to one knee so he could look her more firmly in the eye. "I think of you nearly every day." How could he not? He was responsible for this child, whether she or the rest of the world realized it.

And not only because of the money he sent each month through his solicitor, or the fact that he had purchased this town house, once upon a time. The lump swelled until it felt the approximate size of the London Tower. He wanted to be a part of this child's life. He wanted to be a part of *both* of their lives.

And that meant he needed to spend far more time in London.

The child's eyes grew wide. "You *do*?"

He nodded. "And I would be happy to take you to the park, if your mother says it is all right." Provided, of course, he could come up with a less damning disguise. He wasn't going to attempt navigating Hyde Park in skirts. "But it's our secret." He held a finger to his lips. "Promise?"

The child looked up at her mother, hopeful.

Josephine nodded her agreement. "Yes, duck. It's a secret. Just between us. He is your uncle, but you mustn't tell anyone."

"All right." Ellie smiled. "But *only* if he promises to take me to sail a boat."

LUCY SLIPPED AWAY, her smile lingering long after she boarded the omnibus back to Oxford Street. She would have liked to stay at Golden Square. She was fascinated by the beautiful and mysterious Mrs. Smythe, by the young girl who played the pianoforte so terribly, by the stunned smile she'd seen on Thomas's face. There had been a subtle easing of tension about his eyes, as though the worry of three years was stripped away and replaced with wonder.

She'd wanted to linger, to watch. But it wasn't really her place. She was an outsider. Thomas and his sister had three years to catch up on. And she didn't want the promises she had made to her mother and Lydia to interrupt such a pretty reunion.

The shadows were stretching out in front of Cardwell House by the time she made it back, so she snuck in through the scullery door entrance, keeping her head down and cap pulled low over her eyes. She crept down the hallway, feeling relieved to have made it back unnoticed, and already dreading the predictable pinch of corset that awaited her abovestairs. God knew, she'd need to be tight-laced tonight to fit into her gown, which was already pressed and laid out, eager to begin its reign of torture.

Suddenly, without warning, a hand snaked out of the drawing room door and she was jerked unceremoniously inside.

"Lucy Westmore," Lydia hissed. "Just where do you think you are going dressed like this?" One of Lydia's hands flapped about like a bird, and the other stayed tucked behind her back. "Are you trying to escape tonight's ball?"

Lucy stared at her sister, shocked to a stammer. "Er . . . ah . . . no, that is. I was sneaking *in,* actually. Not out." She reached out a trembling hand to cup her sister's shoulder-length strands of hair. "Oh, Lydia," she groaned, "what have you done?"

Lydia blew a wayward strand from her eyes. "I've cut it, you ninny."

"But . . . *why?*"

Her sister pulled her hand from behind her back and held out the length of her cut hair, as though presenting a bouquet of flowers to an undeserving child. "Because for tonight's ball, *you* need it more than I do. We will pin your hair back and then add a hairpiece. No one will ever need to know the hair isn't your own."

Lucy blinked back a hot wash of tears as she stared at the wispy strands of blond hair clutched in her sister's hand. "You did this . . . for me?"

Lydia heaved a frustrated sigh. "For heaven's sake Lucy, I would do nearly *anything* for you. I should hope that would be obvious by now, given how bloody hard I have worked to save your reputation."

Lucy gaped at her sister. "Did you just say 'bloody'?"

"*I'm* not the one who needs to be a lady tonight," Lydia answered. "*You* are." Her eyes flashed, blue mirrors of Lucy's own. "And if you don't march upstairs *right* now and get into your bath and stand still long enough for us to fix your hair, it will all be lost."

Chapter 29

The noise swept over her, swirling notes from the musicians, the roar of low conversation, melding in a mad mix of sound. Then came the smells, a thousand beeswax candles, flickering in their sconces. The collective perfumes, rising above the crowd and mixing in a fragrance best characterized as *eau de ton*.

The Duchess of Pembroke's ball appeared to be the crush of the Season.

Perhaps *that* was why her heart felt so muffled and bruised in her chest.

Lucy followed her mother through the open doors, holding her breath as their names were announced. What was one more nervous debutante added to the mix? Hardly anyone of significance. And perhaps, if she kept to the corners, hugged the walls, she might escape this night unscathed, the deception corrected, no harm done.

Breathe, she reminded herself.

Though she probably ought to be reminding herself to bow instead.

Finally, they were standing before the Duchess of Pembroke and her mother was sweeping a graceful curtsy. Lucy followed suit, though her stomach insisted on staying somewhere down around her feet.

"I am very pleased to make your acquaintance, your grace," she said.

Quietly and demurely.

She hoped.

The intensity of the duchess's stare felt to Lucy a bit like hot coals dropped down the front of her décolletage. She lifted a gloved hand to her chest, clasping the serpentine pendant to steady her nerves. Tonight she'd replaced the black ribbon with a delicate gold chain, and as a result the pendant hung lower than usual, nestled against the far-too-generous swell of her breasts. And bugger it all, that was precisely where the Duchess of Pembroke was staring.

The older woman raised her quizzing glass, and Lucy braced herself. She knew she had looked her best upon leaving her bedroom. She'd sat for what seemed like hours as the maid and Lydia hovered around her, tugging here, pulling there. With the snood hairpiece, a slew of hairpins, and a frightening amount of pomade, she looked as though her hair had been carefully and elaborately styled on top of her head.

But even at her best, she was hardly the most fetching face in the room. And who knew what had drawn the duchess's attention? Was her hairpiece coming down? Were her nipples popping out of her gown, perchance, a casualty of her perfect curtsy?

"What a *lovely* necklace," the duchess exclaimed. The quizzing glass lowered. "Tell me, wherever did you find such a charming and unusual piece?"

Lucy thought fast—though not, she suspected, particularly well. "There is an . . . ah . . . jeweler in town who specializes in serpentine jewelry. The stone comes from Cornwall." Her mother's elbow in her back served a sharp warning. "Not that I've *been* to Cornwall, you understand," she fumbled, "but the jeweler explained it all. It's a very unusual stone, unique to that part of the country." She bit her lip, realizing she was rambling on.

Perhaps another reminder to breathe would not be out of order.

"It is beautifully designed," the duchess said with a gracious smile. "Which jeweler, did you say?"

Lucy realized she was now in danger of breathing too much. Closer to gasping, actually. She'd wanted to wear the necklace for good luck. A reminder of the things she valued, things that were not found in a glittering ballroom. But it seemed that instead of steadying her nerves, its unusual appearance had only caused her more trouble.

"Er . . . Smythe's," she stammered, then immediately wanted to kick herself.

What had made her say that? Thomas and his sister were clearly still stuck in her head. Now she needed to invent more explanations, more lies. The web was twisting and turning, becoming ever more complicated.

"Well. I would love to have a similar piece." The duchess smiled. "Did the jeweler perchance have any others?"

Through Lucy's racing thoughts and heated cheeks, inspiration somehow struck like a thunderbolt. She nodded numbly. "Several, in fact."

Oh, bugger it all. Why hadn't she seen it before? It was so obvious as to almost be laughable. Lizard Bay needed an industry that would save its residents from ruin.

The town had a nearly unlimited supply of lizardite stones.

And if the Duchess of Pembroke was fascinated by a serpentine charm, wouldn't others in London surely be as well?

THOMAS STEPPED INTO the ballroom, the lurching strains of the music feeling wholly unfamiliar despite the fact he'd once been an active participant in the swirl of London's grand Season. Then again, when he'd last stepped into a ballroom, he was focused on the location of the nearest source of liquor.

Tonight felt different because it *was* different. He was not here because of the obligation or expectations of his position. He felt no urge to seek out the refreshment table and determine if the punch had been properly laced with spirits.

He was here because he wanted to be.

And because he wanted *her*.

When he first realized that Lucy had slipped away from his sister's house, he'd wanted to chase after her. There were things he needed to say, revelations to share. He realized, now, that he could be in London without fear of betraying his sister or succumbing to the temptation of a bottle. If London was where Lucy's family was, he would gladly live here for her. But even as he'd begun to offer his apologies to Josephine, promising to come back soon, he realized what Lucy must have intended. She'd left to give him this moment with his sister, to let their time stretch longer, even as she faced her own penance tonight.

He knew what this evening would cost her in terms of dignity. He well remembered how she'd claimed the expectations of her parents were like a shoe that refused to fit. But her obligations to her family apparently ran deep. She had risked a good deal by coming to Golden Square for him. And now he would gladly do the same for her.

He spied her standing near the Duchess of Pembroke, a highly respected member of the ton who had once been friendly with his parents. He strode in their direction, his mission absolute. He barely registered the parting of the crowd, the shocked whispers that rippled through the mob.

"It's the Marquess of Branston."

"Has he been gone three years?"

"Did you hear about his poor sister?"

Thomas ignored them all. Let them gawk. Let them *talk*.

It no longer mattered.

He came to stop and forced his gaze to shift momentarily from Lucy to their hostess. He executed a bow that felt as unfamiliar as the rusty strains of music. "Your grace, my apologies for coming uninvited."

The Duchess of Pembroke smiled. "Nonsense, Lord Branston, you are welcome here. I would have sent an invitation if I had known you were in London." She cocked her head. "No one has seen you for several years. Have you come back to town for good, then?"

He hesitated. "Not just yet. But I plan to answer my writ of summons and take my seat in the House of Lords next Season."

Beside him, Thomas heard a soft gasp.

Now, finally, his attention could shift to where it wanted.

Where it *demanded*.

And once it landed on Lucy, it never wanted to leave. No longer the wild spirit of his dreams, tonight she was an absolute vision in pale yellow silk, pink rosebuds swirling about the hem of her gown. Her fingers were nervously clutching the serpentine necklace about her neck.

And her hair—holy God, where had *that* come from?

He wanted to pull her away from the crowd and tumble her out onto a darkened terrace. He wanted to press his mouth against her swell of breast, see if her skin tasted as sweet as he remembered. He wanted to—

"Lord Branston," the duchess said, severing that train of thought as cleanly as if she'd brought an axe down across his skull. "May I present Lady Cardwell and her daughter, Miss Lucille Westmore? Miss Westmore has just been presented this Season."

"A pleasure to meet you," he somehow found the composure to murmur. His wayward thoughts were momentarily tamed with the reminder he was not supposed to know this woman. His body, however, was humming with the unspoken awareness that came from knowing her very intimately, indeed. He knew the sound she made in the back of her throat when a kiss caught her by surprise, and he knew the way she tasted, in her most secret places. But to give that away would be to take away her choice in the matter, and so he bent over her gloved hand. "Miss Westmore," he murmured, bowing low. "It is a pleasure to meet you. Would you do me the honor of being my partner for the next dance?"

Lucy's smile was oddly hesitant. She blinked at the woman standing next to her. "Er . . . Mother, may I dance with the Marquess of Branston?"

Her mother's eyes widened in surprise. "Did you say . . . 'marquess'?" Her gaze turned appraising and she nearly shoved Lucy in Thomas's direction. "By all means, dear."

Hiding a smile, Thomas led her onto the dance floor. A new set was beginning, the swirling notes solidifying into a particular three-beat rhythm. His hand settled where it had longed to go since the moment he spied her across the room, settling possessively against the sweet curve of her waist. He led them into a sweeping waltz, remembering the moves well enough, but not remembering this sort of acute anticipation.

He must have danced over a hundred waltzes.

But never, it seemed, with a scandalous spinster.

He smiled down at her, remembering how she had looked in the soft morning light of Cornwall, her skin flushed with pleasure. Her cheeks held something of that glow now, but her hand felt like a trapped bird in his. That was when he realized she was trembling.

"Are you nervous?"

"Aren't *you*?" she retorted. "Everyone in the bloody room is watching."

She sounded so much like the Lucy he knew and loved that he was tempted to laugh, there in the middle of the floor, the eyes of the entire ton upon them. "I probably ought to be nervous," he admitted. "But you see, the only opinion in this room that matters to me is yours."

Her lips lifted, just enough. "I must beg you to keep your false flirtations to yourself, sir." Her words deepened to a whisper. "You see, I am not supposed to know you. It wouldn't be proper."

He cleared his throat. "There once was a spinster by chance . . ."

"This one better not be about my breasts," she warned, but her voice was low and delicious. In an instant his eyes were just there, on the creamy swell of skin that rose up from the yellow silk and appeared to be begging for his kiss.

He swallowed hard, willing his feet to keep to the prescribed rhythm. "Who consented to just one dance."

She ducked her head. "But she tread on his toes . . ."

He nodded, though in truth she'd not stepped on his toes once. "And ought to box his nose . . ." He paused dramatically, letting a few steps go by, then leaned in, his words the merest whisper in her ear. " . . . because he wanted to remove her pants."

She began to shake with laughter. "I am wearing a gown tonight, my lord. Not trousers."

He bent in to whisper again. "But *I* know what you were wearing earlier this afternoon, don't I?"

Chapter 30

*L*ucy hadn't been sure she could do it. Those first, stumbling moments into the crowded ballroom and the nearly disastrous conversation with the Duchess of Pembroke had flayed her nerves. But somehow, on Thomas's arm, she began to think she could do nearly anything.

Flirt, if she must. Smile, if he encouraged it.

Fly, if he but told her she could.

The waltz ended too soon. Would she be permitted another with him tonight? It probably wouldn't be appropriate, but somehow, a reel or a quadrille seemed far too tame. Rules and propriety aside, she only knew she didn't want the moment to end.

"I feel . . . a bit breathless," she said as the last notes drew to a close, not even needing to fabricate the excuse. "A bit of fresh air might be in order."

His eyes darkened promisingly. "A turn in Lady Pembroke's gardens, perhaps?"

She pulled him toward the open French doors, wanting only to escape the notice of her mother and whoever else might be watching. Or waiting. Somewhere, Lydia's viscount was no doubt looking for her, waiting for his chance to pounce. She didn't particularly feel like playing the part of prey at the moment. Not unless it was to snare a marquess.

Outside, the cooler night air was a pleasant balm compared to the too-warm atmosphere of the ballroom. She leaned closer to Thomas, welcoming the warmth that radiated from him. She was tempted to wrap herself around him, but knew she couldn't. At least, not right here. But if they would but go a few more steps, into those shadows, who knew what trouble they might reasonably get up to?

"Did things go well with your sister?" she asked, tugging him deeper into the garden.

"Better than I had ever hoped," he said, his voice a low rumble that did delicious things to her stomach. "I have you to thank for that." He pulled her gently around to face him, leaving them in disappointing view of the ballroom. "I have you to thank for *everything,* Lucy. You've opened my eyes to the world I turned my back on. One can fulfill the obligations of their position as well as find happiness. I can live in London or I can live in Cornwall."

"Or, you can split your time between both." She stepped closer. "With me."

THOMAS SCHOOLED HIS face to a frown, though it took some effort, given the way his heart wanted to pound right out of his chest. "But you don't want a husband," he reminded her.

He'd asked her to marry him—what was it, three times now?

She'd made it clear this needed to be her choice.

And he was enjoying the turnabout.

She swallowed, looking impossibly vulnerable in the darkness. "Don't I?" she whispered.

He let the moment hang. When her hopeful look began to turn pinched, he relented and began to move, pulling her toward the drape of a shadow cast by a pair of well-manicured plum trees, their new spring blossoms sweetly fragrant.

Prunus cerasifera.

Thank God, Lady Pembroke had a deep, lovely set of gardens.

"Well, I imagine that changes things, doesn't it?" he asked, drawing her deeper into the darkness. "If you want a husband, you are in the right place. Most young ladies come to these events to make an exceptional match. Has anyone here caught your eye? I could see you with a fat old viscount, for example. Although, if you want my advice, I suspect you need to find someone who isn't looking for a biddable sort of wife."

She made a sound that sounded suspiciously like a snarl.

He tugged her toward him. She took one step, then another, until she was standing between his braced legs and he was leaning back against the bark of a plum tree, welcoming the chance to kiss her properly.

Though not nearly as properly as he wanted.

HE PULLED HER into a kiss, the gentle press of his lips against hers nearly chaste. But Lucy was having none of his chivalry. She opened her mouth and pressed insistently against him. She sighed into the pleasure of it, though her mind was rattling the bars of the cage. The blasted man. Kissing her like this, instead of proposing. She'd hinted. She'd cajoled.

She'd very nearly begged.

Why wasn't he asking her to marry him again?

And oh, if he only would, there would be no more need for tiresome balls, no more dutiful expectations. She would have fulfilled the entire purpose of a Season: to catch a titled husband. She tried to imagine the look on her mother's face when she learned her wild, ill-mannered, short-haired daughter had landed a marquess instead of a viscount.

Although, "landed" was a bit of a stretch, given that he

seemed content to merely kiss her as though their lives—but not their reputations—depended on it.

It had not escaped her notice that he'd made quite sure to wait for the shadows, after all.

Through the drugging power of his kiss, it suddenly hit her. Why he'd pulled her into the shadows, rather than risk her reputation with this kiss in full view of the ballroom. He'd said he would wait for her decision, and asked her to consider him in the event she ever changed her mind. He didn't want to force her.

He was waiting for *her* to ask *him* this time.

Lucy broke away, gasping for a much-needed breath of air, and then pressed her lips flush against his ear. There was no hesitation, no sense of wondering at her decision.

It was simply made.

It had been, from the moment she'd read Aunt E's final diary entry.

"Thomas," she said, her voice husky with desire. "I love you. I love the way you kiss me, and I love the way you argue with me. I even love your terrible poetry."

She felt the change ripple through him, as though all this time, he'd been holding back a piece of himself, waiting and wanting. "I love you, too, Lucy."

"Then there's only one thing for it." She tipped her forehead against his, wanting to hold her breath, and yet knowing her words had never been so important. "Will you do me the honor of becoming my husband?"

THOMAS PAUSED, ENJOYING the chance to make her squirm.

But he couldn't maintain the ruse for long. There was only one answer on his lips, and it was insisting on tumbling out.

"I would be honored to make you my marchioness, Miss Westmore."

She practically threw herself against him, her arms tight about his neck. "Thank you," she gasped. "I was about to say 'please,' and we both know how much I hate to say *that*."

When it landed on his mouth, her kiss was fevered and hopeful and so bloody right, he couldn't help but take what she offered, sweeping into her mouth with a guttural growl of approval. Whatever hold he'd maintained on his desire until now disintegrated in the face of such a sweet assault. He felt his body respond, his cock swelling to the point of violence, warning him to not stretch the moment out *too* long. Her curves were lush handfuls against his greedy palms, and he gave his hands shameful permission to roam, refamiliarizing himself with territory he'd feared was lost to him forever.

As if deciding he needed a map, she pulled at the edge of her bodice, and he nearly groaned out loud as her rounded breasts spilled out, taunting him with their pert coral tips.

"When?" he groaned against her throat, his tongue sweeping in small circles, drowning in the taste of her. "When should we do it?"

Because God above, if she made him wait, he was going to lose his mind.

"TODAY," LUCY PANTED. "Yesterday, if you can manage it. Post the bans tomorrow." She slipped a hand down and cupped his length in her palm, making him hiss out a breath between his teeth. "Just *please* don't make me wait anymore."

She knew it wasn't proper. Less than a hundred yards away a candlelit ballroom was waiting, with musicians and matrons and probably a viscount, searching for Lydia in every corner. But Lucy was betrothed.

She *loved* this man. They were out of sight, and he had said yes, and she was not leaving here tonight with her maidenhead intact. She'd pay *him* a thousand pounds, if it came down to it.

Thankfully, he was in an agreeable mood, because he

sank down onto the soft grass, drawing her down with him until she was resting on top of him. She kissed him long and hard, struggling to pull her skirts free where they were pinned beneath his legs, not even caring if the expensive silk was collecting grass stains and bits of plum blossoms that would give them away more surely than any bold confession. She never needed to wear another ball gown as long as she lived, but there would be only one first time with the man she loved, and the moment was here.

She struggled at the buttons of his trousers, growing frustrated when they wouldn't give to her needy fingers. But then his hands were there, helping her.

His length spilled out in her hands, the surprise of it making her gasp in wonder. "I didn't expect it to be so soft," she confessed, running her nails lightly across him.

"Trust me, it isn't soft," Thomas choked out.

She ran her hand up the length, pausing to rub her thumb against the tip. Remembering how he had kissed her so intimately in Cornwall, she lowered her head and pressed her tongue against him, smiling to herself to feel him tremble in response to her daring.

"Lucy—" came his protest, but she ignored him, pressing her willing mouth around him, enjoying the sharp hiss of his breath as she ran her tongue in hot, liquid swirls against his straining skin. And then he could no longer form a coherent protest, because his breathing became far too strained for words.

Though she wanted to linger—to punish him, even, for making her wait so long—she finally let him pull her roughly up and away. She followed his lead as he urged her to straddle him. Because she wanted this, too: more of him, more of the feelings he spun up inside her. And she trusted him, now, to not let her down with only half an experience, the way he had before.

She settled over him, and as she lowered herself slowly,

she felt that soft fullness pressing against her in the most perfect place imaginable. She closed her eyes, adjusting to the strange welcome of it all.

"You are chewing on your lip," came his voice. "What are you thinking?"

Lucy opened her eyes. "Truly?" she whispered. When he nodded, she felt her cheeks heat. "I was thinking that perhaps there are some advantages to wearing skirts after all." She shifted, enjoying the way the movement made him groan. "For example, I couldn't do this if we were both wearing trousers."

"For God's sake, hold still, Lucy."

She did. And found that was very nearly as enjoyable as the pursuit of friction.

After a moment his jaw softened, as though preparing himself for a monumental task. "Ready?" he asked, his voice almost a moan.

She blinked. "You mean . . . this isn't it?"

His smile was slow and wicked. "Not even close."

"Then yes. *Please*," she told him.

And that, apparently, was all she needed to say. The delicious, slow glide of his body against hers became a sharp pinch of pain. She drew in a sharp breath, realizing she was now seated on top of him, his body joined with hers.

"Are you all right?" he asked through gritted teeth.

She loosened her breath. "I believe you now. It is not so soft after all."

His chuckle rippled through them both. "It gets better, I promise."

She moved, almost experimentally, to learn that it did, indeed, get better. She felt him move inside her, the sweetest of invasions. He was seated so deeply inside her she felt as though he might very well touch her heart. And it got better still when he pulled her forward so her begging breast was flush against his mouth. He drew her nipple in, suckling gently, rolling it against his tongue until she was thrashing in pleasure.

Yes, this was *much* better.

She tossed her head, enjoying the sheer torment of his lips. Somehow, he guided them into a welcome rhythm, his hands against her hips, showing her how to move. Where their bodies were joined, she felt that building sensation, the one he had shown her that morning in the meadow. But it was different, somehow.

Perhaps because it was a shared experience this time, instead of a one-way gift.

He relinquished his attentions at her breast to both pull her down and rise up to meet her mouth, capturing her soft cries, silencing her with a kiss. "*Shhhhh*. They cannot see us," he whispered, his voice ragged, "but they could perchance hear us if we are not careful."

Lucy tried to be quiet. Oh, how she tried. But she was spiraling out of control now, the friction of their bodies and the slow, building pleasure impossible to fight.

"Thomas!" His name wrenched from her throat, captured by his mouth, protecting her from ruin, even as he tossed her toward the heavens. Her climax rippled through her like a summer windstorm, achingly sweet.

He was close behind, panting against her breast, every bit as devastated.

And then they were floating back down together, arms entwined, breath sounds melding.

Gradually, the scratch of earth beneath her knees began to creep in, and sounds of the distant ballroom and the sweet fragrance of plum blossoms insisted on intruding, reminding her of where they were, and what they had done.

But she didn't care.

How could she, when it was Thomas, and she was finally where she was supposed to be?

She pushed herself up and stared down at him, her eyes

lingering on his smile, just a bit higher on one side than the other. "I love you," she murmured again, unable to say it enough now that she had found the courage to acknowledge it.

"I love you, too," he told her, reaching up to press a kiss against her temple. And then his chuckle came, shaking her with its force, given their bodies were still very much joined. "But after much consideration, I am thinking a special license may be the way to go."

Epilogue

"You're missing the flowers." Thomas turned away from the coach window and regarded his wife with an upraised brow. "It is an entirely different landscape now in July than it was in April. The heath has begun to bloom."

From the opposite seat of the mail coach, Lucy continued to read her book. "I imagine we have plenty of time to see it," she said absently, turning a page. "After all, we'll be here through October, setting up the new jewelry business. I know Josephine is eager to get started."

Thomas frowned. Yes, his sister was eager to begin her new jewelry business, selling the popular serpentine pendants and pins to the most distinguished members of the ton—nary a one who suspected the true origins of the mysterious Mrs. Smythe. They'd started with a few discreet pieces, cutting and polishing the lizardite rock Lucy had brought back to London. The first piece had been delivered to the Duchess of Pembroke, compliments of Smythe Jewelry.

It had worked like . . . well, a charm.

Everyone who was *anyone* wanted one.

Now they needed to deliver more.

Thomas was a little worried, given the potential risks of discovery Josephine faced in her new role, but she had changed enough in appearance in the last few years that it should all be fine. Besides, he had a notion his sister was looking forward to a bit of financial independence and the thought of putting one over on the Society that had once shunned her.

If Josephine were willing to take the risk, it was not his place to try to stop her.

But these next few months in Lizard Bay were bound to be busy. He had a notion the Tanner orphans would be eager enough to collect the lizardite rocks that littered the coast, in between their studies, but he still needed to find townspeople to polish the stones, and he needed to sort out who had a talent for metalworking and artistry. Plus, there was the matter of finishing the repairs on Heathmore Cottage and making sure the Tanner boys had a full complement of shoes. There wouldn't be a lot of time for leisurely walks on the moors.

And more to the point, the landscape next week would be different than the landscape today. That was one of the things he loved about the peninsula: it changed, nearly daily, with a new array of plant life blooming in rapid, wondrous succession.

"We are nearly to Lizard Bay," he said. "And it will be dark soon. Don't you want to look out the window for a minute or two?"

"I want to finish these next few pages first."

Thomas glanced out the window again just as the little town appeared on the horizon. It felt good to be coming back, but better still to be coming back with Lucy on his arm, properly married. Despite the occasional, inevitable argument, three months of marriage roundly agreed with him.

He, lonely for so much of his life, had been thoroughly in-doctrinated into the loud, raucous Cardwell family, though he'd half suspected Lord Cardwell kept a pistol in his jacket right up until the nuptials. With the jewelry business as an excuse, he was able to visit Josephine and his niece as often as he liked, posing as an investor.

And of course, he awakened every morning, a smile on his face and tangled in the arms of a wife who slept like the dead.

But despite their idyll, it seemed they'd regressed a bit in the past hour. His new wife was paying far more attention to her book than to him.

"What are you reading anyway?" he grumbled. "I can't imagine it is more fascinating than Cornish Heath."

"That is a matter of perspective." She turned another page. "I am reading Aunt E's diaries again, and her entries are full of advice for women on how to deal with men."

Thomas eyed the plain-looking cover more curiously. So *that* was where Miss E, the scandalous spinster, had kept all of her secrets. "Are you learning anything new?" he asked, wondering why his new wife's cheeks had gone so pink.

She lowered it, and that was when he realized she wasn't ignoring him at all. "Well, that depends." Her generous mouth curved upward. "For example, how do you feel about ropes?"

He was reminded, then, that his wife might not be a spin-ster anymore, but she was still a bit scandalous, and likely always would be. Not that he minded in the slightest. "I am open to exploration," he told her, shifting on the seat to re-lieve the sudden tightness in his trousers. "And I . . . ah . . . remember from that day on the cliff that you are handy with a knot."

"Good." She smiled, closing the book and blowing him a kiss as the mail coach rolled to a dusty stop. "Because I've a notion to practice my knots on *you*."

LUCY TOOK THOMAS's hand and stepped down onto the single dirt street.

It felt a bit like coming home.

London had its charms, of course. With Thomas poised to formally take his seat in the House of Lords next year, they would need to spend at least half the year in the city. But for now they had time to spend here, and after the busy parliamentary session next year, she suspected she and Thomas would be all too ready to return again to the solitude of the little town.

The arrival of the mail coach was already attracting a crowd. She spied Bentley and Jamieson, both looking happy to see them. Reverend Wellsbury emerged from the door of the little church, raising a hand in welcome. At least two of the Tanner boys launched themselves at Thomas and began to rifle through his pockets, chattering in excitement. Mrs. Wilkins came bustling out her boardinghouse door, flour on her hands and a smile on her wrinkled face.

But this time there were a few new faces in the crowd, faces Lucy didn't recognize. Well-dressed men with neckties and pocket watches and the stink of prosperity about them. Dread slithered through her. In spite of her attempts to save the town, had the Marston Mining Corporation found a foothold here after all?

Grabbing Jamieson by one arm, she pulled him aside. "Who are those men?" she asked uneasily.

The grocer beamed. "Oh, didn't you know, Miss L? We've had *visitors*. They've been flocking here in droves. Ten came just this month."

"It's Lady Branston now, not Miss L," she murmured, still eyeing the new men.

"Oh, you are married?" Mrs. Wilkins clapped her hands and exclaimed, "I just *knew* it!"

Reverend Wellsbury strode forward and slapped Thomas on the back. "Well *done*. Miss E would have been proud to hear it. Although, I confess I would have preferred to have you come back to Lizard Bay so I could do the honors myself."

"We . . . er . . . couldn't wait," Thomas said, smiling warmly in her direction.

Lucy smiled back. No, they couldn't have waited. And given the fact that she had spent most of the last month too nauseated to keep her breakfast down, the special license they had obtained appeared to have been a very smart thing indeed.

In spite of her happiness, she couldn't help but glance at the newcomers again. They looked out of place here among the ragged, aging population of Lizard Bay, but she couldn't quite put her finger on where they looked to belong.

"The visitors . . . do you mean to say they aren't miners?"

"Oh, no, they're naturalists." Mr. Jamieson's whiskers twitched. "From the Linnean Society of London. They've come to see the Cornish heath in bloom. Been a real boon to business here in town. Why, I sold four cans of snuff this week, and Mrs. Wilkins is having to double up on rooms."

Thomas set her bag down on the street, a frown on his handsome face. "But . . . how did they know? I thought the pages I wrote for the Linnean Society had been lost."

Lucy turned to the postmaster, a suspicion dawning. "Mr. Bentley, didn't you give the papers to Lord Branston the way I asked? I told you he needed them most."

Bentley nodded. "Yes, yes, I put them in the post."

"No, Bentley, *most*." Lucy looked back at Thomas, shaking her head. "I am sorry."

Her husband didn't look very upset. In fact, he was already striding toward a few of the gentlemen and reaching out to clasp their hands in welcome. She smiled and curled a hand around her belly as she watched the exchange of greetings. It looked like Lizard Bay was poised to have two solid industries, then.

One grand cause down, a few more dozen to go.

AS THEY SLIPPED through the rocks and Heathmore Cottage came into view, Lucy came to a stop, her hand light against Thomas's arm. "Wait a second."

Thomas stopped and set down the picnic basket Mrs. Wilkins had insisted on packing for them—a "gift for the newlyweds" she had proudly proclaimed. They'd come up to take an inventory of the repairs still needed on Heathmore Cottage. He was pleased to see his wife wasn't out of breath, but he thought taking frequent breaks was a fine idea. He'd been worried about having her make this trek in her condition.

Not that he'd have a prayer in hell of stopping her. He knew better than anyone that you couldn't make Lady Lucy Branston do something she didn't wish to do.

"Are you winded?" he asked in concern.

"No. I am pregnant, not a bloody invalid."

At her words, Thomas smiled down at the woman he could still not quite believe was his wife. It was true: she looked remarkably fit, and it was clear that pregnancy agreed with her, in more ways than one. Last night she'd aptly demonstrated her skill with a knot, a fact he had been all too happy to indulge. Then again, she'd tied up his heart since the first moment she argued with him in her London drawing room.

"Why did we stop, then? You are staring at it as if you've never seen it before," he said, following her line of sight. "I promise you, Heathmore Cottage is the same as you left it."

And it was. He could see just ahead to the whitewashed walls. A partially finished roof.

Cats everywhere.

Actually, *that* part was new.

He squinted, counting five fat tomcats basking in the midday sun. "Er . . . except I believe the rat problem may have been addressed in our absence," he said, laughing.

"It's not just that. Can you hear it?"

He listened a long moment. There was only the sound of waves crashing down below and a subtle clucking from the scrub grass, feral hens settling on their nests. "I don't hear anything."

"Exactly," Lucy said, turning toward him. "Where did the ghostly wind go?"

Thomas listened again. The wind was blowing hard today, Lucy's hair flying about her cheeks. But try as he might, he couldn't hear the whistling sound that had so characterized the property before. "That *is* odd," he admitted. "The landslide must have changed the geography enough to silence our ghost."

Lucy nodded. "That should make it easier to find roofers now," she told him. "And to offer it as a retreat for some of the naturalists cluttering up Mrs. Wilkins's parlor." She smiled up at him. "It will still be ours. Still protected. But useful. I think Aunt E would have liked that."

Thomas glanced back toward the little cottage. It would take a lot of work, but if she was willing, he was as well. The idea that not only did she value the extraordinary beauty of her land, but that she wanted others to enjoy it as well, made him want to give out a whoop of approval.

Instead, he nodded. "If that is what you want, that is what we shall do."

"I like the way you think, husband." She reached up to kiss him once on the mouth, stirring thoughts of other things they might do once their picnic was finished. "And if you are this amenable to my ideas now, I confess I can hardly wait for next year."

"Why?" he drawled. Next year would be lovely, with a tiny heir or future spinster to keep them busy. But *he* was looking forward to the next hour, given that one kiss with Lucy usually led to more. He cocked his head, recognizing all too well the way she was worrying her lower lip. "What are you thinking?" he asked. She may have shown him her skill with knots, but he hadn't yet had an opportunity to show her his.

And if memory served, there was still a rope around here somewhere . . .

She shrugged, looking the opposite of innocent. "Oh, just the grand bit of trouble I could cause with my very own voting member of the House of Lords in my pocket."

"Lucy," he warned, though his own smile had stretched as high as hers. "I am scarcely in your pocket, any more than you are in mine. What are you planning to do?"

She blinked. "Who, *me*? I'm just a plain almost-spinster who somehow managed to attach herself to a handsome, influential husband."

"Mm hmm. Plotting to wreak all the havoc you want, I imagine."

Her smile turned as brilliant as the overhead Cornwall sun. "I only want you," she told him, going up on her toes to kiss him again.

He kissed her back, and gladly. This was not a time to argue with her.

Because for once they were in agreement on something.

Continue reading for an excerpt from the first
Seduction Diaries novel,

Diary of an Accidental Wallflower

Pretty and popular, Miss Clare Westmore knows exactly
what (or rather, who) she wants: the next Duke of Harrington.
But when she twists her ankle on the eve of the Season's
most touted event, Clare is left standing in the wallflower
line watching her best friend dance away with her duke.

Dr. Daniel Merial is tempted to deliver more than a diag-
nosis to London's most unlikely wallflower, but he doesn't
have time for distractions, even one so delectable. Besides,
she's clearly got her sights on more promising prey. So why
can't he stop thinking about her?

All Clare wants to do is return to the dance floor. But as
her former friends try to knock her permanently out of place,
she realizes with horror she is falling for her doctor instead
of her duke. When her ankle finally heals and she faces her
old life again, will she throw herself back into the game?

Or will her time in the wallflower line have given her a
glimpse of who she was really meant to be?

Available now from Avon Books

May 2, 1848

Dear Diary,

If a man's worth is measured in pounds, a woman's is measured in dance steps.

And if those dance steps are with a future duke, surely they are worth all the more.

Mr. Alban, the future Duke of Harrington, asked me to dance again last night, the third time since the start of the Season. My friends are abuzz with what he might ask next, and I confess, I hope it is something more significant than a dance. I know the Season has just begun, but surely a proposal cannot be far from his mind?

When I feel the sting of jealousy from the less fortunate girls lining the walls, I remind myself some casualties are inevitable if I am to dance all the way to a ducal mansion. Any girl who feels tempted to accept the first offer that comes their way would do well to comfort themselves on the arm of a mere marquess.

Miss Clare Westmore
The Future Duchess of Harrington

*M*iss Clare Westmore wasn't the only young woman to fall head-over-heels for Mr. Charles Alban, the newly named heir to the Duke of Harrington.

Though, she was probably the only one to fall quite so literally.

He appeared out of nowhere, broad-shouldered and perfect, trotting his horse down one of the winding paths near the Serpentine. His timing was dreadful. For one, it was three o'clock on a Friday afternoon, hardly a fashionable hour for anyone to be in Hyde Park. For another, she'd come down to the water with her siblings in tow, and the ducks and geese they'd come to feed were already rushing toward them like a great screeching mob.

Her sister, Lucy, poked an elbow into her ribs. "Isn't that your duke?"

Clare's heart galloped well into her throat as the sound of hoofbeats grew closer. What was Mr. Alban *doing* here? Riders tended to contain themselves to Rotten Row, not this inauspicious path near the water. If he saw her now it would be an unmitigated disaster. She was wearing last Season's walking habit—fashionable enough for the ducks, but scarcely the modish image she wished to project to the man who could well be her future husband. Worst of all, she was with Lucy, who brushed her hair approximately once a week, and her brother Geoffrey, who ought to have been finishing his first year at Eton but was expelled just last week for something more than the usual youthful hijinks.

Clare froze in the center of the milling mass of birds, trying to decide if it would be wiser to lift her skirts and run or step behind the cover of a nearby rhododendron bush. One of the geese took advantage of her indecision and its beak jabbed at her calf through layers of silk and cotton. Before she knew what was happening—or even gather her wits into something resembling a plan—her thin-soled slipper twisted out from under her and she pitched over onto the ground with an unladylike *oomph*. She lay there, momentarily stunned.

Well then. The rhododendron it was.

She tucked her head and rolled into the shadow of the bush, ignoring low-hanging branches that reached out for her. The ducks, being intelligent fowl, followed along. They seized the crumpled bag of bread still clutched in her hand and began gulping down its contents. The geese—being, of course, quite the opposite of ducks—shrieked in protest and flapped their wings, stirring up eddies of down and dust.

Clare tucked deeper into the protection of the bush, straining to hear over the avian onslaught. Had she been seen? She didn't think so. Then again, her instincts had also told her no one of importance would be on this path in Hyde Park at three o'clock on a Friday afternoon, and look how well those thoughts had served.

"Oh, what fun!" Lucy laughed, every bit as loud as the geese. "Are you playing the damsel in distress?"

"Perhaps she is studying the mating habits of water fowl," quipped Geoffrey, whose mind always seemed to be on the mating habits of *something* these days. He tossed a forelock full of blond hair out of his eyes as he offered her a hand, but Clare shook her head. She didn't trust her brother a wit. At thirteen years old and five and a half feet, he was as tall as some grown men, but he retained an adolescent streak of mischief as wide as the Serpentine itself.

He was as likely to toss her into Alban's path as help her escape.

Lucy cocked her head. Wisps of tangled blond hair rimmed her face like dandelion fluff and made her appear far younger than her seventeen years, though her tall frame and evident curves left no doubt that she was old enough to show more care with her appearance. "Shall I call Mr. Alban over to request his assistance, then?" she asked, none too innocently.

"Shhhh," Clare hissed. Because the only thing worse than meeting the future Duke of Harrington while dressed in last year's walking habit was meeting him while wallowing in the dirt. Oh, but she should never have worn such inappropriate shoes to go walking in Hyde Park. Then again, such hindsight came close to philosophical brilliance when offered up from the unforgiving ground.

She held her breath until the sound of hoofbeats began to recede into the distance. Dimly, she realized something hurt. In fact, something hurt dreadfully. But she couldn't quite put her finger on the source when her mind was spinning in the more pertinent directions.

"Why are you hiding from Mr. Alban?" Lucy asked pointedly.

"I am not hiding." Clare struggled to a sitting position and blew a wayward brown curl from her eyes. "I am . . . er . . . feeding the ducks."

Geoffrey laughed. "Unless I am mistaken, the ducks have just fed themselves, and that pair over there had a jolly good tup while the rest of them were tussling over the scraps. You should have invited your duke to join us."

"He's not yet a duke," Clare corrected crossly. Much less *her* duke.

But oh, how she wanted him to be.

"Pity to let him go by without saying anything. You could have shown him your overhanded throw, the one you use for Cook's oldest biscuits." Geoffrey pantomimed a great arching throw out into the lake. "*That* would impress him, I'm sure."

The horror of such a scene—and such a brother—made Clare's heart thump in her chest. To be fair, feeding the ducks was something of a family tradition, a ritual born during a time when she hadn't cared whether she was wearing last year's frock. These days, with their house locked in a cold, stilted silence and their parents nearly estranged, they retreated here almost every day. And she *could* throw Cook's biscuits farther than either Lucy or Geoffrey, who took after their father in both coloring and clumsiness. It was almost as if they had been cut from a different bolt of cloth, coarse wool to Clare's smooth velvet.

But these were not facts one ought to share with a future duke—particularly when that future duke was the gentleman you hoped would offer a proposal tonight. No, better to wait and greet Mr. Alban properly this evening at Lady Austerley's annual ball, when Lucy and Geoffrey were stashed safely at home and she would be dressed in tulle and diamonds.

"I don't understand." Lucy stretched out her hand, and this time Clare took it. "Why wouldn't you wish to greet him? He came to call yesterday, after all, and I was given the impression you liked him very much."

Clare pulled herself to standing and winced as a fresh bolt of pain snatched the breath from her lungs. "How do you know about that?" she panted. "I didn't tell anyone." In fact, she'd cajoled their butler, Wilson, to silence. It was imperative word of the visit be kept from their mother, who—if last Season's experience with potential suitors was any indication—would have immediately launched a campaign to put Waterloo to shame.

"I know because I spied on you from the tree outside the picture window." Lucy shrugged. "And didn't you say that he asked you to dance last week?"

"Yes," Clare agreed between gritted teeth. Mr. Alban *had* asked her to dance last week, a breathless waltz that sent the room spinning and held all eyes upon them. It was the third waltz they had shared since the start of the Season—though not all on the same night, more's the pity. But the glory of that dance paled in comparison to the dread exacted by Lucy's confession.

Had her sister really hung apelike from a limb and leered at the man through the window? Except . . . hadn't Alban sat with his back to the window?

She breathed a sigh of relief. Yes, she was almost sure of it.

He'd spent the entire quarter hour with his gaze firmly anchored on her face, their conversation easy. But despite the levity of their exchange, he'd seemed cautious, as though he were hovering on the edge of some question that never materialized but that she fervently wished he'd jus*t hurry up and ask.*

Given his unswerving focus, there was no way he would have seen her clumsy heathen of a sister swinging through the branches, though she shuddered to think that Lucy could have easily lost her balance and come crashing through the window in a shower of broken glass and curse words. But thankfully nothing of the sort had happened. No awkward siblings had intruded on the flushed pleasure of the moment. Her mother had remained oblivious, distracted by her increasing irritation with their father and her shopping on Bond Street.

And to Clare's mind, Mr. Alban had all but declared his intentions out loud.

Tonight, she thought fiercely. Tonight would be the night when he asked for more than just a dance. And that was why it was very important for her to tread carefully, until he was so irrevocably smitten she could risk the introduction of her family.

"I *do* admire him," she admitted, her mind returning reluctantly to the present. "I just do not want him to see me looking like . . ." Clare glanced down at her grass-stained skirts and picked at a twig that had become lodged in the fabric. "Well, like this."

Lucy frowned. "I scarcely think his admiration should be swayed by a little dirt."

"And you didn't look like that before you dove behind that bush," Geoffrey pointed out. "Stunning bit of acrobatics, though. You ought to apply to the circus, sis."

"I didn't dive behind the bush." Clare battled an exasperated sigh. She couldn't expect either of them to understand. Lucy still flitted through life not caring if her hair was falling down. Such obliviousness was sure to give her trouble when she came out next year. Clare herself couldn't remember a time when she hadn't been acutely aware of every hair in its place, every laugh carefully cultivated.

And Geoffrey was . . . well . . . *Geoffrey.*

Loud, male, and far too crude for polite company.

As a child, the pronounced differences between herself and her siblings had often made her wonder if perhaps she had been a foundling, discovered in a basket on the front steps of her parents' Mayfair home. She loved her brother and sister, but who wouldn't sometimes squirm in embarrassment over such a family?

And what young woman wouldn't dream of a dashing duke, destined to take her away from it all and install her within the walls of his country estate?

Clare took a step, but as her toe connected with the ground, the pain in her right ankle punched through the annoyance of her brother's banter. "Oh," she breathed. And then, as she tried another step, "*Ow!* I . . . I must have twisted my ankle when I fell."

"I still say you dove," Geoffrey smirked.

Lucy looked down with a frown. "Why didn't you say something?" she scolded. "Can you put any weight on it at all?"

"I didn't realize at first." Indeed, Clare's mind had been too much on the threat of her looming social ruin to consider what damage had been done to her person. "And I am sure I can walk on it. Just give me a moment to catch my breath."

She somehow made her way to a nearby bench, ducks and geese scattering like ninepins. By the time she sat down, she was gasping in pain and battling tears. As she slid her dainty silk slipper off, all three of them peered down at her stocking-encased foot with collective indrawn breaths. Geoffrey loosened an impressed whistle. "Good God, sis. That thing is swelling faster than a prick at a bawdy show."

"Geoffrey!" Clare's ears stung in embarrassment, though she had to imagine it was an apt description for the swollen contours of her foot. "This is not Eton, we are not your friends, and that will be *quite* enough."

"Don't you have Lady Austerley's ball tonight?" Lucy asked, her blue eyes sympathetic. "I can't imagine you can attend like this. In fact, I feel quite sure we ought to carry you home and call for the doctor, straightaway."

But Clare's mind was already tilting in a far different direction. This evening's ball hadn't even crossed her mind when she had been thinking of the pain, but now she glared down at her disloyal ankle. *No, no, no.* This could not be happening. Not when she was convinced Mr. Alban would seek her out for more than just a single dance tonight.

It didn't hurt so much when she was sitting.

Surely it would be better in an hour or so.

"Of course I can go." She struggled to slip her shoe back on, determined to let neither doubts nor bodily deficiency dissuade her. "Just help me home, and don't tell Mother," she added, "and everything will be fine."